RK
Kipling's
Kingdom

by the same author

PLAIN TALES FROM THE RAJ

RAJ: A SCRAPBOOK OF BRITISH INDIA

TALES FROM THE DARK CONTINENT

A MOUNTAIN IN TIBET

TALES FROM THE SOUTH CHINA SEAS

LIVES OF THE INDIAN PRINCES

A GLIMPSE OF THE BURNING PLAIN

RK

Kipling's Kingdom

Twenty-five of
Rudyard Kipling's
best Indian stories
– known and unknown –
selected and introduced by

Charles
Allen

MICHAEL JOSEPH: LONDON

First published in Great Britain
by Michael Joseph Ltd
27 Wrights Lane, London W8
1987

British Library Cataloguing in Publication Data

Kipling, Rudyard
(Selections). Kiplings kingdom: his best
Indian stories, including two
unpublished ones.
I. Title II. Allen, Charles, 1940-

823'.8[F] PR4852

ISBN 0-7181-2570-3

Typeset by Goodfellow & Egan, Cambridge
Made and Printed in Great Britain by
Hazell, Watson & Viney Ltd., Aylesbury

Contents

INTRODUCTION

When Joseph Rudyard Kipling, aged sixteen years and nine months, stepped ashore at Bombay on 18 October 1882 it was, in his own words, 'as a prince entering his kingdom.'[1] He was returning from exile to his native land, to reclaim the lost years of his childhood.

His parents, Lockwood and Alice Kipling, had first come out to Bombay in 1865 as newly-weds, he to teach sculpture, she carrying the child conceived at the start of their journey east. Rudyard (named after the lake in Staffordshire where his parents first met) was born on 30 December in that same year, in a bungalow within the compound of the Sir Jamsetji Jijibhoy School of Art, off Hornby Road. A first photograph sent back home by the proud parents, showing the baby asleep in the lap of an Indian *ayah*, is said to have caused one of Rudyard's uncles to remark in quiet consternation 'how dark' his mother had become.

Bombay was the seedbed in which the writer's genius was sheltered, watered and nurtured. 'Mother of Cities to me,' he was to write:

> For I was born at her gate,
> Between the palms and the sea
> Where the world-end steamers wait.[2]

Rudyard's first five and a half years were passed here, broken only by a short furlough in England in 1868 for the birth of a sister, Trix. Although only dimly remembered in adulthood, we are left in no doubt that they were years of blissful happiness, full of security and privilege – an infant's vision of paradise, shot through with sensuous tropical effects that excited but rarely threatened:

> My first impression is of daybreak, light and colour and purple fruits at the level of my shoulder . . . Our evening walks were by the sea in the shadow of palm-groves which, I think, were called the Mahim Woods. When the wind blew the great nuts would tumble, and we fled – my ayah, and my sister in her perambulator – to the safety of the open. I have always felt the menacing darkness of tropical eventides, as I have loved the voices of night-winds through palm or banana leaves, and the song of the tree-frogs.[3]

His guardians and mentors were not his parents – benign and loving though they were – but two servants: a Goan Roman Catholic *ayah* and a

1 *From Sea to Sea*, Vol. I.
2 *To the City of Bombay*, 1894.
3 *Something of Myself* (1937 Edition), p.1.

Hindu bearer named Meeta. On their walks the one would stop to pray at wayside crosses – 'and I beside her' – while the other took the boy into Hindu temples where 'being below the age of caste, I held his hand and looked at the dimly-seen friendly gods.' Under their tutelage Rudyard learned to move easily in the several oil-and-water worlds that made up the British India of the Raj, moving freely from one to the other, effortlessly assuming a different persona on each occasion. 'In the afternoon heats before we took our sleep,' he was to write many years later in an unfinished fragment of autobiography,[4] 'she [the *ayah*] or Meeta would tell us stories and Indian nursery songs all unforgotten, and we were sent into the dining-room after we had been dressed with the caution "Speak English now to Papa and Mamma".'

Like other Anglo-Indian children, the young Rudyard absorbed the creed of his kind. He accepted the servants' idolatry of the *chota sahib* or little master as his due, but because they were his friends as well as his social inferiors he responded with equal devotion to them and to others of their kind. There is a story left by a friend of the Kiplings who saw the boy walking hand in hand with a peasant-farmer across a field and calling back over his shoulder to his mother in Hindustani, 'Goodbye, this is my brother.'[5] Although in adulthood 'brother' was paternalised into 'son', Kipling's attachment to Indian *ryots* and others low down the social scale was never lost.

Another revealing childhood vignette comes from a different family friend, J. H. Rivett-Carnac, to whose family Kipling makes obeisance in the first lines of 'The Tomb of His Ancestors':

> One day Master Ruddy had left a small quantity of pudding uneaten. 'You must finish that', said the sister, 'or God will be very angry with you.' 'Boo, boo,' says the delinquent, 'then I shall change my God', (as he might his *dhoby* or washerman). But the sister, who claimed superior theological knowledge, replied authoritatively, 'You can't change your God, it is the *Sirkar*'s (Government) God.' And Rudyard, realising even at that early age, thanks to the gorgeous chuprassy who accompanied him on his morning walks, that he occupied a sort of official position under the Government, which carried with it certain responsibilities, surrendered.[6]

This reveals two aspects of the writer-to-be in conflict: Kipling's readiness to shock, pulling up short before a profound respect for authority. However, before reading too much into the tale of Master Ruddy and his gods we would do well to question Rivett-Carnac's reliability as a witness. He was one of a number of people who claimed to have started the Kiplings in their literary careers – in this case by recommending Lockwood as a Bombay correspondent for the '*Pi*', the leading newspaper of the North-Western Provinces, otherwise known as '*The Pioneer*' – yet he was not close enough to the Kiplings to be able to remember that Rudyard and not

4 *Something of Myself*, (1937 Edition), p.2.
5 C. E. Norton in a note to the 1900 Edition of *Plain Tales from the Hills*.
6 J.H. Rivett-Carnac, *Many Memories*, 1910.

Trix was the older child. He also goes along with the popular belief that the Kiplings were part of the British upper middle-class cadre – the civil and military set – that ran India, which they plainly were not. Lockwood Kipling did not, as is so often stated, come out to Bombay to start the new School of Art as its first Principal. He was a mere subordinate in one of three departments of a flourishing but still insignificant institution, certainly not mighty enough to employ uniformed government servants. He had come out to India not as a gentleman but as an upwardly mobile master-craftsman, the son of a Wesleyan minister educated to fourteen at a Wesleyan school near Bradford. His advancement over the next sixteen years in India was considerable but it could not alter his social position in Anglo-Indian society. Lockwood and his wife – and their son in his turn – were always to remain on the fringes of civil and military India. This uncertainty over social rank, together with the unease that went with it, was to give Rudyard's writing a sharp cutting edge whenever it came to matters of social standing – with the added twist that while his instincts remained those of an outsider he still wanted to belong, to be part of the set.

In 1871 the infant Ruddy's world collapsed. He was cast out of his Bombay Eden and abandoned without warning in a bleak, loveless boarding house in Southsea that he later labelled 'The House of Desolation'. In removing the two children to England for their education the Kiplings were only following Anglo-Indian convention, though the usual custom was to hand them over to relatives – not into the care of strangers. Inexplicably – perhaps for reasons of pride and not wishing to be beholden, perhaps because little Ruddy had already acquired a reputation for being a difficult child – Rudyard and Trix were placed in the hands of a retired sea-captain's wife, 'Auntie Rosa', who did her damnest to break his spirit. The story is told with the barest of fictional disguise in the heart-rending 'Baa, Baa, Black Sheep', the writing of which is known to have been most painful to him. Kipling claimed that Southsea drained him of 'any capacity for real, personal hate' but it certainly did nothing to temper the appetite for revenge that is such a feature of many of Kipling's less attractive stories. These five years of neglect also helped to shape Rudyard in other ways. 'It made me give attention to the lies I soon found it necessary to tell: and this, I presume, is the foundation of literary effort,' writes Kipling in *Something of Myself*. 'Nor was my life an unsuitable preparation for my future, in that it demanded constant wariness, the habit of observation, and attendance on moods and tempers; the noting of discrepancies between speech and action.' Southsea also seems to have left Kipling with an abiding suspicion of the sex that had so devastated his *chota-sahib*'s self-esteem. It taught him never to drop his guard, always to keep his inner self hidden from view.

The five years of bondage at Southsea were followed by five liberating years at United Services College, Westward Ho!, a new but not entirely respectable boarding school for the sons of military officers who could not afford the fees of the smarter public schools. Under the eye of a liberal-minded headmaster, USC did far more for the adolescent Kipling than might have been expected of a school whose primary purpose was to get boys into the Sandhurst and Woolwich military academies. As well as learning to smoke, to bully and to swear, he developed a manner 'so brilliant and cynical', according to one of his schoolmates, 'that he was most cordially hated by his fellow students.'[7] Yet, as well as the cocksure independence celebrated in the *Stalky & Co* stories, Rudyard's aesthetic impulses were also given free rein. Further artistic infusions were received during the holidays when Rudyard went to stay with his Aunt Georgie, the wife of the artist Edward Burne-Jones, at *The Grange* in Fulham, the gathering place of a large circle of bohemian friends which included William Morris and Edward Poynter. In this house of enchantment, charged with romantic visions, the fourteen-year-old schoolboy set down his first known short story, in a family magazine put together with his cousins.

By now the Kiplings had begun to move up in the Anglo-Indian world. After ten years in Bombay, Lockwood had been offered the post of Principal of the new Mayo School of Industrial Art in Lahore, together with the Curatorship of the Lahore Museum. Unlike Bombay – Westernised and dominated by business and box-*wallahs* – Lahore was India for real. Its older inhabitants could remember the days when the one-eyed Ranjit Singh presided over his Sikh Empire from the great fort that dominated the city, when the only whites to be seen were the mercenaries employed to run his artillery. Its largely Muslim population still looked back nostalgically to the golden days of Shah Jahan and Aurangzeb, builders of Lahore's marbled palaces, tombs, pleasure gardens and grand mosque. By contrast, Lahore's newest masters had scarcely begun to make their mark.

Inside the walls of the city the British presence was hardly discernible but to the south a modest Anglo-Indian civil station had recently come into being. Civil lines and a military cantonment were gradually being extended across the open plain, with a Mall as a central boulevard running east and west. A number of government departments and bungalows, set in a generous acreage of compound and garden, provided a base for some sixty to seventy civil officers, together with their wives and families.

Despite their improved standing in the Order of Precedence that determined the ranking of all government employees, an arty couple like the Kiplings could not hope to fit easily into this community of professional administrators, where even to appear at dinner parties without jewellery – as Alice Kipling did – was thought altogether too

7 E. Kay Robinson, 'Kipling in India', *McLure's Magazine*, July 1896.

W Carpenter
Lahore 1855
53.82

bohemian for comfort. As a close friend of Rudyard Kipling was later to point out, this was a community that made up 'the most cultured audience to which an English writer can appeal,'[8] being largely composed (on the male side) of 'competition-*wallahs*' who had passed difficult competitive examinations to get into their respective services. Yet it was also a philistine society, whose shortcomings were to be set out in an angry squib of an article that appeared unsigned in Lahore's '*Civil and Military Gazette*' in January 1887. The article was entitled 'Anglo-Indian Society' and purported to be an extract from a tourist's letter 'showing, in some measure, ourselves as others see us.' It was, however, the work of the twenty-one-year-old Rudyard Kipling, using an old literary device to air some of his views without drawing too much return fire.[9] 'There is no society in India as we understand the word,' is how one passage begins:

> There are no books, no pictures, no conversations worth listening to for recreation's sake. Every man is in some service or other, has a hard day's work to do, and has very little inclination to talk or do anything but sleep at the end of it . . . No one talks lightly or amusingly as in England. Everyone works and talks and thinks about his work . . . Nothing seems to impress the Anglo-Indians except their work. They call the Himalaya mountains 'the hills'; when a man dies he 'pegs out'; when he is ill he is 'sick'. When a mother nearly breaks her heart over the loss of her first child, they say 'she frets about it a little' . . . They have a high opinion of themselves, and I think they have a right to, so far as work goes. But they don't seem to realise any of the beauties of life – perhaps they haven't time.[10]

Despite being different, Lockwood and Alice Kipling quickly became established in the Punjab and up at the summer retreat of Simla as a popular, amusing couple. Lockwood's growing authority in the fields of Indian art and folklore, and his wife's sparkle and wit brought them many invitations that would not normally have come their way. Both also contributed regularly to their local newspaper, the '*Civil and Military Gazette*', and to its far more important sister-paper the '*Pioneer*', six hundred miles away in Allahabad, which had been built up by its founder into the most widely-read paper in Northern India. It is the proud boast of the descendants of this man, Sir George Allen, that it was he and no other who set young Rudyard on his literary course with the blunt telegram 'Kipling will do.' Lacking the means to take his son's education any further, Lockwood had looked to his friends in India for help. The post of Assistant Editor on the *C&MG* at a hundred rupees a month was going and it was Allen, on furlough in London, who confirmed that the precocious talents of Lockwood's son were up to the requirements of the job.

So it was that at the start of the Cold Weather of 1882, sixteen-year-old Rudyard returned to Bombay, 'moving among sights and smells that made

8 Mrs Edmonia Hill, 'The Young Kipling', *Atlantic Monthly*, April 1936.
9 Identified by Thomas Pinney, *Kipling's India: Uncollected Sketches 1884–8*.
10 '*Civil and Military Gazette*', 29 January 1887.

me deliver in the vernacular sentences whose meaning I knew not.' The homecoming was complete when he joined his parents in Lahore three days later – 'where my English years fell away, nor ever, I think, came back in full measure.' Almost his first act was to obey his mother's entreaties and remove his side-whiskers. A moustache that he had been allowed to cultivate at Westward Ho! was spared. It helped to make him appear much older than he was.

The family home was a newly-built brick building known locally as 'Bikanir House', after the desert state of Bikaner, on account of its dusty, treeless garden. The Kiplings, it seems, had a theory that trees and shrubs harboured disease-bearing insects. But for Rudyard these austere surroundings represented the first secure base that he had known for ten years. Though he revelled in the privileges of adulthood – 'my own room in the house; my servant, handed over to me by my father's servant, whose son he was, with the solemnity of a marriage-contract; my own horse, cart, and groom; my own office-hours and direct responsibilities' – this was as nothing compared to the joys of new-found family life based on what his mother liked to call the 'Family Square', made up of Rudyard, his parents and, very soon, his sister Trix. 'I do not remember the smallest friction in any detail of our lives,' Kipling was to write. 'We delighted more in each other's society than in that of strangers; and when my sister came out, a little later, our cup was full to the brim. Not only were we happy but we knew it.'[11] As well as security the family home provided Rudyard with experience and stimulation. It was the perfect base from which to explore the part-familiar, part-alien world that lay outside the compound.

The first corner of this outside world comprised the offices of the *C&MG*, ruled over by a hard taskmaster – known in Bikanir House as the 'Amber Toad' – who did his best to knock the literary stuffing out of his employer's protégé:

> I represented fifty per cent of the 'editorial staff' of the one daily paper of the Punjab . . . and a daily paper comes out every day even though fifty per cent of the staff had fever. My Chief took me in hand, and for three years or so I loathed him . . . I never worked less than ten hours and seldom more than fifteen per diem; and as our paper came out in the evening did not see the midday sun except on Sundays. I had fever too, regular and persistent, to which I added for a while chronic dysentery. Yet I discovered that a man can work with a temperature of 104, even though next day he has to ask the office who wrote the article.[12]

While deriving considerable masochistic pleasure from performing all that his Chief required of him, Rudyard chafed at being denied the opportunity to use what he already knew to be a powerful literary talent. The Amber Toad saw to it that he 'kept his nose to the grindstone of proof-reading, scissors-and-paste work, and the boiling down of government

11 *Something of Myself*, p.40.
12 *Ibid.*, pp.40–1.

Blue Books into summaries for publication.'[13] Creative writing had to be confined to cheerful literary exercises that took place within the Family Square at home. Only on very rare occasions, as when his boss was having one of his bouts of sickness, was Rudyard able to have any say in what went into the paper – although he was sometimes allowed to write the editorial notes known as 'scraps' that went in on the paper's front page after the main news items had been laid out. It was eighteen months before he was given his first major assignment; covering a Viceregal visit to Patiala State in March 1884.

If the *C&MG* was one of the station's main institutions, Montgomery Hall and the Punjab Club – both situated a short ride away at the eastern end of the Mall – were the leading ones. Three times a week the small British community gathered after work at Montgomery Hall, which served the station as a gymkhana club. Here they took tea and exchanged gossip, played tennis and had a drink or two before going home to supper. It was a place where both sexes were welcome – even the lowlier members of the European community in Lahore: the box-*wallahs*, traders, shopkeepers and perhaps the more respectable of the 'country-born' and Eurasian elements who made up the 'railway folk' and lived in their own twilight world on the edge of the civil lines. However, the Lahore Club was not for them. This was the exclusive preserve of the officer cadre, and the fact that young Rudyard was accepted as an honorary member at the age of seventeen says much for his father's improved standing in the community. Though he was later to speak of it somewhat dismissively as a place 'where bachelors, for the most part, gathered to eat meals of no merit among men whose merits they knew well,' Kipling certainly took pride in being a member, for it was at the Club that he met 'none except picked men at their definite work – Civilians, Army, Education, Canals, Forestry, Engineering, Irrigation, Railways, Doctors, and Lawyers – samples of each branch and each talking his own shop.'[14] These were the *C&MG*'s principal readers, who expected their newspaper – and its new assistant editor – to mirror and give voice to their beliefs: 'I was almost nightly responsible for my output to visible and often brutally voluble critics at the Club. They were not concerned with my dreams. They wanted accuracy and interest, but first of all accuracy.' Rudyard had hardly been a club member for more than a month before he was given a brutal demonstration of what the Anglo-Indian community meant by 'accuracy' – and how it dealt with those who stepped out of line.

The occasion of his discomfiture was the presentation of the Ilbert Bill, which gave Indian magistrates in country districts the right to sit in judgement over European defendants. Led by their press, the British in India reacted with fury to this liberal measure imposed on them from on high. After initially supporting the agitation against the bill, '*The Pioneer*'

13 Kay Robinson.
14 *Something of Myself*, p.43.
15 *Ibid*., pp.50–1.
16 'Home', *C&MG*, 25 December 1891.

newspaper in Allahabad suddenly changed sides, with its sister-paper in the Punjab following suit. That night as Rudyard entered the club's dining-room he was greeted by a hostile barrage of hisses: 'It is not pleasant to sit still when one is twenty [seventeen, in fact] while all your universe hisses you. Then uprose a Captain, our Adjutant of Volunteers, and said: "Stop that! The boy's only doing what he's paid to do." The demonstration tailed off, but I had seen a great light. The Adjutant was entirely correct. I was a hireling, paid to do what I was paid to do, and – I did not relish the idea.'[15]

But this was only part of the story. There are at least three known instances when young Ruddy's 'caddish' behaviour at the Club – making disparaging remarks about the Indian Civil Service on one occasion, speaking insolently to a visiting dignitary on another, monopolising the conversation with egotistical remarks on a third – got him into trouble. On the last occasion he was kicked downstairs by a pair of angry lawyers after expressing a wish for a new experience. Clearly, his Westward Ho! bumptiousness was not to everyone's taste.

If these confrontations taught Kipling anything it was the overriding importance of conformity in a community made up of scattered groups of civil and military officers who had set themselves up in fragile authority over some two hundred and fifty million Indians. They were pioneers in an alien land who saw themselves as belonging to 'one big family – and if you do not know the catchwords of the family you must stand outside.'[16] To live at ease among his fellows – and they were the sort of chaps he had

been at school with and whom he admired immensely – meant sharing their views. It was the price of membership of their club:

> Now these are the laws of the jungle,
> And many and mighty are they!
> But the head and the hoof
> And the haunch and the hump is – obey![17]

There was always a part of the cocky young rebel of seventeen and eighteen that wanted nothing more than to be accepted as one of the boys. It was a weakness in his character that showed itself as the anxious-to-please club toady, forever seeking approval with his knowing remarks, demonstrating his loyalty by taunts and bullying. It is there in the crude racism of stories such as 'His Chance in Life', where it is the drop of Yorkshire blood in Michele d'Cruze's veins that enables him to keep his head and act like a sahib in a crisis, and 'The Head of a District', in which the Westernised Bengali Grish Chunder Dé, MA, fails to act like a sahib and so loses his head altogether. What makes these lapses bearable – if not quite forgivable – is that they are put into perspective by the many far greater stories written by Kipling that speak of the human condition in terms that can only be described as having the breadth of true genius.

Kipling was always to remain on uneasy terms with the Lahore Club – but not so the Mess or the barrack-room. While there is not one decent story from him on club life, a dozen of his sharpest stories are built around the British Army in India. Poor physical co-ordination and bad eyesight had put paid to any thoughts of an army career along the lines of so many of his schoolmates, but there was a part of Rudyard that always hankered after the active life, and he thought highly of soldiers as men of action. There was very little active military service in India or along its borders during Kipling's time – but this did not inhibit him from writing about it, drawing heavily on incidents recounted and regimental legends retold.

A few weeks after his arrival he dined 'in awed silence' at the mess of the 30th East Lancashires out in the cantonments at Mian Mir. They were later relieved by the 2nd/5th Northumberland Fusiliers, Kipling's 'first and best beloved Battalion,' whose junior officers and men he got to know well over three years. He was often invited over to dine with the duty subaltern commanding the guard at Fort Lahore, 'where, all among marble-inlaid empty apartments of dead Queens, or under the domes of old tombs, meals began with the regulation thirty grains of quinine in the sherry, and ended – as Allah pleased!'[18]

Perhaps because they asked nothing of him and were happy to take him as he was, Rudyard got on very well with these young officers. His portrait of Bobby Wicks in 'Only a Subaltern' is the most idealised of the many Anglo-Indian characters that he was to create, and in truth, he had much to thank them for as a young bachelor in Lahore. 'It is mainly to them that

17 From *The Jungle Book*.
18 *Something of Myself*, p.55.

any little social festivity is due,' writes the anonymous 'tourist' in the subversive little article in the *C&MG*: 'They organise the races, dances, balls and picnics, and seem to manage most of the flirtations in the country. Nothing can exceed the hospitality and kindness either of a Mess or any officer of one. It is curious to think how little we in England see or know of our army. In India they are one of the most prominent features of the landscape. I owe them many kindnesses.'[19]

His late-night dinners with the Fort guard probably first brought Rudyard into informal contact with ordinary British soldiers as distinct from 'bloomin' orf'cers' – although he seems quite deliberately to have set out to cultivate them. And if the verses entitled 'The Story of Tommy', published in *The Pioneer* in September 1884, about a private soldier 'aged twenty and drunk in his cot' who shoots the barrack-room *punkah-wallah* and is court-martialled and hanged, are by Kipling (and, rough as they are, they have the Kipling touch), it is clear that his interest in the plight of the British soldier had already been aroused by that date. This is supported by the testimony of a former sergeant of the 2nd/5th Fusiliers who was to recall in his old age how 'Mr Kipling, then a man of nineteen', was brought to him one evening by the orderly officer with instructions to introduce him to 'typical scenes of barrack life' so that he could give some account of army life in a series of articles he was writing: 'I knew that the only place to suit his purposes was the regimental canteen and there I conducted him. By chance I found a suitable knot of men in the shape of 8 or 10 "boozing chums" who belonged to the musketry fatigue party, headed by Cpl. MacNamara. I did my best to give them an idea of what Mr Kipling wanted, warning them not to give themselves away by mis-statements and so on, and I left them.'[20]

Whether Corporal Mulvaney and Privates Ortheris and Learoyd were found among this party of 'boozing chums' is not known. The Soldiers Three make their first appearance in the pages of the '*Civil and Military Gazette*' in March 1887 as 'The Three Musketeers', in which the narrator comes upon them in the refreshment rooms at Umballa Station. 'Having no position to consider, and my trade enforcing it, I could move at will in the fourth dimension,' is how Kipling explains his quite extraordinary rapport with the British Other Ranks. His undefined status made it possible for him to bridge the enormous social divide that existed between the officers and the men. Combined with Rudyard's relentless curiosity and his affinity with underdogs, it allowed him to give the BOR a public voice that had never been heard before – an achievement of which he was justifiably proud:

> Lord Roberts, at that time Commander-in-Chief, who knew my people, was interested in the men, and – I had by then written one or two stories about soldiers – the proudest moment of my young life was when I rode

19 *C&MG*, 29 January 1887.

20 Yeoman John Fraser, quoted by Lord Birkenhead in *Rudyard Kipling*, the 'suppressed' authorised biography, finally published in 1978.

> up Simla Mall beside him on his usual explosive red Arab, while he asked me what the men thought about their accommodation, entertainment-rooms and the like. I told him, and he thanked me gravely as though I had been a full Colonel.[21]

Simla, where this encounter took place in the summer of 1889, was well established as the smartest of the British hill-stations in India. Perched on a ridge in the Himalayan foothills 170 miles east of Lahore, the 8000 feet difference in elevation gave its air the sparkle of champagne. For young Rudyard in 1883 it represented the last – and, in many ways, the most thrilling – corner of Anglo-India still to be explored. But Simla had to be preceded by the first Hot Weather Rudyard had known since his infancy. In June 1883, for the first time since his arrival in Lahore eight months earlier, he found himself the sole occupant of the family bungalow, his mother having gone home to England to collect Trix, and Lockwood having taken himself off to the Hills. For a brief period Rudyard was alone in the heat and found it almost unbearable. 'For one weary week', he wrote to his favourite aunt in England, 'my fear in the day time was that I was going to die, and at night my only fear was that I was going to live till morning . . . My eyes began their old tricks again and I was so utterly unstrung . . . I could only avoid the shadows by working every minute.'[22]

At last, in early July, he went off on his first local leave – to Simla and to 'pure joy', where 'every golden hour counted. It began in heat and discomfort, by rail and road. It ended in the cool evening, with a wood fire in one's room.' Simla, where he stayed most comfortably with one of the *C&MG*'s wealthy partners, was 'another new world. There the Hierarchy lived, and one saw and heard the machinery of administration stripped bare. There were the Heads of the Viceregal and Military staffs and the Aides-de-Camp; and playing whist with Great Ones, who gave him special news, was the Correspondent of our big Sister Paper the '*Pioneer*', then a power in the land.'[23]

Despite being the summer headquarters of the Government and the Indian Army, Simla's keynote was relaxation. It offered a refuge from plains' conventions as well as plains' temperatures – a little England free of the suffocating constraints of always being on show. 'The atmosphere of the place is one of pleasure-seeking,' wrote the principal Vicereine of Kipling's time, Lady Dufferin, and the atmosphere was made all the headier by the presence of large numbers of grass widows whose husbands remained at work in the plains. After the rectitude of the plains-station the licence of the hill-station was a revelation to the adolescent Kipling. 'The month was a round of picnics, dances, theatricals and so on – and I flirted with the bottled up energy of a year on my lips,' boasted seventeen-year-old Ruddy to his aunt. Simla excited and shocked him, providing rich grist to his imagination. In his Simla tales he would show his Anglo-Indian

21 *Something of Myself*, p.57.
22 Letter to Miss Edith Macdonald, Kipling Papers, Sussex University.
23 *Something of Myself*, p.57.

readers an aspect of themselves that conflicted directly with their self-image. 'Wonderfully clever as these short stories are,' wrote one well-known Simla resident of Kipling's *Plain Tales from the Hills* and *Under the Deodars*, 'they have, I fear led many to regard Simla as a town populated by Mrs Hauksbees, by frivolous grass-widows, idle hill captains and the genus known as "bow-wows", and no writer has perhaps done more than the brilliant genius I have mentioned to give the outside world the idea of Simla as a centre of frivolity, jealousy and intrigue.'[24] Rudyard would have agreed with every word.

Simla opened Rudyard's eyes to the opposite sex. He had already fallen romantically in love with an English girl before leaving for India and there was the powerful influence of his mother in Lahore (referred to reverentially as 'the Mother' in his autobiography) – who had turned out to be 'more delightful than all my imaginings or memories' and to whom he later dedicated his *Plain Tales from the Hills* as 'The Wittiest Woman in India.' But now he was brought face to face with the full sexuality of Anglo-Indian womanhood – to which even his adored mother was subject – and it unnerved him. Enticing though it was, this sexuality marred his idealised image of English womanhood. It made the sahib prey to the memsahib's wiles – and it let the side down:

I had a little husband
  Who gave me all his pay.
I left him for Mussoorie
  A hundred miles away.
I dragged my little husband's name
  Through heaps of social mire,
And joined him in November
  As good as you'd desire.[25]

But this first visit to Simla lasted barely a month. By August Rudyard was back at work in Lahore, finding its dullness 'something hideous after all the bustle of Simla.' His parents and sister were still away and the civil lines largely untenanted: 'There are 9 men and 2 ladies in the station and most are going away. Practically I am living at the Club. I dine there every night and go home to my big house to sleep.'[26] But sleep was not often to be found. Now, for the first time, he learned what it was to suffer the long drawn-out Indian hot weather; how heat, ennui and isolation combined to tear a young man's nerves to shreds: 'In those months . . . one took up one's bed and walked about with it from room to room, seeking less heated air; or slept on the flat roof with the waterman to throw half-skinfulls of

24 Sir Edward Buck, *Simla Past and Present*, 1904.
25 From an unsigned article entitled 'Music for the Middle-Aged', *C&MG*, 21 June 1884.
26 Letter to Miss Edith Macdonald, 14 August 1883, Kipling Papers.

water on one's parched carcase. This brought on fever but saved heat-stroke.' Unable to sleep and frequently wracked by fevers that sapped body and mind, Rudyard was driven to the verge of a breakdown. 'I had come to the edge of all endurance,' he was to admit years later. 'As I entered my empty house in the dusk there was no more in me except the horror of a great darkness, that I must have been fighting for some days. I came through that darkness alive, but how I do not know.'[27] He had become morbidly obsessed with the threat to his physical existence that India presented. It was as if he was surrounded by death:

> The dead of all times were about us – in the vast forgotten Moslem cemeteries round the Station, where one's horse's hoof of a morning might break through to the corpse below; skulls and bones tumbled out of our mud garden walls, and were turned up among the flowers by the Rains; and at every point were tombs of the dead. Our chief picnic rendezvous and some of our public offices had been memorials to desired dead women; and Fort Lahore, where Ranjit Singh's wives lay, was a mausoleum of ghosts.[28]

The threat of sudden death was a very real one: from typhoid 'which seemed to have something to do with water'; from 'seasonal fever'; from 'what was described as "blood poisoning"'; from cholera 'which was manifestly a breath of the Devil that could kill on one side of a barrack-room and spare the others.' Death was 'always our constant companion . . . My world was filled with boys, but a few years older than I, who lived utterly alone, and died of typhoid mostly at the regulation age of twenty-one.'[29] The taking of opium-based drugs such as chlorodyne (containing morphine, chloroform and cannabis resin) for his dysentery on top of daily doses of quinine can have done nothing to settle an already over-vivid imagination. One outcome was the writing of several bizarre essays and poems on fever and hot weather nights to be found scattered here and there in the *C&MG* and *Pi* during these formative years. One of the earliest was a poem by 'R.K.' published in the *C&MG* in June 1885: 'After the Fever', in which a fever sufferer believes he is dead and buried. Two months later the *Civil and Military Gazette* carried an even stranger piece of writing entitled 'De Profundis', a stage-by-stage account of a night's fever, the first such stage being the 'Purgatory of Sizes and Distances':

> The cold fits have passed away, and you have been burning steadily for the last ten minutes, preparatory to a final glissade down a rolling bank of black cloud and thick darkness, and out into the regions beyond. Here you are alone, utterly alone on the verge of a waste of moonlit sand, stretching away to the horizon. Hundreds and thousands of miles away lies a small silver pool, not bigger than a splash of rain water. A stone is dropped into its bosom, and, as the circles spread, the puddle widens into a devouring, placid sea, advancing in mathematically straight ridges across the sand.

27 *Something of Myself*, pp.53 and 65.
28 *Ibid.*, p.24.
29 *Ibid.*, pp.41–2.

> The silver lines broaden from east to west, and rush up with inconceivable rapidity to the level of your eyes. You shudder and attempt to fly. The innumerable lines retreat with a long drawn '*hesh-sh*' across the levels, and the terrible sea is contracted to the dimensions of a little puddle once more. A moment's breathing space, and the hideous advance and retreat recommences. The unstricken observer would tell you, if you cared to listen (which you do not, for you are deep in a struggle for life), that this phenomenon is simply the result of the quinine taken a few hours ago. But it is a very real Hell to you, for the advancing and receding tide gives place to all manner of strange dreams, wherein you are eternally progressing between infinite parallel straight lines, as eternally being driven back in terror by something that advances and retreats at the further end of the passage, or overwhelmed by immense agitations of the solid earth, all directed against your poor Personality.[30]

Worse visions follow as the victim descends by way of the 'Purgatory of Faces' to the 'Purgatory of Vain Imaginings' before being revived at dawn by a glass of iced water brought to his bedside by the faithful Kadir Baksh, Rudyard's bearer. As much exorcisms as exercises in imaginative prose, these early writings show how Kipling was learning to harness the rioting of his mind and turn it into disciplined sentences.

Insomnia was to harry Kipling for much of his adult life but, typically, he turned it to advantage. When, as he puts it in *Something of Myself*, 'the night got into my head' he used these occasions to extend his experience. Lockwood Kipling had pronounced Lahore to be free of all temptations – 'all that makes Lahore profoundly dull makes it safe for young persons'[31] – but Lockwood had underestimated his son's resourcefulness. Young Ruddy became a night-wanderer. After the paper had been 'put to bed' at around midnight he took to walking the streets, increasingly forsaking the staid Lahore of the Mall and the civil lines for that other infinitely more mysterious Lahore – the City of Dreadful Night – hidden within the city walls, waiting to be entered through one of its many narrow gates:

> A stifling hot blast from the mouth of the Delhi Gate nearly ends my resolution of entering the City of Dreadful Night at this hour. It is a compound of all evil savours, animal and vegetable, that a walled city can brew in a day and a night. The temperature within the motionless groves of plantain and orange trees outside the city walls seems chilly by comparison. . . .
>
> Then silence follows – the silence that is full of the night noises of a great city. A stringed instrument of some kind is just, and only just, audible. High overhead someone throws open a window, and the rattle of the woodwork echoes down the empty street. On one of the roofs a hookah is in full blast: and the men are talking softly as the pipe gutters . . . [32]

Here was a world quite beyond Rudyard's experience – but one whose potential he was quick to grasp: 'The yard-wide gullies into which the

30 Reprinted in full in *Kipling's India*. 31 Kipling Papers.

32 *From Sea to Sea*, 1899. The 'City of Dreadful Night' was borrowed from a poem of that title by James Thomson and was used first to describe Lahore City in a sketch published in the *C&MG* in 1885. It was also used to describe Calcutta in a later series of sketches.

moonlight cannot struggle are full of mystery, stories of life and death and intrigue of which we, the Mall abiding, open-windowed, purdah-less English know nothing and believe less . . . Properly exploited, our City, from the Taksali to the Delhi Gate, and from the wrestling-ground to the Badami Bagh would yield a store of novels to which the *City of Sunshine* would be as "water unto wine."'[33]

And exploit Lahore City was exactly what Kipling did, not only for the novel that began as *Mother Maturin* and ended as *Kim*, but also for a dozen and more of his finest stories (including the one that rounds off the final section of this anthology). More than anything else, it was these nocturnal, fevered excursions into Indian India and into the darkest corners of his imagination that fired Kipling's genius, providing both inspiration and source material:

> I would wander till dawn in all manner of odd places – liquor-shops, gambling and opium-dens, which are not a bit mysterious, wayside entertainments such as puppet-shows, native dances; or in and about the narrow gullies under the Mosque of Wazir Khan for the sheer sake of looking. Sometimes, the Police would challenge, but I knew most of their officers, and many folk in some quarters knew me for the son of my Father, which in the East more than anywhere else is useful. Otherwise, the word 'Newspaper' sufficed; though I did not supply my paper with many accounts of these prowls. One would come home, just as the light broke, in some night-hawk of a hired carriage which stank of hookah-fumes, jasmine-flowers, and sandalwood; and if the driver were inclined to talk, he told one a good deal.[34]

The extent to which Rudyard immersed himself in this shifting, twilight world, whose chaotic, disease-ridden disorder repelled even as it drew him, is a matter for conjecture. We know that he had to spend his second Hot Weather alone in Bikanir House for almost six months while his parents and his sister Trix were away in the less than smart hill-station of Dalhousie. This was a particularly savage summer, with cholera striking Lahore and its shrunken European garrison hard, when 'the men sat up with the men and the women with the women. We lost four of our invalids and thought we had done well.'[35] Late one evening Rudyard himself was struck down with the most severe bout of stomach cramps that he had ever known. It was Kadir Baksh who came to his rescue:

> He lit a lamp and took a look at me and straightaway bolted out of the house. This made me fancy that I must have a touch of the 'sickness that destroyeth in the noonday', as distinguished from the other articles and I poured myself out a pretty stiff dose of chlorodyne and sat down to await the march of events and pray for the morning.
>
> I had hardly rolled onto the floor, however, before my man turned up for the second time with a naked oil lamp, a little bottle and a queer looking weapon in his hand. The fellow had brought me opium and a pipe

33 'The City of Two Creeds', *C&MG*, 1 October 1887. The *City of Sunshine* was the title of a novel by A. Allardyce, published 1887.

34 *Something of Myself*, pp.53–4.

35 *Ibid.*, p.42.

> all complete and then and there insisted upon my smoking as much as I could. Well, I wasn't in a position to argue, so he rolled the pills and I set to. Presently I felt the cramps in my legs dying out and my tummy more settled, and a minute or two later, it seemed to me that I fell through the floor.
>
> When I woke up I found my man waiting at the bedside with a glass of warm milk and a stupendous grin . . . He vows and declares that I was going to have a touch of the sickness that is loose in our city now. Whether he is right or wrong . . . no woman could have tended me more carefully than he through those terrible hours between eleven and two.[36]

That morning Rudyard felt well enough to report for work at the paper – even though he came into the office 'with every sign of advanced intoxication.'

These events took place in mid-September 1884 and on the 28th of that month there appeared in the *Civil and Military Gazette* a bizarre short story entitled 'The Gate of the Hundred Sorrows'. Set in an opium den close by Lahore's Delhi Gate, it dwelt on such morbid themes as darkness, death and decay as perceived through the deteriorating mind of a Eurasian drug-addict. It was Rudyard Kipling's first published short story – and perhaps it was no coincidence that his Chief, the dreaded Amber Toad, happened to be away on local leave with Rudyard in charge.

That Kipling's own powerfully felt experience in taking opium should have provided the inspiration for his first real work of imaginative fiction was not surprising. There was always more than a kernel of hard fact in his stories – an event or a particular personality – that served as the jumping off point for his imagination, which begs the question of how far Kipling went during that long, hot summer of '84. 'I'm in love with the Country,' he wrote to a fellow journalist in India, ' . . . where I find heat and smells of oil and spices and puffs of temple incense, and sweat and darkness, and dirt and lust and cruelty.'[37] How much of his own findings, one has to ask, lie at the heart of such Lahore City tales as 'Beyond the Pale' and 'Without Benefit of Clergy' that turn clubman Kipling's strictures on racial and sexual taboos so topsy-turvy? How could young Kipling have written so feelingly about the young sahibs, Holden and Trejago, and their respective forbidden loves, Ameera and Bisesa, without having shared their delights and agonies in some measure? But the grand old man of letters, the Nobel Prize winner who wrote *Something of Myself*, gives nothing away, and the tidying of his papers, first by his wife and then by his daughter, has ensured that we have little to go on beyond Kipling's genius.

Increasing contact with Indian India, both from his night wanderings and from such journalistic forays as a visit to the agricultural fair at Amritsar in October 1884, did nothing to dampen Rudyard's morbid fears. While he revelled in his greater association with an India that most

36 Letter to Miss Edith Macdonald, Kipling Papers.
37 Letter to E. K. Robinson, 1886, quoted in an article in *Literature*, misquoted by Lord Birkenhead.

Englishmen regarded as off-limits and rejoiced in his fast-growing understanding of Indian ways, he also grew increasingly aware that this native culture was too strong to be budged. Indeed, India put his own culture and his own people at risk – and this threat of being overwhelmed by India becomes a recurrent theme in many of the Kipling stories. Sometimes it takes the form of a hostile landscape – a dust-storm, a drought, a flood or perhaps an outbreak of cholera – sometimes it has a human form, as in the horror story of a young sahib out riding who slides into a sand-pit and finds himself trapped in a living hell peopled by hostile outcasts. This is another of Kipling's earliest published tales, 'The Strange Ride of Morrowbie Jukes', written in December 1884 but not published until a year later.[38] It is an Anglo-Indian nightmare in which British order is displaced by brute chaos, where there is 'no law save that of the strongest.' Whether consciously or not, Rudyard was reflecting many of the fears and preoccupations that lay behind the self-confident facade of the Raj. Almost thirty years after the 1857 Mutiny, the British hold on India was as fragile as ever; the risk (and the fear) of being engulfed by savage, anarchic forces constant. 'Under the shop lights in front of the sweet-meat and *ghee* sellers' booths, the press and din of words is thickest,' is how one passage from Kipling's account of Peshawar City, visited in March 1885, begins:

> Faces of dogs, swine, weazles and goats, all the more hideous for being set on human bodies, and lighted with human intelligence, gather in front of the ring of lamplight, where they may be studied for half an hour at a stretch. Pathans, Afreedees, Logas, Kohistanis, Turkomans, and a hundred other varieties of the turbulent Afghan race, are gathered in the vast human menagerie between the Gate and the Ghor Khutri. As an Englishman passes, they will turn to scowl upon him, and in many cases to spit fluently on the ground after he has passed.[39]

This same year saw Kipling's initiation into the mysteries of freemasonry. Every civil station in India had its Masonic Lodge and in Lahore there were no less than five. Why Kipling chose to become a freemason is not clear but it is surely significant that the Lodge he chose to enter, Hope and Perseverance 782 EC, was not racially exclusive. He records that here he met as equals 'Muslims, Hindus, Sikhs, members of the Arya and Brahmo Samaj, and a Jew tyler, who was priest and butcher to his little community in the city. So yet another world opened to me which I needed.'[40] Perhaps this last sentence holds the key; perhaps freemasonry's cult of universal male brotherhood suggested a bridge between the races – or did it have more to do with Kipling's deep fascination with closed worlds and with those who lived on the fringes of society? Whatever his motives, these masonic ties surely played a part in helping him to achieve that 'veracity of eye and ear' that almost lifts his Indian characters off the page and makes

38 In *Quartette*, Christmas 1885.
39 'The City of Evil Countenances', *C&MG*, 1 April 1885, reprinted in *Kipling's India*.
40 *Something of Myself*, p.52. The Brahmo Samaj was a reformed sect of Hinduism, popular among more Westernised Indians. Arya Samaj was a fundamentalist revivalist movement which in Kipling's time in the Punjab was aggressively anti-Muslim and anti-Christian.

it possible to transliterate their spoken words back into the original vernacular tongue. That, at least, is the assertion of the Indian writer Farrukh Dhondy. 'I can hear the tenor, style and vocabulary of Urdu when I read the English,' he maintains,[41] citing as an example the speech of the Sikh narrator in 'A Sahib's War' (written, it is worth noting, twelve years after Kipling had left India).

Kipling's third Indian summer, in his nineteenth year, heralded his coming of age. His Chief was now allowing him more scope for his talents: letting him insert 'scraps' in the paper when there were spaces to be filled, giving him a weekly column to write on the social round in Lahore, even sending him out to cover such distant events as the reception of the Amir of Afghanistan by the new Viceroy, Lord Dufferin. This took place at Rawalpindi in April 1885 and from there Rudyard proceeded straight to Simla, his reward for lively reporting being five months in the hills as the paper's special Simla correspondent.

This was to be a most glorious summer. Due in large measure to the liberating influence of the Dufferins – a gregarious, sophisticated couple much too sure of themselves to be troubled by Anglo-Indian convention – Simla was about to enter one of its most glittering periods. The Viceroy and Vicereine soon gathered about them a lively circle of friends that included Rudyard's parents and his sister. 'Dullness and Mrs Kipling cannot exist in the same room,' was one of Lord Dufferin's favourite *bons mots*. Lockwood's erudition also went down very well at Peterhoff, the cramped hunting-lodge that had to serve as the Viceroy's summer residence, while pretty young Trix's charms were enough to win her a proposal of marriage from the Viceroy's eldest son (swiftly rejected as unsuitable by both sets of parents). Rudyard must have observed his parents' rapid elevation with considerable satisfaction, although as a newspaper correspondent he limited himself to largely innocuous reporting. Yet, as an excerpt from one of his 'Simla Notes' on the subject of the 'Simla Baby' demonstrates, Rudyard the social observer was hard at work:

> Not long ago it was my exceeding good fortune to come across little Knickerbocker in all his glory. His Mamma had left him in her *ghari* while she stepped into a milliner's shop. The visit was a protracted one, and several other ladies were shopping at the same time. That is to say, there were twenty *jhampanies* or so lounging in the road-way. Scarcely had Mrs Knickerbocker disappeared, than the *rickshaw* was taken with internal convulsions; and above the lap-cloth rim (he had dived below to investigate the structural peculiarities of rickshaws) emerged a tangled brown head, a disreputable sailor's hat, and the upper half of Little Knickerbocker. Then he held his *levee* of *jhampanies*, and I would defy even a Higher Standard, double pressure extra proficient to have done better; the conversation passed beyond his bystander's comprehension. It was flavoured with numberless jokes, for the coolies laughed like the

41 Dhondy, at a discussion of Kipling held at The Bookspace, Royal Festival Hall, 19 March 1986.

> children they are; and Little Knickerbocker the loudest of all. It contained sound moral advice of some kind, for they sat on the ground and stared solemnly into his chubby little face. It enunciated grave truths of life and thought doubtless, for they shook their heads assentingly and said '*Je Han*' '*Such hai*!' to the small philosopher. 'What was it all about?' At this question, the coolies straightway relapsed into stolid *netschies*, and retired to their respective charges. The spell was broken, and the levee dispersed; only Little Knickerbocker was equal to the occasion. He bent forward over the lap-cloth with a grin – an unadulterated boy's grin – 'I was only talking to them about themselves.' Spirit of every ruler and administrator that India has known, has it been reserved for the Simla baby to talk to the people of the land 'about themselves' as Little Knickerbocker did; and to him only will the coolies speak unrestrainedly 'about themselves'? Here were twenty souls, who would have grovelled, cringed and lied with oriental fervour to any district officer who might address a word to them, chattering like daws 'about themselves' to seven-year-old Little Knickerbocker.[42]

Rudyard also observed the adult Anglo-Indian at play, concentrating on 'the female of the species.' In his tourist's guise he informs us that: 'The climate kills good looks, and, taking one thing with another, they are as plain as they can be. Where they aren't plain, they are sickly and sallow. A little beauty goes a very long way in India.' In particular, it was not the pretty young daughters who held his attention but their mothers: 'As a general rule, only the older women try to be "fast", and their fastness is very modified; but it lasts for many years. Women of from forty to fifty and upwards – I'm not exaggerating, I assure you – are the Lillie Langtrys of India, and the youngest men are their worshippers in a lukewarm sort of way . . . They know more of life, death, sickness and trouble than English women, I think; and this makes them broader in their views.'[43]

It was these older, more experienced women, the Lucy Hauksbees and Polly Marlows of Anglo-India, who fascinated him; scheming, flirtatious, caustic, witty women – but also women of great heart, deeply conscious of the vanities and the fragility of their lives – in short, women very like his adored Mother:

The young men come, the young men go,
  Each pink and white and neat,
She's older than their mothers, but
  They grovel at Her feet.
They walk beside Her rickshaw-wheels –
  None ever walk by mine;
And that's because I'm seventeen
  And she is forty-nine.

42 'Simla Notes', *C&MG*, 29 July 1885, reprinted in *Kipling's India*.
43 *C&MG*, 29 January 1887.

This young woman's lament from 'My Rival', one of Kipling's *Departmental Ditties*, gains an extra dimension when one learns that in the summer of 1885 Trix was just seventeen – and her mother forty-nine. We know that Rudyard's strictures on Simla memsahibs did not always go down well with the female half of the Family Square – but what wouldn't one give to have been present in their cottage in Simla at breakfast on 8 July when mother and daughter first set eyes on 'My Rival', set out in stark print in *The Pioneer*!

We can now look upon that long Simla summer as a time of a last gathering of nerve before the great creative surge about to come. In Simla Rudyard picnicked under the deodars, danced, flirted at a distance, joined in the amateur theatricals, wrote light verse and pungent letters home – and yet remained at heart an observer rather than a participant, taking in everything: 'My young head was in a ferment of new things seen and realised at every turn.' Only one Simla story, 'The Phantom Rickshaw', followed on directly, appearing alongside 'The Strange Ride of Morrowbie Jukes' in the Kipling family magazine *Quartette* at the end of the year. It is not at all one of the bitter-sweet comedies of Simla manners popularly associated with Kipling's 'tales from the hills' but a Gothic haunting in the unlikely setting of Simla Mall. In his autobiography Kipling explains how he was more or less driven to write the story by what he termed his 'Personal Daemon':

> Mine came to me early when I sat bewildered among other notions, and said: 'Take this and no other.' I obeyed, and was rewarded. It was a tale in the little Christmas Magazine *Quartette*, which we four wrote together, and it was called 'The Phantom Rickshaw.' Some of it was weak, much was bad and out of key; but it was my first serious attempt to think in another man's skin.
>
> After that I learned to lean upon him and recognise the sign of his approach . . . When your Daemon is in charge, do not try to think consciously. Drift, wait, and obey.[44]

For the first few months after the publication of '*Quartette*' Rudyard did indeed drift and wait. Then at the start of the 1886 Hot Weather comes 'The House of Suddhoo':

> Suddhoo sleeps on the roof generally, except when he sleeps in the street. He used to go to Peshawar in the cold weather to visit his son who sells curiosities near the Edwardes' Gate, and then he slept under a real mud roof. Suddhoo is a great friend of mine, because his cousin had a son who secured, thanks to my commendation, the post of head-messenger to a big firm in the Station. Suddhoo says that God will make me a Lieutenant-Governor one of these days. I daresay his prophecy will come true.[45]

The deceptively simple sentences tell their own story. Kipling the

44 *Something of Myself*, pp. 208–10.
45 *C&MG*, 30 April 1886.

teenager has gone for ever (he had celebrated his twentieth birthday four months earlier). A new voice comes through sharp and clear, with a quiet, gently ironic, seemingly plain conversational tone that does not have to strain to make itself heard. Kipling has also found his means of delivery through the vehicle – to be used again and again – of the reporter-narrator who tells us the story straight as it was told to him. His next two Indian tales, 'Naboth' and 'The Story of Muhammad Din', published in August and September, confirmed that this new-found voice was here to stay. Both are minor masterpieces. The floodgates were about to be opened.

In the spring of 1886 the Kipling family had been visited in Lahore by a thirty-year-old British journalist named Kay Robinson, a recently appointed assistant editor of '*The Pioneer*'. What he later described as the 'family quartette' made a deep impression on him. He found Lockwood 'a rare, genial soul, with happy artistic instincts, a polished literary style, and a generous cynical sense of humour'; Alice Kipling 'preserved all the graces of youth, and had a sprightly, if occasionally caustic wit, which made her society always desirable'; while Trix, a 'statuesque beauty,' had all her mother's vivacity and 'a rare literary memory.' Only Rudyard failed to make a striking first impression:

> His face had not acquired the character of manhood, and contrasted somewhat unpleasantly with his stoop (acquired through much bending over an office table), his heavy eyebrows, his spectacles, and his sallow Anglo-Indian complexion; while his jerky speech and abrupt movements added to the unfavourable impression. But his conversation was brilliant, and his sterling character gleamed through the humorous light which shone through his spectacles, and in ten minutes he fell into his natural place as the most striking member of a remarkably clever and charming family.[46]

When Rudyard returned from a month's leave in Simla – where all the talk had been of his *Departmental Ditties*, collected and published in one volume in June – he found to his delight that the Amber Toad, the Chief who had tyrannised over him for three years, had taken early retirement. His place had been filled by Kay Robinson, sent up from Allahabad by George Allen with written orders to 'put some sparkle' into the *C&MG*. When Robinson read these instructions out to his subordinate the two young men immediately agreed that 'champagne had more of the desired quality than anything else we could think of.' The Sind and Punjab Hotel happened to be opposite the office, so Robinson sent over for a bottle, 'and we inaugurated our first day's work together by drinking to the successful sparkle of "the rag" under its new management.'[47]

Almost the first act of Robinson's 'joyous reign' was to completely revamp the paper, introducing in the process what was known as a 'turnover' that began on the right-hand column of the front page and

46 Robinson, 'Kipling in India'.
47 *Ibid*.

continued on the next. 'Naturally the "office" had to supply most of them,' wrote Kipling, who was given the task of filling these one and a quarter columns 'when and as padding was needed.' Robinson had very quickly caught on to the fact that he was working alongside someone of rare talent. He was later to comment that it had seemed 'almost pathetic to look through the "Civil and Military Gazette" at that time and note where Kipling's bright humour only flashed out in the introductory lines to summaries of government reports, dry semi-political notes, and the side-headings of scissors-and-paste paragraphs . . . My predecessor had done his best to make a sound second-rate journalist out of the youngster by keeping his nose at the grindstone.'[48] Despite this gruelling apprenticeship, Robinson found his assistant's capacity for hard work undiminished: 'My experience of him as a newspaper hack suggests . . . that if you want to find a man who will cheerfully do the office work of three men, you should catch a young genius . . . The amount of "stuff" that Kipling got through in a day was indeed wonderful.'

The two got along extraordinarily well together. 'He was always the best of good company,' Robinson was to recall, 'bubbling over with delightful humour, which found vent in every detail of our day's work together.' However, Rudyard did have his faults:

> There is one peculiarity of Kipling's which I really must mention; namely, the amount of ink he used to throw about. In the heat of summer white cotton trousers and a thin vest constituted his office attire, and by the day's end he was spotted all over like a Dalmatian dog. He had a habit of dipping his pen frequently and deep into the ink-pot, and as all his movements were abrupt, almost jerky, the ink used to fly. When he darted into my room, which he used to do about one thing or another in connection with the paper a dozen times in the morning, I had to shout at him to 'stand off'; otherwise, as I knew by experience, the abrupt halt he would make, and the flourish with which he placed the proof in his hand before me, would send the penful of ink – he always had a *full* pen in his hand – flying over me. Driving or sometimes walking home to breakfast, in his light attire plentifully besprinkled with ink, his spectacled face peeping out under an enormous mushroom-shaped pith hat, Kipling was a quaint-looking object.
>
> This was in the hot weather, when . . . only those men were left who, like Kipling and myself, *had* to stay . . . In the winter when 'society' had returned to Lahore, Kipling was rather scrupulous in the matter of dress.[49]

But Robinson was also to note how terrified his young assistant was of the hot weather months – even though he suffered them bravely enough – and how he 'dreaded dining at the club,' chiefly on account of 'one resident member who disliked him and was always endeavouring to snub him.' Robinson was also astonished, as were many others, then and since, by

48 *Ibid.*
49 *Ibid.*

Kipling's capacity for absorbing and retaining detail on the most esoteric subjects and by the ease with which he penetrated – or appeared to penetrate – every level of society, British and Indian. There was the occasion when Rudyard published some particularly biting verses, filled with racing and stable jargon, satirising a British cavalry regiment. The officers of the regiment were outraged but what chiefly impressed Robinson 'was that a sporting "Vet", who had lived in the pigskin almost all his life, should have gone wandering about the Lahore Club asking people, "Where does the youngster pick it all up?"'

Where, indeed? Part of Rudyard's genius, acccording to Kay Robinson, lay in the fact that he 'neglected no chance and spared no labour' in acquiring experience that he could put to literary use. Robinson was to remember, in particular, Rudyard's capacity for making friends with the strangest people:

> I remember well one long-limbed Pathan, indescribably filthy, but with magnificent mien and features – Mahbub Ali, I think was his name – who regarded Kipling as a man apart from all other 'sahibs'. After each of his wanderings . . . Mahbub Ali always used to turn up travel-stained, dirtier and more majestic than ever, for confidential colloquy with 'Kuppeleen Sahib', his 'friend' . . . And Mahbub Ali, peace to his ashes, was only one link in the strange chain of associations that Kipling riveted round himself in India. No half-note in the wide gamut of native ideas and custom was unfamiliar to him: just as he left no phase of white life in India unexplored.[50]

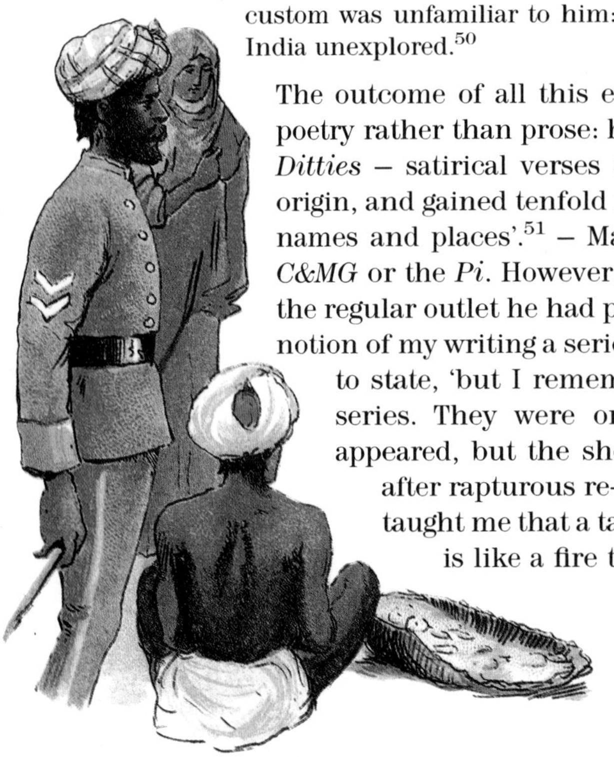

The outcome of all this exploration was, to begin with, a rush of poetry rather than prose: his *Bungalow Ballads* and *Departmental Ditties* – satirical verses that were 'personal and topical in their origin, and gained tenfold in force for readers who could supply the names and places'.[51] – Many of these first appeared either in the *C&MG* or the *Pi*. However, it was the 'turnovers' that gave Rudyard the regular outlet he had previously lacked. 'I forget who started the notion of my writing a series of Anglo-Indian tales,' Kipling was later to state, 'but I remember our council over the naming of the series. They were originally much longer than when they appeared, but the shortening of them, first to my own fancy after rapturous re-readings, and next to the space available, taught me that a tale from which pieces have been raked out is like a fire that has been poked.'

Cutting and re-cutting was only part of the writer's discipline that Rudyard had to learn: 'It was necessary that every word should tell,

50 *Ibid*. Readers familiar with *Kim* will have recognised here the real-life counterpart of Mahbub Ali, the horse-trader – although Robinson's article appeared in print four years before *Kim* was completed.

51 *Ibid*.

carry, weigh, taste and, if need be, smell. Here the Father helped me incomparably by his "judicious leaving alone." "Make your own experiments," said he. "It's the only road."'[52] Thirty-five of these experiments appeared under his own name as 'Plain Tales from the Hills' in *The Civil and Military Gazette* between November 1886 and June 1887, of which twenty-nine, together with eleven other stories, were republished in book form in January 1888. Like his poems, they told 'the tale of our life' for domestic Anglo-Indian consumption, but with a range and a degree of frankness in the telling that quite eclipsed all that had gone before. 'Some I gathered from my friends,' he informed a confidante in verse:

> And some I looted from my foes,
> and some – all's fish that Heaven sends –
> Are histories of private woes.[53]

Plain Tales from the Hills has its weaknesses, but as a body of work produced by a young man just entering his majority it is an astonishing literary *tour de force*, in which the whole emerges as better than the best of its parts. The other astonishing fact is Kipling's productivity. He turned out an average of one short story a week and a poem every fortnight for the whole of 1887 in addition to his office work. In the following year he more than doubled his output, reaching a peak (so far as publication was concerned) in February and March 1888. In March, for instance, we can find three of his short turnover tales in the *C&MG*, nine assorted stories, sketches and travel articles in *The Pioneer*, and five longer stories and one poem in *The Week's News*. As these new outlets indicate, Rudyard had by then undergone a major alteration in his circumstances. 'But mark how discreetly the cards were being dealt me,' he tells us in *Something of Myself*:

> Up till '87 my performances had been veiled in the decent obscurity of the far end of an outlying province, among a specialised community who did not interest any but themselves. I was like a young horse entered for small, up-country events where I could get used to noise and crowds, fall about till I found my feet, and learn to keep my head with the hoofs drumming behind me . . . Here was my modest notion of my own position at the end of my five years' Viceroyalty on the little *Civil and Military Gazette*.[54]

The change had come in the autumn of 1887 when, after one year with Kay Robinson, Rudyard was summoned to Allahabad. The senior proprietor, George Allen, had decided to promote his protégé to the far more important office of *The Pioneer*. The move had its disadvantages. The comforts of the 'family square' at Bikanir House were lost for ever, together with the cross-fertilization of ideas and

52 *Something of Myself*, pp.206–7.
53 Inscribed in the flyleaf on a copy of *Plain Tales from the Hills* given to Mrs Edmonia Hill.
54 *Something of Myself*, p.68.

the stimulation that his family had provided. Rudyard came to Allahabad accompanied only by his Punjabi Muslim bearer, Kadir Baksh, and his own pony and trap, and to begin with he had to put up in the bachelors' quarters of the Allahabad Club, 'full of large-bore officials, and of a respectability all new.' Characteristically, when he transferred to a new Masonic Lodge in Allahabad he made sure that it was one that included non-Europeans, avoiding the station's other more exclusive, Europeans-only Lodge.

Allahabad was an altogether different set-up from Lahore. It was the much larger, more Europeanised headquarters of the populous North-Western Provinces and – despite its name – was a Hindu rather than a Muslim city. It was not a place that Kipling ever grew attached to, for 'my life had lain among Muslims, and a man leans one way or the other according to his first service.' Nor did it improve matters to have his boss practically breathing down his neck:

> The *Pioneer* lived under the eye of its chief proprietor, who spent several months of each year in his bungalow over the way. It is true that I owed him my chance in life, but when one has been second in command of even a third-class cruiser, one does not care to have one's Admiral permanently moored at a cable's length. His love for his paper, which his single genius and ability had largely created, led him sometimes to 'give the boys a hand'. On those hectic days (for he added and subtracted to the last minute) we were relieved when the issue caught the down-country mail.
>
> But he was patient with me, as were the others, and through him again I got a wider field for 'outside stuff'.[55]

Having brought Kipling to Allahabad, Allen made sure that his young prodigy's talents were put to good use. Rudyard was first dispatched on a tour of the princely states of Rajputana, followed by a trip down-river by way of Benares to Calcutta. Almost the first thing to catch his eye as he returned from this last excursion was a large poster on Allahabad railway station which announced that 'Rudyard Kipling, author of *Plain Tales from the Hills,* will write a series of stories for *The Week's News* beginning with the next number.'[56]

Plain Tales from the Hills had only just been published but was already proving to be a phenomenal success. Allen's response was to give Kipling the additional responsibility – though at no extra cost to himself – of editing a weekly supplement called *The Week's News*, 'a rehash of news and views.' What more than outweighed the extra burden of work was that Rudyard could now publish his own stories as and when he liked: 'Henceforth no mere twelve-hundred word Plain Tales jammed into rigid frames, but three- or five-thousand word cartoons once a week.'

Rudyard now abandoned his rooms at the club for the more congenial

55 *Something of Myself*, pp.69–71; 50.
56 Mrs Edmonia Hill, 'The Young Kipling', *Atlantic Monthly*, April 1936.

atmosphere of another family home, moving in with a married couple who had befriended him: Professor Aleck Hill, who taught science at Allahabad's Muir College, and his American wife Edmonia, known as 'Ted'. It was she – a plain, open-hearted woman just turned thirty – who assumed the role previously played by Alice Kipling. She became Rudyard's confidante, chief sounding-board, and it seems, the object of his devotion – albeit a devotion of the 'lukewarm' sort – for all his passions were now concentrated on his work. When at the start of the 1888 Hot Weather the Hills left Allahabad – not for Simla but for the lesser hill-station of Mussoorie – a spate of letters followed, amounting to an intimate running journal of Rudyard's day-to-day affairs. Nothing shows more clearly than these letters to 'Ted' Hill how utterly Rudyard was bound up in his writing; every social contact, every confidence was exploited for his 'copy'. Even the confessions of an unfortunate Captain Beames of the 19th Lancers, who used to pay nightly visits to Rudyard and pour out details of a tortuous love affair, were reported stage by stage to Mrs Hill. 'He was taking down word for word what the gallant captain was saying,' Ted Hill was to recall. 'He intended to use every expression and he did that very thing.' The first episode of what was to evolve into 'The Story of the Gadsbys' appeared in *The Week's News* within the month. 'The man was a fiction, was he?' Rudyard replied when challenged about the authenticity of his Captain Gadsby. 'I've had him under the lens since 8.15 this evening.'[57]

Rudyard was himself soon on the move again, returning to Lahore for six weeks in May and June to 'act' for Kay Robinson, who was going home on leave. So it was back to 'the old, wearying, Godless futile life of a club – same men, same talk, same billiards.' Yet a certain nostalgic satisfaction was to be derived from revisiting old haunts – and it also made good copy:

> To the eye, nothing has changed. The permanent grey dust-cloud dances over the unshifted umber brick-kiln; the venerable Church that is always being built and never finished by the scattered leaven of devout is as unadvanced as ever; the *gharris* at the Station boast no new paint, and their wheels are as 'wobblesome' as of yore; the sun is not dimmed – and the many and manifold stenches have lost nothing of their poignancy. The old Station has assumed no new graces and discarded no blemishes. Here is the identical guard-post against which Timmins riotously ran his trap on that bleak November night, and then laughed futilely to see the spokes fly from the shattered wheel. Timmins laughs no more now; for six feet of rank Irrawaddy mud on mouth and chest do not predispose to merriment. Goyler was with Timmins and was nearly pitched into the road. By the way, where is Goyler? 'Oh! He exchanged ever so long ago, into a battery in Madras. D'you mean to say that you didn't know that?' Old friends have an unpleasant air of superiority about them when you ask questions after an interval. I was in the third seat of the dogcart, and I

57 *Ibid.*

gripped the rails for dear life – and now Timmins is dead and Goyler has drifted into the *Ewigkeit* down South.[58]

With his family already established in Simla for the summer, Rudyard was once more alone in the fierce heat – so fierce that he began to suffer heart palpitations. But he had already made up his mind that this was to be his last Indian Hot Weather. Kay Robinson had repeatedly urged him to return to London and make his mark there – to which he had hitherto 'always returned the answer that when he *knew* he could do work, it would be time for him to strive for a place in the English world of letters . . . The proprietors of the '*Civil and Military Gazette*' had taken him on trust, a boy fresh from school, and he would serve them loyally, like Jacob in the Bible, for his full seven years.' But the publication of *Plain Tales from the Hills* had made Rudyard Kipling a household name throughout the Anglo-Indian community in India and before the year was out his fame would spread even further with the sale of six volumes of his short stories as paperbacks on all Indian railway bookstalls. This idea had come from a fellow poker player at the Allahabad Club, a senior partner in the firm of A. H. Wheeler and Co., which had (and still have) bookstalls on the larger railway stations in India. Picked up by tourists and travellers, these one rupee paperbacks in their grey covers were to take his name overseas. Kipling could no longer remain, as Kay Robinson put it, working 'like a grub of genius, in a remote corner of the Indian Empire, spinning a gold web out of which only stray strands floated ownerless now and then into the side-columns of English newspapers.'[59] It was time for him to move on.

Rudyard's parents also recognised that it was time for them to let go. When Rudyard joined his mother and sister in Simla at the end of June 1888 (Lockwood was in England on business at the time) there was a touch of melancholy in the air. 'I knew in verity that I had come back to the old life and the ways thereof,' he wrote to Ted Hill. 'But not wholly, for it is owned that I am no longer ownable and only a visitor in the land. The Mother says this is so and the Sister too and their eyes see far – "You belong to yourself," says the Mother, and the Maiden says: – "You don't belong to us at any rate," and even in the making of this confession we come together after the wreck of the old home on a new and pleasant platform.'[60]

Rudyard's rise to fame in India had not made him any more popular. 'Ruddy's success in India was doled out drop by drop,' his sister was later to declare. 'People said, "Clever young pup!" and talked about his awful side.'[61] Indeed, as the Hot Weather of 1888 drew to a close *The Pioneer*'s proprietor began to have serious doubts about the wisdom of employing a rather too talented roving correspondent. A hard-hitting set of farewell

58 'The Old Station (by the Visitor)', *C&MG*, 8 May 1888.
59 Kay Robinson.
60 Kipling Papers.
61 Mrs Alice Macdonald Fleming, BBC radio broadcast, August 1947.

verses to speed the departing Viceroy on his way had been followed by verses hinting at the Commander-in-Chief's nepotism. 'I don't think Lord Roberts was pleased with it,' Rudyard was to recall, 'but I know he was not half so annoyed as my chief proprietor.' Then came a sneering article attacking the pretensions of the newly-formed Indian National Congress when it held its annual convention in Allahabad in December. A nasty remark about one of its sympathisers being a 'half-caste' led to an invasion of *The Pioneer*'s office by the supporter in question, a certain Captain Hearsey from a prominent Eurasian family, who proceeded to horsewhip the editor. An exchange of lawsuits for libel and assault followed and Rudyard was left with the feeling that he 'did not quite fit the *Pioneer*'s scheme of things and that my superiors were of the same opinion.'[62]

Other events also helped to speed his departure: his friend Ted Hill had suffered a severe attack of meningitis and talked of returning home to America to recuperate; his sister Trix had become engaged to an officer in the Survey of India and was planning her marriage; his mother had been warned by her doctor not to spend another Hot Weather in India. When George Allen came up with a proposal for Rudyard to do some globe-trotting at the newspaper's expense and to be given six months' salary in lieu of notice, Rudyard jumped at the offer. In February 1889 he returned briefly to Lahore where he and his father bought kites in the bazaar and joined the crowds of kite-fliers that gathered in the evenings on the banks of the Ravi. Then, having made his farewells, Rudyard joined Mr and Mrs Hill in Calcutta. On 9 March 1889 they sailed on the SS *Madura*, bound for Rangoon, Singapore, Hong Kong, Nagasaki, San Francisco – and, for Rudyard Kipling, fame. Of this his colleague Kay Robinson had not the slightest doubt – and he was not alone: 'When he left India I often offered to bet with men out there who dissented from my estimate of his power . . . that before a year had passed he would be one of the most famous writers in England. None of them dissented to the extent of taking my bet, and the result justified my caution.'[63]

This was not quite the end of Rudyard Kipling's contact with the land of his birth and his apprenticeship, his 'seven years hard' (actually, just less than six years and six months). Two years later, in December 1891, he stopped off at Colombo while on a world cruise and spent a week crossing the Indian peninsula by train. He joined his parents at Bikanir House a week before Christmas and was just settling down to the round of festivities when a cable arrived informing him that Wolcott Balestier, an American friend to whom he had become greatly attached, had died of typhoid in Europe. The news had a profound effect on him and without even waiting to spend Christmas Day with his parents, Rudyard left for Bombay. His last act on Indian soil was to call on the old *ayah* who had nursed him as a baby.

62 *Something of Myself*, pp. 73–4.
63 Kay Robinson.

It was a strange and sad end to the Indian years of his life – made all the more bizarre by Rudyard's precipitate marriage to Carrie Balestier, his dead friend's sister, at All Souls' Church, Langham Place, in London. 'A good man marred,' was Lockwood Kipling's terse comment. The wedding took place on 18 January 1892 – less than a month after Rudyard's departure from Lahore.

Although Kipling was never to return to India, in spirit and imagination he never left its shores. For the rest of his life India – and Anglo-India – remained the deepest and the freshest of many sources from which he drew inspiration for his writing, both in his verse and his fiction. As far as the latter is concerned, the list is formidable: the forty *Plain Tales from the Hills* turnovers (1888); the thirty or so stories in the six *Indian Railway Library* paperbacks – *Soldiers Three, The Story of the Gadsbys, In Black and White, Under the Deodars, The Phantom Rickshaw and Other Eerie Tales* and *Wee Willie Winkie and Other Child Stories* (all published in 1889); the twenty-seven Indian tales that made up *Life's Handicap* (1891); the novelette written with Wolcott Balestier, *The Naulahka* (1892); the seven Indian tales included in *Many Inventions* (1893); *The Jungle Book* (1894) and *The Second Jungle Book* (1895), which include the eight Mowgli stories; the six long stories that make up *The Day's Work* (1898); *Kim* (1901); and the twenty or so Indian tales that are scattered through such collections as *From Sea to Sea and Other Sketches* (1900), *Actions and Reactions* (1909) and *Land and Sea Tales for Scouts and Guides* (1923). His last Indian tale, 'The Debt', was included in his final volume of stories, *Limits and Renewals* (1932), published four years before his death. Characteristically, it is a recollection of an Indian childhood in which a little *chota-sahib* communicates far better with his servants than do his elders. Taken together with the many uncollected, suppressed and still to be positively identified fictional scraps that found their way onto the pages of *The Civil and Military Gazette, The Pioneer* and other Indian newspapers between 1883 and 1889, Kipling's Indian tales must number close on two hundred. Some really are mere scraps that follow, thirteen or fourteen have a place in this top league. None of the Mowgli stories are here, forming as they do their own complete masterpieces of English literature. In the selection of twenty-five stories or scraps that follow thirteen or fourteen have a place in this top league. None of the Mowgli stories are here, forming as they do their own complete mythical world that has little to do with the real India of the Raj.
Instead, each story has been chosen to illustrate some aspect of Anglo-India as Rudyard Kipling saw it, showing for the first time in one collection the extraordinary range of his imagination and the diversity and richness of *Kipling's Kingdom*.

SELECTING THE STORIES

My first criterion was quality, my second coverage of the Indian scene. Kipling illuminated some areas more thoroughly than others – eighteen stories about other ranks, for instance, as compared to a third of that number about military officers – so there are tales included here that would not have found their way into my list of the very best twenty-five Indian stories. 'The End of the Passage' is a case in point; marred as it is by a preposterous ending, the picture it gives of life out in the district is so sharp that it had to be included.

Another factor influencing selection was length. Kipling was able to include forty of his early stories in *Plain Tales from the Hills* because they were nearly all under two thousand words in length. But his later stories were in most instances at least twice as long and a number, such as 'The Man Who Would Be King', are really novelettes. Here I have restricted myself to just four of the longer stories: 'The Tomb of His Ancestors', 'Love-o-Women', 'On the City Wall', and 'The Undertakers'. The main casualties have been 'Without Benefit of Clergy', 'William the Conqueror', 'The Bridge Builders' and 'The Maltese Cat' – all very worthy stories but none so inspired as to make me feel they were indispensable. Their exclusion has made it possible to include a number of stories and scraps – to say nothing of an 'Introduction by Kadir Baksh, Khitmatgar' and a very appropriate epilogue entitled 'Home' – that have remained hidden in obscurity since they were first set in type a century ago. One of these is 'The Potted Princess', a delightful story for all that it is wrapped around a rather turgid Indian folk-tale; another is the cheerful scrap called 'Mister Anthony Dawking'. Would that more such forgotten tales could have been included, notably the splendidly entitled 'Collar-wallah and the Poison Stick'. However, a line has to be drawn somewhere – and this is where I have drawn it.

My special thanks in this respect to John Shearman and Lisa Lewis as well as to other members of the Kipling Society who so kindly and generously offered advice and suggestions.

CHARLES ALLEN

INTRODUCTION
BY
KADIR BAKSH, KHITMATGAR

HAZUR

Through your favour this is a book written by my *Sahib*. I know that he wrote it because it was his custom to write far into the night; I greatly desiring to go to my house. But there was no order: therefore it was my fate to sit without the door until the work was accomplished. Then came I and made shut all the papers in the office box, and these papers, by the peculiar operation of Time and owing to the skilful manner in which I picked them up from the floor, became such a book as you now see. God alone knows what is written therein, for I am a poor man, and the *Sahib* is my father and my mother, and I have no concern with his writings until he has left his table and gone to bed.

Nabi Baksh, the clerk, says that it is a book about the black men — common people. This is a manifest lie, for by what road can my *Sahib* have acquired knowledge of the common people? Have I not, for several years, been perpetually with the *Sahib:* and throughout that time have I not stood between him and the other servants who would persecute him with complaints or vex him with idle tales about my work? Did I not smite Dunnoo, the groom, only yesterday in the matter of the badness of the harness composition which I had procured? I am the head of the *Sahib's* household and hold his purse. Without me he does not know where are his rupees or his clean collars. So great is my power over the *Sahib* and the love that he bears to me! Have *I* ever told the *Sahib* about the customs of servants or black men? Am I a fool? I have said "very good talk" upon all occasions. I have cut always smooth his wristbands with scissors, and timely warned him of the passing away of his tobacco that he might not be left smokeless upon a Sunday. More than this I have not done. The *Sahib* cannot go out to dinner lacking my aid. How then should he know aught that I did not tell him? Certainly Nabi Baksh is a liar.

None the less this is a book, and the *Sahib* wrote it, for his name is in it and it is not his washing-book. Now, such is the wisdom of the *Sahib-log* that, upon opening this thing, they will instantly discover the purport. Yet I would of their favour beg them to observe how correct is the order of the pages, which I have counted from the first to the last. Thus, One is followed by Two and Two by Three, and so forward to the end of the book. Even as I picked the pages one by one with great trouble from the floor, when the *Sahib* had gone to bed, so have they been placed: and there is not a fault in the whole account. And this is *my* work. It was a great burden, but I accomplished it; and if the *Sahib* gains reputation by that which he has written — and God knows what he is always writing about — I, Kadir Baksh, his servant, also have a claim to honour.

PART
I
'The Shrine of
the Baba-Logh'

In his fiction Rudyard Kipling returns again and again to the magical years of early childhood, sometimes drawing on his own experiences, sometimes building his own fantasy worlds. 'The Potted Princess' is set in the trouble-free years of Rudyard's Bombay childhood. It is a plain story, perhaps too plain for its author's satisfaction since he withdrew it from public circulation after it had appeared in an American monthly, *'St Nicholas Magazine'* in January 1893. 'The Potted Princess' was written at a particularly happy time in Kipling's life, coinciding with the birth of his first-born, Josephine, in Vermont. There are no clouds in the sky for Punch and his little sister Judy – but they are gathering over the horizon just the same, as readers of 'Baa-Baa Black Sheep' will know.

Six-year old Tods, the 'utterly fearless young pagan' who trots through the pages of the second story in this section, 'Tods' Amendment', is Punch fleshed out and in Simla. Indeed, we have already made his acquaintance as the 'Simla Baby' and the same spoilt, clever little brat pops up in such mawkish tales as 'Wee Willie Winkie' and 'The Son of His Father'. If the memories of one Bombay old-timer are anything to go by,[61] Tods was to be seen and heard in the flesh in the Kiplings' bungalow in Bombay, listening keenly at the dinner-table while his elders talked, and interrupting the conversation with cries of 'I don't agree to that' and 'I don't think so'. It was partly to counter such self-conceit that young Anglo-Indian children like Tods-Ruddy were packed off 'Home' at five or six, away from 'the promiscuous intimacy of the Indian servants, whose propensity to worship at the shrine of the *Baba-log* is unhappily apt to demoralise the small gods and goddesses they serve'.[62]

For native Indian children there was, of course, no sudden casting out of Eden in their lives – but then theirs was indeed a different world. In the third tale of childhood, 'The Story of Muhammad Din', the little Muslim boy is an intruder, a trespasser on British territory who brings his own tragedy along with him.

'The Story of Muhammad Din' was one of Kipling's first 'turnovers', appearing in the *'Civil and Military Gazette'* on 8 September 1886. 'Tods' Amendment' was another turnover, published in the *C&MG* on 16 April 1887. Both stories were republished in *Plain Tales from the Hills*.

Preceding these three childhood tales is an 'Introduction', supposedly written by Kipling's Muslim servant, Kadir Baksh, which originally served to introduce one of the six railway edition paperbacks, *In Black and White*. According to Kipling's confidante, 'Ted' Hill, Kadir Baksh was 'quite a character. He is tall and commanding in appearance and is wholly dependable, which is well, as Rudyard, who lives in the clouds, needs some earthly care.' It was indeed Kadir Baksh who tidied up Rudyard's papers. Mrs Hill also tells us that when Kipling wrote, he would 'push off a sheet from the pad as fast as he had filled it with his tiny fine writing, letting it fall to the floor'.[63]

61 Capt. E.E. Gladstone Soloman, *Kipling Journal* No. 3 1927
62 Maud Diver, *The Englishwoman in India*, 1909
63 Mrs Edmonia Hill, *Atlantic Monthly* April 1936

THE POTTED PRINCESS

Now this is the true tale that was told to Punch and Judy his sister by their nurse, in the city of Bombay. They were playing in the verandah, waiting for their mother to come back from her evening drive. The big pink crane, who generally lived by himself at the bottom of the garden, because he hated horses and carriages, was with them too, and their nurse, who was called the *ayah,* was making him dance by throwing pieces of mud at him. Pink cranes dance very prettily until they grow angry. Then they peck.

This pink crane lost his temper, opened his wings and clattered his beak, and the *ayah* had to sing a song which never fails to quiet all the cranes in Bombay. It is a very old song, and it says:–

Buggle baita nuddee kanara
Toom-toom mushia kaye!
Nuddee kinara kanta lugga
Tullaka-tullaka ju jaye!

That means: A crane sat by the river-bank eating fish, *toom-toom*: and a thorn in the river-bank pricked him, and his life went away, *tullaka-tullaka*—drop by drop. The *ayah* and Punch and Judy always talked Hindustani because they understood it better than English.

'See now,' said Punch, clapping his hands. 'He knows, and he is ashamed. *Tullaka-tullaka ju jaye!* Go away!'

'*Tullaka-tullaka,*' said little Judy, who was five; and the pink crane shut up his beak, and went down to the bottom of the garden to the coconut palms and the aloes and the red peppers. Punch followed, shouting '*Tullaka-tullaka!*' till the crane hopped over an aloe hedge and Punch got pricked by the spikes. Then he

cried, because he was only seven, and because it was so hot that he was wearing only very few clothes and the aloes had pricked a great deal of him; and Judy cried too, because Punch was crying, and she knew that that meant something worth crying for.

'Ohoo!' said Punch, looking at both his fat little legs together. 'I am very badly pricked by the very bad aloe. Perhaps I shall die!'

'Punch will die because he has been pricked by the very bad aloe; and then there will be only Judy,' said Judy.

'No,' said Punch very quickly, putting his legs down. 'Then you will sit up to dinner alone. I will not die; but, *ayah*, I am very badly pricked. What is good for that?'

The *ayah* looked down for a minute, just to see that there were two tiny pink scratches on Punch's legs. Then she looked out across the garden to the blue water of Bombay harbour, where the ships are, and said:–

'Once upon a time there was a Rajah.'

'Will Punch die, *ayah*?' said Judy. She too had seen the pink scratches, and they seemed very dreadful to her.

'No,' said Punch. '*Ayah* is telling a tale. Stop crying, Judy.'

'And the Rajah had a daughter,' said the *ayah*.

'It is a new tale,' said Punch. 'The last Rajah had a son, and he was turned into a monkey. Hssh!'

The *ayah* put out her soft brown arm, picked Judy off the matting of the verandah, and tucked her into her lap. Punch sat cross-legged close by.

'That Rajah's daughter was very beautiful,' the *ayah* went on.

'How beautiful? More beautiful than Mamma? Then I do not believe this tale,' said Punch.

'She was a fairy Princess, Punch *baba*, and she was very beautiful

indeed. And when she grew up the Rajah her father said that she must marry the best Prince in all India.'

'Where did all these things happen?' said Punch.

'In a big forest near Delhi. So it was told to me,' said the *ayah*.

'Very good,' said Punch. 'When I am big I will go to Delhi. Tell the tale, *ayah*.'

'Therefore the king made a talk with his magicians-men with white beards who do *jadoo*, and make snakes come out of baskets, and grow mangoes from little stones, such as you, Punch, and you, Judy *baba*, have seen. But in those days they did much more wonderful things. They turned men into tigers and elephants. And the magicians counted the stars under which the Princess was born.'

'I—I do not understand this,' said Judy, wriggling on the *ayah's* lap. Punch did not understand either, but he looked very wise.

The *ayah* hugged her close. 'How should a babe understand?' she said very softly. 'It is in this way. When the stars are in one position when a child is born, it means well. When they are in another position, it means, perhaps, that the child may be sick or ill-tempered, or she may have to travel very far away.'

'*Must* I travel far away?' said Judy.

'No, no. There were only good little stars in the sky on the night that Judy *baba* was born – little home-keeping stars that danced up and down, they were so pleased.'

'And I—I—I? What did the stars do when I was born?' said Punch.

'There was a new star that night. I saw it. A great star with a fiery tail all across the sky. Punch will travel far.'

'That is true, I have been to Nasik in the railway-train. Never mind the Princess's stars. What did the magic-men do?'

'They consulted the stars, little impatient, and they said that the Princess must be shut up in such a manner that only the very best of all the Princes in India could take her out. So they shut her up, when she was sixteen years old, in a big deep grain-jar of dried clay, with a cover of plaited grass.'

'I have seen them in the Bombay market,' said Judy. 'Was it of the *very* big kind?' The *ayah* nodded, and Judy shivered, for her father had once held her up to look into the mouth of just such a grain-jar, and it was full of empty darkness.

'How did they feed her?' said Punch.

'She was a fairy. Perhaps she did not want food,' the *ayah* replied.

'All people want food. This is not a true tale. I shall go and beat the crane.' Punch got up on his knees.

'No, no. I have forgotten. There was plenty of food-plantains, red and yellow ones, almond curd, boiled rice and peas, fowl stuffed with raisins and red peppers, and cakes fried in oil with coriander seeds, and sweetmeats of sugar and butter. Is that enough food? So the Princess was shut up in the grain-jar, and the Rajah made a proclamation that whoever could take her out should marry her and should govern ten provinces, sitting upon an elephant with tusks of gold. That proclamation was made through all India.'

'We did not hear it, Punch and I,' said Judy. 'Is this a true tale, *ayah*?'

'It was before Punch was born. It was before even I was born; but so my mother told it to me. And when the proclamation was made, there came to Delhi hundreds and thousands of Princes and Rajahs and great men. The grain-jar with the cover of plaited grass was set in the middle of all, and the Rajah said he would allow to each man one year in which to make charms and learn great words that would open the grain-jar.'

'I do not understand,' said Judy again. She had been looking down the garden for her mother's return, and had lost the thread of the tale.

'The jar was a magic one, and it was to be opened by magic,' said Punch. 'Go on, *ayah*; I understand.'

The *ayah* laughed a little. 'Yes, the Rajah's magicians told all the Princes that it was a magic jar, and led them three times round it, muttering under their beards, and bade them come back in a year. So the Princes and the Subadars, and the Wazirs and the Maliks rode away east and west and north and south, and consulted the magicians in their fathers' Courts, and holy men in caves.'

'Like the holy men I saw at Nasik on the mountain? They were all *nungapunga* but they showed me their little Gods, and I burned stuff that smelt in a pot before them all, and they said I was a Hindu, and——' Punch stopped, out of breath.

'Yes. Those were the men. Old men smeared with ashes and yellow paint did the Princes consult, and witches and dwarfs that live in caves, and wise tigers and talking horses and learned parrots. They told all these men and all these beasts of the Princess in the grain-jar; and the holy men and the wise beasts taught them charms and spells that were very strong magic indeed. Some of the Princes they advised to go out and kill giants and dragons, and cut off their heads. And some of the Princes stayed for a year with the holy men in forests, learning charms that would immediately split open great mountains. There was no charm and no magic that these Princes and Subadars did not learn, for they knew that the Rajah's magicians were very strong magicians, and therefore they needed very, very strong charms to open the grain-jar. So they did all these things that I have told, and also cut off the tails of the little devils that live on the sand of the great Desert in the north; and at last there were very few dragons and giants left, and poor people could plough without being bewitched any more.

'Only there was one Prince that did not ride away with the others, for he had neither horse nor saddle nor any men to follow him. He was a Prince of low birth, for his mother had married the son of a potter, and he was the son of his mother. So he sat down on the ground, and the little boys of the city driving the cattle to pasture threw mud at him.'

'Ah,' said Punch. 'Mud is nice. Did they hit him?'

'I am telling the tale of the Princess, and if there are so many questions, how can I finish before bedtime? He sat on the ground, and presently his mother, the Ranee, came by, gathering sticks to cook bread, and he told her of the Princess and the grain-jar. And she said: "Remember that a pot is a pot, and thou art the son of a potter." Then she went away with those dry sticks, and the Potter-Prince waited till the end of the year. Then the Princes returned, as many of them as were left over from the fights that they had fought. They brought with them the terrible cut-off heads of the giants and the dragons, so that people fell down with fright; and the tails of all the little devils, bunch by bunch, tied up with string; and the feathers of magic birds; and their holy men and dwarfs and talking beasts came with them. And there were bullock-carts full of the locked books of magic incantations and spells. The Rajah appointed a day, and his magicians came, and the grain-jar was set in the middle of all, and the Princes began according to their birth and the age of their families to open the grain-jar by means of their charm-work. There were very many Princes, and the charms were very strong, so that, as they performed the ceremonies, the lightning ran about the ground as a broken egg runs over the cook-house floor, and it was thick, dark night, and the people heard the voices of devils and djinns and talking tigers, and saw them running to and fro about the grain-jar till the ground shook. But, none the less, the grain-jar did not open. And the next day the ground was split up as a log of wood is split, and great rivers flowed up and down the plain, and magic armies with banners walked in circles—so great was the strength of the charms! Snakes, too, crawled round the grain-jar and hissed, but none the less the jar did not open. When morning came the holes in the ground had closed up, and the rivers were gone away, and there was only the plain. And that was because it was all magic charmwork, which cannot last.'

'Aha,' said Punch, drawing a deep breath. 'I am glad of that. It was only magic, Judy. Tell the tale, *ayah*.'

'At the very last, when they were all wearied out, and the holy men began to bite their nails with vexation, and the Rajah's magicians laughed, the Potter-Prince came into the plain alone, without even one little talking beast or wise bird, and all the people made jokes at him. But he walked to the grain-jar and cried: "A pot is a pot, and I am the son of a potter!" And he put his two hands upon the grain-jar's cover, and he lifted it up, and the Princess came out! Then the people said, "This is very great magic indeed";

An Ayah.

and they began to chase the talking beasts and the holy men up and down, meaning to kill them. But the Rajah's magicians said: "This is no magic jar at all, for we did not put any charm upon the jar. It *was* a common grain-jar, and it *is* a common grain-jar, such as they buy in the bazar; and a child might have lifted the cover a year ago, or on any day since that day. You are too wise, O Princes and Subadars, who rely on holy men and the heads of dead giants and devils' tails, but do not work with your own hands! You are too cunning! There was no magic, and now one man has taken it all away from you because he was not afraid. Go home, Princes, or, if you will, stay to see the wedding. But remember that a pot is a pot."'

There was a long silence at the end of the tale.

'But the charms were very strong,' said Punch doubtfully.

'They were only words, and how could they touch the pot? Could words turn you into a tiger, Punch *baba*?'

'No. I am Punch.'

'Even so,' said the *ayah*. 'If the pot had been charmed, a charm would have opened it. But it was a common, bazar pot. What did it know of charms? It opened to a hand on the cover.'

'Oh!' said Punch; and then he began to laugh, and Judy followed his example. 'Now I quite understand. I will tell it to Mamma.'

When Mamma came back from her drive, the children told her the tale twice over, while she was dressing for dinner; but as they began in the middle and put the beginning first, and then began at the end and put the middle last, she became a little confused.

'Never mind,' said Punch. 'I will show.' And he reached up to the table for the big eau-de-cologne bottle that he was strictly forbidden to touch, and pulled out the stopper, and upset half the scent down the front of his dress, shouting, 'A pot is a pot, and I am the son of a potter!'

TODS' AMENDMENT

Now Tods' Mamma was a singularly charming woman, and every one in Simla knew Tods. Most men had saved him from death on occasions. He was beyond his *ayah's* control altogether, and perilled his life daily to find out what would happen if you pulled a Mountain Battery mule's tail. He was an utterly fearless young Pagan, about six years old, and the only baby who ever broke the holy calm of the Supreme Legislative Council.

It happened this way: Tods' pet kid got loose, and fled up the hill, off the Boileaugunge Road, Tods after it, until it burst in to the Viceregal Lodge lawn, then attached to 'Peterhoff.' The Council were sitting at the time, and the windows were open because it was warm. The Red Lancer in the porch told Tods to go away; but Tods knew the Red Lancer and most of the Members of Council personally. Moreover, he had firm hold of the kid's collar, and was being dragged all across the flower-beds. 'Give my *salaam* to the long Councillor Sahib, and ask him to help me take *Moti* back!' gasped Tods. The Council heard the noise through the open windows; and, after an interval, was seen the shocking spectacle of a Legal Member and a Lieutenant-Governor helping, under the direct patronage of a Commander-in-Chief and a Viceroy, one small and very dirty boy, in a sailor's suit and a tangle of brown hair, to coerce a lively and rebellious kid. They headed it off down the path to the Mall, and Tods went home in triumph and told his Mamma that *all* the Councillor Sahibs had been helping him to catch *Moti*. Whereat his Mamma smacked Tods for interfering with the administration of the Empire; but Tods met the Legal Member the next day, and told him in confidence that if the Legal Member ever wanted to catch a goat, he, Tods, would give him all the help in his power. 'Thank you, Tods,' said the Legal Member.

Tods was the idol of some eighty *jhampanis,* and half as many *saises*. He saluted them all as 'O Brother.' It never entered his head that any living human being could disobey his orders; and he was the buffer between the servants and his Mamma's wrath. The working of that household turned on Tods, who was adored by every one from the *dhoby* to the dog-boy. Even Futteh Khan, the villainous loafer *khit* from Mussoorie, shirked risking Tods' displeasure for fear his co-mates should look down on him.

So Tods had honour in the land from Boileaugunge to Chota Simla, and ruled justly according to his lights. Of course, he spoke Urdu, but he had also mastered many queer side-speeches like the *chotee bolee* of the women, and held grave converse with shopkeepers and Hill-coolies alike. He was precocious for his age, and his mixing with natives had taught him some of the more bitter truths of life: the meanness and the sordidness of it. He used, over his bread and milk, to deliver solemn and serious aphorisms, translated from the vernacular into the English, that made his Mamma jump and vow that Tods *must* go Home next hot weather.

Just when Tods was in the bloom of his power, the Supreme Legislature were hacking out a Bill for the Sub-Montane Tracts, a revision of the then Act, smaller than the Punjab Land Bill, but affecting a few hundred thousand people none the less. The Legal Member had built, and bolstered, and embroidered, and amended that Bill till it looked beautiful on paper. Then the Council began to settle what they called the 'minor details.' As if any Englishman legislating for natives knows enough to know which are the minor and which are the major points, from the native point of view, of any measure! That Bill was a triumph of 'safe-guarding the interests of the tenant.' One clause provided that land should not be leased on longer terms than five years at a stretch; because, if the landlord had a tenant bound down for, say, twenty years, he would squeeze the very life out of him. The notion was to keep up a stream of independent cultivators in the Sub-Montane Tracts; and ethnologically and politically the notion was correct. The only drawback was that it was altogether wrong. A native's life in India implies the life of his son. Wherefore, you cannot legislate for one generation at a time. You must consider the next from the native point of view. Curiously enough, the native now and then, and in Northern India more particularly, hates being over-protected against himself. There was a Naga village once, where they lived on dead *and* buried Commissariat mules. . . . But that is another story.

For many reasons, to be explained later, the people concerned objected to the Bill. The Native Member in Council knew as much about Punjabis as he knew about Charing Cross. He had said in Calcutta that 'the Bill was entirely in accord with the desires of that large and important class, the cultivators;' and so on, and so on. The Legal Member's knowledge of natives was limited to English-speaking Durbaris, and his own red *chaprassis*, the Sub-Montane Tracts concerned no one in particular, the Deputy Commissioners were a good deal too driven to make representations, and the measure was one which dealt with small land-holders only. Nevertheless, the Legal Member prayed that it might be correct, for he was a nervously conscientious man. He did not know that no man can tell what natives think unless he mixes with them with the varnish off. And not always then. But he did the best he knew. And the measure came up to the Supreme Council for the final touches, while Tods patrolled the Burra Simla Bazar in his morning rides, and played with the monkey belonging to Ditta Mull, the *bunnia*, and listened, as a child listens, to all the stray talk about this new freak of the Lord Sahib's.

One day there was a dinner-party at the house of Tods' Mamma, and the Legal Member came. Tods was in bed, but he kept awake till he heard the bursts of laughter from the men over the coffee. Then he paddled out in his little red flannel dressing-gown and his night-suit, and took refuge by the side of his father, knowing that he would not be sent back. 'See the miseries of having a family!' said Tods' father, giving Tods three prunes, some water in a glass that had been used for claret, and telling him to sit still. Tods sucked the prunes slowly, knowing that he would have to go when they were finished, and sipped the pink water like a man of the world, as he listened to the conversation. Presently, the Legal Member, talking 'shop' to the Head of a Department, mentioned his Bill by its full name—'The Sub-Montane Tracts *Ryotwary* Revised Enactment.' Tods caught the one native word, and lifting up his small voice said—

'Oh, I know *all* about that! Has it been *murramutted* yet, Councillor Sahib?'

'How much?' said the Legal Member.

'*Murramutted*—mended.—Put *theek*, you know—made nice to please Ditta Mull!'

The Legal Member left his place and moved up next to Tods.

'What do you know about *ryotwari*, little man?' he said.

'I'm not a little man, I'm Tods, and I know *all* about it. Ditta Mull, and Choga Lall, and Amir Nath, and—oh, *lakhs* of my friends tell me about it in the bazars when I talk to them.'

'Oh, they do—do they? What do they say, Tods?'

Tods tucked his feet under his red flannel dressing-gown and said—'I must *fink*.'

The Legal Member waited patiently. Then Tods, with infinite compassion—

'You don't speak my talk, do you, Councillor Sahib?'

'No; I am sorry to say I do not,' said the Legal Member.

'Very well,' said Tods, 'I must *fink* in English.'

He spent a minute putting his ideas in order, and began very slowly, translating in his mind from the vernacular to English, as many Anglo-Indian children do. You must remember that the Legal Member helped him on by questions when he halted, for Tods was not equal to the sustained flight of oratory that follows.

'Ditta Mull says, "This thing is the talk of a child, and was made up by fools." But *I* don't think you are a fool, Councillor Sahib,' said Tods hastily. 'You caught my goat. This is what Ditta Mull says—"I am not a fool, and why should the Sirkar say I am a child? I can see if the land is good and if the landlord is good. If I am a fool, the sin is upon my own head. For five years I take my ground for which I have saved money, and a wife I take too, and a little son is born." Ditta Mull has one daughter now, but he *says* he will have a son, soon. And he says, "At the end of five years, by this new *bundobust*, I must go. If I do not go, I must get fresh seals and *takkus*-stamps on the papers, perhaps in the middle of the harvest, and to go to the law-courts once is wisdom, but to go twice is *Jehannum*." That is *quite* true,' explained Tods gravely. 'All my friends say so. And Ditta Mull says, "Always fresh *takkus* and paying money to *vakils* and *chaprassis* and law-courts every five years, or else the landlord makes me go. Why do I want to go? Am I a fool? If I am a fool and do not know, after forty years, good land when I see it, let me die! But if the new *bundobust* says for *fifteen* years, that is good and wise. My little son is a man, and I am burnt, and he takes the ground or another ground, paying only once for the *takkus*-stamps on the papers, and his little son is born, and at the end of fifteen years is a man too. But what profit is there in five years and fresh papers? Nothing but *dikh*, trouble, *dikh*. We are not young men who take these lands, but old ones – not farmers, but tradesmen with a little money – and for fifteen years we shall have peace. Nor are we children that the Sirkar should treat us so."'

Here Tods stopped short, for the whole table were listening. The Legal Member said to Tods, 'Is that all?'

'All I can remember,' said Tods. 'But you should see Ditta Mull's big monkey. It's just like a Councillor Sahib.'

'Tods! Go to bed,' said his father.

Tods gathered up his dressing-gown tail and departed.

The Legal Member brought his hand down on the table with a crash – 'By Jove!' said the Legal Member, 'I believe the boy is right. The short tenure *is* the weak point.'

He left early, thinking over what Tods had said. Now, it was obviously impossible for the Legal Member to play with a *bunnia's* monkey, by way of getting understanding; but he did better. He made inquiries, always bearing in mind the fact that the real native – not the hybrid, University-trained mule – is as timid as a colt, and, little by little, he coaxed some of the men whom the measure concerned most intimately to give in their views, which squared very closely with Tods' evidence.

So the Bill was amended in that clause; and the Legal Member was filled with an uneasy suspicion that the Native Members represent very little except the Orders they carry on their bosoms. But he put the thought from him as illiberal. He was a most Liberal man.

After a time the news spread through the bazars that Tods had got the Bill recast in the tenure-clause, and if Tods' Mamma had not interfered, Tods would have made himself sick on the baskets of fruit and pistachio nuts and Cabuli grapes and almonds that crowded the verandah. Till he went Home, Tods ranked some few degrees before the Viceroy in popular estimation. But for the little life of him Tods could not understand why.

In the Legal Member's private-paper-box still lies the rough draft of the Sub-Montane Tracts *Ryotwari* Revised Enactment; and, opposite the twenty-second clause, pencilled in blue chalk, and signed by the Legal Member, are the words '*Tods' Amendment*.'

THE STORY OF MUHAMMAD DIN

THE POLO-BALL was an old one, scarred, chipped, and dinted. It stood on the mantelpiece among the pipe-stems which Imam Din, *khitmatgar*, was cleaning for me.

'Does the Heaven-born want this ball?' said Imam Din deferentially.

The Heaven-born set no particular store by it; but of what use was a polo-ball to a *khitmatgar*?

'By Your Honour's favour, I have a little son. He has seen this ball, and desires it to play with. I do not want it for myself.'

No one would for an instant accuse portly old Imam Din of wanting to play with polo-balls. He carried out the battered thing into the verandah; and there followed a hurricane of joyful squeaks, a patter of small feet, and the *thud-thud-thud* of the ball rolling along the ground. Evidently the little son had been waiting outside the door to secure his treasure. But how had he managed to see that polo-ball?

Next day, coming back from office half an hour earlier than usual, I was aware of a small figure in the dining-room – a tiny, plump figure in a ridiculously inadequate shirt which came, perhaps, halfway down the tubby stomach. It wandered round the room, thumb in mouth, crooning to itself as it took stock of the pictures. Undoubtedly this was the 'little son.'

He had no business in my room, of course; but was so deeply absorbed in his discoveries that he never noticed me in the doorway. I stepped into the room and startled him nearly into a fit. He sat down on the ground with a gasp. His eyes opened, and his mouth followed suit. I knew what was coming, and fled, followed by a long, dry howl which reached the servants' quarters far more quickly than any command of mine had ever done. In ten seconds Imam Din was in the dining-room. Then despairing sobs arose, and I returned to find Imam Din admonishing the small sinner who was using most of his shirt as a handkerchief.

'This boy,' said Imam Din judicially, 'is a *budmash* – a big *budmash*. He will, without doubt, go to the *jail-khana* for his

behaviour.' Renewed yells from the penitent, and an elaborate apology to myself from Imam Din.

'Tell the baby,' said I, 'that the Sahib is not angry, and take him away.' Imam Din conveyed my forgiveness to the offender, who had now gathered all his shirt round his neck, stringwise, and the yell subsided into a sob. The two set off for the door. 'His name,' said Imam Din, as though the name were part of the crime, 'is Muhammad Din, and he is a *budmash*.' Freed from present danger, Muhammad Din turned round in his father's arms, and said gravely, 'It is true that my name is Muhammad Din, *Tahib*, but I am not a *budmash*. I am a *man*!'

From that day dated my acquaintance with Muhammad Din. Never again did he come into my dining-room, but on the neutral ground of the garden we greeted each other with much state, though our conversation was confined to '*Talaam, Tahib*' from his side, and '*Salaam, Muhammad Din*' from mine. Daily on my return from office, the little white shirt and the fat little body used to rise from the shade of the creeper-covered trellis where they had been hid; and daily I checked my horse here, that my salutation might not be slurred over or given unseemly.

Muhammad Din never had any companions. He used to trot about the compound, in and out of the castor-oil bushes, on mysterious errands of his own. One day I stumbled upon some of his handiwork far down the grounds. He had half buried the polo-ball in dust, and stuck six shrivelled old marigold flowers in a circle round it. Outside that circle again was a rude square, traced out in bits of red brick alternating with fragments of broken china; the whole bounded by a little bank of dust. The water-man from the well-curb put in a plea for the small architect, saying that it was only the play of a baby and did not much disfigure my garden.

Heaven knows that I had no intention of touching the child's work then or later; but, that evening, a stroll through the garden brought me unawares full on it; so that I trampled, before I knew, marigold-heads, dust-bank, and fragments of broken soap-dish into confusion past all hopes of mending. Next morning, I came upon Muhammad Din crying softly to himself over the ruin I had wrought. Some one had told him the Sahib was very angry with him for spoiling the garden, and had scattered his rubbish, using bad language the while. Muhammad Din laboured for an hour at effacing every trace of the dust-bank and pottery fragments, and it was with a tearful and apologetic face that he said, '*Talaam Tahib*,' when I came home from office. A hasty inquiry resulted in Imam Din informing Muhammad Din that, by my singular favour, he was permitted to disport himself as he pleased. Whereat the child took heart and fell to tracing the ground-plan of an edifice which was to eclipse the marigold-polo-ball creation.

For some months the chubby little eccentricity revolved in his humble orbit among the castor-oil bushes and in the dust; always fashioning magnificent palaces from stale flowers thrown away by the bearer, smooth water-worn pebbles, bits of broken glass, and feathers pulled, I fancy, from my fowls – always alone, and always crooning to himself.

A gaily-spotted sea-shell was dropped one day close to the last of his little buildings; and I looked that Muhammad Din should build something more than ordinarily splendid on the strength of it. Nor was I disappointed. He meditated for the better part of an hour, and his crooning rose to a jubilant song. Then he began tracing in the dust. It would certainly be a wondrous palace, this one, for it was two yards long and a yard broad in ground-plan. But the palace was never completed.

Next day there was no Muhammad Din at the head of the carriage-drive, and no '*Talaam, Tahib*' to welcome my return. I had grown accustomed to the greeting, and its omission troubled me. Next day Imam Din told me that the child was suffering slightly from fever and needed quinine. He got the medicine and an English Doctor.

'They have no stamina, these brats,' said the Doctor, as he left Imam Din's quarters.

A week later, though I would have given much to have avoided it, I met on the road to the Mussulman burying-ground Imam Din, accompanied by one other friend, carrying in his arms, wrapped in a white cloth, all that was left of little Muhammad Din.

PART
II
RETURNS
AND
INTRODUCTIONS

These three tales illustrate three very different reactions to the Indian scene. In 'The Bride's Progress' a pair of newly-weds – of the despised species that Kipling always refers to as 'globe-trotters' – tour the Hindu holy city of Benares. Like most Punjab men, Kipling found the manifestations of Hinduism much less easy to tolerate than those of Islam – but he could still satirise the prejudices of the English bride, unable to see further than the city's horrors.

'Thrown Away' and 'The Tomb of His Ancestors' both concern themselves with young men coming to terms with India, one failing and one succeeding. In the first of these the unnamed 'Boy' becomes a casualty because he takes things too much to heart. As a character he is not entirely convincing, but this certainly cannot be said for the circumstances surrounding his death and the cover-up that follows. Suicide was by no means an uncommon occurrence in Kipling's India and in his autobiography Kipling himself cites the case of a man in the Lahore Club who kept 'messing about' with a half-dead viper that someone had brought into dinner until he had to be warned to keep his hands away: 'A few weeks after, some of us realised it would have been better had he accomplished what had been in his foreboding mind that night.'

Lucky young John Chinn in 'The Tomb of His Ancestors' has no such forebodings or doubts about himself. He always lands on his feet, knowing instinctively what to do by virtue of a century of Anglo-Indian ancestry. His is an idealised homecoming, although his meeting with the Bhil tribal leader Bukta and his nephew carries more than an echo of Rudyard's meeting with his father's servant Mir Baksh and his son Kadir Baksh. The original of 'John Chinn the First' is said to be James Outram, the so-called 'Bayard of India' who pacified the Bhils in Khandesh in the 1820s and 30s and was a renowned slayer of tigers.

'The Bride's Progress' appeared in *The Pioneer Mail* on 8 February 1888 as part of a series of travel articles entitled *From Sea to Sea*, later republished in two volumes. 'Thrown Away' was one of the eight previously unpublished stories included in *Plain Tales from the Hills* when it appeared in January 1888. 'The Tomb of His Ancestors' was written in Vermont over the winter of 1895-6 and published in 1898 in *The Day's Work*. It was the last of Kipling's longer Indian stories to be written before he set to work on *Kim*.

THE BRIDE'S PROGRESS

IT WOULD HAVE been presumption and weariness deliberately to have described Benares. No man, except he who writes a guide-book, 'does' the Strand or Westminster Abbey. The foreigner – French or American – tells London what to think of herself, as the visitor tells the Anglo-Indian what to think of India. Our neighbour over the way always knows so much more about us than we ourselves. The Bride interpreted Benares as fresh youth and radiant beauty can interpret a city gray and worn with years. Providence had been very good to her, and she repaid Providence by dressing herself to the best advantage – which, if the French speak truth, is all that a fair woman can do toward religion. Generations of untroubled ease and well-being must have builded the dainty figure and rare face, and the untamable arrogance of wealth looked out of the calm eyes. 'India,' said The Bride philosophically, 'is an incident only in our trip. We are going on to Australia and China, and then Home by San Francisco and New York. We shall be at Home again before the season is quite ended.' And she patted her bracelets, smiling softly to herself over some thought that had little enough to do with Benares or India – whichever was the 'incident.' She went into the city of Benares. Benares of the Buddhists and the Hindus – of Durga of the Thousand Names – of two Thousand Temples, and twice two thousand stenches. Her high heels rang delicately upon the stone pavement of the gullies, and her brow, unmarked as that of a little child, was troubled by the stenches. 'Why does Benares smell so?' demanded The Bride pathetically. '*Must* we do it, if it smells like this?' The Bridegroom was high-coloured, fair-whiskered, and insistent, as an Englishman should be. 'Of course we must. It would never do to go home without having seen Benares. Where is a guide?' The streets were alive with them, and the couple chose him who spoke English most fluently. 'Would you like to see where the Hindus are burnt?' said he. They would, though The Bride shuddered as she spoke, for she feared that it would be very horrible. A ray of gracious sunlight touched her hair as she turned, walking cautiously in the middle of the narrow way, into the maze of the byways of Benares.

The sunlight ceased after a few paces, and the horrors of the Holy City gathered round her. Neglected rainbow-hued sewage sprawled across the

A Street scene. Central India.

path, and a bull, rotten with some hideous disease that distorted his head out of all bestial likeness, pushed through the filth. The Bride picked her way carefully, giving the bull the wall. A lean dog, dying of mange, growled and yelped among her starveling puppies on a threshold that led into the darkness of some unclean temple. The Bride stooped and patted the beast on the head. 'I think she's something like *Bessie*,' said the Bride, and once again her thoughts wandered far beyond Benares. The lanes grew narrower and the symbols of a brutal cult more numerous. Hanuman, red, shameless, and smeared with oil, leaped and leered upon the walls above stolid, black stone bulls, knee-deep in yellow flowers. The bells clamoured from unseen temples, and half-naked men with evil eyes rushed out of dark places and besought her for money, saying that they were priests – *padris*, like the *padris* of her own faith. One young man – who knows in what Mission school he had picked up his speech? – told her this in English, and The Bride laughed merrily, shaking her head. 'These men speak English,' she called back to her husband. 'Isn't it funny!'

But the mirth went out of her face when a turn in the lane brought her suddenly above the burning-*ghat*, where a man was piling logs on some Thing that lay wrapped in white cloth, near the water of the Ganges. 'We can't see well from this place,' said the Bridegroom stolidly. 'Let us get a little closer.' They moved forward through deep grey dust – white sand of the river and black dust of man blended – till they commanded a full view of the steeply sloping bank and the Thing under the logs. A man was laboriously starting a fire at the river end of the pile; stepping wide now and again to avoid the hot embers of a dying blaze actually on the edge of the water. The Bride's face blanched, and she looked appealingly to her husband, but he had eyes only for the newly lit flame. Slowly, very slowly, a white dog crept on his belly down the bank, toward a heap of ashes among which the water was hissing. A plunge, followed by a yelp of pain, told that he had reached food, and that the food was too hot for him. With a deftness that marked long training, he raked the capture from the ashes on to the dust and slobbered, nosing it tentatively. As it cooled, he settled, with noises of animal delight, to his meal and worried and growled and tore. 'Will!' said The Bride faintly. The Bridegroom was watching the newly lit pyre and could not attend. A log slipped sideways, and through the chink showed the face of the man below, smiling the dull thick smile of death, which is such a smile as a very drunken man wears when he has found in his wide-swimming brain a joke of exquisite savour. The dead man grinned up to the sun and the fair face of The Bride. The flames spluttered and caught and spread. A man waded out knee-deep into the water, which was covered with greasy black embers and an oily scum. He chased the bobbing driftwood with a basket, that it might be saved for another occasion, and threw each take on a mound of such economies or on the back of the unheeding dog deep in the enjoyment of his hot dinner.

Slowly, very slowly, as the flames crackled, the Smiling Dead Man lifted one knee through the light logs. He had just been smitten with the idea of rising from his last couch and confounding the spectators. It was easy to see he was tasting the notion of this novel, this stupendous practical joke, and would presently, always smiling, rise up, and up, and up, and . . .

The fire-shrivelled knee gave way, and with its collapse little flames ran forward and whistled and whispered and fluttered from heel to head. 'Come away, Will,' said The Bride, 'come away! It is too horrible. I'm sorry that I saw it.' They left together, she with her arm in her husband's for a sign to all the world that, though Death be inevitable and awful, Love is still the greater, and in its sweet selfishness can set at naught even the horrors of a burning-*ghat*.

'I never thought what it meant before,' said The Bride, releasing her husband's arm as she recovered herself; 'I see now.' 'See what?' 'Don't you know?' said The Bride, 'what Edwin Arnold says:–

For all the tears of all the eyes
  Have room in Gunga's bed,
And all the sorrow is gone to-morrow
  When the white flames have fed.

I see now. I think it is very, *very* horrible.' Then to the guide, suddenly, with a deep compassion, 'And will you be – will you be burnt in that way, too?' 'Yes, your Ladyship,' said the guide cheerfully, 'we are all burnt that way.' 'Poor wretch!' said The Bride to herself. 'Now show us some more temples.' A second time they dived into Benares City, but it was at least five long minutes before The Bride recovered those buoyant spirits which were hers by right of Youth and Love and Happiness. A very pale and sober little face peered into the filth of the Temple of the Cow, where the odour of Holiness and Humanity are highest. Fearful and wonderful old women, crippled in hands and feet, body and back, crawled round her; some even touching the hem of her dress. And at this she shuddered, for the hands were very foul. The walls dripped filth, the pavement sweated filth, and the contagion of uncleanliness walked among the worshippers. There might have been beauty in the Temple of the Cow; there certainly was horror enough and to spare; but The

Bride was conscious only of the filth of the place. She turned to the wisest and best man in the world, asking indignantly, 'Why don't these horrid people clean the place out?' 'I don't know,' said The Bridegroom; 'I suppose their religion forbids it.' Once more they set out on their journey through the city of monstrous creeds – she in front, the pure white hem of her petticoat raised indignantly clear of the mire, and her eyes full of alarm and watchfulness. Closed galleries crossed the narrow way, and the light of day fainted and grew sick ere it could climb down into the abominations of the gullies. A litter of gorgeous red and gold barred the passage to the Golden Temple. 'It is the Maharani of Hazaribagh,' said the guide, 'she coming to pray for a child.' 'Ah!' said The Bride, and turning quickly to her husband, said, 'I wish mother were with us.' The Bridegroom made no answer. Perhaps he was beginning to repent of dragging a young English girl through the iniquities of Benares. He announced his intention of returning to his hotel, and The Bride dutifully followed. At every turn lewd gods grinned and mouthed at her, the still air was clogged with thick odours and the reek of rotten marigold flowers, and disease stood blind and naked before the sun. 'Let us get away quickly,' said The Bride; and they escaped to the main street, having honestly accomplished nearly two-thirds of what was written in the little red guide-book. An instinct inherited from a century of cleanly English housewives made The Bride pause before getting into the carriage, and, addressing the seething crowd generally, murmur, 'Oh! you horrid people! Shouldn't I like to wash you.'

Yet Benares – which name must certainly be derived from *be*, without, and *nares*, nostrils – is not entirely a Sacred Midden. Very early in the morning, almost before the light had given promise of the day, a boat put out from a *ghat* and rowed upstream till it stayed in front of the ruined magnificence of Scindia's Ghat – a range of ruined wall and drunken bastion. The Bride and Bridegroom had risen early to catch their last glimpse of the city. There was no one abroad at that hour, and, except for three or four stone-laden boats rolling down from Mirzapur, they were alone upon the river. In the silence a voice thundered far above their heads: '*I bear witness that there is no God but God.*' It was the mullah, proclaiming the Oneness of God in the city of the Million Manifestations. The call rang across the sleeping city and far over the river, and be sure that the mullah abated nothing of the defiance of his cry for that he looked down upon a sea of temples and smelt the incense of a hundred Hindu shrines. The Bride could make neither head nor tail of the business. 'What is he making that noise for, Will?' she asked. 'Worshipping Vishnu,' was the ready reply; for at the outset of his venture into matrimony a young husband is at the least infallible. The Bride snuggled down under her wraps, keeping her delicate, chill-pinked little nose toward the city. Day broke over Benares, and The Bride stood up and applauded with both her hands. It was finer, she said, than any transformation scene; and so in her gratitude she applauded the earth, the sun, and the everlasting sky. The river turned to a silver flood and the ruled lines of the *ghats* to red gold. 'How can I describe this to mother?' she cried, as the wonder grew, and timeless Benares roused to a fresh day. The Bride nestled down in the boat and gazed round-eyed. As water spurts through a leaky dam, as ants pour out from the invaded nest, so the people of Benares poured down the *ghats* to the river. Wherever The Bride's eye rested, it saw men and women stepping downwards, always downwards, by rotten wall, worn step, tufted bastion, riven water-gate, and stark, bare, dusty bank, to the water. The hundred priests drifted down to their stations under the large mat-umbrellas that all pictures of Benares represent so faithfully. The Bride's face lighted with joy. She had found a simile. 'Will! Do you recollect that pantomime we went to ages and ages ago – before we were engaged – at Brighton? Doesn't it remind you of the scene of the Fairy Mushrooms – just before they all got up and danced, you know? Isn't it splendid?' She leaned forward, her chin in her hand, and watched long and intently; and Nature, who is without doubt a Frenchwoman, so keen is her love for effect, arranged that the shell-like pink of The Bride's cheek should be turned against a dull-red house, in the windows of which sat women in blood-red clothes, letting down crimson turban-cloths for the morning breeze to riot with. From the burning-*ghat* rose lazily a welt of thick blue smoke, and an eddy of the air blew a wreath across the river. The Bride coughed. 'Will,' she said, 'promise me when I die you won't have me cremated – if cremation is the fashion then.' And 'Will' promised lightly, as a man promises who is looking for long years.

The life of the city went forward. The Bride heard, though she did not understand, the marriage-song, and the chant of prayers, and the wail of the mourners. She looked long and steadfastly at the beating heart of Benares and at the Dead for whom no day had dawned. The place was hers to watch and enjoy if she pleased. Her enjoyment was tempered with some thought of regret; for her eyebrows contracted and she thought. Then the trouble was apparent. 'Will!' she said softly, 'they don't seem to think much of *us*, do they?' Did she expect, then, that the whole city would make

obeisance to young Love, robed and crowned in a grey tweed travelling dress and velvet toque?

The boat drifted downstream, and an hour or so later the Dufferin Bridge bore away The Bride and Bridegroom on their travels, in which India was to be 'only an incident.'

THROWN AWAY

To rear a boy under what parents call the 'sheltered life system' is, if the boy must go into the world and fend for himself, not wise. Unless he be one in a thousand he has certainly to pass through many unnecessary troubles; and may, possibly, come to extreme grief simply from ignorance of the proper proportions of things.

Let a puppy eat the soap in the bath-room or chew a newly-blacked boot. He chews and chuckles until, by and by, he finds out that blacking and Old Brown Windsor make him very sick; so he argues that soap and boots are not wholesome. Any old dog about the house will soon show him the unwisdom of biting big dogs' ears. Being young, he remembers and goes abroad, at six months, a well-mannered little beast with a chastened appetite. If he had been kept away from boots, and soap, and big dogs till he came to the trinity full-grown and with developed teeth, consider how fearfully sick and thrashed he would be! Apply that notion to the 'sheltered life,' and see how it works. It does not sound pretty, but it is the better of two evils.

There was a Boy once who had been brought up under the 'sheltered life' theory; and the theory killed him dead. He stayed with his people all his days, from the hour he was born till the hour he went into Sandhurst nearly at the top of the list. He was beautifully taught in all that wins marks by a private tutor, and carried the extra weight of 'never having given his parents an hour's anxiety in his life.' What he learnt at Sandhurst beyond the regular routine is of no great consequence. He looked about him, and he found soap and blacking, so to speak, very good. He ate a little, and came out of Sandhurst not so high as he went in. Then there was an interval and a scene with his people, who expected much from him. Next a year of living unspotted from the world in a third-rate depôt battalion where all the juniors were children and all the seniors old women; and lastly, he came out to India, where he was cut off from the support of his parents, and had no one to fall back on in time of trouble except himself.

Now India is a place beyond all others where one must not take things too seriously – the mid-day sun always excepted. Too much work and too

much energy kill a man just as effectively as too much assorted vice or too much drink. Flirtation does not matter, because everyone is being transferred, and either you or she leave the Station and never return. Good work does not matter, because a man is judged by his worst output, and another man takes all the credit of his best as a rule. Bad work does not matter, because other men do worse, and incompetents hang on longer in India than anywhere else. Amusements do not matter, because you must repeat them as soon as you have accomplished them once, and most amusements only mean trying to win another person's money. Sickness does not matter, because it's all in the day's work, and if you die, another man takes over your place and your office in the eight hours between death and burial. Nothing matters except Home-furlough and acting allowances, and these only because they are scarce. It is a slack country, where all men work with imperfect instruments; and the wisest thing is to escape as soon as ever you can to some place where amusement is amusement and a reputation worth the having.

But this Boy – the tale is as old as the Hills – came out, and took all things seriously. He was pretty and was petted. He took the pettings seriously, and fretted over women not worth saddling a pony to call upon. He found his new free life in India very good. It does look attractive in the beginning, from a subaltern's point of view – all ponies, partners, dancing, and so on. He tasted it as the puppy tastes the soap. Only he came late to the eating, with a grown set of teeth. He had no sense of balance – just like the puppy – and could not understand why he was not treated with the consideration he received under his father's roof. This hurt his feelings.

He quarrelled with other boys and, being sensitive to the marrow, remembered these quarrels, and they excited him. He found whist, and gymkhanas, and things of that kind (meant to amuse one after office) good; but he took them seriously too, just as seriously as he took the 'head' that followed after drink. He lost his money over whist and gymkhanas because they were new to him.

He took his losses seriously, and wasted as much energy and interest over a two-goldmohur race for maiden *ekka*-ponies with their manes hogged, as if it had been the Derby. One-half of this came from inexperience – much as the puppy squabbles with the corner of the hearthrug – and the other half from the dizziness bred by stumbling out of his quiet life into the glare and excitement of a livelier one. No one told him about the soap and the blacking, because an average man takes it for granted that an average man is ordinarily careful in regard to them. It was pitiful to watch The Boy knocking himself to pieces, as an over-handled colt falls down and cuts himself when he gets away from the groom.

This unbridled license in amusements not worth breaking the line for, much less rioting over, endured for six months – all through one cold weather – and then we thought that the heat and the knowledge of having lost his money and health and lamed his horses would sober The Boy down, and he would stand steady. In ninety-nine cases out of a hundred this would have happened. You can see this principle working in any Indian Station. But this particular case fell through because The Boy was sensitive and took things seriously – as I may have said some seven times before. Of course, we could not tell how his excesses struck him personally. They were nothing very heartbreaking or above the average. He might be crippled for life financially, and want a little nursing. Still the memory of his performances would wither away in one hot weather, and the bankers would help him to tide over the money-troubles. But he must have taken another view altogether, and have believed himself ruined beyond redemption. His Colonel talked to him severely when the cold weather ended. That made him more wretched than ever; and it was only an ordinary 'Colonel's wigging'!

What follows is a curious instance of the fashion in which we are all linked together and made responsible for one another. *The* thing that kicked the beam in The Boy's mind was a remark that a woman made when he was talking to her. There is no use repeating it, for it was only a cruel little sentence, rapped out before thinking, that made him flush to the roots of his hair. He kept himself to himself for three days, and then put in for two days' leave to go shooting near a Canal Engineer's Rest House about thirty miles out. He got his leave, and that night at Mess was noisier and more offensive than ever. He said that he was 'going to shoot big game,' and left at half-past ten o'clock in an *ekka*. Partridge – which was the only thing a man could get near the Rest House – is not big game; so every one laughed.

Next morning one of the Majors came in from short leave, and heard that The Boy had gone out to shoot 'big game.' The Major had taken an interest in The Boy, and had, more than once, tried to check him. The Major put up his eyebrows when he heard of the expedition, and went to The Boy's rooms where he rummaged.

Presently he came out and found me leaving cards on the Mess. There was no one else in the ante-room.

He said, 'The Boy has

gone out shooting. *Does* a man shoot *tetur* with a revolver and writing-case?'

I said, 'Nonsense, Major!' for I saw what was in his mind.

He said, 'Nonsense or no nonsense, I'm going to the Canal now – at once. I don't feel easy.'

Then he thought for a minute, and said, 'Can you lie?'

'You know best,' I answered. 'It's my profession.'

'Very well,' said the Major, 'you must come out with me now – at once – in an *ekka* to the Canal to shoot black-buck. Go and put on *shikar*-kit – *quick* – and drive here with a gun.'

The Major was a masterful man, and I knew that he would not give orders for nothing. So I obeyed, and on return found the Major packed up in an *ekka* – gun cases and food slung below – all ready for a shooting trip.

He dismissed the driver and drove himself. We jogged along quietly while in the station; but, as soon as we got to the dusty road across the plains, he made that pony fly. A country-bred can do nearly anything at a pinch. We covered the thirty miles in under three hours, but the poor brute was nearly dead.

Once I said, 'What's the blazing hurry, Major?'

He said quietly, 'The Boy has been alone, by himself for – one, two, five, – fourteen hours now! I tell you, I don't feel easy.'

This uneasiness spread itself to me, and I helped to beat the pony.

When we came to the Canal Engineer's Rest House the Major called for The Boy's servant; but there was no answer. Then we went up to the house, calling for The Boy by name; but there was no answer.

'Oh, he's out shooting,' said I.

Just then I saw through one of the windows a little hurricane-lamp burning. This was at four in the afternoon. We both stopped dead in the verandah, holding our breath to catch every sound; and we heard, inside the room, the '*brr—brr—brr*' of a multitude of flies. The Major said nothing, but he took off his helmet and we entered very softly.

The Boy was dead on the bed in the centre of the bare, lime-washed room. He had shot his head nearly to pieces with his revolver. The gun-cases were still strapped, so was the bedding, and on the table lay The Boy's writing-case with photographs. He had gone away to die like a poisoned rat!

The Major said to himself softly, 'Poor Boy! Poor, *poor* devil!' Then he turned away from the bed and said, 'I want your help in this business.'

Knowing The Boy was dead by his own hand, I saw exactly what that help would be, so I passed over to the table, took a chair, lit a cheroot, and began to go through the writing-case; the Major looking over my shoulder and repeating to himself, 'We came too late! – Like a rat in a hole! – Poor, *poor* devil!'

The Boy must have spent half the night in writing to his people, to his Colonel, and to a girl at Home; and as soon as he had finished, must have shot himself, for he had been dead a long time when we came in.

I read all he had written, and passed over each sheet to the Major as I finished it.

We saw from his accounts how very seriously he had taken everything. He wrote about 'disgrace which he was unable to bear' – 'indelible shame' – 'criminal folly' – 'wasted life,' and so on; besides a lot of private things to his father and mother much too sacred to put into print. The letter to the girl at Home was the most pitiful of all, and I choked as I read it. The Major made no attempt to keep dry-eyed. I respected him for that. He read and rocked himself to and fro, and simply cried like a woman without caring to hide it. The letters were so dreary and hopeless and touching. We forgot all about The Boy's follies, and only thought of the poor Thing on the bed and the scrawled sheets in our hands. It was utterly impossible to let the letters go Home. They would have broken his father's heart and killed his mother after killing her belief in her son.

At last the Major dried his eyes openly, and said, 'Nice sort of thing to spring on an English family! What shall we do?'

I said, knowing what the Major had brought me out for, – 'The Boy died of cholera. We were with him at the time. We can't commit ourselves to half-measures. Come along.'

Then began one of the most grimly comic scenes I have ever taken part in – the concoction of a big, written lie, bolstered with evidence, to soothe The Boy's people at Home. I began the rough draft of the letter, the Major throwing in hints here and there while he gathered up all the stuff that The Boy had written and burnt it in the fireplace. It was a hot, still evening when we began, and the lamp burned very badly. In due course I made the draft to my satisfaction, setting forth how The Boy was the pattern of all virtues, beloved by his regiment, with every promise of a great career before him, and so on; how we had helped him through the sickness – it was no time for little lies, you will understand – and how he had died without pain. I choked while I was putting down these things and thinking of the poor people who would read them. Then I laughed at the grotesqueness of the affair, and the laughter mixed itself up with the choke – and the Major said that we both wanted drinks.

I am afraid to say how much whisky we drank before the letter was finished. It had not the least effect on us. Then we took off The Boy's watch, locket, and rings.

Lastly, the Major said, 'We must send a lock of hair too. A woman values that.'

But there were reasons why we could not find a lock fit to send. The Boy was black-haired, and so was the Major, luckily. I cut off a piece of the

Major's hair above the temple with a knife, and put it into the packet we were making. The laughing-fit and the chokes had got hold of me again, and I had to stop. The Major was nearly as bad; and we both knew that the worst part of the work was to come.

We sealed up the packet, photographs, locket, seals, ring, letter, and lock of hair with The Boy's sealing-wax and The Boy's seal.

Then the Major said, 'For God's sake let's get outside – away from this room – and think!'

We went outside, and walked on the banks of the Canal for an hour, eating and drinking what we had with us, until the moon rose. I know now exactly how a murderer feels. Finally, we forced ourselves back to the room with the lamp and the Other Thing in it, and began to take up the next piece of work. I am not going to write about this. It was too horrible. We burned the bedstead and dropped the ashes into the Canal; we took up the matting of the room and treated that in the same way. I went off to a village and borrowed two big hoes, – I did not want the villagers to help, – while the Major arranged – the other matters. It took us four hours' hard work to make the grave. As we worked, we argued out whether it was right to say as much as we remembered of the Burial of the Dead. We compromised things by saying the Lord's Prayer with a private unofficial prayer for the peace of the soul of The Boy. Then we filled in the grave and went into the verandah – not the house – to lie down to sleep. We were dead-tired.

When we woke the Major said wearily, 'We can't go back till tomorrow. We must give him a decent time to die in. He died early *this* morning, remember. That seems more natural.' So the Major must have been lying awake all the time, thinking.

I said, 'Then why didn't we bring the body back to cantonments?'

The Major thought for a minute. 'Because the people bolted when they heard of the cholera. And the *ekka* has gone!'

That was strictly true. We had forgotten all about the *ekka*-pony, and he had gone home.

So we were left there alone, all that stifling day, in the Canal Rest House, testing and re-testing our story of The Boy's death to see if it was weak in any point. A native appeared in the afternoon but we said that a Sahib was dead of cholera, and he ran away. As the dusk gathered, the Major told me all his fears about The Boy, and awful stories of suicide or nearly-carried-out suicide – tales that made one's hair crisp. He said that he himself had once gone into the same Valley of the Shadow as The Boy, when he was young and new to the country; so he understood how things fought together in The Boy's poor jumbled head. He also said that youngsters, in their repentant moments, consider their sins much more serious and ineffaceable than they really are. We talked together all through the

evening and rehearsed the story of the death of The Boy. As soon as the moon was up, and The Boy, theoretically, just buried, we struck across country for the Station. We walked from eight till six o'clock in the morning; but though we were dead-tired, we did not forget to go to The Boy's rooms and put away his revolver with the proper amount of cartridges in the pouch. Also to set his writing-case on the table. We found the Colonel and reported the death, feeling more like murderers than ever. Then we went to bed and slept the clock round, for there was no more in us.

The tale had credence as long as was necessary; for every one forgot about The Boy before a fortnight was over. Many people, however, found time to say that the Major had behaved scandalously in not bringing in the body for a regimental funeral. The saddest thing of all was the letter from The Boy's mother to the Major and me – with big inky blisters all over the sheet. She wrote the sweetest possible things about our great kindness, and the obligation she would be under to us as long as she lived.

All things considered, she was under an obligation, but not exactly as she meant.

THE TOMB OF HIS ANCESTORS

Some people will tell you that if there were but a single loaf of bread in all India it would be divided equally between the Plowdens, the Trevors, the Beadons, and the Rivett-Carnacs. That is only one way of saying that certain families serve India generation after generation as dolphins follow in line across the open sea.

Let us take a small and obscure case. There has been at least one representative of the Devonshire Chinns in or near Central India since the days of Lieutenant-Fireworker Humphrey Chinn, of the Bombay European Regiment, who assisted at the capture of Seringapatam in 1799. Alfred Ellis Chinn, Humphrey's younger brother, commanded a regiment of Bombay grenadiers from 1804 to 1813, when he saw some mixed fighting; and in 1834 John Chinn of the same family – we will call him John Chinn the First – came to light as a level-headed administrator in time of trouble at a place called Mundesur. He died young, but left his mark on the new country, and the Honourable the Board of Directors of the Honourable the East India Company embodied his virtues in a stately resolution, and paid for the expenses of his tomb among the Satpura hills.

He was succeeded by his son, Lionel Chinn, who left the little old Devonshire home just in time to be severely wounded in the Mutiny. He spent his working life within a hundred and fifty miles of John Chinn's grave, and rose to the command of a regiment of small, wild hill-men, most of whom had known his father. His son John was born in the small thatched-roofed, mud-walled cantonment, which is even today eighty miles from the nearest railway, in the heart of a scrubby, tigerish country. Colonel Lionel Chinn served thirty years and retired. In the Canal his steamer passed the outward-bound troopship, carrying his son eastward to the family duties.

The Chinns are luckier than most folk, because they know exactly what they must do. A clever Chinn passes for the Bombay Civil Service, and gets away to Central India, where everybody is glad to see him. A dull Chinn enters the Police Department or the Woods and Forests, and sooner or later he, too, appears in Central India, and that is what gave rise to the saying, 'Central India is inhabited by Bhils, Mairs, and Chinns, all very much alike.' The breed is small-boned, dark, and silent, and the stupidest of them are good shots. John Chinn the Second was rather clever, but as the eldest son he entered the army, according to Chinn tradition. His duty was to abide in his father's regiment for the term of his natural life, though the corps was one which most men would have paid heavily to avoid. They were irregulars, small, dark, and blackish, clothed in rifle-green with black-leather trimmings; and friends called them the 'Wuddars,' which means a race of low-caste people who dig up rats to eat. But the Wuddars did not resent it. They were the only Wuddars, and their points of pride were these:

Firstly, they had fewer English officers than any native regiment. Secondly, their subalterns were not mounted on parade, as is the general rule, but walked at the head of their men. A man who can hold his own with the Wuddars at their quickstep must be sound in wind and limb. Thirdly, they were the most *pukka shikarries* (out-and-out hunters) in all India. Fourthly – up to one hundredthly – they were the Wuddars – Chinn's Irregular Bhil Levies of the old days, but now, henceforward and for ever, the Wuddars.

No Englishmen entered their mess except for love or through family usage. The officers talked to their soldiers in a tongue not two hundred white folk in India understood; and the men were their children, all drawn from the Bhils, who are, perhaps, the strangest of the many strange races in India. They were, and at heart are, wild men, furtive, shy, full of untold superstitions. The races whom we call natives of the country found the Bhil in possession of the land when they first broke into that part of the world thousands of years ago. The books call them Pre-Aryan, Aboriginal, Dravidian, and so forth; and, in other words, that is what the Bhils call themselves. When a Rajput chief, whose bards can sing his pedigree backwards for twelve hundred years, is set on the throne, his investiture is not complete till he has been marked on the forehead with blood from the veins of a Bhil. The Rajputs say the ceremony has no meaning, but the Bhil knows that it is the last, last shadow of his old rights as the long-ago owner of the soil.

Centuries of oppression and massacre made the Bhil a cruel and half-crazy thief and cattle stealer, and when the English came he seemed to be almost as open to civilisation as the tigers of his own jungles. But John Chinn the First, father of Lionel, grandfather of our John, went into his country, lived with him, learned his language, shot the deer that stole his poor crops, and won his confidence, so that some Bhils learned to plough and sow, while others were coaxed into the Company's service to police their friends.

When they understood that standing in line did not mean instant execution, they accepted soldiering as a cumbrous but amusing kind of sport, and were zealous to keep the wild Bhils under control. That was the thin end of the wedge. John Chinn the First gave them written promises that, if they were good from a certain date, the Government would overlook previous offences; and since John Chinn was never known to break his word – he promised once to hang a Bhil locally esteemed invulnerable, and hanged him in front of his tribe for seven proved murders – the Bhils settled down as steadily as they knew how. It was slow, unseen work, of the sort that is being done all over India today; and though John Chinn's only reward came, as I have said, in the shape of a grave at Government expense, the little people of the hills never forgot him.

Colonel Lionel Chinn knew and loved them too, and they were very fairly civilised, for Bhils, before his service ended. Many of them could hardly be distinguished from low-cast Hindu farmers; but in the south, where John Chinn the First was buried, the wildest still clung to the Satpura ranges, cherishing a legend that some day Jan Chinn, as they called him, would return to his own. In the meantime they mistrusted the white man and his ways. The least excitement would stampede them plundering at random, and now and then killing; but if they were handled discreetly they grieved like children, and promised never to do it again.

The Bhils of the regiment – the uniformed men – were virtuous in many ways, but they needed humouring. They felt bored and homesick unless taken after tigers as beaters; and their cold-blooded daring – all Wuddars shoot tigers on foot: it is their caste-mark – made even the officers wonder. They would follow up a wounded tiger as unconcernedly as though it were a sparrow with a broken wing; and this through a country full of caves and rifts and pits, where a wild beast could hold a dozen men at his mercy. Now and then some little man was brought to barracks with his head smashed in or his ribs torn away; but his companions never learned caution; they contented themselves with settling the tiger.

Young John Chinn was decanted at the verandah of the Wuddars' lonely mess-house from the back seat of a two-wheeled cart, his gun-cases cascading all round him. The slender, little, hookey-nosed boy looked forlorn as a strayed goat when he slapped the white dust off his knees, and the cart jolted down the glaring road. But in his heart he was contented. After all, this was the place where he had been born, and things were not much changed since he had been sent to England, a child, fifteen years ago.

There were a few new buildings, but the air and the smell and the sunshine were the same; and the little green men who crossed the parade-ground looked very familiar. Three weeks ago John Chinn would have said he did not remember a word of the Bhil tongue, but at the mess-door he found his lips moving in sentences he did not understand – bits of old nursery rhymes, and tail-ends of such orders as his father used to give the men.

The Colonel watched him come up the steps, and laughed.

'Look!' he said to the Major. 'No need to ask the young un's breed. He's a *pukka* Chinn. Might be his father in the Fifties over again.'

'Hope he'll shoot as straight,' said the Major. 'He's brought enough ironmongery with him.'

'Wouldn't be a Chinn if he didn't. Watch him blowin' his nose. Regular Chinn beak. Flourishes his handkerchief like his father. It's the second edition – line for line.'

'Fairy tale, by Jove!' said the Major, peering through the slats of the jalousies. 'If he's the lawful heir, he'll . . . Now old Chinn could no more pass that *chick* without fiddling with it than . . .'

'His son!' said the Colonel, jumping up.

'Well, I be blowed!' said the Major. The boy's eye had been caught by a split reed screen that hung on a slew between the verandah pillars, and mechanically he had tweaked the edge to set it level. Old Chinn had sworn three times a day at that screen for many years; he could never get it to his satisfaction. His son entered the anteroom in the middle of a five-fold silence. They made him welcome for his father's sake and, as they took stock of him, for his own. He was ridiculously like the portrait of the Colonel on the wall, and when he had washed a little of the dust from his throat he went to his quarters with the old man's short, noiseless jungle-step.

'So much for heredity,' said the Major. 'That comes of three generations among the Bhils.'

'And the men know it,' said a Wing-officer. 'They've been waiting for this youth with their tongues hanging out. I am persuaded that, unless he absolutely beats 'em over the head, they'll lie down by companies and worship him.'

'Nothin' like having a father before you,' said the Major. 'I'm a parvenu with my chaps. I've only been twenty years in the regiment, and my revered parent he was a simple squire. There's no getting at the bottom of a Bhil's mind. Now, *why* is the superior bearer that young Chinn brought with him fleeing across country with his bundle?' He stepped into the verandah, and shouted after the man – a typical new-joined subaltern's servant who speaks English and cheats his master.

'What is it?' he called.

'Plenty bad men here. I going, sar,' was the reply. 'Have taken Sahib's keys, and say will shoot.'

'Doocid lucid – doocid convincin.' How those up-country thieves can leg it! He has been badly frightened by some one.' The Major strolled to his quarters to dress for mess.

Young Chinn, walking like a man in a dream, had fetched a compass round the entire cantonment before going to his own tiny cottage. The captain's quarters, in which he had been born, delayed him for a little; then he looked at the well on the parade-ground, where he had sat of evenings with his nurse, and at the ten-by-fourteen church, where the officers went to service if a chaplain of any official creed happened to come along. It seemed very small as compared with the gigantic building he used to stare up at, but it was the same place.

From time to time he passed a knot of silent soldiers, who saluted. They might have been the very men who had carried him on their backs when he was in his first knickerbockers. A faint light burned in his room, and, as he entered, hands clasped his feet, and a voice murmured from the floor.

'Who is it?' said young Chinn, not knowing he spoke in the Bhil tongue.

'I bore you in my arms, Sahib, when I was a strong man and you were a small one – crying, crying, crying! I am your servant, as I was your father's before you. We are all your servants.'

Young Chinn could not trust himself to reply, and the voice went on:

'I have taken your keys from that fat foreigner, and sent him away; and the studs are in the shirt for mess. Who should know, if I do not know? And so the baby has become a man, and forgets his nurse; but my nephew shall make a good servant, or I will beat him twice a day.'

Then there rose up, with a rattle, as straight as a Bhil arrow, a little white-haired wizened ape of a man, with medals and orders on his tunic, stammering, saluting, and trembling. Behind him a young and wiry Bhil, in uniform, was taking the trees out of Chinn's mess-boots.

Chinn's eyes were full of tears. The old man held out his keys.

'Foreigners are bad people. He will never come back again. We are all servants of your father's son. Has the Sahib forgotten who took him to see the trapped tiger in the village across the river, when his mother was so frightened and he was so brave?'

The scene came back to Chinn in great magic-lantern flashes. 'Bukta!' he cried; and all in a breath: 'You promised nothing should hurt me. *Is* it Bukta?'

The man was at his feet a second time. 'He has not forgotten. He remembers his own people as his father remembered. Now can I die. But first I will live and show the Sahib how to kill tigers. That *that* yonder is my nephew. If he is not a good servant, beat him and send him to me, and I will surely kill him, for now the Sahib is with his own people. Ai, Jan *baba*—Jan *baba*! My Jan *baba*! I will stay here and see that this does his work well. Take off his boots, fool. Sit down upon the bed, Sahib, and let me look. It *is* Jan *baba*!'

He pushed forward the hilt of his sword as a sign of service, which is an honour paid only to viceroys, governors, generals, or to little children whom one loves dearly. Chinn touched the hilt mechanically with three fingers, muttering he knew not what. It happened to be the old answer of his childhood, when Bukta in jest called him the little General Sahib.

The Major's quarters were opposite Chinn's, and when he heard his servant gasp with surprise he looked across the room. Then the Major sat on the bed and whistled; for the spectacle of the senior native commissioned officer of the regiment, an 'unmixed' Bhil, a Companion of the Order of British India, with thirty-five years' spotless service in the army, and a rank among his own people superior to that of many Bengal princelings, valeting the last-joined subaltern, was a little too much for his nerves.

The throaty bugles blew the Mess-call that has a long legend behind it. First a few piercing notes like the shrieks of beaters in a far-away cover, and next, large, full, and smooth, the refrain of the wild song: 'And oh, and oh, the green pulse of Mundore – Mundore!'

'All little children were in bed when the Sahib heard that call last,' said Bukta, passing Chinn a clean handkerchief. The call brought back memories of his cot under the mosquito-netting, his mother's kiss, and the sound of footsteps growing fainter as he dropped asleep among his men. So he hooked the dark collar of his new mess-jacket, and went to dinner like a prince who has newly inherited his father's crown.

Old Bukta swaggered forth curling his whiskers. He knew his own value, and no money and no rank within the gift of the Government would have induced him to put studs in young officers' shirts, or to hand them clean ties. Yet, when he took off his uniform that night and squatted among his fellows for a quiet smoke, he told them what he had done, and they said that he was entirely right. Thereat Bukta propounded a theory which to a white mind would have seemed raving insanity; but the whispering, level-headed little men of war considered it from every point of view, and thought that there might be a great deal in it.

At mess under the oil-lamps the talk turned as usual to the unfailing subject of *shikar* – big game shooting of every kind and under all sorts of conditions. Young Chinn opened his eyes when he understood that each one of his companions had shot several tigers in the Wuddar style – on foot, that is – making no more of the business than if the brute had been a dog.

'In nine cases out of ten,' said the Major, 'a tiger is almost as dangerous as a porcupine. But the tenth time you come home feet first.'

That set all talking, and long before midnight Chinn's brain was in a whirl with stories of tigers – man-eaters and cattle-killers each pursuing his own business as methodically as clerks in an office; new tigers that had lately come into such-and-such a district; and old, friendly beasts of great cunning, known by nicknames in the mess – such as 'Puggy,' who was lazy, with huge paws, and 'Mrs. Malaprop,' who turned up when you never expected her, and made female noises. Then they spoke of Bhil superstitions, a wide and picturesque field, till young Chinn hinted that they must be pulling his leg.

''Deed we aren't,' said a man on his left. 'We know all about you. You're a Chinn and all that, and you've a sort of vested right here; but if you don't believe what we're telling you, what will you do when old Bukta begins his stories? He knows about ghost-tigers, and tigers that go to a hell of their own; and tigers that walk on their hind feet; and your grandpapa's riding-tiger, as well. Odd he hasn't spoken of that yet.'

'You know you've an ancestor buried down Satpura way, don't you?' said the Major, as Chinn smiled irresolutely.

'Of course I do,' said Chinn, who had the chronicle of the Book of Chinn by heart. It lies in a worn old ledger on the Chinese lacquer table behind the piano in the Devonshire home, and the children are allowed to look at it on Sundays.

'Well, I wasn't sure. Your revered ancestor, my boy, according to the Bhils, has a tiger of his own – a saddle-tiger that he rides round the country whenever he feels inclined. *I* don't call it decent in an ex-Collector's ghost; but that is what the Southern Bhils believe. Even our men, who might be called moderately cool, don't care to beat that country if they hear that Jan Chinn is running about on his tiger. It is supposed to be a clouded animal – not stripy, but blotchy, like a tortoise-shell tom-cat. No end of a brute, it is, and a sure sign of war or pestilence or – or something. There's a nice family legend for you.'

'What's the origin of it, d'you suppose?' said Chinn.

'Ask the Satpura Bhils. Old Jan Chinn was a mighty hunter before the Lord. Perhaps it was the tiger's revenge, or perhaps he's huntin' 'em still. You must go to his tomb one of these days and inquire. Bukta will probably attend to that. He was asking me before you came whether by any ill-luck you had already bagged your tiger. If not, he is going to enter you under his own wing. Of course, for you of all men it's imperative. You'll have a first-class time with Bukta.'

The Major was not wrong. Bukta kept an anxious eye on young Chinn at drill, and it was noticeable that the first time the new officer lifted up his voice in an order the whole line quivered. Even the Colonel was taken aback, for it might have been Lionel Chinn returned from Devonshire with a new lease of life. Bukta had continued to develop his peculiar theory among his intimates, and it was accepted as a matter of faith in the lines, since every word and gesture on young Chinn's part so confirmed it.

The old man arranged early that his darling should wipe out the reproach of not having shot a tiger; but he was not content to take the first or any beast that happened to arrive. In his own villages he dispensed the high, low, and middle justice, and when his people – naked and fluttered – came to him with word of a beast marked down, he bade them send spies to the kills and the watering places, that he might be sure the quarry was such an one as suited the dignity of such a man.

Three or four times the reckless trackers returned, most truthfully saying that the beast was mangy, undersized – a tigress worn with nursing, or a broken-toothed old male – and Bukta would curb young Chinn's impatience.

At last, a noble animal was marked down – a ten-foot cattle-killer with a huge roll of loose skin along the belly, glossy-hided, full-frilled about the neck, whiskered, frisky, and young. He had slain a man in pure sport, they said.

'Let him be fed,' quoth Bukta, and the villagers dutifully drove out cows to amuse him, that he might lie up near by.

Princes and potentates have taken ship to India and spent great moneys for the mere glimpse of beasts one-half as fine as this of Bukta's.

'It is not good,' said he to the Colonel, when he asked for shooting-leave, 'that my Colonel's son who may be – that my Colonel's son should lose his maidenhead on any small jungle beast. That may come after. I have waited long for this which is a tiger. He has come in from the Mair country. In seven days we will return with the skin.'

The mess gnashed their teeth enviously, Bukta, had he chosen, might have invited them all. But he went out alone with Chinn, two days in a shooting-cart and a day on foot, till they came to a rocky, glary valley with a pool of good water in it. It was a parching day, and the boy very naturally stripped and went in for a bathe, leaving Bukta by the clothes. A white skin shows far against brown jungle, and what Bukta beheld on Chinn's back and right shoulder dragged him forward step by step with staring eyeballs.

'I'd forgotten it isn't decent to strip before a man of his position,' said Chinn, flouncing in the water. 'How the little devil stares! What is it, Bukta?'

'The Mark!' was the whispered answer.

'It is nothing. You know how it is with my people!' Chinn was annoyed. The dull-red birth-mark on his shoulder, something like a conventionalised Tartar cloud, had slipped his memory, or he would not have bathed. It occurred, so they said at home, in alternate generations, appearing, curiously enough, eight or nine years after birth, and, save that it was part of the Chinn inheritance, would not be considered pretty. He hurried ashore, dressed again, and went on till they met two or three Bhils, who promptly fell on their faces. 'My people,' grunted Bukta, not condescending to notice them. 'And so your people, Sahib. When I was a young man we were fewer, but not so weak. Now we are many, but poor stock. As may be remembered. How will you shoot him, Sahib? From a tree; from a shelter which my people shall build; by day or by night?'

'On foot and in the daytime,' said young Chinn.

'That was your custom, as I have heard,' said Bukta to himself. 'I will get news of him. Then you and I will go to him. I will carry one gun. You have yours. There is no need of more. What tiger shall stand against *thee*?'

He was marked down by a little water-hole at the head of a ravine, full-gorged and half-asleep in the May sunlight. He was walked up like a partridge, and he turned to do battle for his life. Bukta made no motion to raise his rifle, but kept his eyes on Chinn, who met the shattering roar of the charge with a single shot – it seemed to him hours as he sighted – which tore through the throat, smashing the backbone below the neck and between the shoulders. The brute crouched, choked, and fell, and before Chinn knew well what had happened Bukta bade him stay still while he paced the distance between his feet and the ringing jaws.

'Fifteen,' said Bukta. 'Short paces. No need for a second shot, Sahib. He bleeds cleanly where he lies, and we need not spoil the skin. I said there would be no need of these, but they came – in case.'

Suddenly the sides of the ravine were crowned with the heads of Bukta's people – a force that could have blown the ribs out of the beast had Chinn's shot failed; but their guns were hidden, and they appeared as interested beaters, some five or six, waiting the word to skin. Bukta watched the life fade from the wild eyes, lifted one hand, and turned on his heel.

'No need to show that *we* care,' said he. 'Now, after this, we can kill what we choose. Put out your hand, Sahib.'

Chinn obeyed. It was entirely steady, and Bukta nodded. 'That also was your custom. My men skin quickly. They will carry the skin to cantonments. Will the Sahib come to my poor village for the night and, perhaps, forget that I am his officer?'

'But those men – the beaters. They have worked hard and perhaps——'

'Oh, if they skin clumsily, we will skin them. They are my people. In the lines I am one thing. Here I am another.'

This was very true. When Bukta doffed uniform and reverted to the fragmentary dress of his own people, he left his civilisation to drill in the next world. That night, after a little talk with his subjects, he devoted to an orgie, and a Bhil orgie is a thing not to be safely written about. Chinn, flushed with triumph, was in the thick of it, but the meaning of the mysteries was hidden. Wild folk came and pressed about his knees with offerings. He gave his flask to the elders of the village. They grew eloquent, and wreathed him about with flowers. Gifts and loans, not all seemely, were thrust upon him, and infernal music rolled and maddened round red fires, while singers sang songs of the ancient times, and danced peculiar dances. The aboriginal liquors are very potent, and Chinn was compelled to taste them often, but, unless the stuff had been drugged, how came he to fall asleep suddenly, and to waken late the next day – half a march from the village?

'The Sahib was very tired. A little before dawn he went to sleep,' Bukta explained. 'My people carried him here, and now it is time we should go back to cantonments.'

The voice, smooth and deferential, the step, steady and silent, made it hard to believe that only a few hours before Bukta was yelling and capering with naked fellow-devils of the scrub.

'My people were very pleased to see the Sahib. They will never forget. When next the Sahib goes out recruiting, he will go to my people, and they will give him as many men as we need.'

Chinn kept his own counsel, except as to the shooting of the tiger, and Bukta embroidered that tale with a shameless tongue. The skin was certainly one of the finest ever hung up in the mess, and the first of many. When Bukta could not accompany his boy on shooting-trips, he took care to put him in good hands, and Chinn learned more of the mind and desire

of the wild Bhill in his marches and campings, by talks at twilight or at wayside pools, than an uninstructed man could have come at in a lifetime.

Presently his men in the regiment grew bold to speak of their relatives – mostly in trouble – and to lay cases of tribal custom before him. They would say, squatting in his veranday at twilight, after the easy, confidential style of the Wuddars, that such-and-such a bachelor had run away with such-and-such a wife at a far-off village. Now, how many cows would Chinn Sahib consider a just fine? Or, again, if written order came from the Government that a Bhil was to repair to a walled city of the plains to give evidence in a law-court, would it be wise to disregard that order? On the other hand, if it were obeyed, would the rash voyager return alive?

'But what have I to do with these things?' Chinn demanded of Bukta, impatiently. 'I am a soldier. I do not know the Law.'

'Hoo! Law is for fools and white men. Give them a large and loud order and they will abide by it. Thou art their Law.'

'But wherefore?'

Every trace of expression left Bukta's countenance. The idea might have smitten him for the first time. 'How can I say?' he replied. 'Perhaps it is on account of the name. A Bhil does not love strange things. Give them orders, Sahib – two, three, four words at a time such as they can carry away in their heads. That is enough.'

Chinn gave orders then, valiantly, not realising that a word spoken in haste before mess became the dread unappealable law of villages beyond the smoky hills – was, in truth, no less than the Law of Jan Chinn the First, who, so the whispered legend ran, had come back to earth to oversee the third generation in the body and bones of his grandson.

There could be no sort of doubt in this matter. All the Bhils knew that Jan Chinn reincarnated had honoured Bukta's village with his presence after slaying his first – in this life – tiger; that he had eaten and drunk with the people, as he was used; and – Bukta must have drugged Chinn's liquor very deeply – upon his back and right shoulder all men had seen the same angry red Flying Cloud that the high Gods had set on the flesh of Jan Chinn the First when first he came to the Bhil. As concerned the foolish white world which has no eyes, he was a slim and young officer in the Wuddars; but his own people knew he was Jan Chinn, who had made the Bhil a man; and, believing, they hastened to carry his words, careful never to alter them on the way.

Because the savage and the child who plays lonely games have one horror of being laughed at or questioned, the little folk kept their convictions to themselves; and the Colonel, who thought he knew his regiment, never guessed that each one of the six hundred quick-footed, beady-eyed rank-and-file, at attention beside their rifles, believed serenely and unshakenly that the subaltern on the left flank of the line was a demigod twice born – tutelary deity of their land and people. The Earth-gods themselves had stamped the incarnation, and who would dare to doubt the handiwork of the Earth-gods?

Chinn, being practical above all things, saw that his family name served him well in the lines and in camp. His men gave no trouble – one does not commit regimental offences with a god in the chair of justice – and he was sure of the best beaters in the district when he needed them. They believed that the protection of Jan Chinn the First cloaked them, and were bold in that belief beyond the utmost daring of excited Bhils.

His quarters began to look like an amateur natural-history museum, in spite of duplicate heads and horns and skulls that he sent home to Devonshire. The people, very humanly, learned the weak side of their god. It is true he was unbribable, but bird-skins, butterflies, beetles, and, above all, news of big game pleased him. In other respects, too, he lived up to the Chinn tradition. He was fever-proof. A night's sitting out over a tethered goat in a damp valley, that would have filled the Major with a month's malaria, had no effect on him. He was, as they said, 'salted before he was born.'

Now in the autumn of his second year's service an uneasy rumour crept out of the earth and ran about among the Bhils. Chinn heard nothing of it till a brother-officer said across the mess-table: 'Your revered ancestor's on the rampage in the Satpura country. You'd better look him up.'

'I don't want to be disrespectful, but I'm a little sick of my revered ancestor. Bukta talks of nothing else. What's the old boy supposed to be doing now?'

'Riding cross-country by moonlight on his processional tiger. That's the story. He's been seen by about two thousand Bhils, skipping along the tops of the Satpuras, and scaring people to death. They believe it devoutly, and all the Satpura chaps are worshipping away at his shrine – tomb, I mean – like good 'uns. You really ought to go down there. Must be a queer thing to see your grandfather treated as a god.'

'What makes you think there's any truth in the tale?' said Chinn.

'Because all our men deny it. They say they've never heard of Chinn's tiger. Now that's a manifest lie, because every Bhil *has*.'

'There's only one thing you've overlooked,' said the Colonel, thoughtfully. 'When a local god reappears on earth it's always an excuse for trouble of some kind; and those Satpura Bhils are about as wild as your grandfather left them, young 'un. It means something.'

'Meanin' they may go on the war-path?' said Chinn.

'Can't say – as yet. Shouldn't be surprised a little bit.'

'I haven't been told a syllable.'

'Proves it all the more. They are keeping something back.'

'Bukta tells me everything, too, as a rule. Now, why didn't he tell me that?'

Chinn put the question directly to the old man that night, and the answer surprised him.

'Why should I tell what is well-known? Yes, the Clouded Tiger is out in the Satpura country.'

'What do the wild Bhils think that it means?'

'They do not know. They wait. Sahib, what *is* coming? Say only one little word, and we will be content.'

'We? What have tales from the south, where the jungly Bhils live, to do with drilled men?'

'When Jan Chinn wakes is no time for any Bhil to be quiet.'

'But he has not waked, Bukta.'

'Sahib' – the old man's eyes were full of tender reproof – 'if he does not wish to be seen, why does he go abroad in the moonlight? We know he is awake, but we do not know what he desires. Is it a sign for all the Bhils, or one that concerns the Satpura folk alone? Say one little word, Sahib, that I may carry it to the lines, and send on to our villages. Why does Jan Chinn ride out? Who has done wrong? Is it pestilence? Is it *murrain*? Will our children die? Is it a sword? Remember, Sahib, we are thy people and thy servants, and in this life I bore thee in my arms – not knowing.'

'Bukta had evidently looked on the cup this evening,' Chinn thought; 'but if I can do anything to soothe the old chap I must. It's like the Mutiny rumours on a small scale.'

He dropped into a deep wicker chair, over which was thrown his first tiger-skin, and his weight on the cushion flapped the clawed paws over his shoulders. He laid hold of them mechanically as he spoke, drawing the painted hide, cloak-fashion, about him.

'Now will I tell the truth, Bukta,' he said, leaning forward, the dried muzzle on his shoulder, to invent a specious lie.

'I see that it is the truth,' was the answer, in a shaking voice.

'Jan Chinn goes abroad among the Satpuras, riding on the Clouded Tiger, ye say? Be it so. Therefore the sign of the wonder is for the Satpura Bhils only, and does not touch the Bhils who plough in the north and the east, the Bhils of the Khandesh, or any others, except the Satpura Bhils, who, as we know, are wild and foolish.'

'It is, then, a sign for *them*. Good or bad?'

'Beyond doubt, good. For why should Jan Chinn make evil to those he has made men? The nights over yonder are hot; it is ill to lie in one bed over long without turning, and Jan Chinn would look again upon his people. So he rises, whistles his Clouded Tiger, and goes abroad a little to breathe the cool air. If the Satpura Bhils kept to their villages, and did not wander after dark, they would not see him. Indeed, Bukta, it is no more than that he would see the light again in his own country. Send this news south, and say that it is my word.'

Bukta bowed to the floor. 'Good Heavens!' thought Chinn, 'and this blinking pagan is a first-class officer, and as straight as a die! I may as well round it off neatly.' He went on:

'If the Satpura Bhils ask the meaning of the sign, tell them that Jan Chinn would see how they kept their old promises of good living. Perhaps they have plundered; perhaps they mean to disobey the orders of the Government; perhaps there is a dead man in the jungle; and so Jan Chinn has come to see.'

'Is he, then, angry?'

'Bah! Am *I* ever angry with my Bhils? I say angry words, and threaten many things. *Thou* knowest, Bukta. I have seen thee smile behind the hand. I know, and thou knowest. The Bhils are my children. I have said it many times.'

'Ay. We be thy children,' said Bukta.

'And no otherwise is it with Jan Chinn, my father's father. He would see the land he loved and the people once again. It is a good ghost, Bukta. I say it. Go and tell them. And I do hope devoutly,' he added, 'that it will calm 'em down.' Flinging back the tiger-skin, he rose with a long, unguarded yawn that showed his well-kept teeth.

Bukta fled, to be received in the lines by a knot of panting inquirers.

'It is true,' said Bukta. 'He wrapped himself in the skin and spoke from it. He would see his own country again. The sign is not for us; and, indeed, he is a young man. How should he lie idle of nights? He says his bed is too hot and the air is bad. He goes to and fro for the love of night-running. He has said it.'

The grey-whiskered assembly shuddered.

'He says the Bhils are his children. Ye know he does not lie. He has said it to me.'

'But what of the Satpura Bhils? What means the sign for them?'

'Nothing. It is only night-running, as I have said. He rides to see if they obey the Government, as he taught them to do in his first life.'

'And what if they do not?'

'He did not say.'

The light went out in Chinn's quarters.

'Look,' said Bukta. 'Now he goes away. None the less it is a good ghost, as he has said. How shall we fear Jan Chinn, who made the Bhil a man? His protection is on us; and ye know Jan Chinn never broke a protection spoken or written on paper. When he is older and has found him a wife he will lie in his bed till morning.'

A commanding officer is generally aware of the regimental state of mind a little before the men; and this is why the Colonel said a few days later that some one had been putting the fear of God into the Wuddars. As he was the only person officially entitled to do this, it distressed him to see such unanimous virtue. 'It's too good to last,' he said. 'I only wish I could find out what the little chaps mean.'

The explanation, as it seemed to him, came at the change of the moon, when he received orders to hold himself in readiness to 'allay any possible excitement' among the Satpura Bhils, who were, to put it mildly, uneasy because a paternal Government had sent up against them a Mahratta State-educated vaccinator, with lancets, lymph, an officially registered calf. In the language of State, they had 'manifested a strong objection to all prophylactic measures,' had 'forcibly detained the vaccinator,' and 'were on the point of neglecting or evading their tribal obligations.'

'That means they are in a blue funk – same as they were at the last census-time,' said the Colonel; 'and if we stampede them into the hills we'll never catch 'em, in the first place, and, in the second, they'll whoop off plundering till further orders. Wonder who the God-forsaken idiot is who is trying to vaccinate a Bhil. I knew trouble was coming. One good thing is that they'll only use local corps, and we can knock up something we'll call a campaign, and let them down easy. Fancy us potting our best beaters because they don't want to be vaccinated! They're only crazy with fear.'

'Don't you think, sir,' said Chinn the next day, 'that perhaps you could give me a fortnight's shooting-leave?'

'Desertion in the face of the enemy, by Jove!' The Colonel laughed. 'I might, but I'd have to antedate it a little, because we're warned for service, as you might say. However, we'll assume that you applied for leave three days ago, and are now well on your way south.'

'I'd like to take Bukta with me.'

'Of course, yes. I think that will be the best plan. You've some kind of hereditary influence with the little chaps, and they may listen to you when a glimpse of our uniforms would drive them wild. You've never been in that part of the world before, have you? Take care they don't send you to your family vault in your youth and innocence. I believe you'll be all right if you can get 'em to listen to you.'

'I think so, sir; but if – if they should accidentally put an – make asses of 'emselves – they might, you know – I hope you'll represent that they were only frightened. There isn't an ounce of real vice in 'em, and I should never forgive myself if any one of – of my name got them into trouble.'

The Colonel nodded, but said nothing.

Chinn and Bukta departed at once. Bukta did not say that, ever since the official vaccinator had been dragged into the hills by indignant Bhils, runner after runner had skulked up to the lines, entreating, with forehead in the dust, that Jan Chinn should come and explain this unknown horror that hung over his people.

The portent of the Clouded Tiger was now too clear. Let Jan Chinn comfort his own, for vain was the help of mortal man. Bukta toned down these beseechings to a simple request for Chinn's presence. Nothing would have pleased the old man better than a rough-and-tumble campaign against the Satpuras, whom he, as an 'unmixed' Bhil, despised; but he had a duty to all his nation as Jan Chinn's interpreter, and he devoutly believed that forty plagues would fall on his village if he tampered with that obligation. Besides, Jan Chinn knew all things, and he rode the Clouded Tiger.

They covered thirty miles a day on foot and pony, raising the blue wall-like line of the Satpuras as swiftly as might be. Bukta was very silent.

They began the steep climb a little after noon, but it was near sunset ere they reached the stone platform clinging to the side of a rifted, jungle-covered hill, where Jan Chinn the First was laid, as he had desired, that he might overlook his people. All India is full of neglected graves that date from the beginning of the eighteenth century – tombs of forgotten colonels of corps long since disbanded; mates of East Indiamen who went on shooting expeditions and never came back; factors, agents, writers, and ensigns of the Honourable the East India Company by hundreds and thousands and tens of thousands. English folk forget quickly, but natives have long memories, and if a man has done good in his life it is remembered after his death. The weathered marble four-square tomb of Jan Chinn was hung about with wild flowers and nuts, packets of wax and honey, bottles of native spirits, and infamous cigars, with buffalo horns and plumes of dried grass. At one end was a rude clay image of a white man, in the old-fashioned top-hat, riding on a bloated tiger.

Bukta salaamed reverently as they approached. Chinn bared his head and began to pick out the blurred inscription. So far as he could read it ran thus – word for word, and letter for letter:-

To the Memory of JOHN CHINN, ESQ.
Late Collector of . . . .
. . . . ithout Bloodshed or . . . error of Authority
Employ . only . . . eans of Conciliat . . . and Confiden
accomplished the . . . tire Subjection . . .
a Lawless and Predatory Peop . . .
. . . taching them to . . . . ish Government
by a Conque . . . over . . . . Minds
The most perma . . . and rational Mode of Domini . .

. . . Governor-General and Counc . . . engal
have ordered thi . . . . . . erected
. . . arted this Life Aug. 19, 184 . . . Ag . . .

On the other side of the grave were ancient verses, also very worn. As much as Chinn could decipher said:

. . . the savage band
Forsook their Haunts and b . . . . is Command
. . . . mended . . . rals check a . . . st for spoil
And . . s . . ing Hamlets prove his gene . . . . toil
Humanit . . . survey . . . . . . ights restore . .
A nation . . ield . . subdued without a Sword.

For some little time he leaned on the tomb thinking of this dead man of his own blood, and of the house in Devonshire; then, nodding to the plains: 'Yes; it's a big work – all of it – even my little share. He must have been worth knowing . . . Bukta, where are my people?'

'Not here, Sahib. No man comes here except in full sun. They wait above. Let us climb and see.'

But Chinn, remembering the first law of Oriental diplomacy, in an even voice answered: 'I have come this far only because the Satpura folk are foolish, and dared not visit our lines. Now bid them wait on me *here*. I am not a servant, but the master of Bhils.'

'I go – I go,' clucked the old man. Night was falling, and at any moment Jan Chinn might whistle up his dreaded steed from the darkening scrub.

Now for the first time in a long life Bukta disobeyed a lawful command and deserted his leader; for he did not come back, but pressed to the flat table-top of the hill, and called softly. Men stirred all about him – little trembling men with bows and arrows who had watched the two since noon.

'Where is he?' whispered one.

'At his own place. He bids you come,' said Bukta.

'Now?'

'Now.'

'Rather let him loose the Clouded Tiger upon us. We do not go.'

'Nor I, though I bore him in my arms when he was a child in this his life. Wait here till the day.'

'But surely he will be angry.'

'He will be very angry, for he has nothing to eat. But he has said to me many times that the Bhils are his children. By sunlight I believe this, but – by moonlight I am not so sure. What folly have ye Satpura pigs compassed that ye should need him at all?'

'One came to us in the name of the Government with little ghost-knives and a magic calf, meaning to turn us into cattle by the cutting off of our arms. We were greatly afraid, but we did not kill the man. He is here, bound – a black man; and we think he comes from the West. He said it was an order to cut us all with knives – especially the women and children. We did not hear that it was an order, so we were afraid, and kept to our hills. Some of our men have taken ponies and bullocks from the plains, and others pots and cloths and ear-rings.'

'Are any slain?'

'By our men? Not yet. But the young men are blown to and fro by many rumours like flames upon a hill. I sent runners asking for Jan Chinn lest worse should come to us. It was this fear that he foretold by the sign of the Clouded Tiger.'

'He says it is otherwise,' said Bukta; and he repeated, with amplifications, all that young Chinn had told him at the conference of the wicker chair.

'Think you,' said the questioner, at last, 'that the Government will lay hands on us?'

'Not I,' Bukta rejoined. 'Jan Chinn will give an order, and ye will obey. The rest is between the Government and Jan Chinn. I myself know something of the ghost-knives and the scratching. It is a charm against the Smallpox. But how it is done I cannot tell. Nor need that concern you.'

'If he stands by us and before the anger of the Government we will most strictly obey Jan Chinn, except – except we do not go down to that place tonight.'

They could hear young Chinn below them shouting for Bukta; but they cowered and sat still, expecting the Clouded Tiger. The tomb had been holy ground for nearly half a century. If Jan Chinn chose to sleep there, who had better right? But they would not come within eyeshot of the place till broad day.

At first Chinn was exceedingly angry, till it occurred to him that Bukta most probably had a reason (which, indeed, he had), and his own dignity might suffer if he yelled without answer. He propped himself against the foot of the grave, and alternately dozing and smoking, came through the warm night proud that he was a lawful, legitimate, fever-proof Chinn.

He prepared his plan of action much as his grandfather would have done; and when Bukta appeared in the morning with a most liberal supply of food, said nothing of the overnight desertion. Bukta would have been relieved by an outburst of human anger; but Chinn finished his victual leisurely, and a cheroot, ere he made any sign.

'They are very much afraid,' said Bukta, who was not too bold himself. 'It remains only to give orders. They said they will obey if thou wilt only stand between them and the Government.'

'That I know,' said Chinn, strolling slowly to the table-land. A few of the elder men stood in an irregular semicircle in an open glade; but the ruck of people – women and children – were hidden in the thicket. They had no desire to face the first anger of Jan Chinn the First.

Seating himself on a fragment of split rock, he smoked his cheroot to the butt, hearing men breathe hard all about him. Then he cried, so suddenly that they jumped:

'Bring the man that was bound!'

A scuffle and a cry were followed by the appearance of a Hindu vaccinator, quaking with fear, bound hand and foot, as the Bhils of old were accustomed to bind their human sacrifices. He was pushed cautiously before the presence; but young Chinn did not look at him.

'I said – the man that *was* bound. Is it a jest to bring me one tied like a buffalo? Since when could the Bhil bind folk at his pleasure? Cut!'

Half a dozen hasty knives cut away the thongs, and the man crawled to Chinn, who pocketed his case of lancets and tubes of lymph. Then, sweeping the semicircle with one comprehensive forefinger, and in the voice of compliment, he said, clearly and distinctly: 'Pigs!'

'Ai!' whispered Bukta. 'Now he speaks. Woe to foolish people!'

'I have come on foot from my house' (the assembly shuddered) 'to make clear a matter which any other than a Satpura Bhil would have seen with both eyes from a distance. Ye know the Smallpox, who pits and scars your children so that they look like wasp-combs. It is an order of the Government that whoso is scratched on the arm with these little knives which I hold up is charmed against Her. All Sahibs are thus charmed, and very many Hindus. This is the mark of the charm. Look!'

He rolled back his sleeve to the armpit and showed the white scars of the vaccination-mark on the white skin. 'Come, all, and look.'

A few daring spirits came up, and nodded their heads wisely. There was certainly a mark, and they knew well what other dread marks were hidden by the shirt. Merciful was Jan Chinn, that he had not then and there proclaimed his godhead.

'Now all these things the man whom ye bound told you.'

'I did – a hundred times; but they answered with blows,' groaned the operator, chafing his wrists and ankles.

'But, being pigs, ye did not believe; and so came I here to save you, first from the Smallpox, next from a great folly of fear, and lastly, it may be, from the rope and the jail. It is no gain to me; it is no pleasure to me; but for the sake of that one who is yonder, who made the Bhil a man' – he pointed down the hill – 'I, who am of his blood, the son of his son, come to turn your people. And I speak the truth, as did Jan Chinn.'

The crowd murmured reverently, and men stole out of the thicket by twos and threes to join it. There was no anger in their god's face.

'These are my orders. (Heaven send they'll take 'em, but I seem to have impressed them so far!) I myself will stay among you while this man scratches your arms with knives, after the order of the Government. In three, or it may be five or seven days, your arms will swell and itch and burn. That is the power of Smallpox fighting in your base blood against the orders of the Government. I will therefore stay among you till I see that Smallpox is conquered, and I will not go away till the men and the women and the little children show me upon their arms such marks as I have even now showed you. I bring with me two very good guns, and a man whose name is known among beasts and men. We will hunt together, I and he, and your young men and the others shall eat and lie still. This is my order.'

There was a long pause while victory hung in the balance. A white-haired old sinner, standing on one uneasy leg, piped up:

'There are ponies and some few bullocks and other things for which we need a *kowl*. They were *not* taken in the way of trade.'

The battle was won, and John Chinn drew a breath of relief. The young Bhils had been raiding, but if taken swiftly all could be put straight.

'I will write a *kowl* as soon as the ponies, the bullocks, and the other things are counted before me and sent back whence they came. But first we will put the Government mark on such as have not been visited by Smallpox.' In an undertone, to the vaccinator: 'If you show you are afraid you'll never see Poona again, my friend.'

'There is not sufficient ample supply of vaccine for all this population,' said the man. 'They have destroyed the offeecial calf.'

'They won't know the difference. Scrape 'em all round, and give me a couple of lancets; I'll attend to the elders.'

The aged diplomat who had demanded protection was the first victim. He fell to Chinn's hand, and dared not cry out. As soon as he was freed he dragged up a companion, and held him fast, and the crisis became, as it were, a child's sport; for the vaccinated chased the unvaccinated to treatment, vowing that all the tribe must suffer equally. The women shrieked, and the children ran howling; but Chinn laughed, and waved the pink-tipped lancet.

'It is an honour,' he cried. 'Tell them, Bukta, how great an honour it is that I myself should mark them. Nay, I cannot mark every one – the Hindu must also do his work – but I will touch all marks that he makes, so there will be an equal virtue in them. Thus do the Rajputs stick pigs. Ho, brother with one eye! Catch that girl and bring her to me. She need not run away yet, for she is not married, and I do not seek her in marriage. She will not come? Then she shall be shamed by her little brother, a fat boy, a bold boy. He puts out his arm like a soldier. Look! *He* does not flinch at the blood. Some day he shall be in my regiment. And now, mother of many, we will lightly touch thee, for Smallpox has been before us here. It is a true thing, indeed, that this charm breaks the power of Mata. There will be no more pitted faces among the Satpuras, and so ye can ask many cows for each maid to be wed.'

And so on and so on – quick-poured showman's patter, sauced in the Bhil hunting proverbs and tales of their own brand of coarse humour – till the lancets were blunted and both operators worn out.

But, nature being the same the world over, the unvaccinated grew jealous of their marked comrades, and came near to blows about it. Then Chinn declared himself a court of justice, no longer a medical board, and made formal inquiry into the late robberies.

'We are the thieves of Mahadeo,' said the Bhils, simply. 'It is our fate, and we were frightened. When we are frightened we always steal.'

Simply and directly as children, they gave in the tale of the plunder, all but two bullocks and some spirits that had gone amissing (these Chinn promised to make good out of his own pocket), and ten ringleaders were despatched to the lowlands with a wonderful document, written on the leaf of a note-book, and addressed to an assistant district superintendent of police. There was warm calamity in that note, as Jan Chinn warned them, but anything was better than loss of liberty.

Armed with this protection, the repentant raiders went downhill. They had no desire whatever to meet Mr. Dundas Fawne of the Police, aged twenty-two, and of a cheerful countenance, nor did they wish to revisit the scene of their robberies. Steering a middle course, they ran into the camp of the one Government chaplain allowed to the various irregular corps through a district of some fifteen thousand square miles, and stood before him in a cloud of dust. He was by way of being a priest, they knew, and, what was more to the point, a good sportsman who paid his beaters generously.

When he read Chinn's note he laughed, which they deemed a lucky omen, till he called up policemen, who tethered the ponies and the bullocks by the piled house-gear, and laid stern hands upon three of that smiling band of the thieves of Mahadeo. The chaplain himself addressed them magisterially with a riding whip. That was painful, but Jan Chinn had prophesied it. They submitted, but would not give up the written protection, fearing the jail. On their way back they met Mr. D. Fawne, who had heard about the robberies, and was not pleased.

'Certainly,' said the eldest of the gang, when the second interview was at an end, 'certainly Jan Chinn's protection has saved us our liberty, but it is as though there were many beatings in one small piece of paper. Put it away.'

One climbed into a tree, and stuck the letter into a cleft forty feet from the ground, where it could do no harm. Warmed, sore, but happy, the ten returned to Jan Chinn next day, where he sat among uneasy Bhils, all looking at their right arms, and all bound under terror of their god's disfavour not to scratch.

'It was a good *kowl*,' said the leader. 'First the chaplain, who laughed, took away our plunder, and beat three of us, as was promised. Next, we meet Fawne Sahib, who frowned, and asked for the plunder. We spoke the truth, and so he beat us all, one after another, and called us chosen names. He then gave us these two bundles' – they set down a bottle of whisky and a box of cheroots – 'and we came away. The *kowl* is left in a tree, because its virtue is that so soon as we show it to a Sahib we are beaten.'

'But for that *kowl*,' said Jan Chinn, sternly, 'ye would all have been marching to jail with a policeman on either side. Ye come now to serve as beaters for me. These people are unhappy, and we will go hunting till they are well. Tonight we will make a feast.'

It is written in the chronicles of the Satpura Bhils, together with many other matters not fit for print, that through five days, after the day that he had put his mark upon them, Jan Chinn the First hunted for his people; and on the five nights of those days the tribe was gloriously and entirely drunk. Jan Chinn bought country spirits of an awful strength, and slew wild pig and deer beyond counting, so that if any fell sick they might have two good reasons.

Between head- and stomach-aches they found no time to think of their arms, but followed Jan Chinn obediently through the jungles, and with each day's returning confidence men, women, and children stole away to their villages as the little army passed by. They carried news that it was good and right to be scratched with ghost-knives; that Jan Chinn was indeed reincarnated as a god of free food and drink, and that of all nations the Satpura Bhils stood first in his favour, if they would only refrain from scratching. Henceforward that kindly demi-god would be connected in their minds with great gorgings and the vaccine and lancets of a paternal Government.

'And tomorrow I go back to my home,' said Jan Chinn to his faithful few, whom neither spirits, over-eating, nor swollen glands could conquer. It is hard for children and savages to behave reverently at all times to the idols of their make-belief, and they had frolicked excessively with Jan Chinn. But the reference to his home cast a gloom on the people.

'And the Sahib will not come again?' said he who had been vaccinated first.

'That is to be seen,' answered Chinn, warily.

'Nay, but come as a white man – come as a young man whom we know and love; for, as thou alone knowest, we are a weak people. If we saw thy – thy horse – ' They were picking up their courage.

'I have no horse. I came on foot – with Bukta, yonder. What is this?'

'Thou knowest – the Thing that thou hast chosen for a night-horse.' The little men squirmed in fear and awe.

'Night-horses? Bukta, what is this last tale of children?'

Bukta had been a silent leader in Chinn's presence since the night of his desertion, and was grateful for a chance-flung question.

'They know, Sahib,' he whispered. 'It is the Clouded Tiger. That comes from the place where thou didst once sleep. It is thy horse – as it has been these three generations.'

'My horse! That was a dream of the Bhils.'

'It is no dream. Do dreams leave the tracks of broad pugs on earth? Why make two faces before thy people? They know of the night-ridings, and they — and they —'

'Are afraid, and would have them cease.'

Bukta nodded. 'If thou hast no further need of him. He is thy horse.'

'The thing leaves a trail, then?' said Chinn.

'We have seen it. It is like a village road under the tomb.'

'Can ye find and follow it for me?'

'By daylight – if one comes with us, and, above all, stands near by.'

'I will stand close, and we will see to it that Jan Chinn does not ride any more.'

The Bhils shouted the last words again and again.

From Chinn's point of view the stalk was nothing more than an ordinary one – down hill, through split and crannied rocks, unsafe, perhaps, if a man did not keep his wits by him, but no worse than twenty others he had undertaken. Yet his men – they refused absolutely to beat, and would only trail – dripped sweat at every move. They showed the marks of enormous pugs that ran, always down hill, to a few hundred feet below Jan Chinn's tomb, and disappeared in a narrow-mouthed cave. It was an insolently open road, a domestic highway, beaten without thought of concealment.

'The beggar might be paying rent and taxes,' Chinn muttered ere he asked whether his friend's taste ran to cattle or man.

'Cattle,' was the answer. 'Two heifers a week. We drive them for him at the foot of the hill. It is his custom. If we did not, he might seek us.'

'Blackmail and piracy,' said Chinn. 'I can't say I fancy going into the cave after him. What's to be done?'

The Bhils fell back as Chinn lodged himself behind a rock with his rifle ready. Tigers, he knew, were shy beasts, but one who had been long cattle-fed in this sumptuous style might prove overbold.

'He speaks!' some one whispered from the rear. 'He knows, too.'

'Well, of *all* the infernal cheek!' said Chinn.

There was an angry growl from the cave – a direct challenge.

'Come out, then,' Chinn shouted. 'Come out of that! Let's have a look at you.'

The brute knew well enough that there

was some connection between brown nude Bhils and his weekly allowance; but the white helmet in the sunlight annoyed him, and he did not approve of the voice that broke his rest. Lazily as a gorged snake he dragged himself out of the cave, and stood yawning and blinking at the entrance. The sunlight fell upon his flat right side, and Chinn wondered. Never had he seen a tiger marked after this fashion. Except for his head, which was staringly barred, he was dappled – not striped, but dappled like a child's rocking-horse in rich shades of smoky black on red gold. That portion of his belly and throat which should have been white was orange, and his tail and paws were black.

He looked leisurely for some ten seconds, and then deliberately lowered his head, his chin dropped and drawn in, staring intently at the man. The effect of this was to throw forward the round arch of his skull, with two broad bands across it, while below the bands glared the unwinking eyes; so that, head on, as he stood, he showed something like a diabolically scowling pantomime-mask. It was a piece of natural mesmerism that he had practised many times on his quarry, and though Chinn was by no means a terrified heifer, he stood for a while, held by the extraordinary oddity of the attack. The head – the body seemed to have been packed away behind it – the ferocious, skull-like head, crept nearer to the switching of an angry tail-tip in the grass. Left and right the Bhils had scattered to let John Chinn subdue his own horse.

'My word!' he thought. 'He's trying to frighten me!' and fired between the saucer-like eyes, leaping aside upon the shot.

A big coughing mass, reeking of carrion, bounded past him up the hill, and he followed discreetly. The tiger made no attempt to turn into the jungle; he was hunting for sight and breath – nose up, mouth open, the tremendous fore-legs scattering the gravel in spurts.

'Scuppered!' said John Chinn, watching the flight. 'Now if he was a partridge he'd tower. Lungs must be full of blood.'

The brute had jerked himself over a boulder and fallen out of sight the other side. John Chinn looked over with a ready barrel. But the red trail led straight as an arrow even to his grandfather's tomb, and there, among the smashed spirit bottles and the fragments of the mud image, the life left with a flurry and a grunt.

'If my worthy ancestor could see that,' said John Chinn, 'he'd have been proud of me. Eyes, lower jaw, and lungs. A very nice shot.' He whistled for Bukta as he drew the tape over the stiffening bulk.

'Ten – six – eight – by Jove! It's nearly eleven – call it eleven. Fore-arm, twenty-four – five – seven and a half. A short tail, too; three feet one. But *what* a skin! Oh, Bukta! Bukta! The men with the knives swiftly.'

'Is he beyond question dead?' said an awe-stricken voice behind a rock.

'That was not the way I killed my first tiger,' said Chinn. 'I did not think that Bukta would run. I had no second gun.'

'It – it is the Clouded Tiger,' said Bukta, unheeding the taunt. 'He is dead.'

Whether all the Bhils, vaccinated and unvaccinated, of the Satpuras had lain by to see the kill, Chinn could not say; but the whole hill's flank rustled with little men, shouting, singing, and stamping. And yet, till he had made the first cut in the splendid skin, not a man would take a knife; and, when the shadows fell, they ran from the red-stained tomb, and no persuasion would bring them back till dawn. So Chinn spent a second night in the open, guarding the carcass from jackals, and thinking about his ancestor.

He returned to the lowlands to the triumphal chant of an escorting army three hundred strong, the Mahratta vaccinator close at his elbow, and the rudely dried skin a trophy before him. When that army suddenly and noiselessly disappeared, as quail in high corn, he argued he was near civilisation, and a turn in the road brought him upon the camp of a wing of his own corps. He left the skin on a cart-tail for the world to see, and sought the Colonel.

'They're perfectly right,' he explained earnestly. 'There isn't an ounce of vice in 'em. They were only frightened. I've vaccinated the whole boiling, and they like it awfully. What are – what are we doing here, sir?'

'That's what I'm trying to find out,' said the Colonel. 'I don't know yet whether we're a piece of a brigade or a police force. However, I think we'll call ourselves a police force. How did you manage to get a Bhil vaccinated?'

'Well, sir,' said Chinn, 'I've been thinking it over, and, as far as I can make out, I've got a sort of hereditary influence over 'em.'

'So I know, or I wouldn't have sent you; but *what* exactly?'

'It's rather rummy. It seems, from what I can make out, that I'm my own grandfather reincarnated, and I've been disturbing the peace of the country by riding a pad-tiger of nights. If I hadn't done that, I don't think they'd have objected to the vaccination; but the two together were more than they could stand. And so, sir, I've vaccinated 'em, and shot my tiger-horse as a sort o' proof of good faith. You never saw such a skin in your life'

The Colonel tugged his moustache thoughtfully. 'Now, how the deuce,' said he, 'am I to include that in my report?'

Indeed, the official version of the Bhils' anti-vaccination stampede said nothing about Lieutenant John Chinn, his godship. But Bukta knew, and the corps knew, and every Bhil in the Satpura hills knew.

And now Bukta is zealous that John Chinn shall swiftly be wedded and impart his powers to a son; for if the Chinn succession fails, and the little Bhils are left to their own imaginings, there will be fresh trouble in the Satpuras.

PART III

CIVILIANS

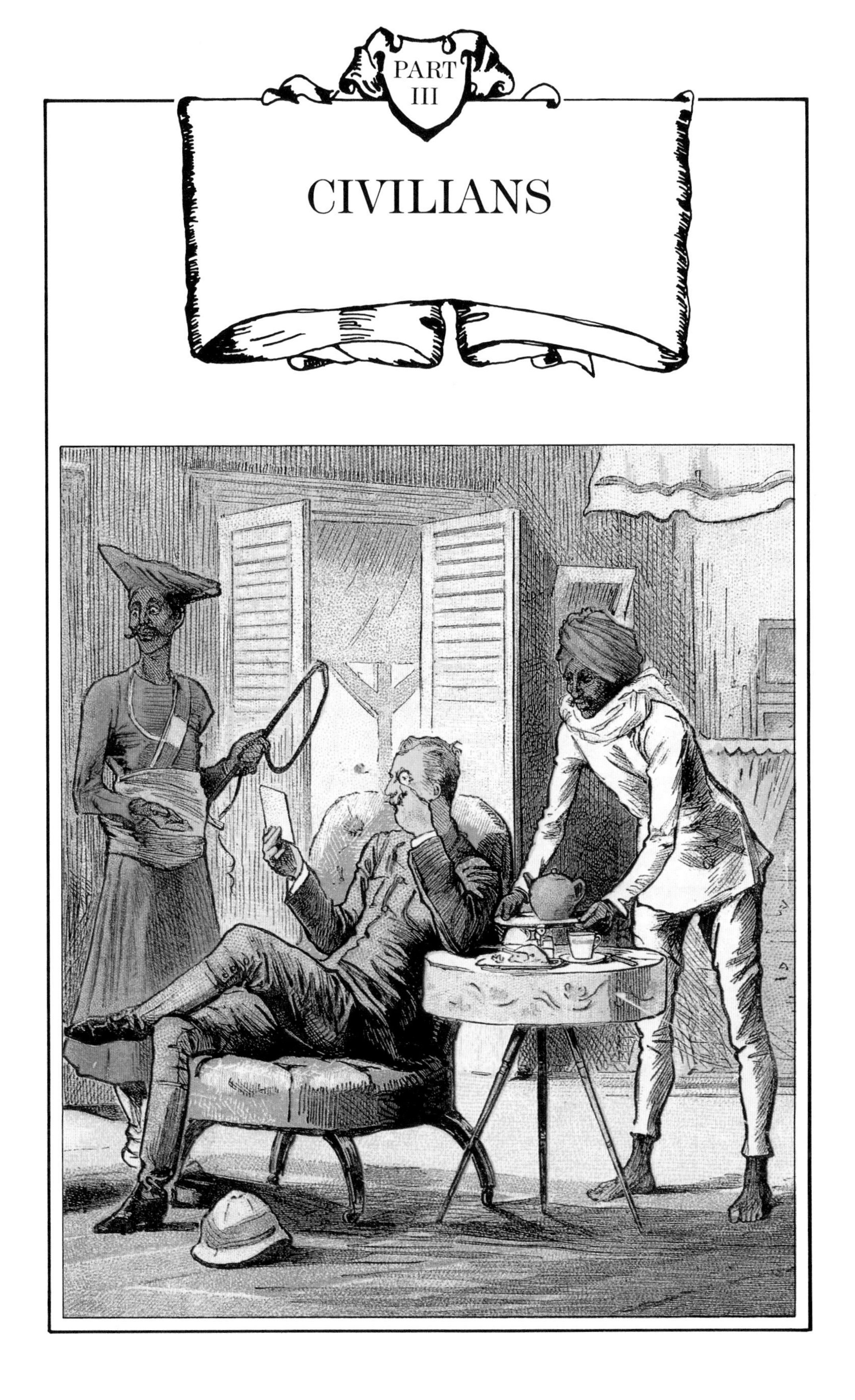

The word 'civilian' had a restricted usage in Kipling's time, relating to government officers not in military employ. In the strictest sense, it was applied only to members of the 'first firing line', the Indian Civil Service, such as Wressley of the Foreign and Political Department in 'Wressley of the Foreign Office'. However, the four protagonists who meet once a week to play bridge in 'At the End of the Passage' would also have regarded themselves as civilians: Hummil the assistant engineer, Mottram of the Indian Survey, Lowndes of the Civil Service and Spurstow of the Medical Service. They would certainly not have regarded the frightful 'Mister Anthony Dawking' as one of their number, whatever his own estimation of himself. Although an engineer by trade, Dawking really belongs to that British sub-species known as the 'loafer' that fascinated Kipling and horrified his contemporaries by letting down the side. We can see him take on a more rounded form in the characters of Carnehan and Dravot in 'The Man Who Would Be King'. Despite the efforts of the authorities to discipline and repatriate them, there were always European drifters and drop-outs to be found eking out an existence of sorts on the fringes of Indian society – just as there are today.

'Wressley of the Foreign Office' first appeared in the *C&MG* on 20 May 1887 and was reprinted in *Plain Tales from the Hills*. 'Mister Anthony Dawking' was one of eight contributions by 'The Traveller' to the *C&MG* in 1888. It has not been republished since. 'At the End of the Passage' reads as if it was written during one of those roasting Lahore summers that Kipling so hated. In fact it was written in London in the summer of 1890, a year after leaving India. First published in *Lippincott's Magazine* in August 1890, it was reprinted in *Life's Handicap*, 1891. The melodramatic overkill in this and other such stories may irritate some readers but those who know India will agree that there is much truth in the opening remarks of 'Wressley of the Foreign Office' about there being no 'half-tints' in India, where 'Men stand out all crude and raw, with nothing to tone them down, and nothing to scale them against.'

WRESSLEY OF THE FOREIGN OFFICE

ONE OF THE many curses of our life in India is the want of atmosphere in the painter's sense. There are no half-tints worth noticing. Men stand out all crude and raw, with nothing to tone them down, and nothing to scale them against. They do their work, and grow to think that there is nothing but their work, and nothing like their work, and that they are the real pivots on which the Administration turns. Here is an instance of this feeling. A half-caste clerk was ruling forms in a Pay Office. He said to me, 'Do you know what would happen if I added or took away one single line on this sheet?' Then, with the air of a conspirator, 'It would disorganise the whole of the Treasury payments throughout the whole of the Presidency Circle! Think of that!'

If men had not this delusion as to the ultra-importance of their own particular employments, I suppose that they would sit down and kill themselves. But their weakness is wearisome, particularly when the listener knows that he himself commits exactly the same sin.

Even the Secretariat believes that it does good when it asks an over-driven Executive Officer to take a census of wheat-weevils through a district of five thousand square miles.

There was a man once in the Foreign Office – a man who had grown middle-aged in the Department, and was commonly said, by irreverent juniors, to be able to repeat Aitchison's *Treaties and Sunnuds* backwards in his sleep. What he did with his stored knowledge only the Secretary knew; and he, naturally, would not publish the news abroad. This man's name was Wressley, and it was the Shibboleth, in those days, to say – 'Wressley knows more about the Central Indian States than any living man.' If you did not say this you were considered one of mean understanding.

Nowadays, the man who says that he knows the ravel of the inter-tribal complications across the Border is of more use; but in Wressley's time, much attention was paid to the Central Indian States. They were called 'foci' and 'factors,' and all manner of imposing names.

And here the curse of Anglo-Indian life fell heavily. When Wressley lifted up his voice and spoke about such-and-such a succession to such-and-such a throne, the Foreign Office were silent, and Heads of Departments repeated the last two or three words of Wressley's sentences, and tacked 'yes, yes,' on to them, and knew that they were assisting the Empire to grapple with serious political contingencies. In most big undertakings one or two men do the work, while the rest sit near and talk till the ripe decorations begin to fall.

Wressley was the working-member of the Foreign Office firm, and, to keep him up to his duties when he showed signs of flagging, he was made much of by his superiors and told what a fine fellow he was. He did not require coaxing because he was of tough build, but what he received confirmed him in the belief that there was no one quite so absolutely and imperatively necessary to the stability of India as Wressley of the Foreign Office. There might be other good men, but the known, honoured, and trusted man among men was Wressley of the Foreign Office. We had a Viceroy in those days who knew exactly when to 'gentle' a fractious big man, and to hearten-up a collar-galled little one, and so keep all his team level. He conveyed to Wressley the impression which I have just set down; and even tough men are apt to be disorganised by a Viceroy's praise. There was a case once – but that is another story.

All India knew Wressley's name and office – it was in Thacker and Spink's Directory – but who he was personally, or what he did, or what his special merits were, not fifty men knew or cared. His work filled all his time, and he found no leisure to cultivate acquaintances beyond those of dead Rajput chiefs with *Ahir* blots in their scutcheons. Wressley would have made a very good Clerk in the Herald's College had he not been a Bengal Civilian.

Upon a day, between office and office, great trouble came to Wressley – overwhelmed him, knocked him down, and left him gasping as though he had been a little schoolboy. Without reason, against prudence, and at a moment's notice, he fell in love with a frivolous, golden-haired girl who used to tear about Simla Mall on a high, rough Waler, with a blue velvet jockey-cap crammed over her eyes. Her name was Venner – Tillie Venner – and she was delightful. She took Wressley's heart at a hand-gallop, and Wressley found that it was not good for man to live alone; even with half the Foreign Office Records in his presses.

Then Simla laughed, for Wressley in love was slightly ridiculous. He did his best to interest the girl in himself – that is to say, his work – and she, after the manner of women, did her best to appear interested in what, behind his back, she called 'Mr. W'essley's Wajahs'; for she lisped very prettily. She did not understand one little thing about them, but she acted as if she did. Men have married on that sort of error before now.

Providence, however, had care of Wressley. He was immensely struck with Miss Venner's intelligence. He would have been more impressed had he heard her private and confidential accounts of his calls. He held peculiar notions as to the wooing of girls. He said that the best work of a man's career should be laid reverently at their feet. Ruskin writes something like this somewhere, I think; but in ordinary life a few kisses are better and save time.

About a month after he had lost his heart to Miss Venner, and had been doing his work vilely in consequence, the first idea of his *Native Rule in Central India* struck Wressley and filled him with joy. It was, as he sketched it, a great thing – the work of his life – a really comprehensive survey of a most fascinating subject – to be written with all the special and laboriously acquired knowledge of Wressley of the Foreign Office – a gift fit for an Empress.

He told Miss Venner that he was going to take leave, and hoped, on his return, to bring her a present worthy of her acceptance. Would she wait? Certainly she would. Wressley drew seventeen hundred rupees a month. She would wait a year for that. Her Mamma would help her to wait.

So Wressley took one year's leave and all the available documents, about a truck-load, that he could lay hands on, and went down to Central India with his notion hot in his head. He began his book in the land he was writing of. Too much official correspondence had made him a frigid workman, and he must have guessed that he needed the white light of local colour on his palette. This is a dangerous paint for amateurs to play with.

Heavens, how that man worked! He caught his Rajahs, analysed his Rajahs and traced them up into the mists of Time and beyond, with their queens and their concubines. He dated and cross-dated, pedigreed and triple-pedigreed, compared, noted, connoted, wove, strung, sorted, selected, inferred, calendared and counter-calendared for ten hours a day. And, because this sudden and new light of Love was upon him, he turned those dry bones of history and dirty records of misdeeds into things to weep or to laugh over as he pleased. His heart and soul were at the end of his pen, and they got into the ink. He was dowered with sympathy, insight, humour, and style for two hundred and thirty days and nights; and his book was a Book. He had his vast special knowledge with him, so to speak; but the spirit, the woven-in human Touch, the poetry and the power of the output, were beyond all special knowledge. But I doubt whether he knew the gift that was in him then, and thus he may have lost

some happiness. He was toiling for Tillie Venner, not for himself. Men often do their best work blind, for some one else's sake.

Also, though this has nothing to do with the story, in India, where every one knows every one else, you can watch men being driven, by the women who govern them, out of the rank-and-file and sent to take up points alone. A good man, once started, goes forward; but an average man, so soon as the woman loses interest in his success as a tribute to her power, comes back to the battalion and is no more heard of.

Wressley bore the first copy of his book to Simla, and, blushing and stammering, presented it to Miss Venner. She read a little of it. I give her review *verbatim* – 'Oh, your book? It's all about those howwid Wajahs. I didn't understand it.'

Wressley of the Foreign Office was broken, smashed, – I am not exaggerating – by this one frivolous little girl. All that he could say feebly was – 'But – but it's my *magnum opus*! The work of my life.' Miss Venner did not know what *magnum opus* meant; but she knew that Captain Kerrington had won three races at the last Gymkhana. Wressley didn't press her to wait for him any longer. He had sense enough for that.

Then came the reaction after the year's strain, and Wressley went back to the Foreign Office and his 'Wajahs,' a compiling, gazetteering, report-writing hack, who would have been dear at three hundred rupees a month. He abided by Miss Venner's review; which proves that the inspiration in the book was purely temporary and unconnected with himself. Nevertheless, he had no right to sink, in a hill-tarn, five packing-cases, brought up at enormous expense from Bombay, of the best book of Indian history ever written.

When he sold off before retiring, some years later, I was turning over his shelves, and came across the only existing copy of *Native Rule in Central India* – the copy that Miss Venner could not understand. I read it, sitting on his mule-trunks, as long as the light lasted, and offered him his own price for it. He looked over my shoulder for a few pages and said to himself drearily –

'Now, how in the world did I come to write such damned good stuff as that?'

Then to me –

'Take it and keep it. Write one of your penny-farthing yarns about its birth. Perhaps – perhaps – the whole business may have been ordained to that end.'

Which, knowing what Wressley of the Foreign Office was once, struck me as about the bitterest thing that I had ever heard a man say of his own work.

AT THE END OF THE PASSAGE

FOUR MEN, each entitled to 'life, liberty, and the pursuit of happiness,' sat at a table playing whist. The thermometer marked – for them – one hundred and one degrees of heat. The room was darkened till it was only just possible to distinguish the pips of the cards and the very white faces of the players. A tattered, rotten *punkah* of whitewashed calico was puddling the hot air and whining dolefully at each stroke. Outside lay gloom of a November day in London. There was neither sky, sun, nor horizon, – nothing but a brown purple haze of heat. It was as though the earth were dying of apoplexy.

From time to time clouds of tawny dust rose from the ground without wind or warning, flung themselves tablecloth-wise among the tops of the parched trees, and came down again. Then a whirling dust-devil would scutter across the plain for a couple of miles, break, and fall outward, though there was nothing to check its flight save a long low line of piled railway-sleepers white with the dust, a cluster of huts made of mud, condemned rails, and canvas, and the one squat four-roomed bungalow that belonged to the assistant engineer in charge of a section of the Gaudhari State line then under construction.

The four, stripped to the thinnest of sleeping-suits, played whist crossly, with wranglings as to leads and returns. It was not the best kind of whist, but they had taken some trouble to arrive at it. Mottram of the Indian Survey had ridden thirty and railed one hundred miles from his lonely post in the desert since the night before; Lowndes of the Civil Service, on special duty in the political department, had come as far to escape for an instant the miserable intrigues of an impoverished native State whose king alternately fawned and blustered for more money from the pitiful revenues contributed by hard-wrung peasants and despairing camel-breeders; Spurstow, the doctor of the line, had left a cholera-stricken camp of coolies to look after itself for forty-eight hours while he associated with white men once more. Hummil, the assistant engineer, was the host. He stood fast and received his friends thus every Sunday if they could come in. When one of them failed to appear, he would send a telegram to his last address, in order that he might know whether the defaulter were dead or alive. There are very many places in the East where it is not good or kind to let your acquaintances drop out of sight even for one short week.

The players were not conscious of any special regard for each other. They squabbled whenever they met; but they ardently desired to meet, as men without water desire to drink. They were lonely folk who understood the dread meaning of loneliness. They were all under thirty years of age, – which is too soon for any man to possess that knowledge.

'Pilsener?' said Spurstow, after the second rubber, mopping his forehead.

'Beer's out, I'm sorry to say, and there's hardly enough soda-water for tonight,' said Hummil.

'What filthy bad management!' Spurstow snarled.

'Can't help it. I've written and wired; but the trains don't come through regularly yet. Last week the ice ran out, – as Lowndes knows.'

'Glad I didn't come. I could ha' sent you some if I had known, though. Phew! it's too hot to go on playing bumblepuppy.' This with a savage scowl at Lowndes, who only laughed. He was a hardened offender.

Mottram rose from the table and looked out of a chink in the shutters.

'What a sweet day!' said he.

The company yawned all together and betook themselves to an aimless investigation of all Hummil's possessions, – guns, tattered novels, saddlery, spurs, and the like. They had fingered them a score of times before, but there was really nothing else to do.

'Got anything fresh?' said Lowndes.

'Last week's *Gazette of India*, and a cutting from a home paper. My father sent it out. It's rather amusing.'

'One of those vestrymen that call 'emselves M.P.'s again, is it?' said Spurstow, who read his newspapers when he could get them.

'Yes. Listen to this. It's to your address, Lowndes. The man was making a speech to his constituents, and he piled it on. Here's a sample. "And I assert unhesitatingly that the Civil Service in India is the preserve — the pet preserve — of the aristocracy of England. What does the democracy — what do the masses — get from that country, which we have step by step fraudulently annexed? I answer, nothing whatever. It is farmed with a single eye to their own interests by the scions of the aristocracy. They take good care to maintain their lavish scale of incomes, to avoid or stifle any inquiries into the nature and conduct of their administration, while they themselves force the unhappy peasant to pay with the sweat of his brow for all the luxuries in which they are lapped."' Hummil waved the cutting above his head. ''Ear! 'ear!' said his audience.

Then Lowndes, meditatively, 'I'd give — I'd give three months' pay to have that gentleman spend one month with me and see how the free and independent native prince works things. Old Timbersides' — this was his flippant title for an honoured and decorated feudatory prince — 'has been wearing my life out this week past for money. By Jove, his latest performance was to send me one of his women as a bribe!'

'Good for you! Did you accept it?' said Mottram.

'No. I rather wish I had, now. She was a pretty little person, and she yarned away to me about the horrible destitution among the king's women-folk. The darlings haven't had any new clothes for nearly a month, and the old man wants to buy a new drag from Calcutta, — solid silver railings and silver lamps, and trifles of that kind. I've tried to make him understand that he has played the deuce with the revenues for the last twenty years and must go slow. He can't see it.'

'But he has the ancestral treasure-vaults to draw on. There must be three millions at least in jewels and coin under his palace,' said Hummil.

'Catch a native king disturbing the family treasure! The priests forbid it except as the last resort. Old Timbersides has added something like a quarter of a million to the deposit in his reign.'

'Where the mischief does it all come from?' said Mottram.

'The country. The state of the people is enough to make you sick. I've known the taxmen wait by a milch-camel till the foal was born and then hurry off the mother for arrears. And what can I do? I can't get the court clerks to give me any accounts; I can't raise more than a fat smile from the commander-in-chief when I find out the troops are three months in arrears; and old Timbersides begins to weep when I speak to him. He has taken to the King's Peg heavily, — liqueur brandy for whisky, and Heidsieck for soda-water.'

'That's what the Rao of Jubela took to. Even a native can't last long at that,' said Spurstow. 'He'll go out.'

'And a good thing, too. Then I suppose we'll have a council of regency, and a tutor for the young prince, and hand him back his kingdom with ten years' accumulations.'

'Whereupon that young prince, having been taught all the vices of the English, will play ducks and drakes with the money and undo ten years' work in eighteen months. I've seen that business before,' said Spurstow. 'I should tackle the king with a light hand if I were you, Lowndes. They'll hate you quite enough under any circumstances.'

'That's all very well. The man who looks on can talk about the light hand; but you can't clean a pig-stye with a pen dipped in rose-water. I know my risks; but nothing has happened yet. My servant's an old Pathan, and he cooks for me. They are hardly likely to bribe him, and I don't accept food from my true friends, as they call themselves. Oh, but it's weary work! I'd sooner be with you, Spurstow. There's shooting near your camp.'

'Would you? I don't think it. About fifteen deaths a day don't incite a man to shoot anything but himself. And the worst of it is that the poor devils look at you as though you ought to save them. Lord knows, I've tried everything. My last attempt was empirical, but it pulled an old man through. He was brought to me apparently past hope, and I gave him gin and Worcester sauce with cayenne. It cured him; but I don't recommend it.'

'How do the cases run generally?' said Hummil.

'Very simply indeed. Chlorodyne, opium pill, chlorodyne, collapse, nitre, bricks to the feet, and then – the burning-*ghaut*. The last seems to be the only thing that stops the trouble. It's black cholera, you know. Poor devils! But I will say, little Bunsee Lal, my apothecary, works like a demon. I've recommended him for promotion if he comes through it all alive.'

'And what are your chances, old man?' said Mottram.

'Don't know; don't care much; but I've sent the letter in. What are you doing with yourself generally?'

'Sitting under a table in the tent and spitting on the sextant to keep it cool,' said the man of the Survey. 'Washing my eyes to avoid ophthalmia, which I shall certainly get, and trying to make a sub-surveyor understand that an error of five degrees in an angle isn't quite so small as it looks. I'm altogether alone, y' know, and shall be till the end of the hot weather.'

'Hummil's the lucky man,' said Lowndes, flinging himself into a long chair. 'He has an actual roof – torn as to the ceiling-cloth, but still a roof – over his head. He sees one train daily. He can get beer and soda-water and ice 'em when God is good. He has books, pictures,' – they were torn from the *Graphic*, – 'and the society of the excellent sub-contractor Jevins, besides the pleasure of receiving us weekly.'

'Hummil smiled grimly. Yes, I'm the lucky man, I suppose. Jevins is luckier.'

'How? Not – '

'Yes. Went out. Last Monday.'

'By his own hand?' said Spurstow quickly, hinting the suspicion that was in everybody's mind. There was no cholera near Hummil's section. Even fever gives a man at least a week's grace, and sudden death generally implies self-slaughter.

'I judge no man this weather,' said Hummil. 'He had a touch of the sun, I fancy; for last week, after you fellows had left, he came into the verandah and told me he was going home to see his wife, in Market Street, Liverpool, that evening.

'I got the apothecary in to look at him, and we tried to make him lie down. After an hour or two he rubbed his eyes and said he believed he had had a fit, – hoped he hadn't said anything rude. Jevins had a great idea of bettering himself socially. He was very like Chucks in his language.'

'Well?'

'Then he went to his own bungalow and began cleaning a rifle. He told the servant that he was going to shoot buck in the morning. Naturally he fumbled with the trigger, and shot himself through the head – accidentally. The apothecary sent in a report to my chief, and Jevins is buried somewhere out there. I'd have wired to you, Spurstow, if you could have done anything.'

'You're a queer chap,' said Mottram. 'If you'd killed the man yourself you couldn't have been more quiet about the business.'

'Good Lord! what does it matter?' said Hummil calmly. 'I've got to do a lot of his overseeing work in addition to my own. I'm the only person that suffers. Jevins is out of it, – by pure accident, of course, but out of it. The apothecary was going to write a long screed on suicide. Trust a *babu* to drivel when he gets the chance.'

'Why didn't you let it go in as suicide?' said Lowndes.

'No direct proof. A man hasn't many privileges in this country, but he might at least be allowed to mishandle his own rifle. Besides, some day I may need a man to smother up an accident to myself. Live and let live. Die and let die.'

'You take a pill,' said Spurstow, who had been watching Hummil's white face narrowly. 'Take a pill, and don't be an ass. That sort of talk is skittles. Anyhow, suicide is shirking your work. If I were Job ten times over, I should be so interested in what was going to happen next that I'd stay on and watch.'

'Ah! I've lost that curiosity,' said Hummil.

'Liver out of order?' said Lowndes feelingly.

'No. Can't sleep. That's worse.'

'By Jove, it is!' said Mottram. 'I'm that way every now and then, and the fit has to wear itself out. What do you take for it?'

'Nothing. What's the use? I haven't had ten minutes' sleep since Friday morning.'

'Poor chap! Spurstow, you ought to attend to this,' said Mottram. 'Now you mention it, your eyes are rather gummy and swollen.'

Spurstow, still watching Hummil, laughed lightly. 'I'll patch him up, later on. Is it too hot, do you think, to go for a ride?'

'Where to?' said Lowndes wearily. 'We shall have to go away at eight, and there'll be riding enough for us then. I hate a horse when I have to use him as a necessity. Oh, heavens! what is there to do?'

'Begin whist again, at *chick* points and a gold *mohur* on the rub,' said Spurstow promptly.

'Poker. A month's pay all round for the pool, — no limit, — and fifty-rupee raises. Somebody would be broken before we got up,' said Lowndes.

'Can't say that it would give me any pleasure to break any man in this company,' said Mottram. 'There isn't enough excitement in it, and it's foolish.' He crossed over to the worn and battered little camp-piano, — wreckage of a married household that had once held the bungalow, — and opened the case.

It's used up long ago,' said Hummil. 'The servants have picked it to pieces.'

The piano was indeed hopelessly out of order, but Mottram managed to bring the rebellious notes into a sort of agreement, and there rose from the ragged keyboard something that might once have been the ghost of a popular music-hall song. The men in the long chairs turned with evident interest as Mottram banged the more lustily.

'That's good!' said Lowndes. 'By Jove! the last time I heard that song was in '79, or thereabouts, just before I came out.'

'Ah!' said Spurstow with pride, 'I was home in '80.' And he mentioned a song of the streets popular at that date.

Mottram executed it roughly. Lowdnes criticised that volunteered emendations. Mottram dashed into another ditty, not of the music-hall character, and made as if to rise.

'Sit down,' said Hummil. 'I didn't know that you had any music in your composition. Go on playing until you can't think of anything more. I'll have that piano tuned up before you come again. Play something festive.'

Very simple indeed were the tunes to which Mottram's art and the limitations of the piano could give effect, but the men listened with pleasure, and in the pauses talked all together of what they had seen or heard when they were last at home. A dense dust-storm sprung up outside, and swept roaring over the house, enveloping it in the choking darkness of midnight, but Mottram continued unheeding, and the crazy tinkle reached the ears of the listeners above the flapping of the tattered ceiling-cloth.

In the silence after the storm he glided from the more directly personal songs of Scotland, half humming as he played, into the Evening Hymn.

'Sunday,' said he, nodding his head.

'Go on. Don't apologise for it,' said Spurstow.

Hummil laughed long and riotously. 'Play it, by all means. You're full of surprises today. I didn't know you had such a gift of finished sarcasm. How does that thing go?'

Mottram took up the tune.

'Too slow by half. You miss the note of gratitude,' said Hummil. 'It ought to go to the "Grasshopper's Polka," — this way.' And he chanted, *prestissimo,—*

'Glory to thee, my God, this night,
For all the blessings of the light.

That shows we really feel our blessings. How does it go on? —

If in the night I sleepless lie,
My soul with sacred thoughts supply;
May no ill dreams disturb my rest,—

Quicker, Mottram! —

Or powers of darkness me molest!'

'Bah! what an old hypocrite you are!'

'Don't be an ass,' said Lowndes. 'You are at full liberty to make fun of anything else you like, but leave that hymn alone. It's associated in my mind with the most sacred recollections — '

'Summer evenings in the country, — stained-glass window, — light going out, and you and she jamming your heads together over one hymn-book,' said Mottram.

'Yes, and a fat old cockchafer hitting you in the eye when you walked home. Smell of hay, and a moon as big as a bandbox sitting on the top of a haycock; bats, — roses, — milk and midges,' said Lowndes.

'Also mothers. I can just recollect my mother singing me to sleep with that when I was a little chap,' said Spurstow.

The darkness had fallen on the room. They could hear Hummil squirming in his chair.

'Consequently,' said he testily, 'you sing it when you are seven fathoms deep in Hell! It's an insult to the intelligence of the Deity to pretend we're anything but tortured rebels.'

'Take *two* pills,' said Spurstow; 'that's tortured liver.'

'The usually placid Hummil is in a vile bad temper. I'm sorry for his coolies tomorrow,' said Lowndes, as the servants brought in the lights and prepared the table for dinner.

As they were settling into their places about the miserable the goat-chops and the smoked tapioca pudding, Spurstow took occasion to whisper to the Mottram, 'Well done, David!'

'Look after Saul, then,' was the reply.

'What are you two whispering about?' said Hummil suspiciously.

'Only saying that you are a damned poor host. This fowl can't be cut,' returned Spurstow with a sweet smile. 'Call this a dinner?'

'I can't help it. You don't expect a banquet, do you?'

Throughout that meal Hummil contrived laboriously to insult directly and pointedly all his guests in succession, and at each insult Spurstow kicked the aggrieved persons under the table; but he dared not exchange a glance of intelligence with either of them. Hummil's face was white and pinched, while his eyes were unnaturally large. No man dreamed for a moment of resenting his savage personalities, but as soon as the meal was over they made haste to get away.

'Don't go. You're just getting amusing, you fellows. I hope I haven't said anything that annoyed you. You're such touchy devils.' Then, changing the note into one of almost abject entreaty, Hummil added, 'I say, you surely aren't going?'

'In the language of the blessed Jorrocks, where I dines I sleeps,' said Spurstow. 'I want to have a look at your coolies tomorrow, if you don't mind. You can give me a place to lie down in, I suppose?'

The others pleaded the urgency of their several duties next day, and, saddling up, departed together, Hummil begging them to come next Sunday. As they jogged off, Lowndes unbosomed himself to Mottram —

'. . . And I never felt so like kicking a man at his own table in my life. He said I cheated at whist, and reminded me I was in debt! Told you you were as good as a liar to your face! You aren't half indignant enough over it.'

'Not I,' said Mottram. 'Poor devil! Did you ever know old Hummy behave like that before or within a hundred miles of it?'

'That's no excuse. Spurstow was hacking my shin all the time, so I kept a hand on myself. Else I should have — '

'No, you wouldn't. You'd have done as Hummy did about Jevins; judge no man this weather. By Jove! the buckle of my bridle is hot in my hand! Trot out a bit, and 'ware rat-holes.'

Ten minutes' trotting jerked out of Lowndes one very sage remark when he pulled up, sweating from every pore —

'Good thing Spurstow's with him tonight.'

'Ye-es. Good man, Spurstow. Our roads turn here. See you again next Sunday, if the sun doesn't bowl me over.'

'S'pose so, unless old Timbersides' finance minister manages to dress some of my food. Good-night, and — God bless you!'

'What's wrong now?'

'Oh, nothing.' Lowndes gathered up his whip, and, as he flicked Mottram's mare on the flank, added, 'You're not a bad little chap, — that's all.' And the mare bolted half a mile across the sand, on the word.

In the assistant engineer's bungalow Spurstow and Hummil smoked the pipe of silence together, each narrowly watching the other. The capacity of a bachelor's establishment is as elastic as its arrangements are simple. A servant cleared away the dining-room table, brought in a couple of rude native bedsteads made of tape strung on a light wood frame, flung a square of cool Calcutta matting over each, set them side by side, pinned two towels to the *punkah* so that their fringes should just sweep clear of the sleeper's nose and mouth, and announced that the couches were ready.

The men flung themselves down, ordering the *punkah*-coolies by all the powers of Hell to pull. Every door and window was shut, for the outside air was that of an oven. The atmosphere within was only 104°, as the thermometer bore witness, and heavy with the foul smell of badly-trimmed kerosene lamps; and this stench, combined with that of native tobacco, baked brick, and dried earth, sends the heart of many a strong man down to his boots, for it is the smell of the Great Indian Empire when she turns herself for six months into a house of torment. Spurstow packed his pillows craftily so that he reclined rather than lay, his head at a safe elevation above his feet. It is not good to sleep on a low pillow in the hot weather if you happen to be of thick-necked build, for you may pass with lively snores and gugglings from natural sleep into the deep slumber of heat-apoplexy.

'Pack your pillows,' said the doctor sharply, as he saw Hummil preparing to lie down at full length.

The night-light was trimmed; the shadow of the *punkah* wavered across the room, and the *'flick'* of the *punkah*-towel and the soft whine of the rope through the wall-hole followed it. Then the *punkah* flagged, almost ceased. The sweat poured from Spurstow's brow. Should he go out and harangue the coolie? It started forward again with a savage jerk, and a pin came out of the towels. When this was replaced, a tomtom in the coolie-lines began to beat with the steady throb of a swollen artery inside some brain-fevered skull. Spurstow turned on his side and swore gently. There was no movement on Hummil's part. The man had composed himself as rigidly as a corpse, his hands clinched at his sides. The respiration was too hurried for any suspicion of sleep. Spurstow looked at the set face. The jaws were clinched, and there was a pucker round the quivering eyelids.

'He's holding himself as tightly as ever he can,' thought Spurstow. 'What in the world is the matter with him? — Hummil!'

'Yes,' in a thick constrained voice.

'Can't you get to sleep?'

'No.'

'Head hot? Throat feeling bulgy? or how?'

'Neither, thanks. I don't sleep much, you know.'

'Feel pretty bad?'

'Pretty bad, thanks. There is a tom-tom outside, isn't there? I thought it was my head at first . . . Oh, Spurstow, for pity's sake give me something that will put me to sleep, — sound asleep, — if it's only for six hours!' He sprang up, trembling from head to foot. 'I haven't been able to sleep naturally for days, and I can't stand it! — I can't stand it!'

'Poor old chap!'

'That's no use. Give me something to make me sleep. I tell you I'm nearly mad. I don't know what I say half my time. For three weeks I've had to think and spell out every word that has come through my lips before I dared say it. Isn't that enough to drive a man mad? I can't see things correctly now, and I've lost my sense of touch. My skin aches — my skin aches! Make me sleep. Oh, Spurstow, for the love of God make me sleep sound. It isn't enough merely to let me dream. Let me sleep!'

'All right, old man, all right. Go slow; you aren't half as bad as you think.'

The flood-gates of reserve once broken, Hummil was clinging to him like a frightened child. 'You're pinching my arm to pieces.'

'I'll break your neck if you don't do something for me. No, I didn't mean that. Don't be angry, old fellow.' He wiped the sweat off himself as he fought to regain composure. 'I'm a bit restless and off my oats, and perhaps you could recommend some sort of sleeping mixture, — bromide of potassium.'

'Bromide of skittles! Why didn't you tell me this before? Let go of my arm, and I'll see if there's anything in my cigarette-case to suit your complaint.' Spurstow hunted among his day-clothes, turned up the lamp, opened a little silver cigarette-case, and advanced on the expectant Hummil with the daintiest of fairy squirts.

'The last appeal of civilisation,' said he, 'and a thing I hate to use. Hold out your arm. Well, your sleeplessness hasn't ruined your muscle; and what a thick hide it is! Might as well inject a buffalo subcutaneously. Now in a few minutes the morphia will begin working. Lie down and wait.'

A smile of unalloyed and idiotic delight began to creep over Hummil's face. 'I think,' he whispered, — 'I think I'm going off now. Gad! It's positively heavenly! Spurstow, you must give me that case to keep; you — ' The voice ceased as the head fell back.

'Not for a good deal,' said Spurstow to the unconscious form. 'And now, my friend, sleeplessness of your kind being very apt to relax the moral fibre in little matters of life and death, I'll just take the liberty of spiking your guns.'

He paddled into Hummil's saddle-room in his bare feet and uncased a twelve-bore rifle, an express, and a revolver. Of the first he unscrewed the nipples and hid them in the bottom of a saddlery-case; of the second he abstracted the lever, kicking it behind a big wardrobe. The third he merely opened, and knocked the doll-head bolt of the grip up with the heel of a riding boot.

'That's settled,' he said, as he shook the sweat off his hands. 'These little precautions will at least give you time to turn. You have too much sympathy with gun-room accidents.'

And as he rose from his knees, the thick muffled voice of Hummil cried in the doorway, 'You fool!'

Such tones they use who speak in the lucid intervals of delirium to their friends before they die.

Spurstow started, dropping the pistol. Hummil stood in the doorway, rocking with helpless laughter.

'That was awf'ly good of you, I'm sure,' he said, very slowly, feeling for his words. 'I don't intend to go out by my own hand at present. I say, Spurstow, that stuff won't work. What shall I do?' And panic terror stood in his eyes.

'Lie down and give it a chance. Lie down at once.'

'I daren't. It will only take me half-way again, and I shan't be able to get away this time. Do you know it was all I could do to come out just now? Generally I am as quick as lightning; but you had clogged my feet. I was nearly caught.'

'Oh yes, I understand. Go and lie down.'

'No, it isn't delirium; but it was an awfully mean trick to play on me. Do you know I might have died?'

As a sponge rubs a slate clean, so some power unknown to Spurstow had wiped out of Hummil's face all that stamped it for the face of a man, and he stood at the doorway in the expression of his lost innocence. He had slept back into terrified childhood.

'Is he going to die on the spot?' thought Spurstow. Then, aloud, 'All right, my son. Come back to bed, and tell me all about it. You couldn't sleep; but what was all the rest of the nonsense?'

'A place, — a place down there,' said Hummil, with simple sincerity. The drug was acting on him by waves, and he was flung from the fear of a strong man to the fright of a child as his nerves gathered sense or were dulled.

'Good God! I've been afraid of it for months past, Spurstow. It has made every night hell to me; and yet I'm not conscious of having done anything wrong.'

'Be still, and I'll give you another dose. We'll stop your nightmares, you unutterable idiot!'

'Yes, but you must give me so much that I can't get away. You must make me quite sleepy, — not just a little sleepy. It's so hard to run then.'

'I know it; I know it. I've felt it myself. The symptoms are exactly as you describe.'

'Oh, don't laugh at me, confound you! Before this awful sleeplessness came to me I've tried to rest on my elbow and put a spur in the bed to sting me when I fell back. Look!'

'By Jove! the man has been rowelled like a horse! Ridden by the nightmare with a vengeance! And we all thought him sensible enough. Heaven send us understanding! You like to talk, don't you?'

'Yes, sometimes. Not when I'm frightened. *Then* I want to run. Don't you?'

'Always. Before I give you your second dose try to tell me exactly what your trouble is.'

Hummil spoke in broken whispers for nearly ten minutes, whilst Spurstow looked into the pupils of his eyes and passed his hand before them once or twice.

At the end of the narrative the silver cigarette-case was produced, and the last words that Hummil said as he fell back for the second time were, 'Put me quite to sleep; for if I'm caught I die, — I die!'

'Yes, yes; we all do that sooner or later, — thank Heaven who has set a term to our miseries,' said Spurstow, settling the cushions under the head. 'It occurs to me that unless I drink something I shall go out before my time. I've stopped sweating, and — I wear a seventeen-inch collar.' He brewed himself scalding hot tea, which is an excellent remedy against heat-apoplexy if you take three or four cups of it in time. Then he watched the sleeper.

'A blind face that cries and can't wipe its eyes, a blind face that chases him down corridors! H'm! Decidedly, Hummil ought to go on leave as soon as possible; and, sane or otherwise, he undoubtedly did rowel himself most cruelly. Well, Heaven send us understanding!'

At mid-day Hummil rose, with an evil taste in his mouth, but an unclouded eye and a joyful heart.

'I was pretty bad last night, wasn't I?' said he.

'I have seen healthier men. You must have had a touch of the sun. Look here: if I write you a swingeing medical certificate, will you apply for leave on the spot?'

'No.'

'Why not? You want it.'

'Yes, but I can hold on till the weather's a little cooler.'

'Why should you, if you can get relieved on the spot?'

'Burkett is the only man who could be sent; and he's a born fool.'

'Oh, never mind about the line. You aren't so important as all that. Wire for leave, if necessary.'

Hummil looked very uncomfortable.

'I can hold on till the Rains,' he said evasively.

'You can't. Wire to headquarters for Burkett.'

'I won't. If you want to know why, particularly, Burkett is married, and his wife's just had a kid, and she's up at Simla, in the cool, and Burkett has a very nice billet that takes him into Simla from Saturday to Monday. That little woman isn't at all well. If Burkett was transferred she'd try to follow him. If she left the baby behind she'd fret herself to death. If she came, — and Burkett's one of those selfish little beasts who are always talking about a wife's place being with her husband, — she'd die. It's murder to bring a woman here just now. Burkett hasn't the physique of a rat. If he came here he'd go out; and I know she hasn't any money, and I'm pretty sure she'd go out too. I'm salted in a sort of way, and I'm not married. Wait till the Rains, and then Burkett can get thin down here. It'll do him heaps of good.'

'Do you mean to say that you intend to face — what you have faced, till the Rains break?'

'Oh, it won't be so bad, now you've shown me a way out of it. I can always wire to you. Besides, now I've once got into the way of sleeping, it'll be all right. Anyhow, I shan't put in for leave. That's the long and the short of it.'

'My great Scott! I thought all that sort of thing was dead and done with.'

'Bosh! You'd do the same yourself. I feel a new man, thanks to that cigarette-case. You're going over to camp now, aren't you?

'Yes; but I'll try to look you up every other day, if I can.'

'I'm not bad enough for that. I don't want you to bother. Give the coolies gin and ketchup.'

'Then you feel all right?'

'Fit to fight for my life, but not to stand out in the sun talking to you. Go along, old man, and bless you!'

Hummil turned on his heel to face the echoing desolation of his bungalow, and the first thing he saw standing in the verandah was the figure of himself. He had met a similar apparition once before, when he was suffering from overwork and the strain of the hot weather.

'This is bad, — already,' he said, rubbing his eyes. 'If the thing slides away from me all in one piece, like a ghost, I shall know it is only my eyes and stomach that are out of order. If it walks — my head is going.'

He approached the figure, which naturally kept at an unvarying distance from him, as is the use of all spectres that are born of overwork. It slid through the house and dissolved into swimming specks within the eyeball as soon as it reached the burning light of the garden. Hummil went about business till even. When he came in to dinner he found himself sitting at the table. The vision rose and walked out hastily. Except that it cast no shadow it was in all respects real.

No living man knows what that week held for Hummil. An increase of the epidemic kept Spurstow in camp among the coolies, and all he could do was to telegraph to Mottram, bidding him go to the bungalow and sleep there. But Mottram was forty miles away from the nearest telegraph, and knew nothing of anything save the needs of the Survey till he met, early on Sunday morning, Lowndes and Spurstow heading towards Hummil's for the weekly gathering.

'Hope the poor chap's in a better temper,' said the former, swinging himself off his horse at the door. 'I suppose he isn't up yet.'

'I'll just have a look at him,' said the doctor. 'If he's asleep there's no need to wake him.'

And an instant later, by the tone of Spurstow's voice calling upon them to enter, the men knew what had happened. There was no need to wake him.

The *punkah* was still being pulled over the bed, but Hummil had departed this life at least three hours.

The body lay on its back, hands clinched by the side, as Spurstow had seen it lying seven nights previously. In the staring eyes was written terror beyond the expression of any pen.

Mottram, who had entered behind Lowndes, bent over the dead and touched the forehead lightly with his lips. 'Oh, you lucky, lucky devil!' he whispered.

But Lowndes had seen the eyes, and withdrew shuddering to the other side of the room.

'Poor chap! poor old chap! And the last time I met him I was angry. Spurstow, we should have watched him. Has he — ?'

Deftly Spurstow continued his investigations, ending by a search round the room.

'No, he hasn't,' he snapped. 'There's no trace of anything. Call the servants.'

They came, eight or ten of them, whispering and peering over each other's shoulders.

'When did your Sahib go to bed?' said Spurstow.

'At eleven or ten, we think,' said Hummil's personal servant.

'He was well then? But how should you know?'

'He was not ill, as far as our comprehension extended. But he had slept very little for three nights. This I know, because I saw him walking much, and specially in the heart of the night.'

As Spurstow was arranging the sheet, a big straight-necked hunting-spur tumbled on the ground. The doctor groaned. The personal servant peeped at the body.

'What do you think, Chuma?' said Spurstow, catching the look on the dark face.

'Heaven-born, in my poor opinion, this that was my master has descended into the Dark Places, and there has been caught because he was not able to escape with sufficient speed. We have the spur for evidence that he fought with Fear. Thus have I seen men of my race do with thorns when a spell was laid upon them to overtake them in their sleeping hours and they dared not sleep.'

'Chuma, you're a mud-head. Go out and prepare seals to be set on the Sahib's property.'

'God has made the Heaven-born. God has made me. Who are we to inquire into the dispensations of God? I will bid the other servants hold aloof while you are reckoning the tale of the Sahib's property. They are all thieves, and would steal.'

'As far as I can make out, he died from — oh, anything; stoppage of the heart's action, heat-apoplexy, or some other visitation,' said Spurstow to his companions. 'We must make an inventory of his effects, and so on.'

'He was scared to death,' insisted Lowndes. 'Look at those eyes! For pity's sake don't let him be buried with them open!'

'Whatever it was, he's clear of all the trouble now,' said Mottram softly.

Spurstow was peering into the open eyes.

'Come here,' said he. 'Can you see anything there?'

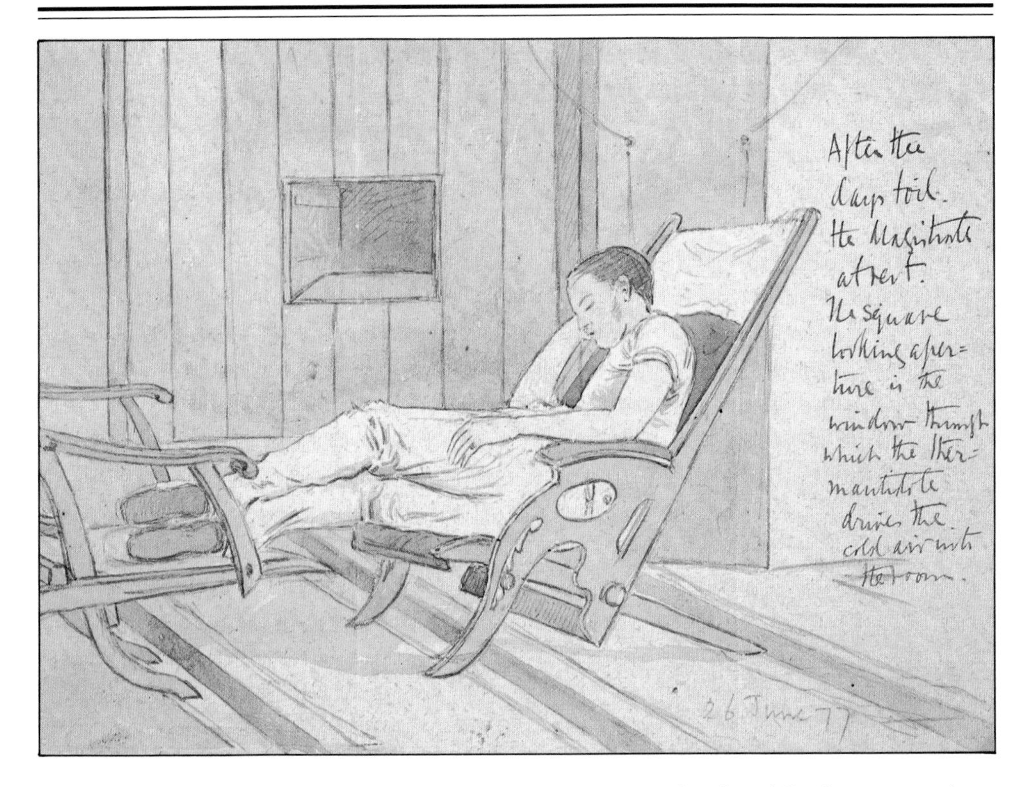

'I can't face it!' whimpered Lowndes. 'Cover up the face! Is there any fear on earth that can turn a man into that likeness? It's ghastly. Oh, Spurstow, cover it up!'

'No fear — on earth,' said Spurstow. Mottram leaned over his shoulder and looked intently.

'I see nothing except some gray blurs in the pupil. There can be nothing there, you know.'

'Even so. Well, let's think. It'll take half a day to knock up any sort of coffin; and he must have died at midnight. Lowndes, old man, go out and tell the coolies to break ground next to Jevins's grave. Mottram, go round the house with Chuma and see that the seals are put on things. Send a couple of men to me here, and I'll arrange.'

The strong-armed servants when they returned to their own kind told a strange story of the doctor Sahib vainly trying to call their master back to life by magic arts, — to wit, the holding of a little green box that clicked to each of the dead man's eyes, and of a bewildered muttering on the part of the doctor Sahib, who took the little green box away with him.

The resonant hammering of a coffin-lid is no pleasant thing to hear, but those who have experience maintain that much more terrible is the soft swish of the bed-linen, the reeving and unreeving of the bed-tapes, when he who has fallen by the roadside is apparelled for burial, sinking gradually as the tapes are tied over, till the swaddled shape touches the floor and there is no protest against the indignity of hasty disposal.

At the last moment Lowndes was seized with scruples of conscience. 'Ought you to read the service, — from beginning to end?' said he to Spurstow.

'I intend to. You're my senior as a civilian. You can take it if you like.'

'I didn't mean that for a moment. I only thought if we could get a chaplain from somewhere, — I'm willing to ride anywhere, — and give poor Hummil a better chance. That's all.'

'Bosh!' said Spurstow, as he framed his lips to the tremendous words that stand at the head of the burial service.

After breakfast they smoked a pipe in silence to the memory of the dead. Then Spurstow said absently —

''Tisn't in medical science.'

'What?'

'Things in a dead man's eye.'

'For goodness' sake leave that horror alone!' said Lowndes. 'I've seen a native die of pure fright when a tiger chivried him. I know what killed Hummil.'

'The deuce you do! I'm going to try to see.' And the doctor retreated into the bath-room with a Kodak camera. After a few minutes there was the sound of something being hammered to pieces, and he emerged, very white indeed.

'Have you got a picture?' said Mottram. 'What does the thing look like?'

'It was impossible, of course. You needn't look, Mottram. I've torn up the films. There was nothing there. It was impossible.'

'That,' said Lowndes, very distinctly, watching the shaking hand striving to relight the pipe, 'is a damned lie.'

Mottram laughed uneasily. 'Spurstow's right,' he said. 'We're all in such a state now that we'd believe anything. For pity's sake let's try to be rational.'

There was no further speech for a long time. The hot wind whistled without, and the dry trees sobbed. Presently the daily train, winking brass, burnished steel, and spouting steam, pulled up panting in the intense glare. 'We'd better go on that,' said Spurstow. 'Go back to work. I've written my certificate. We can't do any more good here, and work'll keep our wits together. Come on.'

No one moved. It is not pleasant to face railway journeys at mid-day in June. Spurstow gathered up his hat and whip, and turning in the doorway, said —

'There may be Heaven, — there may be Hell,
Meantime, there is our life here. We-ell?'

Neither Mottram nor Lowndes had any answer to the question.

MISTER ANTHONY DAWKING

'WHEN I COMES to a gentleman and says, "Look here! you give me a drink," and that gentleman says, "No I won't neither; you've 'ad too much," am I angry? No! what I sez is' . . . At this point, without word or warning, he went deeply and peacefully to sleep in the long-chair in the verandah. The *dak*-bungalow *khansamah* eyed him fearfully from afar. 'He has come again,' said the *dak*-bungalow *khansamah*, 'and God knows when he will depart. I must get dinner.' Towards dusk, Mister Anthony Dawking woke up and demanded refreshment. 'The last time I was 'ere,' said he pensively, 'that there *khansamah* 'e ran away down the road and wouldn't give me no *khana*. So I took a leg off the bed and I broke open the cook'ouse and I made my own *khana*. And now 'e don't run away no more. *Hitherow tum!* Just you *khana lao* and I'll have the same whiskey as I had last time.' While the *khansamah* was preparing the meal, I turned over the pages of the *dak*-bungalow book. They fairly bristled with the name of 'Anthony Dawking,' and opposite each entry were that gentleman's comments on his entertainment. Once he had written 'The food is getting better but their whiskey is dam bad, I am not pleased with this Dork-bungalow.' A month later he had come again and written: 'This day I bete the carsarmer for his beesly cheek and broke two chares. The wiskey is better now.' As I looked, he came and leaned over my shoulder, and there was a spicy fragrance in his breath. 'You never saw such a 'ole,' said he. 'I've written some things there that shows you what you had to expec' but it's worse since I came here last. They've got no good lamps now. I took and chucked the last one into the canal. It wouldn't burn proper. I know this bungalow. It's my reg'lar 'alten' place between Ammedabad an Bhurtpore. My name is Dorking — Mister Anthony Dawking, and I was born in Southsea. I'm none of your measly arf-castes I ain't. I'm a true-born Englishman I am and I ain't afraid of any body.

> Anthony Dawking is my name,
> Hengland is my nation;
> Injy is my dwellin' place,
> An' work my occupation.

That's me! a 'onest pore man who 'as worked on the Hindus State, I've bin there, an' the Rajjputanna-Malwa, I've bin there too, an' the Hindus steamers, an' the Southern M'ratta, an' the Dacca Daily Despatch steamers, I've been there too, an' the Injan Midlan' I was there too, an' the Irrawaddy Flotla I've been there too, fitter, engineer, foreman-fitter, pilot on the rivers that I didn't know — anything you please, for my name is Anthony Dawking and I'm a 'ard workin' man.' All this was delivered, apparently, in one breath. Then Mr. Dawking swayed on his heels for a moment. The *khansamah* peeped in at the door and announced that dinner was on the table.

'Come an' 'ave a snack,' said Mr. Dawking, genially. 'You come an' 'ave dinner with me. Gor blesh you. If I was partic'lar who I spoke to an' 'ad dinner with I wouldn't be the pop'lar man I am now. 'Aven't you 'eard tell o' Anthony Dawking — the fitter? You ask old Beazeley who was a Permanent-way Inspector on the Punjab Northern. You say to 'im: "Beazeley who's Dawking?" an' he'll begin to laugh, laugh 'imself blind. Beazeley was a pop'lar man an' so am I. Many's the time I've said to Beazeley: "Beazeley come an' 'ave a drink," an' many a time 'as Beazeley said to me: "Dawking, you pay for no drinks 'ere this evenin' while Jack Beazeley is 'ere." That was old Beazeley all over. A fine free'earted man was Beazeley. Tell 'im you've seen me an' 'e'll give you a good dinner. Better than this muck. Hi! *khansamah. Kisivasti* 'ave you brought this *krab goshe*?' 'Mister Dawking,' said I meekly, 'do you ever pay for your dinners?' 'Do-I-ever-pay-for-my-dinners?' He looked as though he were about to assault me. 'What d'yer take me for? Me pay? I've bin from Gwalior to Kurrachi on foot an' railway pass an' I've never been asked that yet. Me pay? I'd like to see that *khansamah* ask me. Why on'y the last time I was 'ere the *khansamah* — 'e complained to the Resident because I wouldn't pay an' broke all the crockery, an' the Resident 'e said 'e would send a police guard o' six to look after me. But they never came though I was entitled to 'ave them. So I deducted the cost of that police guard, six men at a rupee a day I made it, from my bill and I stayed four days an' my bill was only twenty rupees. So now I'm waitin' 'ere for the four rupees that that police cost, an' if the *khansamah* complains again I'll 'ave 'is ears off the top of 'is 'ead. Me pay! of course I don't.'

'That is quite true,' said the *khansamah*. 'This sahib never pays. I have never seen a sahib like this sahib. My *bhai*, who keeps the *dak*-bungalow at . . . says that he is *dewanipagal*, and so, your honour, I pay myself. He is a very poor man and he is always drunk.' Mister Anthony Dawking was drinking while this explanation was offered. He roused at the word 'drunk'. 'Who says I am drunk?' he asked with terrific gravity. 'I am sober. Chalk a line on the floor! Chalk a line on the floor and I'll show you whether I'm drunk or not.' There was no chalk, but Mister Anthony Dawking took a juiceful capsicum out of the pickle-bottle and with it smeared an uncertain line upon the floor. This accomplished, he fell flat on his face along the line. 'That's all right,' he said with deep satisfaction, as he lay. 'I knowed I wasn't drunk. *Khansamah*, if I catch you I'll cut your head off for my name is Anthony Dawking and I am a man of my word.' Still prone, he commenced to sing lustily a song that was new to me, beginning

> 'There was a man whose name was Saul,
> An' 'e died in Inji-a.
> But 'e left 'is wife a Kashmir shawl
> Before 'e went away.'

He chaunted ten or twelve verses, and then stopped to explain. 'Me an' old Scott made up that song when we was building the Sone Bridge. You go and sing it to old Beazeley and 'e'll know you've seen me.' The pleasure of gazing upon the dirt-grimed, liquor-blotched face of Mr. Dawking did not strike me as an overwhelming one. It was nearly time to start for the station. I gathered my traps together and left Mister Anthony Dawking fast asleep on the floor, with the *khansamah* timidly trying to thrust a pillow under his head.

A month later I stood in a great down-country factory worked by water-power and full of excited English foremen. 'What's wrong with Number Four Shaft?' 'Nothing much, only some d — d loafer has gone and hampered the turbine — with all these orders to be worked off before Wednesday too!' Strictly speaking Mister Anthony Dawking had done nothing worse than tumble into the dam above the turbine-hatch. They fished him out, as slovenly and unhandsome a corpse as could be desired, and he was buried by order of the Cantonment Magistrate. But in that far away *dak*-bungalow between Ahmedabad and Bhurtpore, the swindled and maltreated *khansamah* picked a bunch of yellow desert-flowers and sent his son by rail to lay them upon Dawking sahib's grave.

The son never found the grave, because there was no mark upon it; but the story is a sufficiently remarkable one, all the same.

PART IV

THE REGIMENT

The greater part of the standing army in India was made up of Indian troops led by British officers. However, Kipling's main army contacts were with the British regiments, based in India for five or six years at a time. In Lahore he got to know their officers well – perhaps too well – which may explain why they rarely appear as fully-rounded characters in his stories. The lighthearted tale of an insensitive colonel who almost provokes a mutiny, told in 'The Rout of the White Hussars' typifies Kipling's cautious approach in dealing with army officers in his fiction.

When it came to writing about the men Rudyard's loyalties were not put to the test, with the result that he wrote as freely as he wished. Of his eighteen 'Soldiers Three' tales at least six must be rated as masterpieces. His first, 'The Three Musketeers', is not among them but this is where a reader new to the characters of Mulvaney, Ortheris and Learoyd ought to begin. It appeared soon after the Queen's Jubilee military review had been held in mid-February 1887 on the maidan in front of Lahore Fort. Kipling watched the parade from the ramparts in the company of some invalid soldiers of the 5th Northumberland Fusiliers, and the first 'Soldiers Three' story appeared in print three weeks later. It was obviously intended as a one-off, since we are told that the three privates are about to embark on the troopship *Serapis*. However, an incident in the war in Burma when a party of British soldiers swam naked across a river to launch an attack, which Rudyard wrote up for his paper, led him to revive Mulvaney so that he could recount the story in 'The Taking of Lungtungpen'.

This second story appeared exactly a month after the first and was followed a month later by a third, by which time the self-destructive, ever-boastful, army-wise Terence Mulvaney had acquired a wife, Dinah, along with a past. A fourth *Plain Tales* story duly put flesh on the cockney Ortheris and the Yorkshireman Learoyd, as well as introducing a more serious undertone to their lives.

The later 'Soldiers Three' stories are longer and, in general, more sombre in tone. 'My Lord the Elephant' is one of the exceptions, being the broadest of farces. The other 'Soldiers Three' story represented here is 'Love-o'-Women', which begins with a chilling first paragraph that must rank as one of the most unsettling to be found anywhere in English literature.

A word of warning – and encouragement – to the reader new to the language of Mulvaney and his mates: Kipling's faithful rendering of each man's speech and pronunciation takes getting used to. But persevere; persistence brings its own reward.

'The Rout of the White Hussars' first appeared in *Plain Tales from the Hills* in January 1888. 'My Lord the Elephant' and 'Love-o'-Women' were both written in America and published in *Many Inventions* in 1893.

THE ROUT OF THE WHITE HUSSARS

SOME PEOPLE HOLD that an English Cavalry regiment cannot run. This is a mistake. I have seen four hundred and thirty-seven sabres flying over the face of the country in abject terror — have seen the best Regiment that ever drew bridle wiped off the Army List for the space of two hours. If you repeat this tale to the White Hussars they will, in all probability, treat you severely. They are not proud of the incident.

You may know the White Hussars by their 'side,' which is greater than that of all the Cavalry Regiments on the roster. If this is not a sufficient mark, you may know them by their old brandy. It has been sixty years in the Mess and is worth going far to taste. Ask for the 'McGaire' old brandy, and see that you get it. If the Mess Sergeant thinks that you are uneducated, and that the genuine article will be lost on you, he will treat you accordingly. He is a good man. But, when you are at Mess, you must never talk to your hosts about forced marches or long-distance rides. The Mess are very sensitive; and, if they think that you are laughing at them, will tell you so.

As the White Hussars say, it was all the Colonel's fault. He was a new man, and he ought never to have taken the Command. He said that the Regiment was not smart enough. This to the White Hussars, who knew they could walk round any Horse and through any Guns, and over any Foot on the face of the earth! That insult was the first cause of offence.

Then the Colonel cast the Drum-Horse — the Drum-Horse of the White Hussars! Perhaps you do not see what an unspeakable crime he had committed. I will try to make it clear. The soul of the Regiment lives in the Drum-Horse who carries the silver kettle-drums. He is nearly always a big piebald Waler. That is a point of honour; and a Regiment will spend anything you please on a piebald. He is beyond the ordinary laws of casting. His work is very light, and he only manœuvres at a footpace. Wherefore, so long as he can step out and look handsome, his well-being is assured. He knows more about the Regiment than the Adjutant, and could not make a mistake if he tried.

The Drum-Horse of the White Hussars was only eighteen years old, and perfectly equal to his duties. He had at least six years' more work in him, and carried himself with all the pomp and dignity of a Drum-Major of the Guards. The Regiment had paid Rs. 1200 for him.

But the Colonel said that he must go, and he was cast in due form and replaced by a washy, bay beast, as ugly as a mule, with a ewe-neck, rat-tail, and cow-hocks. The Drummer detested that animal, and the best of the Band-horses put back their ears and showed the whites of their eyes at the very sight of him. They knew him for an upstart and no gentleman. I fancy that the Colonel's ideas of smartness extended to the Band, and that he wanted to make it take part in the regular parade movements. A Cavalry band is a sacred thing. It only turns out for Commanding Officers' parades, and the Band Master is one degree more important than the Colonel. He is a High Priest and the 'Keel Row' is his holy song. The 'Keel Row' is the Cavalry Trot; and the man who has never heard that tune rising, high and shrill, above the rattle of the Regiment going past the saluting-base, has something yet to hear and understand.

When the Colonel cast the Drum-Horse of the White Hussars there was nearly a mutiny.

The officers were angry, the Regiment were furious, and the Bandsmen swore — like troopers. The Drum-Horse was going to be put up to auction — public auction — to be bought, perhaps, by a Parsee and put into a cart!

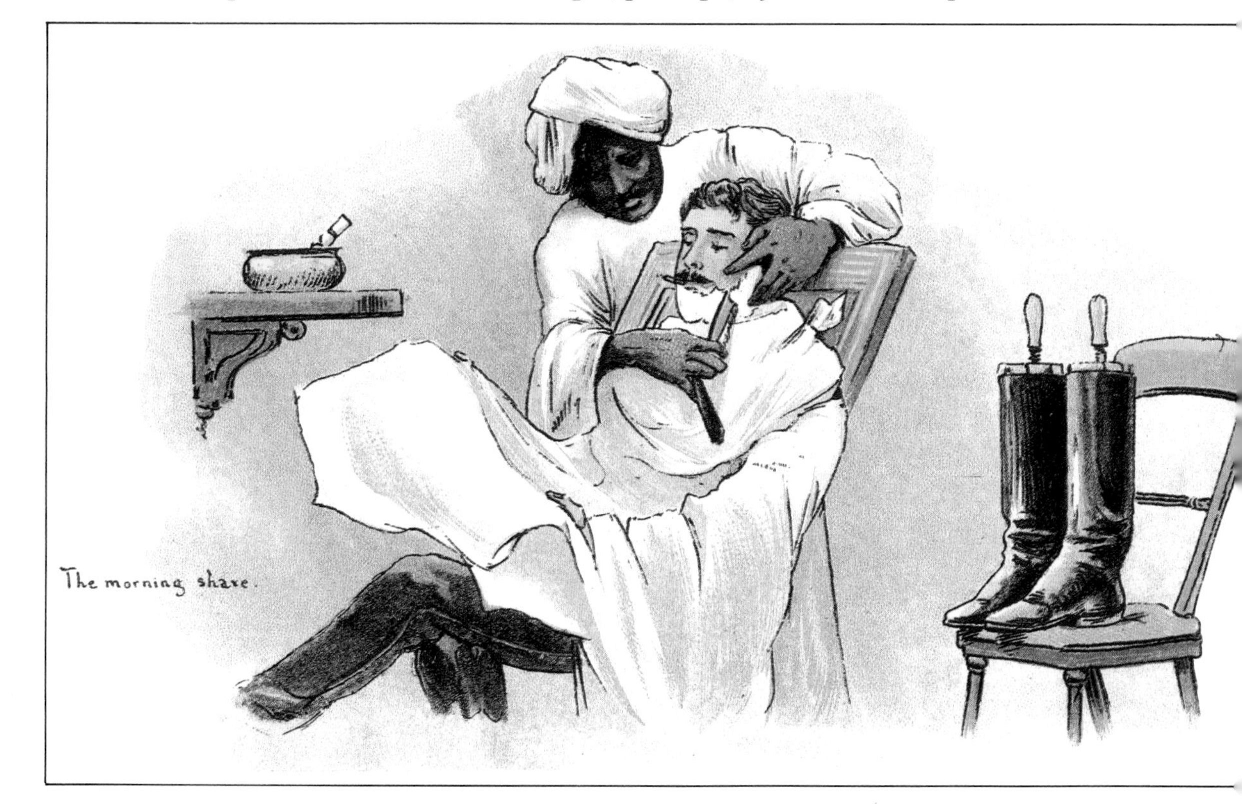

The morning shave.

It was worse than exposing the inner life of the Regiment to the whole world, or selling the Mess Plate to a Jew – a Black Jew.

The Colonel was a mean man and a bully. He knew what the Regiment thought about his action; and, when the troopers offered to buy the Drum-Horse, he said that their offer was mutinous and forbidden by the Regulations. But one of the Subalterns — Hogan-Yale, an Irishman — bought the Drum-Horse for Rs. 160 at the sale; and the Colonel was wroth. Yale professed repentance — he was unnaturally submissive — and said that, as he had only made the purchase to save the horse from possible illtreatment and starvation, he would now shoot him and end the business. This appeared to soothe the Colonel, for he wanted the Drum-Horse disposed of. He felt that he had made a mistake, and could not of course acknowledge it. Meantime, the presence of the Drum-Horse was an annoyance to him.

Yale took to himself a glass of the old brandy, three cheroots, and his friend Martyn; and they all left the Mess together. Yale and Martyn conferred for two hours in Yale's quarters; but only the bull-terrier who keeps watch over Yale's boot-trees knows what they said. A horse, hooded and sheeted to his ears, left Yale's stables and was taken, very unwillingly, into the Civil Lines. Yale's groom went with him. Two men broke into the Regimental Theatre and took several paint-pots and some large scenery-brushes. Then night fell over the Cantonments, and there was a noise as of a horse kicking his loose-box to pieces in Yale's stables. Yale had a big, old, white Waler trap-horse.

The next day was a Thursday, and the men, hearing that Yale was going to shoot the Drum-Horse in the evening, determined to give the beast a regular regimental funeral — a finer one than they would have given the Colonel had he died just then. They got a bullock-cart and some sacking, and mounds and mounds of roses, and the body, under sacking, was carried out to the place where the anthrax cases were cremated; two-thirds of the Regiment following. There was no Band, but they all sang 'The Place where the old Horse died' as something respectful and appropriate to the occasion. When the corpse was dumped into the grave, and the men began throwing down armfuls of roses to cover it, the Farrier-Sergeant ripped out an oath and said aloud, 'Why, it ain't the Drum-Horse any more than it's me!' The Troop-Sergeant-Majors asked him whether he had left his head in the Canteen. The Farrier-Sergeant said that he knew the Drum-Horse's feet as well as he knew his own; but he was silenced when he saw the regimental number burnt in on the poor stiff, upturned near-fore.

Thus was the Drum-Horse of the White Hussars buried; the Farrier-Sergeant grumbling. The sacking that covered the corpse was smeared in places with black paint; and the Farrier-Sergeant drew attention to this fact. But the Troop-Sergeant-Major of E Troop kicked him severely on the shin, and told him that he was undoubtedly drunk.

On the Monday following the burial, the Colonel sought revenge on the White Hussars. Unfortunately, being at that time temporarily in Command of the Station, he ordered a Brigade field-day. He said that he wished to make the Regiment 'sweat for their damned insolence,' and he carried out his notion thoroughly. That Monday was one of the hardest days in the memory of the White Hussars. They were thrown against a skeleton-enemy, and pushed forward, and withdrawn, and dismounted, and 'scientifically handled' in every possible fashion over dusty country, till they sweated profusely. Their only amusement came late in the day when they fell upon the battery of Horse Artillery and chased it for two miles. This was a personal question, and most of the troopers had money on the event; the Gunners saying openly that they had the legs of the White Hussars. They were wrong. A march-past concluded the campaign, and when the Regiment got back to their Lines the men were coated with dirt from spur to chin-strap.

The White Hussars have one great and peculiar privilege. They won it at Fontenoy, I think.

Many Regiments possess special rights, such as wearing collars with undress uniform, or a bow of riband between the shoulders, or red and white roses in their helmets on certain days of the year. Some rights are connected with regimental saints, and some with regimental successes. All are valued highly; but none so highly as the right of the White Hussars to have the Band playing when their horses are being watered in the Lines. Only one tune is played, and that tune never varies. I don't know its real name, but the White Hussars call it, 'Take me to London again.' It sounds very pretty. The Regiment would sooner be struck off the roster than forego their distinction.

After the 'dismiss' was sounded, the officers rode off home to prepare for stables; and the men filed into the lines riding easy. That is to say, they opened their tight buttons, shifted their helmets, and began to joke or to swear as the humour took them; the more careful slipping off and easing girths and curbs. A good trooper values his mount exactly as much as he values himself, and believes, or should believe, that the two together are irresistible where women or men, girls or guns, are concerned.

Then the Orderly-Officer gave the order, 'Water horses,' and the Regiment loafed off to the squadron-troughs which were in the rear of the stables, and between these and the barracks. There were four huge troughs, one for each squadron, arranged *en échelon*, so that the whole Regiment could water in ten minutes if it liked. But it lingered for seventeen, as a rule, while the Band played.

The Band struck up as the squadrons filed off to the troughs, and the men slipped their feet out of the stirrups and chaffed each other. The sun was just setting in a big, hot bed of red cloud, and the road to the Civil Lines seemed to run straight into the sun's eye. There was a little dot on the road. It grew and grew till it showed as a horse, with a sort of gridiron-thing on his back. The red cloud glared through the bars of the gridiron. Some of the troopers shaded their eyes with their hands and said — 'What the mischief 'as that there 'orse got on 'im?'

In another minute they heard a neigh that every soul — horse and man — in the Regiment knew, and saw, heading straight towards the Band, the dead Drum-Horse of the White Hussars!

On his withers banged and bumped the kettle-drums draped in crape, and on his back, very stiff and soldierly, sat a bareheaded skeleton.

The Band stopped playing, and, for a moment, there was a hush.

Then some one in E Troop — men said it was the Troop-Sergeant-Major — swung his horse round and yelled. No one can account exactly for what happened afterwards; but it seems that, at least, one man in each troop set an example of panic, and the rest followed like sheep. The horses that had barely put their muzzles into the troughs reared and capered; but as soon as the Band broke, which it did when the ghost of the Drum-Horse was about a furlong distant, all hooves followed suit, and the clatter of the stampede — quite different from the orderly throb and roar of a movement on parade, or the rough horse-play of watering in camp — made them only more terrified. They felt that the men on their backs were afraid of something. When horses once know that, all is over except the butchery.

Troop after troop turned from the troughs and ran — anywhere and everywhere — like spilt quicksilver. It was a most extraordinary spectacle,

THE AFGHAN
OR ALI MUSJID
GALOP
Published by E. Griffith & Son, Birkenhead.
COMPOSED BY W. H. WESTOVER.

for men and horses were in all stages of easiness, and the carbine-buckets flopping against their sides urged the horses on. Men were shouting and cursing, and trying to pull clear of the Band which was being chased by the Drum-Horse whose rider had fallen forward and seemed to be spurring for a wager.

The Colonel had gone over to the Mess for a drink. Most of the officers were with him, and the Subaltern of the Day was preparing to go down to the Lines, and receive the watering reports from the Troop-Sergeant-Majors. When 'Take me to London again' stopped, after twenty bars, every one in the Mess said, 'What on earth has happened?' A minute later, they heard unmilitary noises, and saw, far across the plain, the White Hussars scattered and broken, and flying.

The Colonel was speechless with rage, for he thought that the Regiment had risen against him or was unanimously drunk. The Band, a disorganised mob, tore past, and at its heels laboured the Drum-Horse — the dead and buried Drum-Horse — with the jolting, clattering skeleton. Hogan-Yale whispered softly to Martyn — 'No wire will stand that treatment,' and the Band, which had doubled like a hare, came back again. But the rest of the Regiment was gone, was rioting all over the Province, for the dusk had shut in, and each man was howling to his neighbour that the Drum-Horse was on his flank. Troop-horses are far too tenderly treated as a rule. They can, on emergencies, do a great deal, even with seventeen stone on their backs; as the troopers found out.

How long this panic lasted I cannot say. I believe that when the moon rose the men saw they had nothing to fear, and, by twos and threes and half-troops, crept back into Cantonments very much ashamed of themselves. Meantime, the Drum-Horse, disgusted at his treatment by old friends, pulled up, wheeled round, and trotted up to the Mess verandah-steps for bread. No one liked to run; but no one cared to go forward till the Colonel made a movement and laid hold of the skeleton's foot. The Band had halted some distance away, and now came back slowly. The Colonel called it, individually and collectively, every evil name that occurred to him at the time; for he had set his hand on the bosom of the Drum-Horse and found flesh and blood. Then he beat the kettle-drums with his clenched fist, and discovered that they were but made of silvered paper and bamboo. Next, still swearing, he tried to drag the skeleton out of the saddle, but found that it had been wired into the cantle. The sight of the Colonel, with his arms round the skeleton's pelvis and his knee in the old Drum-Horse's stomach, was striking; not to say amusing. He worried the thing off in a minute or two, and threw it down on the ground, saying to the Band — 'Here, you curs, that's what you're afraid of.' The skeleton did not look pretty in the twilight. The Band-Sergeant seemed to recognise it, for he began to chuckle and choke. 'Shall I take it away, sir?' said the

Band-Sergeant. 'Yes,' said the Colonel, 'take it to Hell, and ride there yourselves!'

The Band-Sergeant saluted, hoisted the skeleton across his saddle-bow, and led off to the stables. Then the Colonel began to make inquiries for the rest of the Regiment, and the language he used was wonderful. He would disband the Regiment — he would court-martial every soul in it — he would not command such a set of rabble, and so on, and so on. As the men dropped in, his language grew wilder, until at last it exceeded the utmost limits of free speech allowed even to a Colonel of Horse.

Martyn took Hogan-Yale aside and suggested compulsory retirement from the Service as a necessity when all was discovered. Martyn was the weaker man of the two. Hogan-Yale put up his eyebrows and remarked, firstly, that he was the son of a Lord, and, secondly, that he was as innocent as the babe unborn of the theatrical resurrection of the Drum-Horse.

'My instructions,' said Yale, with a singularly sweet smile, 'were that the Drum-Horse should be sent back as impressively as possible. I ask you, *am* I responsible if a mule-headed friend sends him back in such a manner as to disturb the peace of mind of a regiment of Her Majesty's Cavalry?'

Martyn said, 'You are a great man, and will in time become a General; but I'd give my chance of a troop to be safe out of this affair.'

Providence saved Martyn and Hogan-Yale. The Second-in-Command led the Colonel away to the little curtained alcove wherein the Subalterns of the White Hussars were accustomed to play poker of nights; and there, after many oaths on the Colonel's part, they talked together in low tones. I fancy that the Second-in-Command must have represented the scare as the work of some trooper whom it would be hopeless to detect; and I know that he dwelt upon the sin and the shame of making a public laughing-stock of the scare.

'They will call us,' said the Second-in-Command, who had really a fine imagination — 'they will call us the "Fly-by-Nights"; they will call us the "Ghost Hunters"; they will nickname us from one end of the Army List to the other. All the explanation in the world won't make outsiders understand that the officers were away when the panic began. For the honour of the Regiment and for your own sake keep this thing quiet.'

The Colonel was so exhausted with anger that soothing him down was not as difficult as might be imagined. He was made to see, gently and by degrees, that it was obviously impossible to court-martial the whole Regiment, and equally impossible to proceed against any subaltern who, in his belief, had any concern in the hoax.

'But the beast's alive! He's never been shot at all!' shouted the Colonel. 'It's flat flagrant disobedience! I've known a man broke for less — dam sight less. They're mocking me, I tell you, Mutman! They're mocking me!'

Once more the Second-in-Command set himself to soothe the Colonel, and wrestled with him for half an hour. At the end of that time the Regimental Sergeant-Major reported himself. The situation was rather novel to him; but he was not a man to be put out by circumstances. He saluted and said, 'Regiment all come back, Sir.' Then, to propitiate the Colonel — 'An' none of the 'orses any the worse, Sir.'

The Colonel only snorted and answered — 'You'd better tuck the men into their cots, then, and see that they don't wake up and cry in the night.' The Sergeant withdrew.

His little stroke of humour pleased the Colonel, and, further, he felt slightly ashamed of the language he had been using. The Second-in-Command worried him again, and the two sat talking far into the night.

Next day but one there was a Commanding Officer's parade, and the Colonel harangued the White Hussars vigorously. The pith of his speech was that, since the Drum-Horse in his old age had proved himself capable of cutting up the whole Regiment, he should return to his post of pride at the head of the Band, *but* the Regiment were a set of ruffians with bad consciences.

The White Hussars shouted, and threw everything movable about them into the air, and when the parade was over they cheered the Colonel till they couldn't speak. No cheers were put up for Lieutenant Hogan-Yale, who smiled very sweetly in the background.

Said the Second-in-Command to the Colonel, unofficially —

'These little things ensure popularity, and do not the least affect discipline.'

'But I went back on my word,' said the Colonel.

'Never mind,' said the Second-in-Command. 'The White Hussars will follow you anywhere from today. Regiments are just like women. They will do anything for trinketry.'

A week later, Hogan-Yale received an extraordinary letter from some one who signed himself 'Secretary, *Charity and Zeal*, 3709, E.C.,' and asked for 'the return of our skeleton which we have reason to believe is in your possession.'

'Who the deuce is this lunatic who trades in bones?' said Hogan-Yale.

'Beg your pardon, Sir,' said the Band-Sergeant, 'but the skeleton is with me, an' I'll return it if you'll pay the carriage into the Civil Lines. There's a coffin with it, Sir.'

Hogan-Yale smiled and handed two rupees to the Band-Sergeant, saying, 'Write the date on the skull, will you?'

If you doubt this story, and know where to go, you can see the date on the skeleton. But don't mention the matter to the White Hussars.

I happen to know something about it, because I prepared the Drum-Horse for his resurrection. He did not take kindly to the skeleton at all.

MY LORD THE ELEPHANT

Touching the truth of this tale there need be no doubt at all, for it was told to me by Mulvaney at the back of the elephant-lines, one warm evening when we were taking the dogs out for exercise. The twelve Government elephants rocked at their pickets outside the big mud-walled stables (one arch, as wide as a bridge-arch, to each restless beast), and the *mahouts* were preparing the evening meal. Now and again some impatient youngster would smell the cooking flour-cakes and squeal; and the naked little children of the elephant-lines would strut down the row shouting and commanding silence, or, reaching up, would slap at the eager trunks. Then the elephants feigned to be deeply interested in pouring dust upon their heads, but, so soon as the children passed, the rocking, fidgeting, and muttering broke out again.

The sunset was dying, and the elephants heaved and swayed dead black against the one sheet of rose-red low down in the dusty gray sky. It was at the beginning of the hot weather, just after the troops had changed into their white clothes, so Mulvaney and Ortheris looked like ghosts walking through the dusk. Learoyd had gone off to another barrack to buy sulphur ointment for his last dog under suspicion of mange, and with delicacy had put his kennel into quarantine at the back of the furnace where they cremate the anthrax cases.

'*You* wouldn't like mange, little woman?' said Ortheris, turning my terrier over on her fat white back with his foot. 'You're no end bloomin' partic'lar, you are. 'Oo wouldn't take no notice o' me t'other day 'cause she was goin' 'ome all alone in 'er dorg-cart, eh? Settin' on the box-seat like a bloomin' little tart, you was, Vicy. Now you run along an' make them *'uttees* 'oller. Sick 'em, Vicy, loo!'

Elephants loathe little dogs. Vixen barked herself down the pickets, and in a minute all the elephants were kicking and squealing and clucking together.

'Oh, you soldier-men,' said a *mahout* angrily, 'call off your she-dog. She is frightening our elephant-folk.'

'Rummy beggars!' said Ortheris meditatively. 'Call 'em people, same as if they was. An' they are too. Not so bloomin' rummy when you come to think of it, neither.'

Vixen returned yapping to show that she could do it again if she liked, and established herself between Ortheris's knees, smiling a large smile at his lawful dogs who dared not fly at her.

''Seed the battery this mornin'?' said Ortheris. He meant the newly-arrived elephant-battery; otherwise he would have said simply 'guns.' Three elephants harnessed tandem go to each gun, and those who have not seen the big forty-pounders of position trundling along in the wake of their gigantic team have yet something to behold. The lead-elephant had behaved very badly on parade; and had been cut loose, sent back to the lines in disgrace, and was at that hour squealing and lashing out with his trunk at the end of the line; a picture of blind, bound, bad temper. His *mahout*, standing clear of the flail-like blows, was trying to soothe him.

'That's the beggar that cut up on p'rade. 'E's *must*,' said Ortheris pointing. 'There'll be murder in the lines soon, and then, per'aps, 'e'll get loose an' we'll 'ave to be turned out to shoot 'im, same as when one o' they native king's elephants *musted* last June. 'Ope 'e will.'

'*Must* be sugared!' said Mulvaney contemptuously from his resting-place on a pile of dried bedding. 'He's no more than in a powerful bad timper wid bein' put upon. I'd lay my kit he's new to the gun-team, an' by natur' he hates haulin'. Ask the *mahout*, sorr.'

I hailed the old white-bearded *mahout* who was lavishing pet words on his sulky red-eyed charge.

'He is not *musth*,' the man replied indignantly; 'only his honour has been touched. Is an elephant an ox or a mule that he should tug at a trace? His strength is in his head — Peace, peace, my Lord! It was not *my* fault that they yoked thee this morning! — Only a low-caste elephant will pull a gun, and *he* is a Kumeria of the Doon. It cost a year and the life of a man to break him to burden. They of the Artillery put him in the gun-team because one of their base-born brutes had gone lame. No wonder that he was, and is wrath.'

'Rummy! Most unusual rum,' said Ortheris. 'Gawd, 'e is in a temper, though! S'pose 'e got loose!'

Mulvaney began to speak but checked himself, and I asked the *mahout* what would happen if the heel-chains broke.

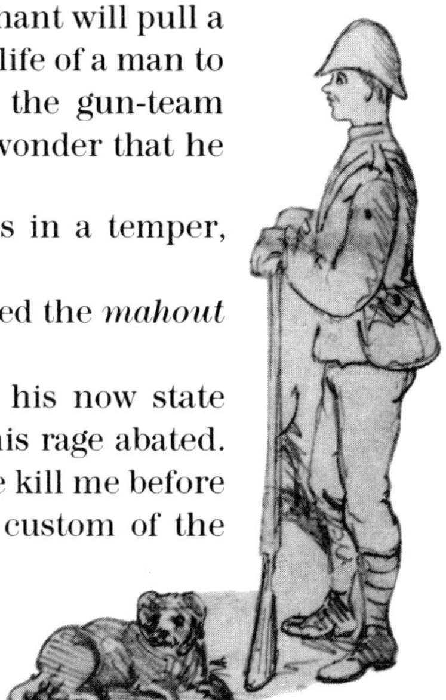

'God knows, who made elephants,' he said simply. 'In his now state peradventure he might kill you three, or run at large till his rage abated. He would not kill me, except he were *musth*. *Then* would he kill me before any one in the world, because he loves me. Such is the custom of the elephant-folk; and the custom of us *mahout*-people matches it for foolishness. We trust each our own elephant, till our own elephant kills us. Other castes trust women, but we the elephant-folk. I have seen men deal with enraged elephants and live; but never was man yet born of woman that met my lord the elephant in his *musth* and lived to tell of the taming. They are enough bold who meet him angry.'

I translated. Then said Terence: 'Ask the heathen if he iver saw a man tame an elephint, — anyways — a white man.'

'Once,' said the *mahout*, 'I saw a man astride of such a beast in the town of Cawnpore; a bare-headed man, a white man, beating it upon the head with a gun. It was said he was possessed of devils or drunk.'

'Is ut like, think you, he'd be doin' it sober?' said Mulvaney after interpretation, and the chained elephant roared.

'There's only one man top of earth that would be the partic'lar kind o' sorter bloomin' fool to do it!' said Ortheris. 'When was that, Mulvaney?'

'As the naygur sez, in Cawnpore; an' I was that fool — in the days av my youth. But it came about as naturil as wan thing leads to another, — me an' the elephint, and the elephint and me; an' the fight betune us was the most naturil av all.'

'That's just wot it would ha' been,' said Ortheris. 'Only you must ha' been more than usual full. You does one queer trick with an elephant that I know of, why didn't you never tell us the other one?'

'Bekase, onless you had heard the naygur here say what he has said spontaneous, you'd ha' called me for a liar, Stanley, my son, an' it would ha' bin my duty an' my delight to give you the father an' mother av a beltin'! There's only wan fault about you, little man, an' that's thinking you know all there is in the world, an' a little more. 'Tis a fault that has made away wid a few orf'cers I've served undher, not to spake av ivry man but two that I iver thried to make into a privit.'

'Ho!' said Ortheris with ruffled plumes, 'an' 'oo was your two bloomin' little Sir Garnets, eh?'

'Wan was mesilf,' said Mulvaney with a grin that darkness could not hide; 'an' — seein' that he's not here there's no harm speakin' av him — t'other was Jock.'

'Jock's no more than a 'ayrick in trousies. 'E be'aves *like* one; an' 'e can't '*it* one at a 'undred; 'e was born *on* one, an' s'welp me 'e'll die *under* one for not bein' able to say wot 'e wants in a Christian lingo,' said Ortheris, jumping up from the piled fodder only to be swept off his legs. Vixen leaped upon his stomach, and the other dogs followed and sat down there.

'I know what Jock is like,' I said. 'I want to hear about the elephant, though.'

'It's another o' Mulvaney's bloomin' panoramas,' said Ortheris, gasping under the dogs. ''Im an' Jock for the 'ole bloomin' British Army! You'll be

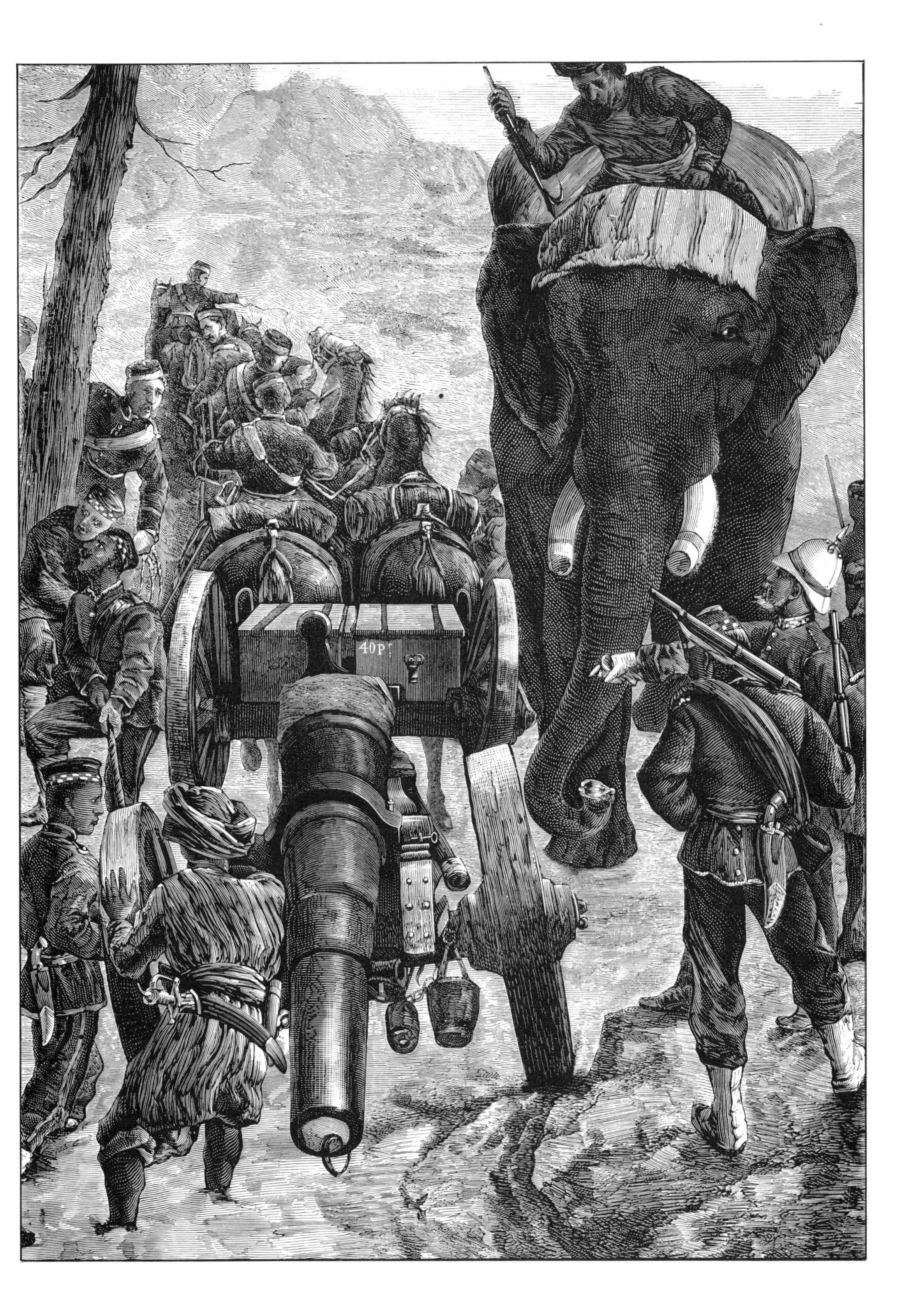
40 Pr.

sayin' you won Waterloo next, — you an' Jock. Garn!'

Neither of us thought it worth while to notice Ortheris. The big gun-elephant threshed and muttered in his chains, giving tongue now and again in crashing trumpet-peals, and to this accompaniment Terence went on: 'In the beginnin',' said he, 'me bein' what I was, there was a misunderstandin' wid my sergeant that was then. He put his spite on me for various reasons,' —

The deep-set eyes twinkled above the glow of the pipe-bowl, and Ortheris grunted, 'Another petticoat!'

— 'For various an' promiscuous reasons; an' the upshot av it was that he come into barricks wan afternoon whin' I was settlin' my cowlick before goin' walkin', called me a big baboon (which I was not), an' a demoralisin' beggar (which I was), an' bid me go on fatigue thin an' there, helpin' shift E.P. tents, fourteen av thim from the rest-camps. At that, me bein' set on my walk — '

'Ah!' from under the dogs, 'He's a Mormon, Vic. Don't you 'ave nothin' to do with 'im, little dorg.'

— 'Set on my walk, I tould him a few things that came up in my mind, an' wan thing led on to another, an' betune talkin' I made time for to hit the nose av him so that he'd be no Venus to any woman for a week to come. 'Twas a fine big nose, and well it paid for a little groomin'. Afther that I was so well pleased wid my handicraftfulness that I niver raised fist on the gyard that came to take me to Clink. A child might ha' led me along, for I knew old Kearney's nose was ruined. That summer the Ould Rig'ment did not use their own Clink, bekase the cholera was hangin' about there like mildew on wet boots, an' 'twas murdher to confine in ut. We borrowed the Clink that belonged to the Holy Christians (the rig'ment that has never seen service yet), and that lay a matther av a mile away, acrost two p'rade grounds an' the main road, an' all the ladies av Cawnpore goin' out for their afternoon dhrive. So I moved in the best av society, my shadow dancin' along forninst me, an' the gyard as solemn as putty, the bracelets on my wrists, an' my heart full contint wid the notion av Kearney's pro — pro — probosculum in a shling.

'In the middle av ut all I perceived a gunner-orf'cer in full rig'mentals perusin' down the road, hell-for-leather, wid his mouth open. He fetched wan woild despairin' look on the dog-kyarts an' the polite society av Cawnpore, an' thin he dived like a rabbut into a dhrain by the side av the road.

'"Bhoys," sez I, "that orfcer's dhrunk. 'Tis cand'lus. Let's take him to Clink too."

'The corp'ril of the gyard made a jump for me, unlocked my stringers, an' he sez: "If it comes to runnin', run for your life. If it doesn't, I'll trust your honour. Anyways," sez he. "come to Clink whin you can".'

'Then I behild him runnin' wan way, stuffin' the bracelets in his pocket, they bein' Gov'ment property, and the gyard runnin' another, an' all the dog-kyarts runnin' all ways to wanst, an' me alone lookin' down the red bag av a mouth av an elephint forty-two feet high at the shoulder, tin feet wide, wid tusks as long as the Ochterlony Monumint. That was my first reconnaissance. Maybe he was not quite so contagious, nor quite so tall, but I didn't stop to throw out pickets. Mother av Hiven, how I ran down the road! The baste began to inveshtigate the dhrain wid the gunner-orf'cer in ut; an' that was the makin' av me. I tripped over wan of the rifles that my gyard had discarded (onsoldierly blackguards they was!), an' whin I got up I was facin' t'other way about an' the elephint was huntin' for the gunner-orf'cer. I can see his big fat back yet. Excipt that he didn't dig, he car'ied on for all the world like little Vixen here at a rat-hole. He put his head down (by my sowl he nearly stood on ut!) to shquint down the dhrain; thin he'd grunt, and run round to the other ind in case the orf'cer was gone out by the backdoor; an' he'd shtuff his trunk down the flue an' get ut filled wid mud, an' blow ut out, an' grunt, an' swear! My troth, he swore all hiven down upon that orf'cer; an' what a commissariat elephint had to do wid a gunner-orf'cer passed me. Me havin' nowhere to go except to Clink, I stud in the road wid the rifle, a Snider an' no amm'nition, philosophisin' upon the rear ind av the animal. All round me, miles and miles, there was howlin' desolation, for ivry human sowl wid two legs, or four for the matther av that, was ambuscadin', an' this ould rapparee stud on his head tuggin' an' gruntin' above the dhrain, his tail stickin' up to the sky, an' he thryin' to thrumpet through three feet av road-sweepin's up his thrunk. Begad, t'was wickud to behold!

'Subsequint he caught sight av me standin' alone in the wide, wide world lanin' on the rifle. That dishcomposed him, bekase he thought I was the gunner-orf'cer got out unbeknownst. He looked betune his feet at the dhrain, an' he looked at me, an' I sez to myself: "Terence, my son, you've been watchin' this Noah's ark too long. Run for your life." Dear knows I wanted to tell him I was only a poor privit on my way to Clink, an' no orf'cer at all, at all; but he put his ears forward av his thick head, an' I rethreated down the road grippin' the rifle, my back as cowld as a tombstone, an' the slack av my trousies, where I made sure he'd take hould, crawlin' wid, — wid invidjus apprehension.

'I might ha' run till I dhropped, bekase I was betune the two straight lines av the road, an' a man, or a thousand men for the matther av that, are the like av sheep in keepin' betune right an' left marks.'

'Same as canaries,' said Ortheris from the darkness. 'Draw a line on a bloomin' little board, put their bloomin' little beakses there; stay so for hever an' hever, amen, they will. 'Seed a 'ole reg'ment, I 'ave, walk crabways along the edge of a two-foot water-cut 'stid o' thinkin' to cross it.

Men *is* sheep — bloomin' sheep. Go on.'

'But I saw his shadow wid the tail av my eye,' continued the man of experience, 'an' "Wheel," I sez, "Terence, wheel!" an' I wheeled. 'Tis truth that I cud hear the shparks flyin' from my heels; an' I shpun into the nearest compound, fetched wan jump from the gate to the verandah av the house, an' fell over a tribe of naygurs wid a half-caste boy at a desk, all manufacturin' harness. 'Twas Antonio's Carriage Emporium at Cawnpore. You know ut, sorr?

'Ould Grambags must ha' wheeled abreast wid me, for his trunk came lickin' into the verandah like a belt in a barrick-room row, before I was in the shop. The naygurs an' the half-caste boy howled an' wint out at the backdoor, an' I stud lone as Lot's wife among the harness. A powerful thirsty thing is harness, by reason av the smell to ut.

'I wint into the backroom, nobody bein' there to invite, an' I found a bottle av whisky and a goglet av wather. The first and the second dhrink I never noticed bein' dhry, but the fourth an' the fifth tuk good hould av me an' I begun to think scornful av elephints. "Take the upper ground in manœ'vrin', Terence," I sez; "an' you'll be a gen'ral yet," sez I. An wid that I wint up to the flat mud roof av the house an' looked over the edge av the parapit, threadin' delicate. Ould Barrel-belly was in the compound, walkin' to an' fro, pluckin' a piece av grass here an' a weed there, for all the world like our colonel that is now whin his wife's given him a talkin' down an' he's prom'nadin' to ease his timper. His back was to me, an' by the same token I hiccupped. He checked in his walk, wan ear forward like a deaf ould lady wid an ear-thrumpet, an' his thrunk hild out in a kind av fore-reaching hook. Thin he wagged his ear sayin', "Do my sinses deceive me?" as plain as print, an' he recomminst promenadin'. You know Antonio's compound? 'Twas as full thin as 'tis now av new kyarts and ould kyarts, an' second-hand kyarts an' kyarts for hire, — landos, an' b'rooshes, an' brooms, an' wag'nettes av ivry description. Thin I hiccupped again, an' he began to study the ground beneath him, his tail whistlin' wid emotion. Thin he lapped his thrunk round the shaft av a wag'nette an' dhrew it out circumspectuous an' thoughtful. "He's not there," he sez, fumblin' in the cushions wid his thrunk. Thin I hiccupped again, an' wid that he lost his patience good an' all, same as this wan in the lines here.'

The gun-elephant was breaking into peal after peal of indignant trumpetings, to the disgust of the other animals who had finished their food and wished to drowse. Between the outcries we could hear him picking restlessly at his ankle ring.

'As I was sayin',' Mulvaney went on, 'he behaved dishgraceful. He let out wid his fore-fut like a steam-hammer, bein' convinced that I was in ambuscade adjacent; an' that wag'nette ran back among the other carriages like a field-gun in charge. Thin he hauled ut out again an' shuk ut, an' by nature it came all to little pieces. Afther that he went sheer damn, slam, dancin', lunatic, double-shuffle demented wid the whole of Antonio's shtock for the season. He kicked, an' he straddled, and he stamped, an' he pounded all at wanst, his big bald head bobbin' up an' down, solemn as a rigadoon. He tuk a new shiny broom an' kicked ut on wan corner, an' ut opened out like a blossomin' lily; an' he shtuck wan fool-foot through the flure av ut an' a wheel was shpinnin on his tusk. At that he got scared, an' by this an' that he fair sat down plump among the carriages, an' they pricked 'im wid splinters till he was a boundin' pincushin. In the middle av the mess, whin the kyarts was climbin' wan on top av the other, an' rickochettin' off the mud walls, an' showin' their agility, wid him tearin' their wheels off, I heard the sound av distressful wailin' on the housetops, an' the whole Antonio firm an' fam'ly was cursin' me an' him from the roof next door; me bekase I'd taken refuge wid them, and he bekase he was playin' shtep-dances wid the carriages av the aristocracy.

' "Divart his attention," sez Antonio, dancin' on the roof in his big white waistcoat. "Divart his attention," he sez, "or I'll prosecute you." An' the whole fam'ly shouts, "Hit him a kick, mister soldier."

' "He's divartin' himself," I sez, for it was just the worth av a man's life to go down into the compound. But by way av makin' show I threw the whisky-bottle ('twas not full whin I came there) at him. He shpun round from what was left av the last kyart, an' shtuck his head into the verandah not three feet below me. Maybe 'twas the temptin'ness av his back or the whisky. Anyways, the next thing I knew was me, wid my hands full av mud an' mortar, all fours on his back, an' the Snider just slidin' off the slope av his head. I grabbed that an' scuffled on his neck, dhruv my knees undher his big flappin' ears, an' we wint to glory out av that compound wid a shqueal that crawled up my back an' down my belly. Thin I remimbered the Snider, an' I grup ut by the muzzle an' hit him on the head. 'Twas most forlorn — like tappin' the deck av a throopship wid a cane to stop the engines whin you're sea-sick. But I parsevered till I sweated, an' at last from takin' no notice at all he began to grunt. I hit wid the full strength that was in me in those days, an' it might ha' discommoded him. We came back to the p'rade-groun' forty miles an hour, trumpetin' vainglorious. I never stopped hammerin' him for a minut'; 'twas by way av divartin' him from runnin' undher the trees an' scrapin' me off like a poultice. The p'rade-groun' an' the road was all empty, but the throops was on the roofs av the barricks, an' betune Ould Thrajectory's gruntin' an' mine (for I was winded wid my stone-breakin'), I heard them clappin' and cheerin'. He was growin' more confused an' tuk to runnin' in circles.

' "Begad," sez I to mesilf, "there's dacincy in all things, Terence. 'Tis like you've shplit his head, and whin you come out av Clink you'll be put under stoppages for killin' a Gov'ment elephint." At that I caressed him.'

''Ow the devil did you do that? Might as well pat a barrick,' said Ortheris.

'Thried all manner av endearin' epitaphs, but bein' more than a little shuk up I disremimbered what the divil would answer to. So, "Good dog," I sez; "Pretty puss," sez I; "Whoa mare," I sez; an' at that I fetched him a shtroke av the butt for to conciliate him, an' he stud still among the barricks.

'Will no one take me off the top av this murderin volcano?' I sez at the top av my shout; an' I heard a man yellin', "Hould on, faith an' patience, the other elephints are comin'." "Mother av Glory," I sez, "will I rough-ride the whole stud? Come an' take me down, ye cowards!"

'Thin a brace av fat she-elephants wid *mahouts* an' a commissariat sergint came shuffling round the corner av the barricks; an' the *mahouts* was abusin' ould Potiphar's mother an' blood-kin.

' "Obsarve my reinforcements," I sez. "The're goin' to take you to Clink, my son;" an' the child av calamity put his ears forward an' swung head on to those females. The pluck av him, afther my oratorio on his brain-pan, wint to the heart av me. "I'm in dishgrace mesilf," I sez, "but I'll do what I can for ye. Will ye go to Clink like a man, or fight like a fool whin there's no chanst?" Wid that I fetched him wan last lick on the head, an' he fetched a tremenjus groan an' dhropped his thrunk. "Think," sez I to him, an' "Halt!" I sez to the *mahouts*. They was anxious so to do. I could feel the ould reprobit meditating undher me. At last he put his thrunk straight out an' gave a most melancholious toot (the like av a sigh wid an elephint); an' by that I knew the white flag was up an' the rest was no more than considherin' his feelin's.

' "He's done," I sez. "Kape open ordher left an' right alongside. We'll go to Clink quiet."

'Sez the commissariat sergeant to me from his elephant, "Are you a man or a mericle?" sez he.

' "I'm betwixt an' betune," I sez, thryin' to set up stiff-back. "An' what," sez I, "may ha' set this animal off in this opprobrious shtyle?" I sez, the gun-butt light an' easy on my hip an' my left hand dhropped, such as throopers behave. We was bowlin' on to the elephint-lines under escort all this time.

' "I was not in the lines whin the throuble began," sez the sergeant. "They tuk him off carryin' tents an' such like, an' put him to the gun-team. I knew he would not like ut, but by token it fair tore his heart out."

' "Faith, wan man's meat is another's poison," I sez. "'Twas bein' put on to carry tents that was the ruin av me." An' my heart warrumed to Ould Double Ends bekase he had been put upon.

' "We'll close on him here," sez the sergeant, whin we got to the elephint-lines. All the *mahouts* an' their childher was round the pickets cursin' my poney from a mile to hear. "You skip off on to my elephint's back," he sez. "There'll be throuble."

' "Sind that howlin' crowd away," I sez, "or he'll thrample the life out av thim." I cud feel his ears beginnin' to twitch. "An' do you an' your immoril she-elephints go well clear away. I will get down here. He's an Irishman," I sez, "for all his long Jew's nose, an' he shall be threated like an Irishman."

' "Are ye tired av life?" sez the sergeant.

' "Divil a bit," I sez; "but wan av us has to win, an' I'm av opinion 'tis me. Get back," I sez.

'The two elephints wint off, an' Smith O'Brine came to a dead halt above his own pickuts. "Down," sez I, whackin' him on the head, an' down he wint, shouldher over shouldher like a hill-side slippin' afther rain. "Now," sez I, slidin' down his nose an' runnin' to the front av him, "you will see the man that's betther than you."

'His big head was down betune his big forefeet, an' they was twisted in sideways like a kitten's. He looked the picture av innocince an' forlornsomeness, an' by this an' that his big hairy undherlip was thremblin', an' he winked his eyes together to kape from cryin'. "For the love av God," I sez, clean forgettin' he was a dumb baste; "don't take ut to heart so! Aisy, be aisy," I sez; an' wid that I rubbed his cheek an' betune his eyes an' the top av his thrunk, talkin' all the time. "Now," sez I, "I'll make you comfortable for the night. Send wan or two childher here," I sez to the sergeant who was watchin' for to see me killed. "He'll rouse at the sight av a man."'

'You got bloomin' clever all of a sudden,' said Ortheris. ''Ow did you come to know 'is funny little ways that soon?'

'Bekase,' said Terence with emphasis, 'bekase I had conquered the beggar, my son.'

'Ho!' said Ortheris between doubt and derision. 'G'on.'

'His *mahout*'s child an' wan or two other line-babies came runnin' up, not bein' afraid av anything, an' some got wather, an' I washed the top av his poor sore head (begad, I had done him a turn!), an' some picked the pieces av cart out av his hide, an' we scraped him, an' handled him all over, an' we put a thunderin' big poultice av neem-leaves (the same that ye stick on a pony's gall) on his head, an' it looked like a smokin'-cap, an' we put a pile av young sugar-cane forninst him, an' he began to pick at ut. "Now," sez I, settin' down on his fore-foot, "we'll have a dhrink, an' let bygones be." I sent a naygur-child for a quart av arrack, an' the sergeant's wife she sint me out four fingers av whisky, an' whin the liquor came I cud see by the twinkle in Ould Typhoon's eye that he was no more a stranger to ut than me, — worse luck, than me! So he tuk his quart like a Christian, an' *thin* I put his shackles on, chained him fore an' aft to the pickets, an' gave him my blessin', an' wint back to barricks.'

'And after?' I said in the pause.

'Ye can guess,' said Mulvaney. 'There was confusion, an' the colonel gave me ten rupees, an' the adj'tant gave me five, an' my comp'ny captain gave me five, an' the men carried me round the barricks shoutin'.'

'Did you go to Clink?' said Ortheris.

'I niver heard a word more about the misundherstandin' wid Kearney's beak, if that's what you mane; but sev'ril av the bhoys was tuk off sudden to the Holy Christians' Hotel that night. Small blame to thim, — they had twenty rupees in dhrinks. I wint to lie down an' sleep ut off, for I was as done an' double done as him there in the lines. 'Tis no small thing to go ride elephants.

'Subsequint, me an' the Venerable Father av Sin became mighty friendly. I wud go down to the lines, whin I was in dishgrace, an' spend an afthernoon collogin' wid him; he chewin' wan stick av sugar-cane an' me another, as thick as thieves. He'd take all I had out av my pockets an' put ut back again, an' now an' thin I'd bring him beer for his dijistin', an' I'd give him advice about bein' well behaved an' keepin' off the books. Afther that he wint the way av the Army, an' that's bein' thransferred as soon as you've made a good friend.'

'So you never saw him again?' I demanded.

'Do you belave the first half av the affair?' said Terence.

'I'll wait till Learoyd comes,' I said evasively. Except when he was carefully tutored by the other two and the immediate money-benefit explained, the Yorkshireman did not tell lies; and Terence, I knew, had a profligate imagination.

'There's another part still,' said Mulvaney. 'Ortheris was in that.'

'Then I'll believe it all,' I answered, not from any special belief in Ortheris's word, but from desire to learn the rest. Ortheris stole a pup from me when our acquaintance was new, and with the little beast stifling under his overcoat denied not only the theft but that he ever was interested in dogs.

'That was at the beginnin' av the Afghan business,' said Mulvaney; 'years afther the men that had seen me do the thrick was dead or gone home. I came not to speak av ut at the last bekase, — bekase I do *not* care to knock the face av ivry man that calls me a liar. At the very beginnin' av the marchin' I wint sick like a fool. I had a boot-gall, but I was all for keepin' up wid the rig'ment and such like foolishness. So I finished up wid a hole in my heel that you cud ha' dhruv a tent-peg into. Faith, how often have I preached that to recruities since, for a warnin' to thim to look afther their feet! Our docthor, who knew our business as well as his own, he sez to me, in the middle av the Tangi Pass it was: "That's sheer damned carelessness," sez he. "How often have I tould you that a marchin' man is no stronger than his feet, — his feet, — his feet!" he sez. "Now to hospital you go," he sez, "for three weeks, an expense to your Quane an' a nuisince to your counthry. Next time," sez he, "perhaps you'll put some av the whisky you pour down your throat, an' some av the tallow you put into your hair, into your socks," sez he. Faith he was a just man. So soon as we come to the head av the Tangi I wint to hospital, hoppin' on wan fut, woild wid disappointment. 'Twas a field-hospital (all flies an' native apothecaries an' liniment) dhropped, in a way av speakin', close by the head av the Tangi. The hospital guard was ravin' mad wid us sick for keepin' thim there, an' we was ravin' mad at bein' kept; an' through the Tangi, day an' night an' night an' day, the fut an' horse an' guns an' commissariat an' tents an' followers av the brigades was pourin' like a coffee-mill. The doolies came dancin' through, scores an' scores av thim, an' they'd turn up the hill to hospital wid their sick, an' I lay in bed nursin' my heel, an' hearin' the men bein' tuk out. I remimber wan night (the time I was tuk wid fever) a man came rowlin' through the tents an', "Is there any room to die here?" he sez; "there's none wid the columns"; an' at that he dhropped dead across a cot, an' thin the man in ut began to complain against dyin' all alone in the dust undher dead men. Thin I must ha' turned mad wid the fever, an' for a week I was prayin' the saints to stop the noise av the columns movin' through the Tangi. Gun-wheels it was that wore my head thin. Ye know how 'tis wid fever?'

We nodded; there was no need to explain.

'Gun-wheels an' feet an' people shoutin', but mostly gun-wheels. 'Twas neither night nor day to me for a week. In the mornin' they'd rowl up the tent-flies, an' we sick cud look at the Pass an' considher what was comin' next. Horse, fut, or guns, they'd be sure to dhrop wan or two sick wid us an' we'd get news. Wan mornin', whin the fever hild off of me, I was watchin' the Tangi, an' 'twas just like the picture on the backside av the Afghan medal, — men an' elephints an' guns comin' wan at a time crawlin' out of a dhrain.'

'It were a dhrain,' said Ortheris with feeling. 'I've fell out an' been sick in the Tangi twice; an' wot turns my innards ain't no bloomin' vi'lets neither.'

'The Pass give a twist at the ind, so everything shot out suddint an' they'd built a throop-bridge (mud an' dead mules) over a nullah at the head av ut. I lay an' counted the elephints (gun-elephints) thryin' the bridge wid their thrunks an' rollin' out sagacious. The fifth elephint's head came round the corner, an' he threw up his thrunk, an' he fetched a toot, an' there he shtuck at the head of the Tangi like a cork in a bottle. "Faith," thinks I to mysilf, "he will not thrust the bridge; there will be throuble."'

'Trouble! My Gawd!' said Ortheris. 'Terence, *I* was be'ind that bloomin' '*uttee* up to my stock in dust. Trouble!'

'Tell on then, little man; I only saw the hospital ind av ut.' Mulvaney knocked the ashes out of his pipe, as Ortheris heaved the dogs aside and went on.

'We was escort to them guns, three comp'nies of us,' he said. 'Dewcy was our major, an' our orders was to roll up anything we come across in the Tangi an' shove it out t'other end. Sort o' pop-gun picnic, see? We'd rolled up a lot o' lazy beggars o' native followers, an' some commissariat supplies that was bivoo-whackin' for ever seemin'ly, an' all the sweepin's of 'arf a dozen things what ought to 'ave bin at the front weeks ago, an' Dewcy, he says to us: "You're most 'eart-breakin' sweeps," 'e sez. "For 'eving's sake," sez 'e, "do a little sweepin' now." So we swep', — s'welp me, 'ow we did sweep 'em along! There was a full reg'ment be'ind us; most anxious to get on they was; an' they kep' on sendin' to us with the colonel's compliments, an' what in 'ell was we stoppin' the way for, please? Oh, they was partic'lar polite! So was Dewcy! 'E sent 'em back wot-for, an' 'e give us wot-for, an' we give the guns wot-for, an' they give the commissariat wot-for, an' the commissariat give first-class extry wot-for to the native followers, an' on we'd go again till we was stuck, an' the 'ole Pass 'ud be swimmin' Allelujah for a mile an' a 'arf. We 'adn't no tempers, nor no seats to our trousies, an' our coats an' our rifles was chucked in the carts, so as we might ha' been cut up any minute, an' we was doin' drover-work. That was wot it was; drovin' on the Islin'ton road!

'I was close up at the 'ead of the column when we saw the end of the Tangi openin' out ahead of us, an' I sez: "The door's open, boys. 'Oo'll git to the gall'ry fust?" I sez. Then I saw Dewcy screwin' 'is bloomin' eyeglass in 'is eye an' lookin' straight on. "Propped, —*ther* beggar!" he sez; an' the be'ind end o' that bloomin' old '*uttee* was shinin' through the dust like a bloomin old moon made o' tarpaulin. Then we 'alted, all chock-a-block, one atop o' the other, an' right at the back o' the guns there sails in a lot o' silly grinnin' camels, what the commissariat was in charge of — sailin' away as if they was at the Zoological Gardens an' squeezin' our men most awful. The dust was that up you couldn't see your 'and; an' the more we 'it 'em on the 'ead the more their drivers sez, "Accha! Accha!" an' by Gawd it was "at yer" before you knew where you was. An' that '*uttee*'s be'ind end stuck in the Pass good an' tight, an' no one knew wot for.

'Fust thing we 'ad to do was to fight they bloomin' camels. I wasn't goin' to be eat by no bull-*oont*; so I 'eld up my trousies with one 'and, standin' on a rock, an' 'it away with my belt at every nose I saw bobbin' above me. Then the camels fell back, an' they 'ad to fight to keep the rear-guard an' the native followers from crushin' into them; an' the rear-guard 'ad to send down the Tangi to warn the other reg'ment that we was blocked. I 'eard the *mahouts* shoutin' in front that the *'uttee* wouldn't cross the bridge; an' I saw Dewcy skippin' about through the dust like a musquito worm in a tank. Then our comp'nies got tired o' waitin' an' begun to mark time, an' some goat struck up *Tommy, make room for your Uncle*. After *that*, you couldn't neither see nor breathe nor 'ear; an' there we was, singin' bloomin' serenades to the end of a' elephant that don't care for tunes! I sung too; I couldn't do nothin' else. They was strengthenin' the bridge in front, all for the sake of the *'uttee*. By an' by a' orf'cer caught me by the throat an' choked the sing out of me. So I caught the next man I could see by the throat an' choked the sing out of *'im*.'

'What's the difference between being choked by an officer and being hit?' I asked, remembering a little affair in which Ortheris's honour had been injured by his lieutenant.

'One's a bloomin' lark, an' one's a bloomin' insult!' said Ortheris. 'Besides, we was on service, an' no one cares what an orf'cer does then, s'long as 'e gets our rations an' don't get us unusual cut up. After that we got quiet, an' I 'eard Dewcy say that 'e'd court-martial the lot of us as soon as we was out of the Tangi. Then we give three cheers for Dewcy an' three more for the Tangi; an' the *'uttee*'s be'ind end was stickin' in the Pass, so we cheered *that*. Then they said the bridge had been strengthened, an' we give three cheers for the bridge; but the *'uttee* wouldn't move a bloomin' hinch. Not 'im! Then we cheered 'im again, an' Kite Dawson, that was corner-man at all the sing-songs ('e died on the way down) began to give a nigger lecture on the be'ind ends of elephants, an' Dewcy, 'e tried to keep 'is face for a minute, but Lord, you couldn't do such when Kite was playin' the fool an' askin' whether 'e mightn't 'ave leave to rent a villa an' raise 'is orphan children in the Tangi, 'cos 'e couldn't get 'ome no more. Then up come a orf'cer (mounted, like a fool, too) from the reg'mint at the back with some more of his colonel's pretty little compliments, an' what was this delay, please. We sung 'im, *There's another bloomin' row downstairs* till 'is 'orse bolted, an' then we give 'im three cheers; an' Kite Dawson sez 'e was goin' to write to *The Times* about the awful state of the streets in Afghanistan. The *'uttee*'s be'ind end was stickin' in the Pass all the time. At last one of the mahouts came to Dewcy and sez something. "Oh Lord!" sez Dewcy, "*I* don't know the beggar's visiting-list! I'll give him another ten minutes an' then I'll shoot 'im." Things was gettin' pretty dusty in the Tangi, so we all listened. "'E wants to see a friend," sez Dewcy out loud to the men, an' 'e mopped 'is forehead an' sat down on a gun-tail.

'I leave it to you to judge 'ow the reg'ment shouted. "That's all right," we sez. "Three cheers for Mister Winterbottom's friend," sez we. "Why didn't you say so at first? Pass the word for old Swizzletail's wife," — and such like. Some o' the men they didn't laugh. They took it same as if it might have been a' introduction like, 'cos they knew about '*uttees*. Then we all run forward over the guns an' in an' out among the elephants' legs, — Lord, I wonder 'arf the comp'nies wasn't squashed — an' the next thing I saw was Terence 'ere, lookin' like a sheet o' wet paper, comin' down the 'illside wid a sergeant. "'Strewth," I sez. "I might ha' knowed 'e'd be at the bottom of any cat's trick," sez I. Now you tell wot 'appened your end?'

'I lay be the same as you did, little man, listenin' to the noises and the bhoys singin'. Presintly I heard whisperin' an' the doctor sayin', "Get out av this, wakin' my sick wid your jokes about elephints." An' another man sez, all angry:"'Tis a joke that is stoppin' two thousand men in the Tangi. That son av sin av a haybag av an elephint sez, or the *mahouts* sez for him, that he wants to see a friend, an' he'll not lift hand or fut till he finds him. I'm wore out wid inthrojucin' sweepers an' coolies to him, an' his hide's as full o' bay'net pricks as a mosquito-net av holes, an' I'm here undher ordhers, docther dear, to ask if anyone, sick or well, or alive or dead, knows an elephint. I'm not mad," he sez, settin' on a box av medical comforts. "'Tis my ordhers, an' 'tis my mother," he sez, "that would laugh at me for the father av all fools to-day. Does any wan here know an elephint?" We sick was all quiet.

' "Now you've had your answer," sez the doctor. "Go away."

' "Hould on," I sez, thinkin' mistiways in my cot, an' I did not know my own voice. "I'm by way av bein' acquainted wid an elephant, myself," I sez.

' "That's delirium," sez the doctor. "See what you've done, sergeant. Lie down, man," he sez, seein' me thryin' to get up.

' " 'Tis not," I sez. "I rode him round Cawnpore barricks. He will not ha' forgotten. I bruk his head wid a rifle."

' "Mad as a coot," sez the doctor, an' thin he felt my head. "It's quare," sez he. "Man," he sez, "if you go, d'you know 'twill either kill or cure?"

' "What do I care?" sez I. "If I'm mad, 'tis better dead."

' "Faith, that's sound enough," sez the doctor. "You've no fever on you now."

' "Come on," sez the sergeant. "We're all mad to-day, an' the throops are wantin' their dinner." He put his arm around av me an' I came into the sun, the hills an' the rocks skippin' big giddy-go-rounds. "Seventeen years have I been in the army," sez the sergeant, "an' the days av mericles are not done. They'll be givin' us more pay next. Begad," he sez, "the brute knows you!"

'Ould Obstructionist was screamin' like all possist whin I came up, an' I heard forty million men up the Tangi shoutin', "He knows him!" Thin the big thrunk came round me an' I was nigh fainting wid weakness. "Are you well, Malachi?" I sez, givin' him the name he answered to in the lines. "Malachi, my son, are you well?" sez I, "for I am not." At that he thrumpeted again till the Pass rang to ut, an' the other eliphants tuk it up.

Thin I got a little strength back. "Down, Malachi," I sez, "an' put me up, but touch me tendher for I am not good." He was on his knees in a minut' an' he slung me up as gentle as a girl. "Go on now, my son," I sez. "You're blockin' the road." He fetched wan more joyous toot, an' swung grand out av the head av the Tangi, his gun-gear clankin' on his back; an' at the back av him there wint the most 'mazin' shout I iver heard. An' thin I felt my head shpin, an' a mighty sweat bruk out on me, an' Malachi was growin' taller an' taller to me settin' on his back, an' I sez, foolish like an' weak, smilin' all round an' about, "Take me down," I sez, "or I'll fall."

'The next I remimber was lyin' in my cot again, limp as a chewed rag but cured av the fever, an' the Tangi as empty as the back av my hand. They'd all gone up to the front, an' ten days later I wint up too, havin' blocked an' unblocked an entire army corps. What do you think av ut, sorr?'

'I'll wait till I see Learoyd,' I repeated.

'Ah'm here,' said a shadow from among the shadows. 'Ah've heard t'tale too.'

'Is it true, Jock?'

'Ay; true as t'owd bitch has getten t'mange. Orth'ris, yo' maun't let t'dawgs hev owt to do wi' her.'

'LOVE-O'-WOMEN'

THE HORROR, THE CONFUSION, and the separation of the murderer from his comrades were all over before I came. There remained only on the barrack-square the blood of man calling from the ground. The hot sun had dried it to a dusky goldbeater-skin film, cracked lozenge-wise by the heat; and as the wind rose, each lozenge, rising a little, curled up at the edges as if it were a dumb tongue. Then a heavier gust blew all away down wind in grains of dark coloured dust. It was too hot to stand in the sunshine before breakfast. The men were in barracks talking the matter over. A knot of soldiers' wives stood by one of the entrances to the married quarters, while inside a woman shrieked and raved with wicked filthy words.

A quiet and well-conducted sergeant had shot down, in broad daylight just after early parade, one of his own corporals, had then returned to barracks and sat on a cot till the guard came for him. He would, therefore, in due time be handed over to the High Court for trial. Further, but this he could hardly have considered in his scheme of revenge, he would horribly upset my work; for the reporting of that trial would fall on me without a relief. What that trial would be like I knew even to weariness. There would be the rifle carefully uncleaned, with the fouling marks about breach and muzzle, to be sworn to by half a dozen superfluous privates; there would be heat, reeking heat, till the wet pencil slipped sideways between the fingers; and the *punkah* would swish and the pleaders would jabber in the verandahs, and his Commanding Officer would put in certificates to the prisoner's moral character, while the jury would pant and the summer uniforms of the witnesses would smell of dye and soaps; and some abject barrack-sweeper would lose his head in cross-examination, and the young barrister who always defended soldiers' cases for the credit that they never brought him, would say and do wonderful things, and would then quarrel with me because I had not reported him correctly. At the last, for he would surely not be hanged, I might meet the prisoner again, ruling blank account-forms in the Central Jail, and cheer him with the hope of his being made a warder in the Andamans.

The Indian Penal Code and its interpreters do not treat murder, under any provocation whatever, in any spirit of jest. Sergeant Raines would be

very lucky indeed if he got off with seven years, I thought. He had slept the night upon his wrongs, and killed his man at twenty yards before any talk was possible. That much I knew. Unless, therefore, the case was doctored a little, seven years would be his least; and I fancied it was exceedingly well for Sergeant Raines that he had been liked by his Company.

That same evening — no day is so long as the day of a murder — I met Ortheris with the dogs, and he plunged defiantly into the middle of the matter. 'I'll be one o' the witnesses,' said he. 'I was in the verandah when Mackie come along. 'E come from Mrs. Raines's quarters. Quigley, Parsons, an' Trot, they was in the inside verandah, so *they* couldn't 'ave 'eard nothing. Sergeant Raines was in the verandah talkin' to me, an' Mackie 'e come along acrost the square an' 'e sez, "Well," sez 'e, "'ave they pushed your 'elmet off yet, Sergeant?" 'e sez. An' at that Raines 'e catches 'is breath an' 'e sez, "My Gawd, I can't stand this!" sez 'e, an' 'e picks up my rifle an' shoots Mackie. See?'

'But what were you doing with your rifle in the outer verandah an hour after parade?'

'Cleanin' 'er,' said Ortheris, with the sullen brassy stare that always went with his choicer lies.

He might as well have said that he was dancing naked, for at no time did his rifle need hand or rag on her twenty minutes after parade. Still, the High Court would not know his routine.

'Are you going to stick to that — on the Book?' I asked.

'Yes. Like a bloomin' leech.'

'All right, I don't want to know any more. Only remember that Quigley, Parsons, and Trot couldn't have been where you say without hearing something; and there's nearly certain to be a barrack-sweeper who was knocking about the square at the time. There always is.'

''Twasn't the sweeper. It was the *beastie*. 'E's all right.'

Then I knew that there was going to be some spirited doctoring, and I felt sorry for the Government Advocate who would conduct the prosecution.

When the trial came on I pitied him more, for he was always quick to lose his temper and made a personal matter of each lost cause. Raines's young barrister had for once put aside his unslaked and welling passion for alibis and insanity, had forsworn gymnastics and fireworks, and worked soberly for his client. Mercifully the hot weather was yet young, and there had been no flagrant cases of barrack-shootings up to the time; and the jury was a good one, even for an Indian jury, where nine men out of every twelve are accustomed to weighing evidence. Ortheris stood firm and was not shaken by any cross-examination. The one weak point in his tale — the presence of his rifle in the outer verandah — went unchallenged by civilian wisdom, though some of the witnesses could not help smiling. The Government Advocate called for the rope, contending throughout that the murder had been a deliberate one. Time had passed, he argued, for that reflection which comes so naturally to a man whose honour is lost. There was also the Law, ever ready and anxious to right the wrongs of the common soldier if, indeed, wrong had been done. But he doubted much whether there had been any sufficient wrong. Causeless suspicion over-long brooded upon had led, by his theory, to deliberate crime. But his attempts to minimise the motive failed. The most disconnected witness knew — had known for weeks — the causes of offence; and the prisoner, who naturally was the last of all to know, groaned in the dock while he listened. The one question that the trial circled round was whether Raines had fired under sudden and blinding provocation given that very morning; and in the summing-up it was clear that Ortheris's evidence told. He had contrived most artistically to suggest that he personally hated the Sergeant, who had come into the verandah to give him a talking to for insubordination. In a weak moment the Government Advocate asked one question too many. 'Beggin' *your* pardon, sir,' Ortheris replied, ''e was callin' me a dam' impudent little lawyer.' The Court shook. The jury brought it in a killing, but with every provocation and extenuation known to God or man, and the Judge put his hand to his brow before giving sentence, and the Adam's apple in the prisoner's throat went up and down like mercury pumping before a cyclone.

In consideration of all considerations, from his Commanding Officer's certificate of good conduct to the sure loss of pension, service, and honour, the prisoner would get two years, to be served in India, and — there need be no demonstration in Court. The Government Advocate scowled and picked up his papers; the guard wheeled with a clash, and the prisoner was relaxed to the Secular Arm, and driven to the jail in a broken-down *ticca-gharri*.

His guard and some ten or twelve military witnesses, being less important, were ordered to wait till what was officially called the cool of the evening before marching back to cantonments. They gathered together in one of the deep red brick verandahs of a disused lock-up and congratulated Ortheris, who bore his honours modestly. I sent my work into the office and joined them. Ortheris watched the Government Advocate driving off to lunch.

'That's a nasty little bald-'eaded little butcher, that is,' he said. ''E don't please me. 'E's got a colley dog wot do, though. I'm goin' up to Murree in a week. That dawg'll bring fifteen rupees anywheres.'

'You had better spend ut in Masses,' said Terence, unbuckling his belt; for he had been on the prisoner's guard, standing helmeted and bolt upright for three long hours.

'Not me,' said Ortheris cheerfully. 'Gawd'll put it down to B Comp'ny's barrick-damages one o' these days. You look strapped, Terence.'

'Faith, I'm not so young as I was. That gyard-mountin' wears on the sole av the fut, and this' — he sniffed contemptuously at the brick verandah — 'is as hard setting as standin'!'

'Wait a minute. I'll get the cushions out of my cart,' I said.

''Strewth — sofies. We're going it gay,' said Ortheris, as Terence dropped himself section by section on the leather cushions, saying prettily, 'May ye niver want a soft place wheriver you go, an' power to share ut wid a frind. Another for yourself? That's good. It lets me sit longways. Stanley, pass me a pipe. Augrrh! An' that's another man gone all to pieces bekaze av a woman. I must ha' been on forty or fifty prisoners' gyards, first and last; an' I hate ut new ivry time.'

'Let's see. You were on Losson's, Lancey's, Dugard's, and Stebbins's, that I can remember,' I said.

'Ay, an' before that an' before that — scores av thim,' he answered with a worn smile. ''Tis better to die than to live for them, though. Whin Raines comes out — he'll be changin' his kit at the jail now — he'll think that too. He shud ha' shot hemself an' the woman by rights an' made a clean bill av all. Now he's left the woman — she tuk tay wid Dinah Sunday gone last — an' he's left hemself. Mackie's the lucky man.'

'He's probably getting it hot where he is,' I ventured, for I knew something of the dead Corporal's record.

'Be sure av that,' said Terence, spitting over the edge of the verandah. 'But fwhat he'll get there is light marchin'-ordher to fwhat he'd ha' got here if he'd lived.'

'Surely not. He'd have gone on and forgotten — like the others.'

'Did ye know Mackie well, sorr?' said Terence.

'He was on the Pattiala guard of honour last winter, and I went out shooting with him in an *ekka* for the day, and I found him rather an amusing man.'

'Well, he'll ha' got shut av amusemints, excipt turnin' from wan side to the other, these few years to come. I knew Mackie, an' I've seen too many to be mistuk in the muster av wan man. He might ha' gone on an' forgot as you say, sorr, but he was a man wid an educashin, an' he used ut for his schames; an' the same educashin, an' talkin', an' all that made him able to do fwhat he had a mind to wid a woman, that same wud turn back again in the long-run an' tear him alive. I can't say fwhat that I mane to say bekaze I don't know how, but Mackie was the spit an' livin' image av a man that I saw march the same march *all but*; an' 'twas worse for him that he did not come by Mackie's ind. Wait while I remember now. 'Twas whin I was in the Black Tyrone, an' he was drafted us from Portsmouth; an' fwhat was his misbegotten name? Larry — Larry Tighe ut was; an' wan of the draft said he was a gentleman-ranker, an' Larry tuk an' three-parts killed him for saying so. An' he was a big man, an' a strong man, an' a handsome man, an' that tells heavy in practice wid some women, but takin' them by an' large, not wid all. Yet 'twas wid all that Larry dealt — *all* — for he cud put the comether on any woman that trod the green earth av God, an' he knew ut. Like Mackie that's roastin' now, he knew ut, an' niver did he put the comether on any woman save an' excipt for the black shame. 'Tis not me that shud be talkin', dear knows, dear knows, but the most av my mis — misallinces was for pure devilry, an' mighty sorry I have been whin harm came; an' time an' again wid a girl, ay, an' a woman too, for the matter av that, whin I have seen by the eyes av her that I was makin' more throuble than I talked, I have hild off an' let be for the sake av the mother that bore me. But Larry, I'm thinkin', he was suckled by a she-divil, for he niver let wan go that came nigh to listen to him. 'Twas his business, as if it might ha' ben sinthry-go. He was a good soldier too. Now there was the Colonel's governess — an' he a privit too! — that was never known in barricks; an' wan av the Major's maids, and she was promised to a man; an' some more outside; an' fwhat ut was amongst *us* we'll never know till Judgement Day. 'Twas the nature av the baste to put the comether on the best av thim — but the like av such women as you cud lay your hand on the Book an' swear there was niver thought av foolishness in. An' for that very reason, mark you, he was niver caught. He came close to ut wanst or twice, but caught he niver was, an' that cost him more at the ind than the beginnin'. He talked to me more than most, bekaze he tould me, barrin' the accident av my educashin, I'd av been the same kind av divil he was. "An' is ut like," he wud say, houldin' his head high — "is ut like that I'd iver be thrapped? For fwhat am I when all's said an' done?" he sez. "A damned privit," sez he. "An' is ut like, think you, that thim I know wud be connect wid a privit like me? Number tin thousand four hundred an' sivin," he sez grinnin'. I knew by the turn av his spache when he was not takin' care to talk rough-shod that he was a gentleman-ranker.

' "I do not undherstan' ut at all," I sez; "but I know," sez I, "that the divil looks out av your eyes, an' I'll have no share wid you. A little fun by way av amusemint where 'twill do no harm, Larry, is right and fair, but I am mistook if 'tis any amusemint to you," I sez.

' "You are much mistook," he sez. "An' I counsel you not to judge your betters."

' "My betthers!" I sez. "God help you, Larry. There's no betther in this; 'tis all bad, as ye will find for yoursilf."

' "You're not like me," he says, tossin' his head.

' "Praise the Saints, I am not," I sez. "Fwhat I have done I have done an' been crool sorry for. Fwhin your time comes," sez I, "ye'll remember fwhat I say."

'"An' whin that time comes," sez he, "I'll come to you for ghostly consolation, Father Terence," an' at that he wint off afther some more divil's business — for to get expayrience, he tould me. He was wicked — rank wicked — wicked as all Hell! I'm not construct by nature to go in fear of any man, but, begad, I was afraid of Larry. He'd come in to barricks wid his cap on three hairs, an' lie on his cot and stare at the ceilin', an' now an' again he'd fetch a little laugh, the like av a splash in the bottom av a well, an' by that I knew he was schamin' new wickedness, an' I'd be afraid. All this was long an' long ago, but ut hild me straight — for a while.

'I tould you, did I not, sorr, that I was caressed an' pershuaded to lave the Tyrone on account av a throuble?'

'Something to do with a belt and a man's head wasn't it?' Terence had never given the tale in full.

'It was. Faith, ivry time I go on prisoner's gyard in coort I wondher fwhy I was not where the pris'ner is. But the man I struk tuk it in fair fight an' he had the good sinse not to die. Considher now, fwhat wud ha' come to the Army if he had! I was enthreated to exchange, an' my Commandin' Orf'cer pled wid me. I wint, not to be disobligin', and Larry tould me he was powerful sorry to lose me, though fwhat I'd done to make him sorry I do not know. So to the Ould Reg'mint I came, lavin' Larry to go to the divil his own way, an' niver expectin' to see him again excipt as a shootin'-case in barracks . . . Who's that quittin' the compound?' Terence's quick eye had caught sight of a white uniform skulking behind the hedge.

'The Sergeant's gone visiting,' said a voice.

'Thin I command here, an' I will have no sneakin' away to the bazar, an' huntin' for you wid a pathrol at midnight. Nalson, for I know ut's you, come back to the verandah.'

Nalson, detected, slunk back to his fellows. There was a grumble that died away in a minute or two, and Terence turning on the other side went on:—

'That was the last I saw av Larry for a while. Exchange is the same as death for not thinkin', an' by token I married Dinah, an' that kept me from remimberin' ould times. Thin we went up to the Front, an' ut tore my heart in tu to lave Dinah at the Depôt in Pindi. Consequint, whin I was at the Front I fought circumspectuous till I warrmed up, an' thin I fought double tides. You remember fwhat I tould you in the gyard-gate av the fight at Silver's Theatre?'

'Wot's that about Silver's Theayter?' said Ortheris quickly, over his shoulder.

'Nothin', little man. A tale that ye know. As I was sayin', afther that fight, us av the Ould Rig'mint an' the Tyrone was all mixed together takin' shtock av the dead, an' av coorse I wint about to find if there was any man that remembered me. The second man I came acrost — an' how I'd missed him in the fight I do not know — was Larry, an' a fine man he looked, but oulder, by reason that he had fair call to be. "Larry," sez I, "how is ut wid you?"

' "Ye're callin' the wrong man," he sez, wid his gentleman's smile, "Larry has been dead these three years. They call him 'Love-o'-Women' now," he sez. By that I knew the ould divil was in him yet, but the ind av a fight is no time for the beginnin' av confession, so we sat down an' talked av times.

' "They tell me you're a married man," he sez, puffin' slow at his poipe. "Are ye happy?"

' "I will be whin I get back to Depôt," I sez. "'Tis a reconnaissance-honeymoon now."

' "I'm married too," he sez, puffin' slow an' more slow, an' stopperin' wid his forefinger.

' "Send you happiness," I sez. "That's the best hearin' for a long time."

' "Are ye av that opinion?" he sez; an' thin he began talkin' av the campaign. The sweat av Silver's Theatre was not dhry upon him an' he was prayin' for more work. I was well contint to lie and listen to the cook-pot lids.

'Whin he got up off the ground he shtaggered a little, an' laned over all twisted.

' "Ye've got more than ye bargained for," I sez. "Take an inventory, Larry. 'Tis like you're hurt."

'He turned round stiff as a ramrod an' damned the eyes av me up an' down for an impartinent Irish ape. If that had been in barracks, I'd ha' stretched him an' no more said, but 'twas at the Front, an' afther such a fight as Silver's Theatre I knew there was no callin' a man to account for his tempers. He might as well ha' kissed me. Aftherwards I was well pleased I kept my fists home. Thin our Captain Crook — Cruik-na-bulleen — came up. He'd been talkin' to the little orf'cer bhoy av the Tyrone. "We're all cut to windystraws," he sez, "but the Tyrone are damned short for noncoms. Go you over there, Mulvaney, an' be Deputy-Sergeant, Corp'ral, Lance, an' everything else ye can lay hands on till I bid you stop."

'I wint over an' tuk hould. There was wan sergeant left standin', and they'd pay no heed to him. The remnint was me, an' 'twas full time I came. Some I talked to, an' some I did not, but before night the bhoys av the

Tyrone stud to attention, by gad, if I sucked on my poipe above a whishper. Betune you an' me an' Bobbs I was commandin' the company, an' that was what Crook had thransferred me for; an' the little orf'cer bhoy knew ut, and I knew ut, but the comp'ny did not. And *there*, mark you, is the vartue that no money an' no dhrill can buy — the vartue av the ould soldier that knows his orf'cer's work an' does ut for him at the salute!

'Thin the Tyrone, wid the Ould Rig'mint in touch, was sint maraudin' an' prowlin' acrost the hills promishcuous an' onsatisfactory. 'Tis my privat opinion that a gin'ral does not know half the time fwhat to do wid three-quarters his command. So he shquats on his hunkers an' bids them run round an' round forninst him while he considhers on it. Whin by the process av nature they get sejuced into a big fight that was none av their seekin' , he sez: "Observe my shuperior janius. I meant ut to come so." We ran round an' about, an' all we got was shootin' into the camp at night, an' rushin' empty *sungars* wid the long bradawl, an' bein' hit from behind rocks till we was wore out — all excipt Love-o'-Women. That puppy-dog business was mate an' dhrink to him. Begad he cud niver get enough av ut. Me well knowin' that it is just this desultorial campaignin' that kills the best men, an' suspicionin' that if I was cut, the little orf'cer bhoy wud expind all his men in thryin' to get out, I wud lie most powerful doggo whin I heard a shot, an' curl my long legs behind a bowlder, an' run like blazes whin the ground was clear. Faith, if I led the Tyrone in rethreat wanst I led thim forty times! Love-o'-Women wud stay pottin' an' pottin' from behind a rock and wait till the fire was heaviest, an' thin stand up an' fire man-height clear. He wud lie out in camp too at night, snipin' at the shadows, for he never tuk a mouthful av slape. My commandin' orf'cer — save his little soul! — cud not see the beauty av my strategims, an' whin the Ould Rig'mint crossed us, an' that was wanst a week, he'd throt off to Crook, wid his big blue eyes as round as saucers, an' lay an information against me. I heard thim wanst talkin' through the tent wall, an' I nearly laughed.

' "He runs — runs like a hare," sez the little orf'cer bhoy. "'Tis demoralisin' my men."

' "Ye damned little fool," sez Crook laughin'. "He's larnin' you your business. Have ye been rushed at night yet?"

' "No," sez that child; wishful he had been.

' "Have you any wounded?" sez Crook.

' "No," he sez. "There was no chanst for that. They follow Mulvaney too quick," he sez.

' "Fwhat more do you want, thin?" sez Crook. "Terence is bloodin' you neat an' handy," he sez. "He knows fwhat you do not, an' that's that there's a time for ivrything. He'll not lead you wrong," he sez, "but I'd give a month's pay to larn fwhat he thinks av you."

'That kept the babe quiet, but Love-o'-Women was pokin' at me for ivrything I did, an' specially my manœuvres.

' "Mr. Mulvaney," he sez wan evenin', very contempshus, "you're grown very *jeldy* on your feet. Among gentlemen," he sez, "among gentlemen that's called no pretty name."

' "Among privits 'tis different," I sez. "Get back to your tent. I'm sergeant here," I sez.

'There was just enough in the voice av me to tell him he was playin' wid his life betune his teeth. He wint off, an' I noticed that this man that was contempshus set off from the halt wid a shunt as tho' he was bein' kicked behind. That same night there was a Paythan picnic in the hills about, an' firin' into our tents fit to wake the livin' dead. "Lie down all," I sez. "Lie down an' kape still. They'll no more than waste ammunition."

'I heard a man's feet on the ground, an' thin a 'Tini joinin' in the chorus. I'd been lyin' warm, thinkin' av Dinah an' all, but I crup out wid the bugle for to look round in case there was a rush; an' the 'Tini was flashin' at the fore-ind av the camp, an' the hill near by was fair flickerin' wid long-range fire. Undher the starlight I behild Love-o'-Women settin' on a rock wid his belt and helmet off. He shouted wanst or twice, an' thin I heard him say: "They shud ha' got the range long ago. Maybe they'll fire at the flash." Thin he fired again, an' that dhrew a fresh volley, and the long slugs that they chew in their teeth came floppin' among the rocks like tree-toads av a hot night. "That's better," sez Love-o'-Women. "Oh Lord, how long, how long!" he sez, an' at that he lit a match and held ut above his head.

' "Mad," thinks I, "mad as a coot," an' I tuk wan stip forward, an' the nixt I knew was the sole av my boot flappin' like a cavalry gydon an' the funny-bone av my toes tinglin'. 'Twas a clane-cut shot — a slug — that niver touched sock or hide, but set me bare-fut on the rocks. At that I tuk Love-o'-Women by the scruff an' threw him under a bowlder, an' whin I sat down I heard the bullets patterin' on that same good stone.

' "Ye may dhraw your own wicked fire," I sez, shakin' him, "but I'm not goin' to be kilt too."

' "Ye've come too soon," he sez. "Ye've come too soon. In another minute they cudn't ha' missed me. Mother av God," he sez, "fwhy did ye not lave me be? Now 'tis all to do again," an' he hides his face in his hands.

' "So that's it," I sez, shakin' him again. "That's the manin' av your disobeyin' ordhers."

' "I dare not kill meself," he sez, rockin' to and fro. "My own hand wud not let me die, and there's not a bullet this month past wud touch me. I'm to die slow," he sez. "I'm to die slow. But I'm in hell now," he sez, shriekin' like a woman. "I'm in hell now!"

' "God be good to us all," I sez, for I saw his face. "Will ye tell a man the throuble? If 'tis not murder, maybe we'll mend it yet."

'At that he laughed. "D'you remember fwhat I said in the Tyrone barricks about comin' to you for ghostly consolation. I have not forgot," he sez. "That came back, and the rest av my time is on me now, Terence. I've fought ut off for months an' months, but the liquor will not bite any more. Terence," he sez, "I can't get dhrunk!"

'Thin I knew he spoke the truth about bein' in hell, for whin liquor does not take hould the sowl av a man is rotten in him. But me bein' such as I was, fwhat could I say to him?

' "Di'monds an' pearls," he begins again. "Di'monds an' pearls I have thrown away wid both hands — an' fwhat have I left? Oh, fwhat have I left?"

'He was shakin' an' thremblin' up against my shouldher, an' the slugs were singin' overhead, an' I was wonderin' whether my little bhoy wud have sinse enough to kape his men quiet through all this firin'.

' "So long as I did not think," sez Love-o'-Women, "so long I did not see — I wud not see, but I can now, what I've lost. The time an' the place," he sez, "an' the very words I said whin ut pleased me to go off alone to hell. But thin, even thin," he sez, wrigglin' tremenjous, "I wud not ha' been happy. There was too much behind av me. How cud I ha' believed her sworn oath — me that have bruk mine again an' again for the sport av seein' thim cry? An' there are the others," he sez. "Oh, what will I do — what will I do?" He rocked back an' forward again, an' I think he was cryin' like wan av the women he talked av.

'The full half of fwhat he said was Brigade Ordhers to me, but from the rest an' the remnint I suspicioned somethin' av his throuble. 'Twas the judgemint av God had grup the heel av him, as I tould him 'twould in the Tyrone barricks. The slugs was singin' over our rock more an' more, an' I sez for to divart him: "Let bad alone," I sez. "They'll be tryin' to rush the camp in a minut'."

'I had no more than said that whin a Paythan man crep' up on his belly wid his knife betune his teeth, not twinty yards from us. Love-o'-Women jumped up an' fetched a yell, an' the man saw him an' ran at him (he'd left his rifle under the rock) wid the knife. Love-o'-Women niver turned a hair, but by the Living Power, for I saw ut, a stone twisted under the Paythan man's feet an' he came down full sprawl, an' his knife wint tinkling acrost the rocks! "I tould you I was Cain," sez Love-o'-Women. "Fwhat's the use av killin' him? He's an honest man — by compare."

'I was not dishputin' about the morils av Paythans that tide, so I dhropped Love-o'-Women's butt acrost the man's face, an' "Hurry into camp," I sez, "for this may be the first av a rush."

'There was no rush after all, though we waited undher arms to give them a chanst. The Paythan man must ha' come alone for the mischief, an' afther a while Love-o'-Women wint back to his tint wid that quare lurchin' sind-off in his walk that I cud niver understand. Begad, I pitied him, an' the more bekase he made me think for the rest av the night av the day whin I was confirmed Corp'ril, not actin' Lef'tinant, an' my thoughts was not good to me.'

'Ye can ondersthand that afther that night we came to talkin' a dale together, an' bit by bit ut came out fwhat I'd suspicioned. The whole av his carr'in's on an' divilments had come back on him hard, as liquor comes back whin you've been on the dhrink for a wake. All he'd said an' all he'd done, an' only he cud tell how much that was, come back, and there was niver a minut's peace in his sowl. 'Twas the Horrors widout any cause to see, an' yet, an' yet — fwhat am I talkin' av? He'd ha' taken' the Horrors wid thankfulness. Beyon' the repentince av the man, an' that was beyon' the nature av man — awful, awful, to behould! — there was more that was worst than any repentince. Av the scores an' scores that he called over in his mind (and they were drivin' him mad), there was, mark you, wan woman av all an' she was not his wife, that cut him to the quick av his marrow. 'Twas there he said that he'd thrown away di'monds an' pearls past count, an' thin he'd begin again like a blind *byle* in an oil-mill, walkin' round and round, to considher (him that was beyond all touch av bein' happy this side hell!) how happy he wud ha' been wid *her*. The more he considhered, the more he'd consate himself that he'd lost mighty happiness, an' thin he wud work ut all backwards, an' cry that he niver cud ha' been happy anyway.

'Time an' time again in camp, on p'rade, ay, an' in action, I've seen that man shut his eyes an' duck his head as ye wud duck to the flicker av a bay'nit. For 'twas thin, he tould me, that the thought av all he'd missed came and stud forninst him like red-hot irons. For what he'd done wid the others he was sorry, but he did not care; but this wan woman that I've tould of, by the Hilts av God, she made him pay for all the others twice over! Niver did I know that a man cud enjure such tormint widout his heart crackin' in his ribs, an' I have been' — Terence turned the pipe-stem slowly between his teeth — 'I have been in some black cells. All I iver suffered tho' was not to be talked of alongside av *him* . . . an' what could I do? Paternosters was no more than peas on plates for his sorrows.

'Evenshually we finished our prom'nade acrost the hills, and, thanks to me for the same, there was no casualties an' no glory. The campaign was comin' to an ind, an' all the rig'mints was being drawn together for to be sint back home. Love-o'-Women was mighty sorry bekaze he had no work to do, an' all his time to think in. I've heard that man talkin' to his belt-plate an' his side-arms while he was soldierin' thim, all to prevent himself from thinkin', an' ivry time he got up afther he had been settin' down or wint on from the halt, he'd start wid that kick an' traverse that I tould you of — his legs sprawlin' all ways to wanst. He wud niver go to see the docthor, tho' I tould him to be wise. He'd curse me up an' down for my advice; but I knew he was no more a man to be reckoned wid than the little bhoy was a commandin' orf'cer, so I let his tongue run if it aised him.

'Wan day — 'twas on the way back — I was walkin' round camp wid him, and he stopped an' struck ground wid his right fut three or four times doubtful. "Fwhat is ut?" I sez. "Is that ground?" sez he; an' while I was thinkin' his mind was goin', up comes the docthor, who'd been anatomisin' a dead bullock. Love-o'-Women starts to go on quick, an' lands me a kick on the knee while his legs was gettin' into marchin' ordher.

' "Hould on there," sez the docthor; an' Love-o'-Women's face, that was lined like a gridiron, turns red as brick.

' "'Tention," says the docthor; an' Love-o'-Women stud so. "Now shut your eyes," sez the docthor. "No, ye must not hould by your comrade."

' "'Tis all up," sez Love-o'-Women, thryin to smile. "I'd fall, docthor, an' you know ut."

' "Fall?" I sez. "Fall at attention wid your eyes shut! Fwhat do you mane?"

' "The docthor knows," he sez. "I've hild up as long as I can, but begad I'm glad 'tis all done. But I will die slow," he sez, "I will die very slow."

'I cud see by the docthor's face that he was mortial sorry for the man, an' he ordered him to hospital. We wint back together, an' I was dumb-struck. Love-o'-Women was cripplin' and crumblin' at ivry step. He walked wid a hand on my shoulder all slued sideways, an' his right leg swingin' like a lame camel. Me not knowin' more than the dead fwhat ailed him, 'twas just as though the docthor's word had done ut all — as if Love-o'-Women had but been waitin' for the word to let go.

'In hospital he sez somethin' to the docthor that I could not catch.

' "Holy Shmoke!" sez the docthor, "an' who are you, to be givin' names to your diseases? 'Tis agin all the reg'lations."

' "I'll not be a privit much longer," sez Love-o'-Women in his gentleman's voice, an' the docthor jumped.

' "Thrate me as a study, Doctor Lowndes," he sez; an' that was the first time I'd iver heard a docthor called his name.

' "Good-bye, Terence," sez Love-o'-Women. "'Tis a dead man I am widout the pleasure av dyin'. You'll come an' set wid me sometimes for the peace av my sowl."

'Now I had been minded to ask Crook to take me back to the Ould Rig'mint; the fightin' was over, an' I was wore out wid the ways av the bhoys in the Tyrone; but I shifted my will, an' hild on, and wint to set wid Love-o'-Women in the hospital. As I have said, sorr, the man bruk all to little pieces under my hand. How long he had hild up an' forced himself fit to march I cannot tell, but in hospital but two days later he was such as I hardly knew. I shuk hands wid him, an' his grip was fair strong, but his hands wint all ways to wanst, an' he cud not button his tunic.

' "I'll take long an' long to die yet," he sez, "for the wages av sin they're like interest in the rig'mintal savin's-bank — sure, but a damned long time bein' paid."

'The docthor sez to me, quiet one day, "Has Tighe there anythin' on his mind?" he sez. "He's burnin' himself out."

' "How shud I know, sorr?" I sez, as innocint as putty.

' "They call him Love-o'-Women in the Tyrone, do they not?" he sez. "I was a fool to ask. Be wid him all you can. He's houldin' on to your strength."

' "But fwhat ails him, docthor?" I sez.

' "They call ut Locomotus attacks us," he sez, "bekaze," sez he, "ut attacks us like a locomotive, if ye know fwhat that manes. An' ut comes," sez he, lookin' at me, "ut comes from bein' called Love-o'-Women."

' "You're jokin', docthor," I sez.

' "Jokin'!" sez he. "If iver you feel that you've got a felt sole in your boot instid av a Government bull's-wool, come to me," he sez, "an' I'll show you whether 'tis a joke."

'You would not belave ut, sorr, but that, an' seein' Love-o'-Women overtuk widout warnin', put the cowld fear av Attacks us on me so strong that for a week an' more I was kickin' my toes against stones an' stumps for the pleasure av feelin' thim hurt.

'An' Love-o'-Women lay in the cot (he might have gone down wid the wounded before an' before, but he asked to stay wid me), and fwhat there was in his mind had full swing at him night an' day an' ivry hour av the day an' night, and he shrivelled like beef-rations in a hot sun, an' his eyes was like owls' eyes, an' his hands was mut'nous.

'They was gettin' the rig'mints away wan by wan, the campaign bein' inded, but as ushuil they was behavin' as if niver a rig'mint had been moved before in the mem'ry av man. Now, fwhy is that, sorr? There's fightin', in an' out, nine months av the twelve somewhere in the army.

There has been — for years an' years an' years; an' I wud ha' thought they'd begin to get the hang av providin' for throops. But no! Ivry time 'tis like a girls' school meetin' a big red bull whin they're goin' to church; an' "Mother av God," sez the Commissariat an' the Railways an' the Barrick-masters, "fwhat will we do now?" The ordhers came to us av the Tyrone an' the Ould Rig'mint an' half a dozen more to go down, an' there the ordhers stopped dumb. We wint down, by the special grace av God — down the Khaiber anyways. There was sick wid us, an' I'm thinkin' that some av thim was jolted to death in the doolies, but they was anxious to be kilt so if they cud get to Peshawur alive the sooner. I walked by Love-o'-Women — there was no marchin', an' Love-o'-Women was not in a stew to get on. "If I'd only ha' died up there," sez he through the dooli-curtains, an' thin he'd twist up his eyes an' duck his head for the thoughts that come an' raked him.

'Dinah was in Depôt at Pindi, but I wint circumspectuous, for well I knew 'tis just at the rump-ind av all things that his luck turns on a man. By token I had seen a dhriver of a batthery goin' by at a trot singin' "Home swate home" at the top av his shout, and takin' no heed to his bridle-hand — I had seen that man dhrop under the gun in the middle of a word, and come out by the limber like — like a frog on a pavestone. No. I wud *not* hurry, though, God knows, my heart was all in Pindi. Love-o'-Women saw fwhat was in my mind, an' "Go on, Terence," he sez, "I know fwhat's waitin' for you." "I will not," I sez. "'Twill kape a little yet."

'Ye know the turn of the pass forninst Jumrood and the nine-mile road on the flat to Peshawur? All Peshawur was along that road day and night waitin' for frinds — men, women, childer, and bands. Some av the throops was camped round Jumrood, an' some wint on to Peshawur to get away down to their cantonmints. We came through in the early mornin', havin' been awake the night through, and we dhruv sheer into the middle av the mess. Mother av Glory, will I iver forget that comin' back? The light was not fair lifted, and the first we heard was "For 'tis my delight av a shiny night," frum a band that thought we was the second four comp'nies av the Lincolnshire. At that we was forced to sind them a yell to say who we was, an' thin up wint "The wearin' av the Green." It made me crawl all up my backbone, not havin' taken my brequist. Then right smash into our rear came fwhat was left av the Jock Elliott's — wid four pipers an' not half a kilt among thim, playin' for the dear life, an' swingin' their rumps like buck-rabbits, an' a native rig'mint shriekin' blue murther. Ye niver heard the like! There was men cryin' like women that did — an' faith I do not blame them! Fwhat bruk me down was the Lancers' Band — shinin' an' spick like angils, wid the ould dhrum-horse at the head an' the silver kettle-dhrums an' all an' all, waitin' for their men that was behind us. They shtruck up the Cavalry Canter; an' begad those poor ghosts that had not a

sound fut in a throop they answered to ut; the men rockin' in their saddles. We thried to cheer them as they wint by, but ut came out like a big gruntin' cough, so there must have been many that was feelin' like me. Oh, but I'm forgettin'! The Fly-by-Nights was waitin' for their second battalion, an' whin ut came out, there was the Colonel's horse led at the head — saddle empty. The men fair worshipped him, an' he'd died at Ali Musjid on the road down. They waited till the remnint av the battalion was up and thin — clane against ordhers, for who wanted *that* chune that day? — they went back to Peshawur slow-time an' tearin' the bowils out av ivry man that heard, wid "The Dead March." Right acrost our line they wint, an' ye know their uniforms are as black as the Sweeps, crawlin' past like the dead, an' the other bands damnin' them to let be.

'Little they cared. The carpse was wid them, an' they'd ha taken ut so through a Coronation. Our Ordhers was to go into Peshawur, an' we wint hot-fut past The Fly-by-Nights, not singin', to lave that chune behind us. That was how we tuk the road av the other corps.

''Twas ringin' in my ears still whin I felt in the bones of me that Dinah was comin', an' I heard a shout, an' thin I saw a horse an' a tattoo latherin' down the road, hell-to-shplit, under women. I knew — I knew! Wan was the Tyrone Colonel's wife — ould Beeker's lady — her grey hair flyin' an' her fat round carkiss rowlin' in the saddle, an' the other was Dinah, that shud ha' been at Pindi. The Colonel's lady she charged the head av our column like a stone wall, an' she all but knocked Beeker off his horse, throwin' her arms round his neck and blubberin', "Me bhoy! me bhoy!" an' Dinah wheeled left an' came down on our flank, an' I let a yell that had suffered inside av me for months and – Dinah came! Will I iver forget that while I live! She'd come on pass from Pindi, an' the Colonel's lady had lint her the tattoo. They'd been huggin' an' cryin' in each other's arms all the long night.

'So she walked along wid her hand in mine, asking forty questions to wanst, an' beggin' me on the Virgin to make oath that there was not a bullet consaled in me, unbeknownst somewhere, an' thin I remembered Love-o'-Women. He was watchin' us, an' his face was like the face av a divil that has been cooked too long. I did not wish Dinah to see ut, for whin a woman's runnin' over with happiness she's like to be touched, for harm afterwards, by the laste little thing in life. So I dhrew the curtain, an' Love-o'-Women lay back and groaned.

'Whin we marched into Peshawur Dinah wint to barricks to wait for me, an', me feelin' so rich that tide, I wint on to take Love-o'-Women to hospital. It was the last I cud do, an' to save him the dust an' the smother I turned the dooli-men down a road well clear av the rest av the throops, an' we wint along, me talkin' through the curtains. Av a sudden I heard him say:

'"Let me look. For the mercy av Hiven, let me look." I had been so tuk up wid gettin' him out av the dust an' thinkin' av Dinah that I had not kept my eyes about me. There was a woman ridin' a little behind av us; an' talkin' ut over wid Dinah afterwards, that same woman must ha' rid out far on the Jumrood road. Dinah said that she had been hoverin' like a kite on the left flank av the columns.

'I halted the dooli to set the curtains, an' she rode by, walkin' pace, an' Love-o'-Women's eyes wint afther her as if he wud fair haul her down from the saddle.

'"Follow there," was all he sez, but I niver heard a man speak in that voice before or since; an' I knew by those two wan words an' the look in his face that she was Di'monds-an'-Pearls that he'd talked av in his disthresses.

'We followed till she turned into the gate av a little house that stud near Edwardes' Gate. There was two girls in the verandah, an' they ran in whin they saw us. Faith, at long eye-range it did not take me a wink to see fwhat kind av house ut was. The throops bein' there an' all, there was three or four such; but aftherwards the polis bade thim go. At the verandah Love-o'-Women sez, catchin' his breath, "Stop here," an' thin, an' thin, wid a grunt that must ha' torn the heart up from his stomick, he swung himself out av the dooli, an' my troth he stud up on his feet wid the sweat pourin' down his face! If Mackie was to walk in here now I'd be less tuk back than I was thin. Where he'd dhrawn his power from, God knows — or the Divil — but 'twas a dead man walkin' in the sun, wid the face av a dead man and the breath av a dead man, hild up by the Power, an' the legs an' the arms av the carpse obeyin' ordhers.

'The woman stud in the verandah. She'd been a beauty too, though her

eyes was sunk in her head, an' she looked Love-o'-Women up an' down terrible. "An'," she sez, kicking back the tail av her habit, – "An'," she sez, "fwhat are you doin' *here*, married man?"

'Love-o'-Women said nothin', but a little froth came to his lips, an' he wiped ut off wid his hand an' looked at her an' the paint on her, an' looked, an' looked, an' looked.

"'An' yet," she sez, wid a laugh. (Did you hear Raines' wife laugh whin Mackie died? Ye did not? Well for you.) "An' yet," she sez, "who but you have betther right," sez she. "You taught me the road. You showed me the way," she sez. "Ay, look," she sez, "for 'tis your work; you that tould me — d'you remimber it? — that a woman who was false to wan man cud be false to two. I have been that," she sez, "that an' more, for you always said I was a quick learner, Ellis. Look well," she sez, "for it is me that you called your wife in the sight av God long since." An' she laughed.

'Love-o'-Women stud still in the sun widout answerin'. Thin he groaned an' coughed to wanst, an' I thought 'twas the death-rattle, but he niver tuk his eyes off her face, not fur a blink. Ye cud ha' put her eyelashes through the flies av an E.P. tent, they were so long.

'"Fwhat do you do here?" she sez, word by word, "that have taken away my joy in my man this five years gone — that have broken my rest an' killed my body an' damned my soul for the sake av seein' how 'twas done. Did your expayrience aftherwards bring you acrost any woman that give you more than I did? Wud I not ha' died for you, an' wid you, Ellis? Ye know that, man! If iver your lyin' sowl saw truth in uts life ye know that."

'An' Love-o'-Women lifted up his head and said, "I knew," an' that was all. While she was spakin' the Power hild him up parade-set in the sun, an' the sweat dhripped undher his helmet. 'Twas more an' more throuble for him to talk, an' his mouth was running twistways.

'"Fwhat do you do *here*?" she sez, an' her voice wint up. 'Twas like bells tollin' before. "Time was whin you were quick enough wid your words, — you that talked me down to hell. Are ye dumb now?" An' Love-o'-Women got his tongue, an' sez simple, like a little child, "May I come in?" he sez.

'"The house is open day an' night," she sez, wid a laugh; an' Love-o'-Women ducked his head an' hild up his hand as tho' he was gyardin'. The Power was on him still — it hild him up still, for, by my sowl, as I'll never save ut, he walked up the verandah steps that had been a livin' carpse in hospital for a month!

'"An' now?" she sez, lookin' at him; an' the red paint stud lone on the white av her face like a bull's eye on a target.

'He lifted up his eyes, slow an' very slow, an' he looked at her long an' very long, an' he tuk his spache betune his teeth wid a wrench that shuk him.

'"I'm dyin', Aigypt — dyin'," he sez. Ay, those were his words, for I remimber the name he called her. He was turnin' the death-colour, but his eyes niver rowled. They were set — set on her. Widout word or warnin' she opened her arms full stretch, an' "Here!" she sez. (Oh, fwhat a golden mericle av a voice ut was!) "Die here!" she sez; an' Love-o'-Women dhropped forward, an' she hild him up, for she was a fine big woman.

'I had no time to turn, bekaze that minut' I heard the sowl quit him — tore out in the death-rattle — an' she laid him back in a long chair, an' she sez to me, "Misther soldier," she sez, "will ye not wait an' talk to wan av the girls? This sun's too much for him."

'Well I knew there was no sun he'd iver see, but I cud not spake, so I wint away wid the empty dooli to find the docthor. He'd been breakfastin' an' lunchin' iver since we'd come in, an' he was as full as a tick.

'"Faith, ye've got dhrunk mighty soon," he sez, whin I'd tould him, "to see that man walk. Barrin' a puff or two av life, he was a carpse before we left Jumrood. I've a great mind," he sez, "to confine you."

'"There's a dale av liquor runnin' about, docthor," I sez, solemn as a hard-boiled egg. "Maybe 'tis so; but will ye not come and see the carpse at the house?"

'"'Tis dishgraceful," he sez, "that I would be expected to go to a place like that. Was she a pretty woman?" he sez, an' at that he set off double-quick.

'I cud see that the two was in the verandah where I'd left them, an' I knew by the hang av her head an' the noise av the crows fwhat had happened. 'Twas the first and the last time I'd iver known woman to use the pistol. They fear the shot as a rule, but Di'monds-an'-Pearls she did not — she did not.

'The doctor touched the long black hair av her head ('twas all loose upon Love-o'-Women's tunic), an' that cleared the liquor out av him. He stud considherin' a long time, his hands in his pockets, an' at last he sez to me, "Here's a double death from naturil causes, most naturil causes; an' in the present state av affairs the rig'mint will be thankful for wan grave the less to dig. *Issiwasti*," he sez. "*Issiwasti*, Privit Mulvaney, these two will be buried together in the Civil Cemet'ry at my expinse; an' may the good God," he sez, "make it so much for me whin my time comes. Go you to your wife," he sez. "Go an' be happy. I'll see to this all."

'I left him still considherin'. They was buried in the Civil Cemet'ry together, wid a Church av England service. There was too many buryin's thin to ask questions, an' the docthor — he ran away wid Major — Major Van Dyce's lady that year — he saw to ut all. Fwhat the right an' the wrong av Love-o'-Women and Di'monds-an'-Pearls was I niver knew, an' I will niver know; but I've tould ut as I came acrost ut — here an' there in little pieces. *So*, being fwhat I am, an' knowing fwhat I knew, that's fwhy I say in this shootin'-case here, Mackie that's dead an' in hell is the lucky man. There are times, sorr, whin 'tis better for the man to die than to live, an' by consequince forty million times betther for the woman.'

'H'up there!' said Ortheris. 'It's time to go.'

The witness and guard formed up in the thick white dust of the parched twilight and swung off, marching easy and whistling. Down the road to the green by the church I could hear Ortheris, the black Book-lie still uncleansed on his lips, setting, with a fine sense of the fitness of things, the shrill quickstep that runs —

'Oh, do not despise the advice of the wise,
  Learn wisdom from those that are older,
And don't try for things that are out of your reach —
An' that's what the Girl told the Soldier!
  Soldier! soldier!
Oh, that's what the Girl told the Soldier!'

PART
V
IN BLACK
AND WHITE

Nothing fascinated the young Kipling more than taboos and the breaking of them – and in his day no taboo was as strong as that of race. So it is no surprise that two of his most powerful stories should take the breaking of racial barriers as their theme. It is also significant that he chose to open his selection of *Plain Tales from the Hills* stories with a tart little tale about a missionary couple's hypocritical treatment of the adopted hill-woman christened 'Lispeth'. Did Kipling put 'Lispeth' first for effect or was it intended to set the tone for the other stories that followed? Lispeth's fate certainly concerned him enough for him to revise her circumstances twelve years later when she reappeared in *Kim* as 'the woman from Shamlegh', no longer a ravaged old drunk but a well-preserved ruler of her own people.

'Beyond the Pale' and 'Without Benefit of Clergy' are both about love across the racial divide and so well do they complement each other that it was extremely difficult to exclude or reject one in favour of the other. The first is very much a product of Rudyard's early years in India, the second the work of the mature artist writing without the constraints that bound him in Lahore and Allahabad but 'Without Benefit of Clergy' is twice as long – and so it had to go. Mawkish it may be – Kipling could be horribly sentimental – but it is still a most tender love story that should be compulsory reading for anyone who considers Kipling a commited rascist. 'Beyond the Pale' is less straightforward. Just as the well-known lines of Kipling's 'Ballad of East and West' about 'the twain' never meeting are consistently misinterpreted as being about the impossibility of understanding between the races, so the opening sentences of 'Beyond the Pale' are taken literally as evidence of the author's racism. This is to ignore the fact that Kipling's sympathies lie always with the breakers of the taboo – even when he seems to support the taboo.

One more story abut the crossing of racial barriers also deserves a place in this section – if only as an antidote to the previous two. 'On the City Wall' also deals with sex across the divide but that is only part of what is the most openly political of Kipling's Indian tales. The setting is Lahore City at the time of the Muslim festival of Mohurrum, when tall wood and paper structures called *tazias* were carried in procession through the streets by the faithful. This was always a trying occasion for the authorities since these processions frequently led to outbreaks of inter-communal rioting. One such Mohurrum riot – which Rudyard witnessed and reported on – took place in Lahore in September 1885.

Again, Kipling's sympathies are with the Indians who so thoroughly outwit the narrator of the story, although he makes it quite clear that any idea of India ever 'standing alone' without British administration is an absurd dream, albeit a 'pretty one'. Along with his British contemporaries in India he had a very low opinion of Indian accomplishments – and these views he never abandoned.

LISPETH

SHE WAS THE daughter of Sonoo, a Hill-man of the Himalayas, and Jadéh his wife. One year their maize failed, and two bears spent the night in their only opium poppy-field just above the Sutlej Valley on the Kotgarh side; so, next season, they turned Christian, and brought their baby to the Mission to be baptized. The Kotgarh Chaplain christened her Elizabeth, and 'Lispeth' is the Hill or *pahari* pronunciation.

Later, cholera came into the Kotgarh Valley and carried off Sonoo and Jadéh, and Lispeth became half servant, half companion, to the wife of the then Chaplain of Kotgarh. This was after the reign of the Moravian missionaries in that place, but before Kotgarh had quite forgotten her title of 'Mistress of the Northern Hills.'

Whether Christianity improved Lispeth, or whether the gods of her own people would have done as much for her under any circumstances, I do not know; but she grew very lovely. When a Hill-girl grows lovely, she is worth travelling fifty miles over bad ground to look upon. Lispeth had a Greek face — one of those faces people paint so often, and see so seldom. She was of a pale, ivory colour, and, for her race, extremely tall. Also, she possessed eyes that were wonderful; and, had she not been dressed in the abominable print-cloths affected by Missions, you would, meeting her on the hillside unexpectedly, have thought her the original Diana of the Romans going out to slay.

Lispeth took to Christianity readily, and did not abandon it when she reached womanhood, as do some Hill-girls. Her own people hated her because she had, they said, become a white woman and washed herself daily; and the Chaplain's wife did not know what to do with her. One cannot ask a stately goddess, five feet ten in her shoes, to clean plates and dishes. She played with the Chaplain's children and took classes in the Sunday School, and read all the books in the house, and grew more and more beautiful, like the Princesses in fairy tales. The Chaplain's wife said that the girl ought to take service in Simla as a nurse or something 'genteel.' But Lispeth did not want to take service. She was very happy where she was.

When travellers — there were not many in those years — came in to Kotgarh, Lispeth used to lock herself into her own room for fear they

might take her away to Simla, or out into the unknown world.

One day, a few months after she was seventeen years old, Lispeth went out for a walk. She did not walk in the manner of English ladies — a mile and a half out, with a carriage-ride back again. She covered between twenty and thirty miles in her little constitutionals, all about and about, between Kotgarh and Narkunda. This time she came back at full dusk, stepping down the break-neck descent into Kotgarh with something heavy in her arms. The Chaplain's wife was dozing in the drawing-room when Lispeth came in breathing heavily and very exhausted with her burden. Lispeth put it down on the sofa, and said simply, 'This is my husband. I found him on the Bagi Road. He has hurt himself. We will nurse him, and when he is well your husband shall marry him to me.'

This was the first mention Lispeth had ever made of her matrimonial views, and the Chaplain's wife shrieked with horror. However, the man on the sofa needed attention first. He was a young Englishman, and his head had been cut to the bone by something jagged. Lispeth said she had found him down the hillside, and had brought him in. He was breathing queerly and was unconscious.

He was put to bed and tended by the Chaplain, who knew something of medicine; and Lispeth waited outside the door in case she could be useful. She explained to the Chaplain that this was the man she meant to marry; and the Chaplain and his wife lectured her severely on the impropriety of her conduct. Lispeth listened quietly, and repeated her first proposition. It takes a great deal of Christianity to wipe out uncivilised Eastern instincts, such as falling in love at first sight. Lispeth, having found the man she worshipped, did not see why she should keep silent as to her choice. She had no intention of being sent away, either. She was going to nurse that Englishman until he was well enough to marry her. This was her programme.

After a fortnight of slight fever and inflammation, the Englishman recovered coherence and thanked the Chaplain and his wife, and Lispeth — especially Lispeth — for their kindness. He was a traveller in the East, he said — they never talked about 'globe-trotters' in those days, when the P. & O. fleet was young and small — and had come from Dehra Dun to hunt for plants and butterflies among the Simla hills. No one at Simla, therefore, knew anything about him. He fancied that he must have fallen over the cliff while reaching out for a fern on a rotten tree-trunk, and that his coolies must have stolen his baggage and fled. He thought he would go back to Simla when he was a little stronger. He desired no more mountaineering.

He made small haste to go away, and recovered his strength slowly. Lispeth objected to being advised either by the Chaplain or his wife; therefore the latter spoke to the Englishman, and told him how matters stood in Lispeth's heart. He laughed a good deal, and said it was very pretty and romantic, but, as he was engaged to a girl at Home, he fancied that nothing would happen. Certainly he would behave with discretion. He did that. Still he found it very pleasant to talk to Lispeth, and walk with Lispeth, and say nice things to her, and call her pet names while he was getting strong enough to go away. It meant nothing at all to him, and everything in the world to Lispeth. She was very happy while the fortnight lasted, because she had found a man to love.

Being a savage by birth, she took no trouble to hide her feelings, and the Englishman was amused. When he went away, Lispeth walked with him up the Hill as far as Narkunda, very troubled and very miserable. The Chaplain's wife, being a good Christian and disliking anything in the shape of fuss or scandal — Lispeth was beyond her management entirely — had told the Englishman to tell Lispeth that he was coming back to marry her. 'She is but a child, you know, and, I fear, at heart a heathen,' said the Chaplain's wife. So all the twelve miles up the Hill the Englishman, with his arm round Lispeth's waist, was assuring the girl that he would come back and marry her; and Lispeth made him promise over and over again. She wept on the Narkunda Ridge till he had passed out of sight along the Muttiani path.

Then she dried her tears and went in to Kotgarh again, and said to the Chaplain's wife, 'He will come back and marry me. He has gone to his own people to tell them so.' And the Chaplain's wife soothed Lispeth and said, 'He will come back.' At the end of two months Lispeth grew impatient, and was told that the Englishman had gone over the seas to England. She knew where England was, because she had read little geography primers; but, of course, she had no conception of the nature of the sea, being a Hill-girl. There was an old puzzle-map of the World in the house. Lispeth had played with it when she was a child. She unearthed it again, and put it together of evenings, and cried to herself, and tried to imagine where her Englishman was. As she had no idea of distance or steamboats her notions were somewhat wild. It would not have made the least difference had she been perfectly correct; for the Englishman had no intention of coming back to marry a Hill-girl. He forgot all about her by the time he was butterfly-hunting in Assam. He wrote a book on the East afterwards. Lispeth's name did not appear there.

At the end of three months Lispeth made daily pilgrimage to Narkunda to see if her Englishman was coming along the road. It gave her comfort, and the Chaplain's wife finding her happier thought she was getting over her 'barbarous and most indelicate folly.' A little later the walks ceased to help Lispeth, and her temper grew very bad. The Chaplain's wife thought this a profitable time to let her know the real state of affairs — that the Englishman had only promised his love to keep her quiet — that he had never meant anything, and that it was wrong and improper of Lispeth to think of marriage with an Englishman, who was of a superior clay, besides being promised in marriage to a girl of his own people. Lispeth said that all this was clearly impossible because he had said he loved her, and the Chaplain's wife had, with her own lips, asserted that the Englishman was coming back.

'How can what he and you said be untrue?' asked Lispeth.

'We said it as an excuse to keep you quiet, child,' said the Chaplain's wife.

'Then you have lied to me,' said Lispeth, ' you and he?'

The Chaplain's wife bowed her head, and said nothing. Lispeth was silent too for a little time; then she went out down the valley, and returned in the dress of a Hill-girl — infamously dirty, but without the nose-stud and ear-rings. She had her hair braided into the long pigtail, helped out with black thread, that Hill-women wear.

'I am going back to my own people,' said she. 'You have killed Lispeth. There is only left old Jadéh's daughter — the daughter of a *pahari* and the servant of *Tarka Devi*. You are all liars, you English.'

By the time that the Chaplain's wife had recovered from the shock of the announcement that Lispeth had 'verted to her mother's gods the girl had gone; and she never came back.

She took to her own unclean people savagely, as if to make up the arrears of the life she had stepped out of; and, in a little time, she married a woodcutter who beat her after the manner of *paharis*, and her beauty faded soon.

'There is no law whereby you can account for the vagaries of the heathen,' said the Chaplain's wife, 'and I believe that Lispeth was always at heart an infidel.' Seeing that she had been taken into the Church of England at the mature age of five weeks, this statement does not do credit to the Chaplain's wife.

Lispeth was a very old woman when she died. She had always a perfect command of English, and when she was sufficiently drunk could sometimes be induced to tell the story of her first love-affair.

It was hard then to realise that the bleared, wrinkled creature, exactly like a wisp of charred rag, could ever have been 'Lispeth of the Kotgarh Mission.'

BEYOND THE PALE

A MAN SHOULD, whatever happens, keep to his own caste, race, and breed. Let the White go to the White and the Black to the Black. Then, whatever trouble falls is in the ordinary course of things — neither sudden, alien, nor unexpected.

This is the story of a man who wilfully stepped beyond the safe limits of decent everyday society, and paid for it heavily.

He knew too much in the first instance; and he saw too much in the second. He took too deep an interest in native life; but he will never do so again.

Deep away in the heart of the City, behind Jitha Megji's *bustee*, lies Amir Nath's Gully, which ends in a dead-wall pierced by one grated window. At the head of the Gully is a big cowbyre, and the walls on either side of the Gully are without windows. Neither Suchet Singh nor Gaur Chand approve of their women-folk looking into the world. If Durga Charan had been of their opinion he would have been a happier man today, and little Bisesa would have been able to knead her own bread. Her room looked out through the grated window into the narrow dark Gully where the sun never came and where the buffaloes wallowed in the blue slime. She was a widow, about fifteen years old, and she prayed the Gods, day and night, to send her a lover; for she did not approve of living alone.

One day, the man — Trejago his name was — came into Amir Nath's Gully on an aimless wandering; and, after he had passed the buffaloes, stumbled over a big heap of cattle-food.

Then he saw that the Gully ended in a trap, and heard a little laugh from behind the grated window. It was a pretty little laugh, and Trejago, knowing that, for all practical purposes, the old *Arabian Nights* are good guides, went forward to the window, and whispered the verse of 'The Love Song of Har Dyal' which begins: —

> Can a man stand upright in the face of the naked Sun;
> or a Lover in the Presence of his Beloved?
> If my feet fail me, O Heart of my Heart, am I to blame,
> being blinded by the glimpse of your beauty?

There came the faint *tchink* of a woman's bracelets from behind the grating, and a little voice went on with the song at the fifth verse: —

Alas! alas! Can the Moon tell the Lotus of her love
when the Gate of Heaven is shut and the clouds gather for the rains?
They have taken my Beloved, and driven her with the pack-horses to the North.
There are iron chains on the feet that were set on my heart.
Call to the bowmen to make ready —

The voice stopped suddenly, and Trejago walked out of Amir Nath's Gully, wondering who in the world could have capped 'The Love Song of Har Dyal!' so neatly.

Next morning, as he was driving to office, an old woman threw a packet into his dogcart. In the packet was the half of a broken glass-bangle, one flower of the blood-red *dhak*, a pinch of *bhusa* or cattle-food, and eleven cardamoms. That packet was a letter — not a clumsy compromising letter, but an innocent unintelligible lover's epistle.

Trejago knew far too much about these things, as I have said. No Englishman should be able to translate object-letters. But Trejago spread all the trifles on the lid of his office-box and began to puzzle them out.

A broken glass-bangle stands for a Hindu widow all India over; because when her husband dies, a woman's bracelets are broken on her wrists. Trejago saw the meaning of the little bit of the glass. The flower of the *dhak* means diversely 'desire,' 'come,' 'write,' or 'danger,' according to the other things with it. One cardamom means 'jealousy'; but when any article is duplicated in an object-letter, it loses its symbolic meaning and stands merely for one of a number indicating time, or, if incense, curds, or saffron be sent also, place. The message ran then — 'A widow — *dhak* flower and *bhusa*, — at eleven o'clock.' He saw — this kind of letter leaves much to instinctive knowledge — that the *bhusa* referred to the big heap of cattle-food over which he had fallen in Amir Nath's Gully, and that the message must come from the person behind the grating; she being a widow. So the message ran then — 'A widow, in the Gully in which there is the heap of *bhusa*, desires you to come at eleven o'clock.'

Trejago threw all the rubbish into the fireplace and laughed. He knew that men in the East do not make love under windows at eleven in the forenoon, nor do women fix appointments a week in advance. So he went, that very night at eleven, into Amir Nath's Gully, clad in a *boorka*, which cloaks a man as well as a woman. Directly the gongs of the City made the hour, the little voice behind the grating took up 'The Love Song of Har Dyal' at the verse where the Pathan girl calls upon Har Dyal to return. The song is really pretty in the Vernacular. In English you miss the wail of it. It runs something like this:—

Alone upon the housetops, to the North
I turn and watch the lightning in the sky,—

The glamour of thy footsteps in the North,
Come back to me, Beloved, or I die!

Below my feet the still bazar is laid,
Far, far, below the weary camels lie,—
The camels and the captives of thy raid.
Come back to me, Beloved, or I die!

My father's wife is old and harsh with years,
And drudge of all my father's house am I.—
My bread is sorrow and my drink is tears,
Come back to me, Beloved, or I die!

As the song stopped, Trejago stepped up under the grating and whispered — 'I am here.'

Bisesa was good to look upon.

That night was the beginning of many strange things, and of a double life so wild that Trejago today sometimes wonders if it were not all a dream. Bisesa, or her old handmaiden who had thrown the object-letter, had detached the heavy grating from the brick-work of the wall; so that the window slid inside, leaving only a square of raw masonry into which an active man might climb.

In the day-time, Trejago drove through his routine of office-work, or put on his calling clothes and called on the ladies of the Station, wondering how long they would know him if they knew of poor little Bisesa. At night, when all the City was still, came the walk under the evil-smelling *boorka*, the patrol through Jitha Megji's *bustee*, the quick turn into Amir Nath's Gully between the sleeping cattle and the dead walls, and then, last of all, Bisesa, and the deep, even breathing of the old woman who slept outside the door of the bare little room that Durga Charan allotted to his sister's daughter. Who or what Durga Charan was, Trejago never inquired; and why in the world he was not discovered and knifed never occurred to him till his madness was over, and Bisesa . . . But this comes later.

Bisesa was an endless delight to Trejago. She was as ignorant as a bird; and her distorted versions of the rumours from the outside world, that had reached her in her room, amused Trejago almost as much as her lisping attempts to pronounce his name — 'Christopher.' The first syllable was always more than she could manage, and she made funny little gestures with her roseleaf hands, as one throwing the name away, and then, kneeling before Trejago, asked him, exactly as an Englishwoman would do, if he were sure he loved her. Trejago swore that he loved her. Trejago swore that he loved her more than anyone else in the world. Which was true.

After a month of this folly, the exigencies of his other life compelled Trejago to be especially attentive to a lady of his acquaintance. You may take it for a fact that anything of this kind is not only noticed and discussed by a man's own race, but by some hundred and fifty natives as well. Trejago had to walk with this lady and talk to her at the band-stand, and once or twice to drive with her; never for an instant dreaming that this would affect his dearer, out-of-the-way life. But the news flew, in the usual mysterious fashion, from mouth to mouth, till Bisesa's duenna heard of it and told Bisesa. The child was so troubled that she did the housework evilly, and was beaten by Durga Charan's wife in consequence.

A week later Bisesa taxed Trejago with the flirtation. She understood no gradations and spoke openly. Trejago laughed, and Bisesa stamped her little feet — little feet, light as marigold flowers, that could lie in the palm of a man's one hand.

Much that is written about Oriental passion and impulsiveness is exaggerated and compiled at second-hand, but a little of it is true; and when an Englishman finds that little, it is quite as startling as any passion in his own proper life. Bisesa raged and stormed, and finally threatened to kill herself if Trejago did not at once drop the alien Memsahib who had come between them. Trejago tried to explain, and to show her that she did not understand these things from a Western standpoint. Bisesa drew herself up, and said simply —

'I do not. I know only this — it is not good that I should have made you dearer than my own heart to me, Sahib. You are an Englishman. I am only a black girl' — she was fairer than bar-gold in the Mint, — 'and the widow of a black man.'

Then she sobbed and said — 'But on my soul and my Mother's soul, I love you. There shall be no harm come to you, whatever happens to me.'

Trejago argued with the child, and tried to soothe her, but she seemed quite unreasonably disturbed. Nothing would satisfy her save that all relations between them should end. He was to go away at once. And he went. As he dropped out of the window, she kissed his forehead twice, and he walked home wondering.

A week, and then three weeks, passed without a sign from Bisesa. Trejago, thinking that the rupture had lasted quite long enough, went down to Amir Nath's Gully for the fifth time in three weeks, hoping that his rap at the sill of the shifting grating would be answered. He was not disappointed.

There was a young moon, and one stream of light fell down into Amir Nath's Gully, and struck the grating which was drawn away as he knocked. From the black dark Bisesa held out her arms in the moonlight. Both hands had been cut off at the wrists, and the stumps were nearly healed.

Then, as Bisesa bowed her head between her arms and sobbed, some one in the room grunted like a wild beast, and something sharp — knife, sword, or spear, — thrust at Trejago in his *boorka*. The stroke missed his body, but cut into one of the muscles of the groin, and he limped slightly from the wound for the rest of his days.

The grating went into its place. There was no sign whatever from inside the house, — nothing but the moonlight strip on the high wall, and the blackness of Amir Nath's Gully behind.

The next thing Trejago remembers, after raging and shouting like a madman between those pitiless walls, is that he found himself near the river as the dawn was breaking, threw away his *boorka* and went home bareheaded.

What was the tragedy — whether Bisesa had, in a fit of causeless despair, told everything, or the intrigue had been discovered and she tortured to tell; whether Durga Charan knew his name; and what became of Bisesa — Trejago does not know to this day. Something horrible had happened, and the thought of what it must have been comes upon Trejago in the night now and again, and keeps him company till the morning. One special feature of the case is that he does not know where lies the front of Durga Charan's house. It may open on to a courtyard common to two or more houses, or it may lie behind any one of the gates of Jitha Megji's *bustee*. Trejago cannot tell. He cannot get Bisesa — poor little Bisesa — back again. He has lost her in the City where each man's house is as guarded and as unknowable as the grave; and the grating that opens into Amir Nath's Gully has been walled up.

But Trejago pays his calls regularly, and is reckoned a very decent sort of man.

There is nothing peculiar about him, except a slight stiffness, caused by a riding-strain, in the right leg.

ON THE CITY WALL

LALUN IS A member of the most ancient profession in the world. Lilith was her very-great-grandmamma, and that was before the days of Eve, as every one knows. In the West, people say rude things about Lalun's profession, and write lectures about it, and distribute the lectures to young persons in order that Morality may be preserved. In the East, where the profession is hereditary, descending from mother to daughter, nobody writes lectures or takes any notice; and that is a distinct proof of the inability of the East to manage its own affairs.

Lalun's real husband, for even ladies of Lalun's profession in the East must have husbands, was a big jujube-tree. Her Mamma, who had married a fig-tree, spent ten thousand rupees on Lalun's wedding, which was blessed by forty-seven clergymen of Mamma's Church, and distributed five thousand rupees in charity to the poor. And that was the custom of the land. The advantages of having a jujube-tree for a husband are obvious. You cannot hurt his feelings, and he looks imposing.

Lalun's husband stood on the plain outside the City walls, and Lalun's house was upon the east wall facing the river. If you fell from the broad window-seat you dropped thirty feet sheer into the City Ditch. But if you stayed where you should and looked forth, you saw all the cattle of the City being driven down to water, the students of the Government College playing cricket, the high grass and trees that fringed the river-bank, the great sand-bars that ribbed the river, the red tombs of dead Emperors beyond the river, and very far away through the blue heat-haze a glint of the snows of the Himalayas.

Wali Dad used to lie in the window-seat for hours at a time watching this view. He was a young Muhammadan who was suffering acutely from education of the English variety and knew it. His father had sent him to a Mission-school to get wisdom, and Wali Dad had absorbed more than ever his father or the Missionaries intended he should. When his father died, Wali Dad was independent and spent two years experimenting with the creeds of the Earth and reading books that are of no use to anybody.

After he had made an unsuccessful attempt to enter the Roman Catholic Church and the Presbyterian fold at the same time (the Missionaries found him out and called him names, but they did not understand his trouble), he discovered Lalun on the City wall and became the most constant of her few admirers. He possessed a head that English artists at home would rave over and paint amid impossible surroundings — a face that female novelists would use with delight through nine hundred pages. In reality he was only a clean-bred young Muhammadan, with pencilled eyebrows, small-cut nostrils, little feet and hands, and a very tired look in his eyes. By virtue of his twenty-two years he had grown a neat black beard which he stroked with pride and kept delicately scented. His life seemed to be divided between borrowing books from me and making love to Lalun in the window-seat. He composed songs about her, and some of the songs are sung to this day in the City from the Street of the Mutton-Butchers to the Copper-Smiths' ward.

One song, the prettiest of all, says that the beauty of Lalun was so great that it troubled the hearts of the British Government and caused them to lose their peace of mind. That is the way the song is sung in the streets; but, if you examine it carefully and know the key to the explanation, you will find that there are three puns in it — on 'beauty,' 'heart,' and 'peace of mind,' — so that it runs: 'By subtlety of Lalun the administration of the Government was troubled and it lost such and such a man.' When Wali Dad sings that song his eyes glow like hot coals, and Lalun leans back among the cushions and throws bunches of jasmine-buds at Wali Dad.

But first it is necessary to explain something about the Supreme Government which is above all and below all and behind all. Gentlemen come from England, spend a few weeks in India, walk round this great Sphinx of the Plains, and write books upon its ways and its works, denouncing or praising it as their own ignorance prompts. Consequently all the world knows how the Supreme Government conducts itself. But no one, not even the Supreme Government, knows everything about the administration of the Empire. Year by year England sends out fresh drafts for the first fighting-line, which is officially called the Indian Civil Service. These die, or kill themselves by overwork, or are worried to death, or broken in health and hope in order that the land may be protected from death and sickness, famine and war, and may eventually become capable of standing alone. It will never stand alone, but the idea is a pretty one, and men are willing to die for it, and yearly the work of pushing and coaxing and scolding and petting the country into good living goes forward. If an advance be made all credit is given to the native, while the Englishmen stand back and wipe their foreheads. If a failure occurs the Englishmen step forward and take the blame. Overmuch tenderness of this kind has bred a strong belief among many natives that the native is capable of administering the country, and many devout Englishmen believe this also, because the theory is stated in beautiful English with all the latest political colour.

There be other men who, though uneducated, see visions and dream dreams, and they, too, hope to administer the country in their own way — that is to say, with a garnish of Red Sauce. Such men must exist among two hundred million people, and, if they are not attended to, may cause trouble and even break the great idol called *Pax Britannica*, which, as the newspapers say, lives between Peshawar and Cape Comorin. Were the Day of Doom to dawn tomorrow, you would find the Supreme Government 'taking measures to allay popular excitement,' and putting guards upon the graveyards that the Dead might troop forth orderly. The youngest Civilian would arrest Gabriel on his own responsibility if the Archangel could not produce a Deputy Commissioner's permission to 'make music or other noises' as the licence says.

Whence it is easy to see that mere men of the flesh who would create a tumult must fare badly at the hands of the Supreme Government. And they do. There is no outward sign of excitement; there is no confusion; there is no knowledge. When due and sufficient reasons have been given, weighed and approved, the machinery moves forward, and the dreamer of dreams and the seer of visions is gone from his friends and following. He enjoys the hospitality of Government; there is no restriction upon his movements within certain limits; but he must not confer any more with his brother dreamers. Once in every six months the Supreme Government assures itself that he is well and takes formal acknowledgement of his existence. No one protests against his detention, because the few people who know about it are in deadly fear of seeming to know him; and never a single newspaper 'takes up his case' or organises demonstrations on his behalf, because the newspapers of India have got behind that lying proverb which says the Pen is mightier than the Sword, and can walk delicately.

So now you know as much as you ought about Wali Dad, the educational mixture, and the Supreme Government.

Lalun has not yet been described. She would need, so Wali Dad says, a thousand pens of gold and ink scented with musk. She has been variously compared to the Moon, the Dil Sagar Lake, a spotted quail, a gazelle, the Sun on the Desert of Kutch, the Dawn, the Stars, and the young bamboo. These comparisons imply that she is beautiful exceedingly according to the native standards, which are practically the same as those of the West. Her eyes are black and her hair is black, and her eyebrows are as black as leeches; her mouth is tiny and says witty things; her hands are tiny and have saved much money; her feet are tiny and have trodden on the naked hearts of many men. But, as Wali Dad sings: 'Lalun *is* Lalun, and when you have said that, you have only come to the Beginnings of Knowledge.'

The little house on the City wall was just big enough to hold Lalun, and her maid, and a pussy-cat with a silver collar. A big pink and blue cut-glass

chandelier hung from the ceiling of the reception room. A petty Nawab had given Lalun the horror, and she kept it for politeness' sake. The floor of the room was of polished *chunam*, white as curds. A latticed window of carved wood was set in one wall; there was a profusion of squabby pluffy cushions and fat carpets everywhere, and Lalun's silver *huqa*, studded with turquoises, had a special little carpet all to its shining self. Wali Dad was nearly as permanent a fixture as the chandelier. As I have said, he lay in the window-seat and meditated on Life and Death and Lalun — specially Lalun. The feet of the young men of the City tended to her doorways and then — retired, for Lalun was a particular maiden, slow of speech, reserved of mind, and not in the least inclined to orgies which were nearly certain to end in strife. 'If I am of no value, I am unworthy of this honour,' said Lalun. 'If I am of value, they are unworthy of Me.' And that was a crooked sentence.

In the long hot nights of latter April and May all the City seemed to assemble in Lalun's little white room to smoke and to talk. Shiahs of the grimmest and most uncompromising persuasion; Sufis who had lost all belief in the Prophet and retained but little in God; wandering Hindu priests passing southward on their way to the Central India fairs and other

affairs; Pundits in black gowns, with spectacles on their noses and undigested wisdom in their insides; bearded head-men of the wards; Sikhs with all the details of the latest ecclesiastical scandal in the Golden Temple; red-eyed priests from beyond the Border, looking like trapped wolves and talking like ravens; M.A.'s of the University, very superior and very voluble — all these people and more also you might find in the white room. Wali Dad lay in the window-seat and listened to the talk.

'It is Lalun's *salon*,' said Wali Dad to me, 'and it is electic — is not that the word? Outside of a Freemasons' Lodge I have never seen such gatherings. *There* I dined once with a Jew — a Yahoudi!' He spat into the City Ditch with apologies for allowing national feelings to overcome him. 'Though I have lost every belief in the world,' said he, 'and try to be proud of my losing, I cannot help hating a Jew. Lalun admits no Jews here.'

'But what in the world do all these men do?' I asked.

'The curse of our country,' said Wali Dad. 'They talk. It is like the Athenians — always hearing and telling some new thing. Ask the Pearl and she will show you how much she knows of the news of the City and the Province. Lalun knows everything.'

'Lalun,' I said at random — she was talking to a gentleman of the Kurd persuasion who had come in from God-knows-where — 'when does the 175th Regiment go to Agra?'

'It does not go at all,' said Lalun, without turning her head. 'They have ordered the 118th to go in its stead. That Regiment goes to Lucknow in three months, unless they give a fresh order.'

'That is so,' said Wali Dad, without a shade of doubt. 'Can you, with your telegrams and your newspapers, do better? Always hearing and telling some new thing,' he went on. 'My friend, has your God ever smitten a European nation for gossiping in the bazars? India has gossiped for centuries — always standing in the bazars until the soldiers go by. Therefore — you are here today instead of starving in your own country, and I am not a Muhammadan — I am a Product — a Demnition Product. That also I owe to you and yours: that I cannot make an end to my sentence without quoting from your authors.' He pulled at the *huqa* and mourned, half feelingly, half in earnest, for the shattered hopes of his youth. Wali Dad was always mourning over something or other — the country of which he despaired, or the creed in which he had lost faith, or the life of the English which he could by no means understand.

Lalun never mourned. She played little songs on the *sitar*, and to hear her sing, '*O Peacock, cry again*,' was always a fresh pleasure. She knew all the songs that have ever been sung, from the war songs of the South, that make the old men angry with the young men and the young men angry with the State, to the love-songs of the North, where the swords whinny-whicker like angry kites in the pauses between the kisses, and the Passes fill with armed men, and the Lover is torn from his Beloved and cries, *Ai! Ai! Ai!* evermore. She knew how to make up tobacco for the *huqa* so that it smelt like the Gates of Paradise and wafted you gently through them. She could embroider strange things in gold and silver, and dance softly with the moonlight when it came in at the window. Also she knew the hearts of men, and the heart of the City, and whose wives were faithful and whose untrue, and more of the secrets of the Government Offices than are good to be set down in this place. Nasiban, her maid, said that her jewelry was worth ten thousand pounds, and that, some night, a thief would enter and murder her for its possession; but Lalun said that all the City would tear the thief limb from limb, and that he, whoever he was, knew it.

So she took her *sitar* and sat in the window-seat, and sang a song of old days that had been sung by a girl of her profession in an armed camp on the eve of a great battle — the day before the Fords of the Jumna ran red and Sivaji fled fifty miles to Delhi with a Toorkh stallion at his horse's tail and another Lalun on his saddle-bow. It was what men called a Mahratta *laonee*, and it said: —

Their warrior forces Chimnajee
Before the Peishwa led,
The Children of the Sun and Fire
Behind him turned and fled.

And the chorus said: —

With them there fought who rides so free
With sword and turban red,
The warrior-youth who earns his fee
At peril of his head.

'At peril of his head,' said Wali Dad in English to me. 'Thanks to your Government, all our heads are protected, and with the educational facilities at my command' — his eyes twinkled wickedly — 'I might be a distinguished member of the local administration. Perhaps, in time, I might even be a member of a Legislative Council.'

'Don't speak English,' said Lalun, bending over her *sitar* afresh. The chorus went out from the City wall to the blackened wall of Fort Amara which dominates the City. No man knows the precise extent of Fort Amara. Three kings built it hundreds of years ago, and they say that there are miles of underground rooms beneath its walls. It is peopled with many ghosts, a detachment of Garrison Artillery, and a Company of Infantry. In its prime it held ten thousand men and filled its ditches with corpses.

'At peril of his head,' sang Lalun again and again.

A head moved on one of the ramparts — the gray head of an old man — and a voice, rough as shark-skin on a sword-hilt, sent back the last line of the chorus and broke into a song that I could not understand, though Lalun and Wali Dad listened intently.

'What is it?' I asked. 'Who is it?'

'A consistent man,' said Wali Dad. 'He fought you in '46, when he was a warrior-youth; refought you in '57, and he tried to fight you in '71, but you had learned the trick of blowing men from guns too well. Now he is old; but he would still fight if he could.'

'Is he a Wahabi, then? Why should he answer to a Mahratta *laonee* if he be Wahabi — or Sikh?' said I.

'I do not know,' said Wali Dad. 'He has lost, perhaps, his religion. Perhaps he wishes to be a King. Perhaps he is a King. I do not know his name.'

'That is a lie, Wali Dad. If you know his career you must know his name.'

'That is quite true. I belong to a nation of liars. I would rather not tell you his name. Think for yourself.'

Lalun finished her song, pointed to the Fort, and said simply: 'Khem Singh.'

'Hm,' said Wali Dad. 'If the Pearl chooses to tell you the Pearl is a fool.'

I translated to Lalun, who laughed. 'I choose to tell what I choose to tell. They kept Khem Singh in Burma,' said she. 'They kept him there for many years until his mind was changed in him. So great was the kindness of the Government. Finding this, they sent him back to his own country that he might look upon it before he died. He is an old man, but when he looks upon this his country his memory will come. Moreover, there be many who remember him.'

'He is an Interesting Survival,' said Wali Dad, pulling at the *huqa*. 'He returns to a country now full of educational and political reform, but, as the Pearl says, there are many who remember him. He was once a great man. There will never be any more great men in India. They will all, when they are boys, go whoring after strange gods, and they will become citizens—"fellow-citizens" — "illustrious fellow-citizens." What is it that the native papers call them?'

Wali Dad seemed to be in a very bad temper. Lalun looked out of the window and smiled into the dust-haze. I went away thinking about Khem Singh who had once made history with a thousand followers, and would have been a princeling but for the power of the Supreme Government aforesaid.

The Senior Captain Commanding Fort Amara was away on leave, but the Subaltern, his Deputy, had drifted down to the Club, where I found him and inquired of him whether it was really true that a political prisoner had been added to the attractions of the Fort. The Subaltern explained at great length, for this was the first time that he had held Command of the Fort, and his glory lay heavy upon him.

'Yes,' said he, 'a man was sent in to me about a week ago from down the line — a thorough gentleman, whoever he is. Of course I did all I could for him. He had his two servants and some silver cooking-pots, and he looked for all the world like a native officer. I called him Subadar Sahib; just as well to be on the safe side, y'know. "Look here, Subadar Sahib," I said, "you're handed over to my authority, and I'm supposed to guard you. Now I don't want to make your life hard, but you must make things easy for me. All the Fort is at your disposal, from the flagstaff to the dry ditch, and I shall be happy to entertain you in any way I can, but you mustn't take advantage of it. Give me your word that you won't try to escape, Subadar Sahib, and I'll give you my word that you shall have no heavy guard put over you." I thought the best way of getting at him was by going at him straight, y'know; and it was, by Jove! The old man gave me his word, and moved about the Fort as contented as a sick crow. He's a rummy chap — always asking to be told where he is and what the buildings about him are. I had to sign a slip of blue paper when he turned up, acknowledging receipt of his body and all that, and I'm responsible, y'know, that he doesn't get away. Queer thing, though, looking after a Johnnie old enough to be your grandfather, isn't it? Come to the Fort one of these days and see him?'

For reasons which will appear, I never went to the Fort while Khem Singh was then within its walls. I knew him only as a gray head seen from Lalun's window — a gray head and a harsh voice. But natives told me that, day by day, as he looked upon the fair lands round Amara, his memory came back to him and, with it, the old hatred against the Government that had been nearly effaced in far-off Burma. So he raged up and down the West face of the Fort from morning till noon and from evening till the night, devising vain things in his heart, and croaking war-songs when Lalun sang on the City wall. As he grew more acquainted with the Subaltern he unburdened his old heart of some of the passions that had withered it. 'Sahib,' he used to say, tapping his stick against the parapet, 'when I was a young man I was one of twenty thousand horsemen who came out of the City and rode round the plain here. Sahib, I was the leader of a hundred, then of a thousand, then of five thousand, and now!' — he pointed to his two servants. 'But from the beginning to today I would cut the throats of all the Sahibs in the land if I could. Hold me fast, Sahib, lest I get away and return to those who would follow me. I forgot them when I was in Burma, but now that I am in my own country again, I remember everything.'

'Do you remember that you have given me your Honour not to make your tendance a hard matter?' said the Subaltern.

'Yes, to you, only to you, Sahib,' said Khem Singh. 'To you because you are of a pleasant countenance. If my turn comes again, Sahib, I will not hang you nor cut your throat.'

'Thank you,' said the Subaltern gravely, as he looked along the line of guns that could pound the City to powder in half an hour. 'Let us go into our own quarters, Khem Singh. Come and talk with me after dinner.'

Khem Singh would sit on his own cushion at the Subaltern's feet, drinking heavy, scented anise-seed brandy in great gulps, and telling strange stories of Fort Amara, which had been a palace in the old days, of Begums and Ranees tortured to death — ay, in the very vaulted chamber that now served as a Mess-room; would tell stories of Sobraon that made the Subaltern's cheeks flush and tingle with pride of race, and of the Kuka rising from which so much was expected and the fore-knowledge of which was shared by a hundred thousand souls. But he never told tales of '57 because, as he said, he was the Subaltern's guest, and '57 is a year that no man, Black or White, cares to speak of. Once only, when the aniseseed brandy had slightly affected his head, he said: 'Sahib, speaking now of a matter which lay between Sobraon and the affair of the Kukas, it was ever a wonder to us that you stayed your hand at all, and that, having stayed it, you did not make the land one prison. Now I hear from without that you do great honour to all men of our country and by your own hands are destroying the Terror of your Name which is your strong rock and defence. This is a foolish thing. Will oil and water mix? Now in '57 — '

'I was not born then, Subadar Sahib,' said the Subaltern, and Khem Singh reeled to his quarters.

The Subaltern would tell me of these conversations at the Club, and my desire to see Khem Singh increased. But Wali Dad, sitting in the window-seat of the house on the City wall, said that it would be a cruel thing to do,

and Lalun pretended that I preferred the society of a grizzled old Sikh to hers.

'Here is tobacco, here is talk, here are many friends and all the news of the City, and, above all, here is myself. I will tell you stories and sing you songs, and Wali Dad will talk his English nonsense in your ears. Is that worse than watching the caged animal yonder? Go tomorrow then, if you must, but today such and such an one will be here, and he will speak of wonderful things.'

It happened that Tomorrow never came, and the warm heat of the latter Rains gave place to the chill of early October almost before I was aware of the flight of the year. The Captain Commanding the Fort returned from leave and took over charge of Khem Singh according to the laws of seniority. The Captain was not a nice man. He called all natives 'niggers,' which, besides being extreme bad form, shows gross ignorance.

'What's the use of telling off two Tommies to watch that old nigger?' said he.

'I fancy it soothes his vanity,' said the Subaltern. 'The men are ordered to keep well out of his way, but he takes them as a tribute to his importance, poor old wretch.'

'I won't have Line men taken off regular guards in this way. Put on a couple of Native Infantry.'

'Sikhs?' said the Subaltern, lifting his eyebrows.

'Sikhs, Pathans, Dogras — they're all alike, these black vermin,' and the Captain talked to Khem Singh in a manner which hurt that old gentleman's feelings. Fifteen years before, when he had been caught for the second time, every one looked upon him as a sort of tiger. He liked being regarded in this light. But he forgot that the world goes forward in fifteen years, and many Subalterns are promoted to Captaincies.

'The Captain-pig is in charge of the Fort?' said Khem Singh to his native guard every morning. And the native guard said: 'Yes, Subadar Sahib,' in deference to his age and his air of distinction; but they did not know who he was.

In those days the gathering in Lalun's little white room was always large and talked more than before.

'The Greeks,' said Wali Dad who had been borrowing my books, 'the inhabitants of the city of Athens, where they were always hearing and telling some new thing, rigorously secluded their women — who were fools.

Hence the glorious institution of the heterodox women — is it not? — who were amusing and *not* fools. All the Greek philosophers delighted in their company. Tell me, my friend, how it goes now in Greece and the other places upon the Continent of Europe. Are your women-folk also fools?'

'Wali Dad,' I said, 'you never speak to us about your women-folk and we never speak about ours to you. That is the bar between us.'

'Yes,' said Wali Dad, 'it is curious to think that our common meeting-place should be here, in the house of a common — how do you call *her?*' He pointed with the pipe-mouth to Lalun.

'Lalun is nothing but Lalun,' I said, and that was perfectly true. 'But if you took your place in the world, Wali Dad, and gave up dreaming dreams — '

'I might wear an English coat and trouser. I might be a leading Muhammadan pleader. I might be received even at the Commissioner's tennis-parties where the English stand on one side and the natives on the other, in order to promote social intercourse throughout the Empire. Heart's Heart,' said he to Lalun quickly, 'the Sahib says I ought to quit you.'

'The Sahib is always talking stupid talk,' returned Lalun with a laugh. 'In this house I am a Queen and thou art a King. The Sahib' — she put her arms above her head and thought for a moment — 'the Sahib shall be our Vizier — thine and mine, Wali Dad — because he has said that thou shouldst leave me.'

Wali Dad laughed immoderately, and I laughed too. 'Be it so,' said he. 'My friend, are you willing to take this lucrative Government appointment? Lalun, what shall his pay be?'

But Lalun began to sing, and for the rest of the time there was no hope of getting a sensible answer from her or Wali Dad. When the one stopped, the other began to quote Persian poetry with a triple pun in every other line. Some of it was not strictly proper, but it was all very funny, and it only came to an end when a fat person in black, with gold *pince-nez*, sent up his name to Lalun, and Wali Dad dragged me into the twinkling night to walk in a big rose-garden and talk heresies about Religion and Governments and a man's career in life.

The Mohurrum, the great mourning-festival of the Muhammadans, was close at hand, and the things that Wali Dad said about religious fanaticism would have secured his expulsion from the loosest-thinking Muslim sect. There were the rose-bushes round us, the stars above us, and from every quarter of the City came the boom of the big Mohurrum drums. You must know that the City is divided in fairly equal proportions between the Hindus and the Mussulmans, and where both creeds belong to the fighting races, a big religious festival gives ample chance for trouble. When they can — that is to say, when the authorities are weak enough to allow it — the Hindus do their best to arrange some minor feast-day of their own in time to clash with the period of general mourning for the martyrs Hasan and Hussain, the heroes of the Mohurrum. Gilt and painted paper presentations of their tombs are borne with shouting and wailing, music, torches, and yells, through the principal thoroughfares of the City; which fakements are called *tazias*. Their passage is rigorously laid down beforehand by the Police, and detachments of Police accompany each *tazia*, lest the Hindus should throw bricks at it and the peace of the Queen and the heads of Her loyal subjects should thereby be broken. Mohurrum time in a 'fighting' town means anxiety to all the officials, because, if a riot breaks out, the officials and not the rioters are held responsible. The former must foresee everything, and while not making their precautions ridiculously elaborate, must see that they are at least adequate.

'Listen to the drums!' said Wali Dad. 'That is the heart of the people — empty and making much noise. How, think you, will the Mohurrum go this year? *I* think that there will be trouble.'

He turned down a side-street and left me alone with the stars and a sleepy Police patrol. Then I went to bed and dreamed that Wali Dad had sacked the City and I was made Vizier, with Lalun's silver *huqa* for mark of office.

All day the Mohurrum drums beat in the City, and all day deputations of tearful Hindu gentlemen besieged the Deputy Commissioner with assurances that they would be murdered ere next dawning by the Muhammadans. 'Which,' said the Deputy Commissioner, in confidence to the Head of Police, 'is a pretty fair indication that the Hindus are going to make 'emselves unpleasant. I think we can arrange a little surprise for them. I have given the heads of both Creeds fair warning. If they choose to disregard it, so much the worse for them.'

There was a large gathering in Lalun's house that night, but of men that I had never seen before, if I except the fat gentleman in black with the gold *pince-nez*. Wali Dad lay in the window-seat, more bitterly scornful of his Faith and its manifestations than I had ever known him. Lalun's maid was very busy cutting up and mixing tobacco for the guests. We could hear the thunder of the drums as the processions accompanying each *tazia* marched to the central gathering-place in the plain outside the City, preparatory to their triumphant re-entry and circuit within the walls. All the streets seemed ablaze with torches, and only Fort Amara was black and silent.

When the noise of the drums ceased, no one in the white room spoke for a time. 'The first *tazia* has moved off,' said Wali Dad, looking to the plain.

'That is very early,' said the man with the *pince-nez*. 'It is only half-past eight.' The company rose and departed.

'Some of them were men from Ladakh,' said Lalun, when the last had gone. 'They brought me brick-tea such as the Russians sell, and a tea-urn from Peshawur. Show me, now, how the English Memsahibs make tea.'

The brick-tea was abominable. When it was finished Wali Dad suggested going into the streets. 'I am nearly sure that there will be trouble tonight,' he said. 'All the City thinks so, and *Vox Populi* is *Vox Dei*, as the Babus say. Now I tell you that at the corner of the Padshahi Gate you will find my horse all this night if you want to go about and see things. It is a most disgraceful exhibition. Where is the pleasure of saying "*Ya Hasan, Ya Hussain*" twenty thousand times in a night?'

All the processions — there were two-and-twenty of them — were now well within the City walls. The drums were beating afresh, the crowd were howling '*Ya Hasan! Ya Hussain!*' and beating their breasts, the brass bands were playing their loudest, and at every corner where space allowed, Muhammadan preachers were telling the lamentable story of the death of the Martyrs. It was impossible to move except with the crowd, for the streets were not more than twenty feet wide. In the Hindu quarters the shutters of all the shops were up and cross-barred. As the first *tazia*, a gorgeous erection ten feet high, was borne aloft on the shoulders of a score of stout men into the semi-darkness of the Gully of the Horsemen, a brickbat crashed through its talc and tinsel sides.

'Into thy hands, O Lord!' murmured Wali Dad profanely, as a yell went up from behind, and a native officer of Police jammed his horse through the crowd. Another brickbat followed, and the *tazia* staggered and swayed where it had stopped.

'Go on! In the name of the *Sirkar*, go forward!' shouted the Policeman; but there was an ugly cracking and splintering of shutters, and the crowd halted, with oaths and growlings, before the house whence the brickbat had been thrown.

Then, without any warning, broke the storm — not only in the Gully of the Horsemen, but in half-a-dozen other places. The *tazias* rocked like ships at sea, the long pole-torches dipped and rose round them while the men shouted: 'The Hindus are dishonouring the *tazias!* Strike! strike! Into their temples for the Faith!' The six or eight Policemen with each *tazia* drew their batons, and struck as long as they could in the hope of forcing the mob forward, but they were overpowered, and as contingents of Hindus poured into the streets, the fight became general. Half a mile away where the *tazias* were yet untouched the drums and the shrieks of '*Ya Hasan! Ya Hussain!*' continued, but not for long. The priests at the corners of the streets knocked the legs from the bedsteads that supported their pulpits and smote for the Faith, while stones fell from the silent houses upon friend and foe, and the packed streets bellowed: '*Din! Din! Din!*' A *tazia* caught fire, and was dropped for a flaming barrier between Hindu and Mussulman at the corner of the Gully. Then the crowd surged forward, and Wali Dad drew me close to the stone pillar of a well.

'It was intended from the beginning!' he shouted in my ear, with more heat than blank unbelief should be guilty of. 'The bricks were carried up to the houses beforehand. These swine of Hindus! We shall be gutting kine in their temples tonight!'

Tazia after *tazia*, some burning, others torn to pieces, hurried past us and the mob with them, howling, shrieking, and striking at the house doors in their flight. At last we saw the reason of the rush. Hugonin, the Assistant District Superintendent of Police, a boy of twenty, had got together thirty constables and was forcing the crowd through the streets. His old gray Policehorse showed no sign of uneasiness as it was spurred breast-on into the crowd, and the long dog-whip with which he had armed himself was never still.

'They know we haven't enough Police to hold 'em,' he cried as he passed me, mopping a cut on his face. 'They *know* we haven't! Aren't any of the men from the Club coming down to help? Get on, you sons of burnt fathers!' The dog-whip cracked across the writhing backs, and the constables smote afresh with baton and gun-butt. With these passed the lights and the shouting, and Wali Dad began to swear under his breath. From Fort Amara shot up a single rocket; then two side by side. It was the signal for troops.

Petitt, the Deputy Commissioner, covered with dust and sweat, but calm and gently smiling, cantered up the clean-swept street in rear of the main body of the rioters. 'No one killed yet,' he shouted. 'I'll keep 'em on the run till dawn! Don't let em halt, Hugonin! Trot 'em about till the troops come.'

The science of the defence lay solely in keeping the mob on the move. If they had breathing-space they would halt and fire a house, and then the work of restoring order would be more difficult, to say the least of it. Flames have the same effect on a crowd as blood has on a wild beast.

Word had reached the Club and men in evening-dress were beginning to show themselves and lend a hand in heading off and breaking up the shouting masses with stirrup-leathers, whips, or chance-found staves. They were not very often attacked, for the rioters had sense enough to know that the death of a European would not mean one hanging but many, and possibly the appearance of the thrice-dreaded Artillery. The clamour in the City redoubled. The Hindus had descended into the streets in real earnest and ere long the mob returned. It was a strange sight. There were no *tazias* — only their riven platforms — and there were no Police. Here and there a City dignitary, Hindu or Muhammadan, was vainly imploring his co-religionists to keep quiet and behave themselves — advice for which his white beard was pulled. Then a native officer of Police, unhorsed but still using his spurs with effect, would be borne along, warning all the crowd of the danger of insulting the Government. Everywhere men struck aimlessly with sticks, grasping each other by the

throat, howling and foaming with rage, or beat with their bare hands on the doors of the houses.

'It is a lucky thing that they are fighting with natural weapons,' I said to Wali Dad, 'else we should have half the City killed.'

I turned as I spoke and looked at his face. His nostrils were distended, his eyes were fixed, and he was smiting himself softly on the breast. The crowd poured by with renewed riot — a gang of Mussulmans hard pressed by some hundred Hindu fanatics. Wali Dad left my side with an oath, and shouting: '*Ya Hasan! Ya Hussain!*' plunged into the thick of the fight where I lost sight of him.

I fled by a side alley to the Padshahi Gate where I found Wali Dad's horse, and thence rode to the Fort. Once outside the City wall, the tumult sank to a dull roar, very impressive under the stars and reflecting great credit on the fifty thousand angry able-bodied men who were making it. The troops who, at the Deputy Commissioner's instance, had been ordered to rendezvous quietly near the Fort, showed no signs of being impressed. Two companies of Native Infantry, a squadron of Native Cavalry, and a company of British Infantry were kicking their heels in the shadow of the East face, waiting for orders to march in. I am sorry to say that they were all pleased, unholily pleased, at the chance of what they called 'a little fun.' The senior officers, to be sure, grumbled at having been kept out of bed, and the English troops pretended to be sulky, but there was joy in the hearts of all the subalterns, and whispers ran up and down the line: 'No ball-cartridge — what a beastly shame!' 'D'you think the beggars will really stand up to us?' ''Hope I shall meet my money-lender there. I owe him more than I can afford.' 'Oh, they won't let us even unsheathe swords.' 'Hurrah! Up goes the fourth rocket. Fall in, there!'

The Garrison Artillery, who to the last cherished a wild hope that they might be allowed to bombard the City at a hundred yards' range, lined the parapet above the East gateway and cheered themselves hoarse as the British Infantry doubled along the road to the Main Gate of the City. The Cavalry cantered on to the Padshahi Gate, and the Native Infantry marched slowly to the Gate of the Butchers. The surprise was intended to be of a distinctly unpleasant nature, and to come on top of the defeat of the Police, who had been just able to keep the Muhammadans from firing the houses of a few leading Hindus. The bulk of the riot lay in the north and north-west wards. The east and south-east were by this time dark and silent, and I rode hastily to Lalun's house for I wished to tell her to send some one in search of Wali Dad. The house was unlighted, but the door was open, and I climbed upstairs in the darkness. One small lamp in the white room showed Lalun and her maid leaning half out of the window, breathing heavily and evidently pulling at something that refused to come.

'Thou art late — very late,' gasped Lalun without turning her head. 'Help us now, O Fool, if thou hast not spent thy strength howling among the *tazias*. Pull! Nasiban and I can do no more! O Sahib, is it you? The Hindus have been hunting an old Muhammadan round the Ditch with clubs. If they find him again they will kill him. Help us to pull him up.'

I put my hands to the long red silk waist-cloth that was hanging out of the window, and we three pulled and pulled with all the strength at our command. There was something very heavy at the end, and it swore in an unknown tongue as it kicked against the City wall.

'Pull, oh, pull!' said Lalun at the last. A pair of brown hands grasped the window-sill and a venerable Muhammadan tumbled upon the floor, very much out of breath. His jaws were tied up, his turban had fallen over one eye, and he was dusty and angry.

Lalun hid her face in her hands for an instant and said something about Wali Dad that I could not catch.

Then, to my extreme gratification, she threw her arms round my neck and murmured pretty things. I was in no haste to stop her; and Nasiban, being a handmaiden of tact, turned to the big jewel-chest that stands in the corner of the white room and rummaged among the contents. The Muhammadan sat on the floor and glared.

'One service more, Sahib, since thou hast come so opportunely,' said Lalun. 'Wilt thou' — it is very nice to be thou-ed by Lalun — 'take this old man across the City — the troops are everywhere, and they hurt him for he is old — to the Kumharsen Gate? There I think he may find a carriage to take him to his house. He is a friend of mine, and thou art — more than a friend — therefore I ask this.'

Nasiban bent over the old man, tucked something into his belt, and I raised him up, and led him into the streets. In crossing from the east to the west of the City there was no chance of avoiding the troops and the crowd. Long before I reached the Gully of the Horsemen I heard the shouts of the British Infantry crying cheerily: 'Hutt, ye beggars! Hutt, ye devils! Get along! Go forward, there!' Then followed the ringing of rifle-butts and shrieks of pain. The troops were banging the bare toes of the mob with their gun-butts — for not a bayonet had been fixed. My companion mumbled and jabbered as we walked on until we were carried back by the crowd and had to force our way back to the troops. I caught him by the wrist and felt a bangle there — the iron bangle of the Sikhs — but I had no suspicions, for Lalun had only ten minutes before put her arms round me. Thrice we were carried back by the crowd, and when we made our way past the British Infantry it was to meet the Sikh Cavalry driving another mob before them with the butts of their lances.

'What are these dogs?' said the old man.

'Sikhs of the Cavalry, Father,' I said, and we edged our way up the line of horses two abreast and found the Deputy Commissioner, his helmet smashed on his head, surrounded by a knot of men who had come down from the Club as amateur constables and had helped the Police mightily.

'We'll keep 'em on the run till dawn,' said Petitt. 'Who's your villainous friend?'

I had only time to say: 'The Protection of the *Sirkar!*' when a fresh crowd flying before the Native Infantry carried us a hundred yards nearer the Kumharsen Gate, and Petitt was swept away like a shadow.

'I do not know — I cannot see — this is all new to me!' moaned my companion. 'How many troops are there in the City?'

'Perhaps five hundred,' I said.

'A lakh of men beaten by five hundred — and Sikhs among them! Surely, surely, I am an old man, but — the Kumharsen Gate is new. Who pulled down the stone lions? Where is the conduit? Sahib, I am a very old man, and, alas, I — I cannot stand.' He dropped in the shadow of the Kumharsen Gate where there was no disturbance. A fat gentleman wearing gold *pince-nez* came out of the darkness.

'You are most kind to bring my old friend,' he said suavely. 'He is a landholder of Akala. He should not be in a big City when there is religious excitement. But I have a carriage here. You are quite truly kind. Will you help me to put him into the carriage? It is very late.'

We bundled the old man into a hired victoria that stood close to the gate, and I turned back to the house on the City wall. The troops were driving the people to and fro, while the Police shouted, 'To your houses! Get to your houses!' and the dog-whip of the Assistant District Superintendent cracked remorselessly. Terror-stricken *bunnias* clung to the stirrups of the cavalry, crying that their houses had been robbed (which was a lie), and the burly Sikh horsemen patted them on the shoulder and bade them return to those houses lest a worse thing should happen. Parties of five or six British soldiers, joining arms, swept down the side-gullies, their rifles on their backs, stamping, with shouting and song, upon the toes of Hindu and Mussulman. Never was religious enthusiasm more systematically squashed; and never were poor breakers of the peace more utterly weary and footsore. They were routed out of holes and corners, from behind well-pillars and byres, and bidden to go to their houses. If they had no houses to go to, so much the worse for their toes.

On returning to Lalun's door I stumbled over a man at the threshold. He was sobbing hysterically and his arms flapped like the wings of a goose. It was Wali Dad, Agnostic and Unbeliever, shoeless, turbanless, and frothing at the mouth, the flesh on his chest bruised and bleeding from the vehemence with which he had smitten himself. A broken torch-handle lay by his side, and his quivering lips murmured, '*Ya Hasan! Ya Hussain!*' as I stooped over him. I pushed him a few steps up the staircase, threw a pebble at Lalun's City window and hurried home.

Most of the streets were very still, and the cold wind that comes before the dawn whistled down them. In the centre of the Square of the Mosque a man was bending over a corpse. The skull had been smashed in by gun-butt or bamboo-stave.

'It is expedient that one man should die for the people,' said Petitt grimly, raising the shapeless head. 'These brutes were beginning to show their teeth too much.'

And from afar we could hear the soldiers singing 'Two Lovely Black Eyes,' as they drove the remnants of the rioters within doors.

Of course you can guess what happened? I was not so clever. When the news went abroad that Khem Singh had escaped from the Fort, I did not, since I was then living this story, not writing it, connect myself, or Lalun, or the fat gentleman of the gold *pince-nez*, with his disappearance. Nor did it strike me that Wali Dad was the man who should have conveyed him across the City, or that Lalun's arms around my neck were put there to hide the money that Nasiban gave to Khem Singh, and that Lalun had used me and my white face as even a better safeguard than Wali Dad who proved himself so untrustworthy. All that I knew at the time was that, when Fort Amara was taken up with the riots, Khem Singh profited by the confusion to get away, and that his two Sikh guards also escaped.

But later on I received full enlightenment; and so did Khem Singh. He fled to those who knew him in the old days, but many of them were dead and more were changed, and all knew something of the Wrath of the Government. He went to the young men, but the glamour of his name had passed away, and they were entering native regiments or Government offices, and Khem Singh could give them neither pension, decorations, nor influence — nothing but a glorious death with their back to the mouth of a gun. He wrote letters and made promises, and the letters fell into bad hands, and a wholly insignificant subordinate officer of Police tracked them down and gained promotion thereby. Moreover, Khem Singh was old, and anise-seed brandy was scarce, and he had left his silver cooking-pots in Fort Amara with his nice warm bedding, and the gentleman with the gold *pince-nez* was told by Those who had employed him that Khem Singh as a popular leader was not worth the money paid.

'Great is the mercy of these fools of English!' said Khem Singh when the situation was put before him. 'I will go back to Fort Amara of my own free will and gain honour. Give me good clothes to return in.'

So, at his own time, Khem Singh knocked at the wicket-gate of the Fort and walked to the Captain and the Subaltern, who were nearly gray-headed on account of correspondence that daily arrived from Simla marked 'Private.'

'I have come back, Captain Sahib,' said Khem Singh. 'Put no more guards over me. It is no good out yonder.'

A week later I saw him for the first time to my knowledge, and he made as though there were an understanding between us.

'It was well done, Sahib,' said he, 'and greatly I admired your astuteness in thus boldly facing the troops when I, whom they would have doubtless torn to pieces, was with you. Now there is a man in Fort Ooltagarh whom a bold man could with ease help to escape. This is the position of the Fort as I draw it on the sand — '

But I was thinking how I had become Lalun's Vizier after all.

PART VI

MAN AND BEAST

Kipling's entry into the animal kingdom really dates from his arrival in America in 1892. I have found only one 'animal' story that was written while he was in India: an account of a struggle between two colonies of ants that the writer claims to have witnessed in the bathroom of his bungalow in Allahabad. The article appeared unsigned in *The Pioneer* on 5 July 1886 as 'The Battle of the Bathroom: Fought at Allahabad, July 1st 1886' – which is a puzzle because at that time Rudyard was in Lahore prior to joining his family in Simla in August. However, everything about the article points to it being the work of young Rudyard, so we must assume that the details of the title were changed to suit *The Pioneer*, which had already published several uncredited articles and poems by Kipling. My own theory is that the article was placed in *The Pioneer* by Rudyard's new acquaintance, Kay Robinson.

There are no such doubts about the other two animal tales in this section. 'Rikki-Tikki-Tavi' was written in the autumn of 1893 in Vermont but its setting is the garden of the Hills' bungalow in Allahabad, 'only half cultivated, with bushes as big as summer houses of Marshal Niel roses, lime and orange trees, clumps of bamboos, and thickets of high grass'. Like so many of Kipling's animal and jungle stories it has its roots in the ancient Indian moral fables known as the *Jataka*, to which Rudyard was introduced by his father, although Rudyard himself did have his own experiences and observations to draw upon. We know, for instance, that a 'perfectly wild mongoose' used to come and sit on his shoulder in his office and occasionally 'burn his inquisitive nose on the end of my cigar, just as Rikki did in the tale'.

The most obvious choice for a third animal tale ought to be the story of that stout-hearted polo pony, 'The Maltese Cat', but I have plumped instead for a less popular tale that covers more ground and has a lot more bite to it: 'The Undertakers', with its three delightful villains – the blunt-nosed crocodile, the 'Mugger of Mugger-Ghaut', and his two fellow scavengers, the Jackal and the Adjutant-Bird. The references to the 'Mutiny' of 'thirty seasons ago' relate to the Indian Mutiny of 1857 and its attendant massacres – references that most of Kipling's Anglo-Indian readers would have found in very bad taste.

'Rikki-Tikki-Tavi' first appeared in *St. Nicholas Magazine* in November 1893, reprinted in *The Jungle Book*, 1894. 'The Undertakers' was published in *The Second Jungle Book*, 1895.

THE BATTLE OF THE BATHROOM

FOUGHT AT ALLAHABAD, JULY 1st, 1886

IT ALL CAME about through a dead beetle. I had been seeking relaxation in light literature, say the Bengal Administration Report for 1862-63, and found that Summaries of statistics in numbered paragraphs are not good for the temper; so when — just as I began to wade through the final Resolution of the Government, and to wish that they had deleted all the reflections which appeared above the signature of Mr. Acting Sub-Secretary Somebody or Other, — a bulletty beetle flopped for the fifth time on to the book. I shut it with a snap. A Bengal Administration Report may be light literature, but it measures about six foot by three; and that beetle was flattened out to the shape of a damaged eighteen-penny rupee. I then cast him forth, with ignominy, into the verandah; and went to bed. But one crime breeds many, and that murdered beetle had bloody obsequies. At the extreme corner of the bungalow is a bathroom where a large colony of fierce black ants have established themselves. They belong to a warlike sect which from time immemorial have garrisoned the peepul behind the house. They have branch establishments in the cook house, in the back verandah, and in the mud wall down to the left hand gate, both of the posts of which are held in strength as a kind of scientific frontier against the roving ant tribes of the maidan beyond. The other gate belongs to another sect, — a very fanatical sect who carry their tails in the air, and whose headquarters are in three neem trees in the front garden, with settlements in the road before the house, and fortified posts all down the garden drive towards the right hand gate. They had also a formidable strategic outpost in the extreme right hand corner of the front verandah. At the extreme left of this same verandah I had thrown out the beetle's corpse among the flowerpots. The normal relations of these two sects were a kind of armed and mutually respectful neutrality. The neem tree or front garden ants patrolled the front verandah and the drawing-room: the peepul tree or bathroom ants ventured no further than the dressing-room. But in front of the house the line of demarcation ran along the edge of the verandah, the Neemtreeites above and the Peepulites below. In the small hours of the morning a Neemtreeite worker, one of the small sized ants that venture themselves into perilous places where the bullet-headed soldier ant dare not climb, discovered the beetle's corpse on the rim of a flowerpot. After vain attempts to drag it along, he rushed off to get help, running down a long leaf and dropping thence to the ground. Presently he returned with a fatigue party of three soldiers and four workers — all in single file, and a loafer or two behind. They laboriously circumvented the perils of the sloping leaf, and one by one struggled over the summit of the flowerpot. At once they set to work and proceeded to drag the beetle from his dangerous position, whence the slightest push might precipitate him to the Peepulites below. All might have gone well but for one of the loafers who, rushing officiously up at the last moment, climbed upon the beetle's body, ran along one of his outstretched legs, and overbalanced the whole concern. Down they went flop into Peepulite territory — three soldiers, one loafer, and a worker. Scarcely had they touched the ground than each of the soldiers found himself desperately engaged with half a dozen of the enemy, and in spite of their desperate headwagging defence they were torn limb from limb, their own jaws fixed tight, even in death, upon the foe they seized first. The loafer with tail in air had escaped by sheer speed across country, while the worker hurried back into the verandah to report the disaster. Meanwhile the victors carried off the dismembered corpses of their enemies, and proceeded to disembowel the beetle, with a strong contingent of soldiers to guard the working party.

Presently came hurrying in, tail in air, messengers from the front, who reported unusual signs of activity in the Neemtreeite fort in the corner of the verandah. A worker told how, following the usual trade-route to the rubbish heap behind the fowl-house, she had fallen almost into the midst of a regiment of the enemy; a loafer told how he had slain sixteen Peepulites in buckram who had endeavoured to arrest him, while a wounded veteran staggered in with half his legs gone, to tell how he was all that remained of the picket opposite the enemy's fort. 'A sudden sally, — deeds of heroism worthy of the Peepulite traditions, — fearful odds — sole survivor,' such was the substance of his report. The gathering Peepulites listened with growing wrath, and then, seeing that the veteran was too damaged to be of any use again, they cut him up and carried off his joints to the larder under the bathroom. Tremendous was the excitement there when the news was brought. Scouts rushed off in every direction, stumbling over each other round corners, climbing up the sides of the bath and tumbling in, swarming all over the walls, and clustering in serried groups round each door of the citadel.

Meanwhile the first battalion of the Neemtreeites had started on the war path. In parallel lines, covering the whole width of the verandah, they advanced about 50,000 strong, in small companies of about a dozen

each, — the fighting unit in ant-warfare, — composed of six or seven warriors and the rest workers, to carry off the dead and wounded, to act as scouts, to feed the weary, and generally perform the functions of Transport, Commissariat, Ambulance, and Intelligence departments. In single file the advance guard, following the worker who had brought the news, climbed up the sloping leaf, hurried across the pot to the place whence the beetle fell, and without a moment's hesitation dropped plumb down among the swarming Peepulites. Scarcely had they touched ground before they were at death grips with the eager foe, and still others came dropping down, an endless stream of shiny sharp-jawed warriors, till the spot beneath was piled high with a conical heap of struggling combatants. In their eagerness to discover whence this sudden waterspout of enemies came from, the Peepulite scouts had climbed across the frontier into the verandah, and, darting here and there, stumbled upon the main body of the enemy; who fell upon them, killing and driving them back upon their supports, till the edge of the verandah was reached and then the two armies closed. The Neemtreeites had immense numerical odds, and overbearing all opposition took position after position, fought inch by inch all down the side of the house, round the corner right away to the bathroom pipe. Here the fight waxed stubborn. In vain the assailants poured themselves into the

The Indian Bathroom. A sponge would be too convenient a lurking place for scorpions so a tin cup takes its place.

pipe. The Peepulites were there in thousands too, and the gutter was inches deep in struggling forms.

Meanwhile some of the bathroom scouts who had gone off reconnoitring through the house penetrated to the drawing-room, and there fell in with the skirmishers of the Neemtreeite rearguard. The alarm was given and the Neemtreeites poured through the drawing-room, fought a long skirmish across the bedroom and so to the bathroom beyond; taking the Peepulite defenders in flank. The bathroom position consisted of eleven independent forts — the two largest at each end of the water pipe and the others at distances round the wall. From all of these, defenders in long streams were pouring to the water pipe when the new assault through the doorway diverted their attention; and they swarmed to defend the raised rim round the bath place. In a minute they swept this clear, and tumbling over, hundreds at a time, met the main body of the assailants on the strip of carpet. Here the fight was unusually desperate, because the hairy nature of the field of battle enabled the combatants to hold on like grim death to it and to each other till the troops advancing from behind had to march over a substratum of combatants.

Here, indeed, victory inclined to the Peepulites, but at a fatal cost. For lack of supports the defenders of the twin forts in the water pipe were annihilated, and the key of the whole position lost. In quick succession the others were taken; and when the first returning Peepulite victors from the strip of carpet came tumbling into the bath place, laden with corpses of the slain, they found each of their own camps in the possession of the enemy. They fought nobly, but in isolated groups as they struggled in. Ere an hour was over all the bathroom Peepulites were destroyed; and when I came in for my bath I crushed scores of corpses at every step. Throughout the day the victorious invaders were busy enough, deporting the loot. At the entrance of each hole a picquet was posted, and all day long files of workers passed in and out with grubs, eggs, cocoons, and provisions. All day long, too, ants of every species prowled scavengering on the field of battle and carrying off the corpses to their respective larders. I visited the peepul tree, the metropolis of the sect whose fort had been captured, and found the trunk black with wag-headed warriors and patrols busy in every direction. Communications had been kept open by a circuitous route with the other outposts in the mud banks and the gate post opposite the maidan; and at one time I thought the whole Peepulite force, some millions strong, were going to advance and retake the bathroom, but they thought better of it. The Neemtreeites were, as might have been expected, marching and countermarching all over the garden and house. The three neemtree trunks were alive with troops, hurrying up and down and counting the spoil as it came in.

Next day, save for a sentry or two at each hole, the bathroom was deserted; and the Neemtreeites deliberately attacked the Peepulite positions in the mud bank. These they appeared to have taken separately by assault, for each had only a small ring of corpses round it. Finally they stormed the gate-posts after a battle almost as bloody as that of the bathroom.

The peepul tree itself they seemed to think too formidable; for they left it unassaulted: and now, as before, the relations of the two sects are those of armed neutrality, only the Peepulites are sulkily confined to the compound at the back and the Neemtreeite sentries, tail in air, keep vigorous watch day and night at each of the captured forts. The bodies of the wounded and dead of both sides were all used for food; but such Neemtreeite warriors as were not quite disabled were carefully tended; and the heads of their dead enemies sticking to them were carefully picked off by the workers. These heads it seems are the only indigestible part of a dead soldier ant, for though the bodies were all stored up and eaten, the heads were thrown away on the path, and still gave a black tinge to yards of the gravel around each spot where the battle had raged fiercely. About two quarters of heads were swept out of the bathroom.

RIKKI-TIKKI-TAVI

THIS IS THE story of the great war that Rikki-tikki-tavi fought single-handed, through the bathrooms of the big bungalow in Segowlee cantonment. Darzee, the tailor-bird, helped him, and Chuchundra, the musk-rat, who never comes out into the middle of the floor, but always creeps round by the wall, gave him advice; but Rikki-tikki did the real fighting.

He was a mongoose, rather like a little cat in his fur and his tail, but quite like a weasel in his head and his habits. His eyes and the end of his restless nose were pink; he could scratch himself anywhere he pleased, with any leg, front or back, that he chose to use; he could fluff up his tail till it looked like a bottle-brush, and his war-cry, as he scuttled through the long grass, was: '*Rikki-tikk-tikki-tikki-tchk!*'

One day, a high summer flood washed him out of the burrow where he lived with his father and mother, and carried him, kicking and clucking, down a road-side ditch. He found a little wisp of grass floating there, and clung to it till he lost his senses. When he revived, he was lying in the hot sun on the middle of a garden path, very draggled indeed, and a small boy was saying: 'Here's a dead mongoose. Let's have a funeral.'

'No.' said his mother; 'let's take him in and dry him. Perhaps he isn't really dead.'

They took him into the house, and a big man picked him up between his finger and thumb, and said he was not dead but half choked; so they wrapped him in cotton-wool, and warmed him, and he opened his eyes and sneezed.

'Now,' said the big man (he was an Englishman who had just moved into the bungalow); 'don't frighten him, and we'll see what he'll do.'

It is the hardest thing in the world to frighten a mongoose, because he is eaten up from nose to tail with curiosity. The motto of all the mongoose family is, 'Run and find out'; and Rikki-tikki was a true mongoose. He looked at the cotton-wool, decided that it was not good to eat, ran all round the table, sat up and put his fur in order, scratched himself, and jumped on the small boy's shoulder.

'Don't be frightened, Teddy,' said his father. 'That's his way of making friends.'

'Ouch! He's tickling under my chin,' said Teddy.

Rikki-tikki looked down between the boy's collar and neck, snuffed at

his ear, and climbed down to the floor, where he sat rubbing his nose.

'Good gracious,' said Teddy's mother, 'and that's a wild creature! I suppose he's so tame because we've been kind to him.'

'All mongooses are like that,' said her husband. 'If Teddy doesn't pick him up by the tail, or try to put him in a cage, he'll run in and out of the house all day long. Let's give him something to eat.'

They gave him a little piece of raw meat. Rikki-tikki liked it immensely, and when it was finished he went out into the verandah and sat in the sunshine and fluffed up his fur to make it dry to the roots. Then he felt better.

'There are more things to find out about in this house,' he said to himself, 'than all my family could find out in all their lives. I shall certainly stay and find out.'

He spent all that day roaming over the house. He nearly drowned himself in the bath-tubs, put his nose into the ink on a writing-table, and burnt it on the end of the big man's cigar, for he climbed up in the big man's lap to see how writing was done. At nightfall he ran into Teddy's nursery to watch how kerosene-lamps were lighted, and when Teddy went to bed Rikki-tikki climbed up too; but he was a restless companion, because he had to get up and attend to every noise all through the night, and find out what made it. Teddy's mother and father came in, the last thing, to look at their boy, and Rikki-tikki was awake on the pillow. 'I don't like that,' said Teddy's mother; 'he may bite the child.' 'He'll do no such thing,' said the father. 'Teddy's safer with that little beast than if he had a bloodhound to watch him. If a snake came into the nursery now — '

But Teddy's mother wouldn't think of anything so awful.

Early in the morning Rikki-tikki came to early breakfast in the verandah riding on Teddy's shoulder, and they gave him banana and some boiled egg; and he sat on all their laps one after the other, because every well-brought-up mongoose always hopes to be a house-mongoose some day and have rooms to run about in, and Rikki-tikki's mother (she used to live in the General's house at Segowlee) had carefully told Rikki what to do if ever he came across white men.

Then Rikki-tikki went out into the garden to see what was to be seen. It was a large garden, only half cultivated, with bushes as big as summer-houses of Marshal Niel roses, lime and orange trees, clumps of bamboos, and thickets of high grass. Rikki-tikki licked his lips. 'This is a splendid hunting-ground,' he said, and his tail grew bottle-brushy at the thought of it, and he scuttled up and down the garden, snuffing here and there till he heard very sorrowful voices in a thorn-bush.

It was Darzee, the tailor-bird, and his wife. They had made a beautiful nest by pulling two big leaves together and stitching them up the edges with fibres, and had filled the hollow with cotton and downy fluff. The nest swayed to and fro, as they sat on the rim and cried.

'What is the matter?' asked Rikki-tikki.

'We are very miserable,' said Darzee. 'One of our babies fell out of the nest yesterday, and Nag ate him.'

'H'm!' said Rikki-tikki, 'that is very sad — but I am a stranger here. Who is Nag?'

Darzee and his wife only cowered down in the nest without answering, for from the thick grass at the foot of the bush there came a low hiss — a horrid cold sound that made Rikki-tikki jump back two clear feet. Then inch by inch out of the grass rose up the head and spread hood of Nag, the big black cobra, and he was five feet long from tongue to tail. When he had lifted one-third of himself clear of the ground, he stayed balancing to and fro exactly as a dandelion-tuft balances in the wind, and he looked at Rikki-tikki with the wicked snake's eyes that never change their expression, whatever the snake may be thinking of.

'Who is Nag?' said he. '*I* am Nag. The great god Brahm put his mark upon all our people when the first cobra spread his hood to keep the sun off Brahm as he slept. Look, and be afraid!'

He spread out his hood more than ever, and Rikki-tikki saw the spectacle-mark on the back of it that looks exactly like the eye part of a hook-and-eye fastening. He was afraid for the minute; but it is impossible for a mongoose to stay frightened for any length of time, and though Rikki-tikki had never met a live cobra before, his mother had fed him on dead ones, and he knew that all a grown mongoose's business in life was to fight and eat snakes. Nag knew that too, and at the bottom of his cold heart he was afraid.

'Well,' said Rikki-tikki, and his tail began to fluff up again, 'marks or no marks, do you think it is right for you to eat fledglings out of a nest?'

Nag was thinking to himself, and watching the least little movement in the grass behind Rikki-tikki. He knew that mongooses in the garden meant death sooner or later for him and his family, but he wanted to get Rikki-tikki off his guard. So he dropped his head a little, and put it on one side.

'Let us talk,' he said. 'You eat eggs. Why should not I eat birds?'

'Behind you! Look behind you!' sang Darzee.

Rikki-tikki knew better than to waste time in staring. He jumped up in the air as high as he could go, and just under him whizzed by the head of Nagaina, Nag's wicked wife. She had crept up behind him as he was talking, to make an end of him; and he heard her savage hiss as the stroke missed. He came down almost across her back, and if he had been an old mongoose he would have known that then was the time to break her back with one bite; but he was afraid of the terrible lashing return-stroke of the cobra. He bit, indeed, but did not bite long enough, and he jumped clear of the whisking tail, leaving Nagaina torn and angry.

'Wicked, wicked Darzee!' said Nag, lashing up as high as he could reach toward the nest in the thorn-bush, but Darzee had built it out of reach of snakes, and it only swayed to and fro.

Rikki-tikki felt his eyes growing red and hot (when a mongoose's eyes grow red, he is angry), and he sat back on his tail and hind legs like a little kangaroo, and looked all round him, and chattered with rage. But Nag and Nagaina had disappeared into the grass. When a snake misses its stroke, it never says anything or gives any sign of what it means to do next. Rikki-tikki did not care to follow them, for he did not feel sure that he could manage two snakes at once. So he trotted off to the gravel path near the house, and sat down to think. It was a serious matter for him.

If you read the old books of natural history, you will find they say that when the mongoose fights the snake and happens to get bitten, he runs off and eats some herb that cures him. That is not true. The victory is only a matter of quickness of eye and quickness of foot, — snake's blow against mongoose's jump, — and as no eye can follow the motion of a snake's head when it strikes, that makes things much more wonderful than any magic herb. Rikki-tikki knew he was a young mongoose, and it made him all the more pleased to think that he had managed to escape a blow from behind. It gave him confidence in himself, and when Teddy came running down the path, Rikki-tikki was ready to be petted.

But just as Teddy was stooping, something flinched a little in the dust, and a tiny voice said: 'Be careful. I am death!' It was Karait, the dusty

"AN UNWELCOME VISITOR"—A FREQUENT INCIDENT OF ANGLO-INDIAN LIFE

brown snakeling that lies for choice on the dusty earth; and his bite is as dangerous as the cobra's. But he is so small that nobody thinks of him, and so he does the more harm to people.

Rikki-tikki's eyes grew red again, and he danced up to Karait with the peculiar rocking, swaying motion that he had inherited from his family. It looks very funny, but it is so perfectly balanced a gait that you can fly off from it at any angle you please; and in dealing with snakes this is an advantage. If Rikki-tikki had only known, he was doing a much more dangerous thing than fighting Nag, for Karait is so small, and can turn so quickly, that unless Rikki bit him close to the back of the head, he would get the return-stroke in his eye or lip. But Rikki did not know: his eyes were all red, and he rocked back and forth, looking for a good place to hold. Karait struck out. Rikki jumped sideways and tried to run in, but the wicked little dusty grey head lashed within a fraction of his shoulder, and he had to jump over the body, and the head followed his heels close.

Teddy shouted to the house: 'Oh, look here! Our mongoose is killing a snake'; and Rikki-tikki heard a scream from Teddy's mother. His father ran out with a stick, but by the time he came up, Karait had lunged out once too far, and Rikki-tikki had sprung, jumped on the snake's back, dropped his head far between his fore-legs, bitten as high up the back as he could get hold, and rolled away. That bite paralysed Karait, and

Rikki-tikki was just going to eat him up from the tail, after the custom of his family at dinner, when he remembered that a full meal makes a slow mongoose, and if he wanted all his strength and quickness ready, he must keep himself thin.

He went away for a dust-bath under the castor-oil bushes, while Teddy's father beat the dead Karait. 'What is the use of that?' thought Rikki-tikki. 'I have settled it all'; and then Teddy's mother picked him up from the dust and hugged him, crying that he had saved Teddy from death, and Teddy's father said that he was a providence, and Teddy looked on with big scared eyes. Rikki-tikki was rather amused at all the fuss, which, of course, he did not understand. Teddy's mother might just as well have petted Teddy for playing in the dust. Rikki was thoroughly enjoying himself.

That night, at dinner, walking to and fro among the wine-glasses on the table, he could have stuffed himself three times over with nice things; but he remembered Nag and Nagaina, and though it was very pleasant to be patted and petted by Teddy's mother, and to sit on Teddy's shoulder, his eyes would get red from time to time, and he would go off into his long war-cry of '*Rikki-tikk-tikki-tikki-tchk!*'

Teddy carried him off to bed, and insisted on Rikki-tikki sleeping under his chin. Rikki-tikki was too well-bred to bite or scratch, but as soon as Teddy was asleep he went off for his nightly walk round the house, and in the dark he ran up against Chuchundra, the musk-rat, creeping round by the wall. Chuchundra is a broken-hearted little beast. He whimpers and cheeps all the night, trying to make up his mind to run into the middle of the room, but he never gets there.

'Don't kill me,' said Chuchundra, almost weeping. 'Rikki-tikki, don't kill me.'

'Do you think a snake-killer kills musk-rats?' said Rikki-tikki scornfully.

'Those who kill snakes get killed by snakes,' said Chuchundra, more sorrowfully than ever. 'And how am I to be sure that Nag won't mistake me for you some dark night?'

'There's not the least danger,' said Rikki-tikki; 'but Nag is in the garden, and I know you don't go there.'

'My cousin Chua, the rat, told me — ' said Chuchundra, and then he stopped.

'Told you what?'

'H'sh! Nag is everywhere, Rikki-tikki. You should have talked to Chua in the garden.'

'I didn't — so you must tell me. Quick, Chuchundra, or I'll bite you!'

Chuchundra sat down and cried till the tears rolled off his whiskers. 'I am a very poor man,' he sobbed. 'I never had spirit enough to run out into the middle of the room. H'sh! I mustn't tell you anything. Can't you *hear*, Rikki-tikki?'

Rikki-tikki listened. The house was as still as still, but he thought he could just catch the faintest *scratch-scratch* in the world, — a noise as faint as that of a wasp walking on a window-pane, — the dry scratch of a snake's scales on brickwork.

'That's Nag or Nagaina,' he said to himself; 'and he is crawling into the bath-room sluice. You're right, Chuchundra, I should have talked to Chua.'

He stole off to Teddy's bath-room, but there was nothing there, and then to Teddy's mother's bath-room. At the bottom of the smooth plaster wall there was a brick pulled out to make a sluice for the bath-water, and as Rikki-tikki stole in by the masonry curb where the bath is put, he heard Nag and Nagaina whispering together outside in the moonlight.

'When the house is emptied of people,' said Nagaina to her husband, '*he* will have to go away, and then the garden will be our own again. Go in quietly, and remember that the big man who killed Karait is the first one to bite. Then come out and tell me, and we will hunt for Rikki-tikki together.'

'But are you sure that there is anything to be gained by killing the people?' said Nag.

'Everything. When there were no people in the bungalow, did we have any mongoose in the garden? So long as the bungalow is empty, we are king and queen of the garden; and remember that as soon as our eggs in the melon-bed hatch (as they may tomorrow), our children will need room and quiet.'

'I had not thought of that,' said Nag. 'I will go, but there is no need that we should hunt for Rikki-tikki afterward. I will kill the big man and his wife, and the child if I can, and come away quietly. Then the bungalow will be empty, and Rikki-tikki will go.'

Rikki-tikki tingled all over with rage and hatred at this, and then Nag's head came through the sluice, and his five feet of cold body followed it. Angry as he was, Rikki-tikki was very frightened as he saw the size of the big cobra. Nag coiled himself up, raised his head, and looked into the bath-room in the dark, and Rikki could see his eyes glitter.

'Now, if I kill him here, Nagaina will know; and if I fight him on the open floor, the odds are in his favour. What am I to do?' said Rikki-tikki-tavi.

Nag waved to and fro, and then Rikki-tikki heard him drinking from the biggest water-jar that was used to fill the bath. 'That is good,' said the snake. 'Now, when Karait was killed, the big man had a stick. He may have that stick still, but when he comes in to bathe in the morning he will not have a stick. I shall wait here till he comes. Nagaina — do you hear me? — I shall wait here in the cool till daytime.'

There was no answer from outside, so Rikki-tikki knew Nagaina had gone away. Nag coiled himself down, coil by coil, round the bulge at the bottom of the water jar, and Rikki-tikki looked at his big back, wondering which would be the best place for a good hold. 'If I don't break his back at the first jump,' said Rikki, 'he can still fight; and if he fights — oh, Rikki!' He looked at the thickness of the neck below the hood, but that was too much for him; and a bite near the tail would only make Nag savage.

'It must be the head,' he said at last; 'the head above the hood; and when I am once there, I must not let go.'

Then he jumped. The head was lying a little clear of the water-jar, under the curve of it; and, as his teeth met, Rikki braced his back against the bulge of the red earthenware to hold down the head. This gave him just one second's purchase, and he made the most of it. Then he was battered to and fro as a rat is shaken by a dog — to and fro on the floor, up and down, and round in great circles; but his eyes were red, and he held on as the body cart-whipped over the floor, upsetting the tin dipper and the soap-dish and the flesh-brush, and banged against the tin side of the bath. As he held he closed his jaws tighter and tighter, for he made sure he would be banged to death, and, for the honour of his family, he preferred to be found with his teeth locked. He was dizzy, aching, and felt shaken to pieces when something went off like a thunderclap just behind him; a hot wind knocked him senseless, and red fire singed his fur. The big man had been wakened by the noise, and had fired both barrels of a shot-gun into Nag just behind the hood.

Rikki-tikki held on with his eyes shut, for now he was quite sure he was dead; but the head did not move, and the big man picked him up and said:

'It's the mongoose again, Alice; the little chap has saved *our* lives now.' Then Teddy's mother came in with a very white face, and saw what was left of Nag, and Rikki-tikki dragged himself to Teddy's bed-room and spent half the rest of the night shaking himself tenderly to find out whether he really was broken into forty pieces, as he fancied.

When morning came he was very stiff, but well pleased with his doings. 'Now I have Nagaina to settle with, and she will be worse than five Nags, and there's no knowing when the eggs she spoke of will hatch. Goodness! I must go and see Darzee,' he said.

Without waiting for breakfast, Rikki-tikki ran to the thorn-bush where Darzee was singing a song of triumph at the top of his voice. The news of Nag's death was all over the garden, for the sweeper had thrown the body on the rubbish-heap.

'Oh, you stupid tuft of feathers!' said Rikki-tikki angrily. 'Is this the time to sing?'

'Nag is dead — is dead — is dead!' sang Darzee. 'The valiant Rikki-tikki caught him by the head and held fast. The big man brought the bang-stick, and Nag fell in two pieces! He will never eat my babies again.'

'All that's true enough; but where's Nagaina?' said Rikki-tikki, looking carefully round him.

'Nagaina came to the bathroom sluice and called for Nag,' Darzee went on; 'and Nag came out on the end of a stick — the sweeper picked him up on the end of a stick and threw him upon the rubbish-heap. Let us sing about the great, the red-eyed Rikki-tikki!' and Darzee filled his throat and sang.

'If I could get up to your nest, I'd roll all your babies out!' said Rikki-tikki. 'You don't know when to do the right thing at the right time. You're safe enough in your nest there, but it's war for me down here. Stop singing a minute, Darzee.'

'For the great, the beautiful Rikki-tikki's sake I will stop,' said Darzee. 'What is it, O Killer of the terrible Nag?'

'Where is Nagaina, for the third time?'

'On the rubbish-heap by the stables, mourning for Nag. Great is Rikki-tikki with the white teeth.'

'Bother my white teeth! Have you ever heard where she keeps her eggs?'

'In the melon-bed, on the end nearest the wall, where the sun strikes nearly all day. She hid them there weeks ago.'

'And you never thought it worth while to tell me? The end nearest the wall, you said?'

'Rikki-tikki, you are not going to eat her eggs?'

'Not eat exactly; no. Darzee, if you have a grain of sense you will fly off to the stables and pretend that your wing is broken, and let Nagaina chase you away to this bush. I must get to the melon-bed, and if I went there now she'd see me.'

Darzee was a feather-brained little fellow who could never hold more than one idea at a time in his head; and just because he knew that Nagaina's children were born in eggs like his own, he didn't think at first that it was fair to kill them. But his wife was a sensible bird, and she knew that cobra's eggs meant young cobras later on; so she flew off from the nest, and left Darzee to keep the babies warm, and continue his song about the death of Nag. Darzee was very like a man in some ways

She fluttered in front of Nagaina by the rubbish-heap, and cried out: 'Oh, my wing is broken! The boy in the house threw a stone at me and broke it.' Then she fluttered more desperately than ever.

Nagaina lifted up her head and hissed: 'You warned Rikki-tikki when I would have killed him. Indeed and truly, you've chosen a bad place to be lame in.' And she moved toward Darzee's wife, slipping along over the dust.

'The boy broke it with a stone!' shrieked Darzee's wife.

'Well, it may be some consolation to you when you're dead to know that I shall settle accounts with the boy. My husband lies on the rubbish-heap this morning, but before night the boy in the house will lie very still. What is the use of running away? I am sure to catch you. Little fool, look at me!'

Darzee's wife knew better than to do *that*, for a bird who looks at a snake's eyes gets so frightened that she cannot move. Darzee's wife fluttered on, piping sorrowfully, and never leaving the ground, and Nagaina quickened her pace.

Rikki-tikki heard them going up the path from the stables, and he raced for the end of the melon-patch near the wall. There, in the warm litter about the melons, very cunningly hidden, he found twenty-five eggs, about the size of a bantam's eggs, but with a whitish skin instead of shell.

'I was not a day too soon,' he said; for he could see the baby cobras curled up inside the skin, and he knew that the minute they were hatched they could each kill a man or a mongoose. He bit off the tops of the eggs as fast as he could, taking care to crush the young cobras, and turned over the litter from time to time to see if he had missed any. At last there were only three eggs left, and Rikki-tikki began to chuckle to himself, when he heard Darzee's wife screaming:

'Rikki-tikki, I led Nagaina toward the house, and she has gone into the verandah, and — oh, come quickly — she means killing!'

Rikki-tikki smashed two eggs, and tumbled backward down the melon-bed with the third egg in his mouth, and scuttled to the verandah as hard as he could put foot to the ground. Teddy and his mother and father were there at early breakfast; but Rikki-tikki saw that they were not eating anything. They sat stone-still, and their faces were white. Nagaina was coiled up on the matting by Teddy's chair, within easy striking-distance of Teddy's bare leg, and she was swaying to and fro singing a song of triumph.

'Son of the big man that killed Nag,' she hissed, 'stay still. I am not ready yet. Wait a little. Keep very still, all you three. If you move I strike, and if you do not move I strike. Oh, foolish people, who killed my Nag!'

Teddy's eyes were fixed on his father, and all his father could do was to whisper: 'Sit still, Teddy. You mustn't move. Teddy, keep still.'

Then Rikki-tikki came up and cried: 'Turn round, Nagaina; turn and fight!'

'All in good time,' said she, without moving her eyes. 'I will settle my account with *you* presently. Look at your friends, Rikki-tikki. They are still and white; they are afraid. They dare not move, and if you come a step nearer I strike.'

'Look at your eggs,' said Rikki-tikki, 'in the melon-bed near the wall. Go and look, Nagaina.'

The big snake turned half-round, and saw the egg on the verandah. 'Ah-h! Give it to me,' she said.

Rikki-tikki put his paws on each side of the egg, and his eyes were blood-red. 'What price for a snake's egg? For a young cobra? For a young king-cobra? For the last — the very last of the brood? The ants are eating all the others down by the melon-bed.'

Nagaina spun clear round, forgetting everything for the sake of the one egg; and Rikki-tikki saw Teddy's father shoot out a big hand, catch Teddy by the shoulder, and drag him across the little table with the tea-cups, safe and out of reach of Nagaina.

'Tricked! Tricked! Tricked! *Rikk-tck-tck!*' chuckled Rikki-tikki. 'The boy is safe, and it was I — I — I that caught Nag by the hood last night in the bath-room.' Then he began to jump up and down, all four feet together, his head close to the floor. 'He threw me to and fro, but he could not shake me off. He was dead before the big man blew him in two. I did it. *Rikki-tikki-tck-tck!* Come then, Nagaina. Come and fight with me. You shall not be a widow long.'

Nagaina saw that she had lost her chance of killing Teddy, and the egg lay between Rikki-tikki's paws. 'Give me the egg, Rikki-tikki. Give me the last of my eggs, and I will go away and never come back,' she said, lowering her hood.

'Yes, you will go away, and you will never come back; for you will go to the rubbish-heap with Nag. Fight, widow! The big man has gone for his gun! Fight!'

Rikki-tikki was bounding all round Nagaina, keeping just out of reach of her stroke, his little eyes like hot coals. Nagaina gathered herself together, and flung out at him. Rikki-tikki jumped up and backward. Again and again and again she struck, and each time her head came with a whack on the matting of the verandah, and she gathered herself together like a watch-spring. Then Rikki-tikki danced in a circle to get behind her, and Nagaina spun round to keep her head to his head, so that the rustle of her tail on the matting sounded like dry leaves blown along by the wind.

He had forgotten the egg. It still lay on the verandah, and Nagaina came nearer and nearer to it, till at last, while Rikki-tikki was drawing breath, she caught it in her mouth, turned to the verandah steps, and flew like an arrow down the path, with Rikki-tikki behind her. When the cobra runs for her life, she goes like a whiplash flicked across a horse's neck.

Rikki-tikki knew that he must catch her, or all the trouble would begin again. She headed straight for the long grass by the thorn-bush, and as he was running Rikki-tikki heard Darzee still singing his foolish little song of triumph. But Darzee's wife was wiser. She flew off her nest as Nagaina came along, and flapped her wings about Nagaina's head. If Darzee had helped they might have turned her; but Nagaina only lowered her hood and went on. Still, the instant's delay brought Rikki-tikki up to her, and as she plunged into the rat-hole where she and Nag used to live, his little white teeth were clenched on her tail, and he went down with her — and very few mongooses, however wise and old they may be, care to follow a cobra into its hole. It was dark in the hole; and Rikki-tikki never knew when it might open out and give Nagaina room to turn and strike at him.

He held on savagely, and struck out his feet to act as brakes on the dark slope of the hot, moist earth.

Then the grass by the mouth of the hole stopped waving, and Darzee said: 'It is all over with Rikki-tikki! We must sing his death-song. Valiant Rikki-tikki is dead! For Nagaina will surely kill him underground.'

So he sang a very mournful song that he made up on the spur of the minute, and just as he got to the most touching part the grass quivered again, and Rikki-tikki, covered with dirt, dragged himself out of the hole leg by leg, licking his whiskers. Darzee stopped with a little shout. Rikki-tikki shook some of the dust out of his fur and sneezed. 'It is all over,' he said. 'The widow will never come out again.' And the red ants that live between the grass-stems heard him, and began to troop down one after another to see if he had spoken the truth.

Rikki-tikki curled himself up in the grass and slept where he was — slept and slept till it was late in the afternoon, for he had done a hard day's work.

'Now,' he said, when he awoke, 'I will go back to the house. Tell the Coppersmith, Darzee, and he will tell the garden that Nagaina is dead.'

The Coppersmith is a bird who makes a noise exactly like the beating of a little hammer on a copper pot; and the reason he is always making it is because he is the town-crier to every Indian garden, and tells all the news to everybody who cares to listen. As Rikki-tikki went up the path, he heard his 'attention' notes like a tiny dinner-gong; and then the steady '*Ding-dong-tock!* Nag is dead — *dong!* Nagaina is dead! *Ding-dong-tock!*' That set all the birds in the garden singing, and the frogs croaking; for Nag and Nagaina used to eat frogs as well as little birds.

When Rikki got to the house, Teddy and Teddy's mother (she still looked very white, for she had been fainting) and Teddy's father came out and almost cried over him; and that night he ate all that was given to him till he could eat no more, and went to bed on Teddy's shoulder, where Teddy's mother saw him when she came to look late at night.

'He saved our lives and Teddy's life,' she said to her husband. 'Just think, he saved all our lives!'

Rikki-tikki woke up with a jump, for all the mongooses are light sleepers.

'Oh, it's you,' said he. 'What are you bothering for? All the cobras are dead; and if they weren't, I'm here.'

Rikki-tikki had a right to be proud of himself; but he did not grow too proud, and he kept that garden as a mongoose should keep it, with tooth and jump and spring and bite, till never a cobra dared show its head inside the walls.

THE UNDERTAKERS

Respect the aged!'

It was a thick voice — a muddy voice that would have made you shudder — a voice like something soft breaking in two. There was a quaver in it, a croak and a whine.

'Respect the aged! O Companions of the River — respect the aged!'

Nothing could be seen on the broad reach of the river except a little fleet of square-sailed, wooden-pinned barges, loaded with building-stone, that had just come under the railway bridge, and were driving down-stream. They put their clumsy helms over to avoid the sand-bar made by the scour of the bridge-piers, and as they passed, three abreast, the horrible voice began again:

'O Brahmins of the River — respect the aged and infirm!'

A boatman turned where he sat on the gunwale, lifted up his hand, said something that was not a blessing, and the boats creaked on through the twilight. The broad Indian river, that looked more like a chain of little lakes than a stream, was as smooth as glass, reflecting the sandy-red sky in mid-channel, but splashed with patches of yellow and dusky purple near and under the low banks. Little creeks ran into the river in the wet season, but now their dry mouths hung clear above the water-line. On the left shore, and almost under the railway bridge, stood a mud-and-brick and thatch-and-stick village, whose main street, full of cattle going back to their byres, ran straight to the river, and ended in a sort of rude brick pier-head, where people who wanted to wash could wade in step by step. That was the Ghaut of the village of Mugger-Ghaut.

Night was falling fast over the fields of lentils and rice and cotton in the low-lying ground yearly flooded by the river; over the reeds that fringed the elbow of the bend, and the tangled jungle of the grazing-grounds behind the still reeds. The parrots and crows, who had been chattering and shouting over their evening drink, had flown inland to roost, crossing the out-going battalions of the flying-foxes; and cloud upon cloud of water-birds came whistling and 'honking' to the cover of the reed-beds. There were geese, barrel-headed and black-backed, teal, widgeon, mallard, and sheldrake, with curlews, and here and there a flamingo.

A lumbering Adjutant-crane brought up the rear, flying as though each slow stroke would be his last.

'Respect the aged! Brahmins of the River — respect the aged!'

The Adjutant half turned his head, sheered a little in the direction of the voice and landed stiffly on the sand-bar below the bridge. Then you saw what a ruffianly brute he really was. His back view was immensely respectable, for he stood nearly six feet high, and looked rather like a very proper bald-headed parson. In front it was different, for his Ally Sloper-like head and neck had not a feather to them, and there was a horrible raw-skin pouch on his neck under his chin — a hold-all for the things his pick-axe beak might steal. His legs were long and thin and skinny, but he moved them delicately, and looked at them with pride as he preened down his ashy-grey tail-feathers, glanced over the smooth of his shoulder, and stiffened into 'Stand at attention.'

A mangy little Jackal, who had been yapping hungrily on a low bluff, cocked up his ears and tail, and scuttered across the shallows to join the Adjutant.

He was the lowest of his caste — not that the best of jackals are good for much, but this one was peculiarly low, being half a beggar, half a criminal — a cleaner-up of village rubbish heaps, desperately timid or wildly bold, everlastingly hungry, and full of cunning that never did him any good.

'Ugh!' he said, shaking himself dolefully as he landed. 'May the red mange destroy the dogs of this village! I have three bites for each flea upon me, and all because I looked — only looked, mark you — at an old shoe in a cow-byre. Can I eat mud?' He scratched himself under his left ear.

'I heard,' said the Adjutant, in a voice like a blunt saw going through a thick board — 'I *heard* there was a new-born puppy in that same shoe.'

'To hear is one thing; to know is another,' said the Jackal, who had a very fair knowledge of proverbs, picked up by listening to men round the village fires of an evening.

'Quite true. So, to make sure, I took care of that puppy while the dogs were busy elsewhere,'

'They were *very* busy,' said the Jackal. 'Well, I must not go to the village hunting for scraps yet awhile. And so there truly was a blind puppy in that shoe?'

'It is here,' said the Adjutant, squinting over his beak at his full pouch. 'A small thing, but acceptable now that charity is dead in the world.'

'Ahai! The world is iron in these days,' wailed the Jackal. Then his restless eye caught the least possible ripple on the water, and he went on quickly: 'Life is hard for us all, and I doubt not that even our excellent master, the Pride of the Ghaut and the Envy of the River — '

'A liar, a flatterer, and a Jackal were all hatched out of the same egg,' said the Adjutant to nobody in particular; for he was rather a fine sort of a liar on his own account when he took the trouble.

'Yes, the Envy of the River,' the Jackal repeated, raising his voice. 'Even he, I doubt not, finds that since the bridge has been built good food is more scarce. But on the other hand, though I would by no means say this to his noble face, he is so wise and so virtuous — as I, alas!, am not — '

'When the Jackal owns he is grey, how black must the Jackal be!' muttered the Adjutant. He could not see what was coming.

'That *his* food never fails, and in consequence — '

There was a soft grating sound, as though a boat had just touched in shoal water. The Jackal spun round quickly and faced (it is always best to face) the creature he had been talking about. It was a twenty-four-foot crocodile, cased in what looked like treble-riveted boiler-plate, studded and keeled and crested; the yellow points of his upper teeth just overhanging his beautifully fluted lower jaw. It was the blunt-nosed Mugger of Mugger-Ghaut, older than any man in the village, who had given his name to the village; the demon of the ford before the railway bridge came — murderer, man-eater, and local fetish in one. He lay with his chin in the shallows, keeping his place by an almost invisible rippling of his tail, and well the Jackal knew that one stroke of that same tail in the water would carry the Mugger up the bank with the rush of a steam-engine.

'Auspiciously met, Protector of the Poor!' he fawned, backing at every word. 'A delectable voice was heard, and we came in the hopes of sweet conversation. My tailless presumption, while waiting here, led me, indeed, to speak of thee. It is my hope that nothing was overheard.'

Now the Jackal had spoken just to be listened to, for he knew flattery was the best way of getting things to eat, and the Mugger knew that the Jackal had spoken for this end, and the Jackal knew that the Mugger knew, and the Mugger knew that the Jackal knew that the Mugger knew, and so they were all very contented together.

The old brute pushed and panted and grunted up the bank, mumbling, 'Respect the aged and infirm!' and all the time his little eyes burned like coals under the heavy, horny eyelids on the top of his triangular head, as he shoved his bloated barrel-body along between his crutched legs. Then he settled down, and accustomed as the Jackal was to his ways, he could not help starting, for the hundredth time, when he saw how exactly the Mugger imitated a log adrift on the bar. He had even taken pains to lie at the exact angle a naturally stranded log would make with the water, having regard to the current of the season at the time and place. All this was only a matter of habit, of course, because the Mugger had come ashore for pleasure; but a crocodile is never quite full, and if the Jackal had been deceived by the likeness he would not have lived to philosophise over it.

'My child, I heard nothing,' said the Mugger, shutting one eye. 'The water

was in my ears, and also I was faint with hunger. Since the railway bridge was built my people at my village have ceased to love me; and that is breaking my heart.'

'Ah, shame!' said the Jackal. 'So noble a heart, too! But men are all alike, to my mind.'

'Nay, there are very great differences indeed,' the Mugger answered gently. 'Some are as lean as boat-poles. Others again are as fat as young ja — dogs. Never would I causelessly revile men. They are of all fashions, but the long years have shown me that, one with another, they are very good. Men, women, and children — I have no fault to find with them. And remember, child, he who rebukes the World is rebuked by the World.'

'Flattery is worse than an empty tin can in the belly. But that which we have just heard is wisdom,' said the Adjutant, bringing down one foot.

'Consider, though, their ingratitude to this excellent one,' began the Jackal tenderly.

'Nay, nay, not ingratitude!' the Mugger said. 'They do not think for others; that is all. But I have noticed, lying at my station below the ford, that the stairs of the new bridge are cruelly hard to climb, both for old people and young children. The old, indeed, are not so worthy of consideration, but I am grieved — I am truly grieved — on account of the fat children. Still, I think, in a little while, when the newness of the bridge has worn away, we shall see my people's bare brown legs bravely splashing through the ford as before. Then the old Mugger will be honoured again.'

'But surely I saw marigold wreaths floating off the edge of the Ghaut only this noon,' said the Adjutant.

Marigold wreaths are a sign of reverence all India over.

'An error — an error. It was the wife of the sweetmeat-seller. She loses her eyesight year by year, and cannot tell a log from me — the Mugger of the Ghaut. I saw the mistake when she threw the garland, for I was lying at the very foot of the Ghaut, and had she taken another step I might have shown her some little difference. Yet she meant well, and we must consider the spirit of the offering.'

'What good are marigold wreaths when one is on the rubbish-heap?' said the Jackal, hunting for fleas, but keeping one wary eye on his Protector of the Poor.

'True, but they have not yet begun to make the rubbish-heap that shall carry *me*. Five times have I seen the river draw back from the village and make new land at the foot of the street. Five times have I seen the village rebuilt on the banks, and I shall see it built yet five times more. I am no faithless, fish-hunting Gavial, I, at Kasi today and Prayag tomorrow, as the saying is, but the true and constant watcher of the ford. It is not for nothing, child, that the village bears my name, and "he who watches long", as the saying is, "shall at last have his reward." '

'*I* have watched long — very long — nearly all my life, and my reward has been bites and blows,' said the Jackal.

'Ho! ho! ho!' roared the Adjutant.

'In August was the Jackal born;
The Rains fell in September;
"Now such a fearful flood as this,"
Says he, "I can't remember!" '

There is one very unpleasant peculiarity about the Adjutant. At uncertain times he suffers from acute attacks of the fidgets or cramp in his legs, and though he is more virtuous to behold than any of the cranes, who are all immensely respectable, he flies off into wild, cripple-stilt war-dances, half-opening his wings and bobbing his bald head up and down; while for reasons best known to himself he is very careful to time his worst attacks with his nastiest remarks. At the last word of his song he came to attention again, ten times adjutaunter than before.

The Jackal winced, though he was full three seasons old, but you cannot resent an insult from a person with a beak a yard long, and the power of driving it like a javelin. The Adjutant was a most notorious coward, but the Jackal was worse.

'We must live before we can learn,' said the Mugger, 'and there is this to say: Little jackals are very common, child, but such a mugger as I am is not common. For all that, I am not proud, since pride is destruction; but take notice, it is Fate, and against his Fate no one who swims or walks or runs should say anything at all. I am well contented with Fate. With good luck, a keen eye, and the custom of considering whether a creek or a backwater has an outlet to it ere you ascend, much may be done.'

'Once I heard that even the Protector of the Poor made a mistake,' said the Jackal viciously.

'True; but there my Fate helped me. It was before I had come to my full growth — before the last famine but three (by the Right and Left of Gunga, how full used the streams to be in those days!). Yes, I was young and unthinking, and when the flood came, who so pleased as I? A little made me very happy then. The village was deep in flood, and I swam above the Ghaut and went far inland, up to the rice-fields, and they were deep in good mud. I remember also a pair of bracelets (glass they were, and troubled me not a little) that I found that evening. Yes, glass bracelets; and, if my memory serves me well, a shoe. I should have shaken off both shoes, but I was hungry. I learned better later. Yes. And so I fed and rested me; but when I was ready to go to the river again the flood had fallen, and I walked through the mud of the main street. Who but I? Came out all my people, priests and women and children, and I looked upon them with benevolence. The mud is not a good place to fight in. Said a boatman, "Get axes and kill him, for he is the Mugger of the ford." "Not so," said the Brahmin. "Look, he is driving the flood before him! He is the godling of the village." Then they threw many flowers at me, and by happy thought one led a goat across the road.'

'How good — how very good is goat!' said the Jackal.

'Hairy — too hairy, and when found in the water more than likely to hide a cross-shaped hook. But that goat I accepted, and went down to the Ghaut in great honour. Later, my Fate sent me the boatman who had desired to cut off my tail with an axe. His boat grounded upon an old shoal which you would not remember.'

'We are not *all* jackals here,' said the Adjutant. 'Was it the shoal made where the stone-boats sank in the year of the great drouth — a long shoal that lasted three floods?'

'There were two,' said the Mugger; 'an upper and a lower shoal.'

'Ay, I forgot. A channel divided them, and later dried up again,' said the Adjutant, who prided himself on his memory.

'On the lower shoal my well-wisher's craft grounded. He was sleeping in the bows, and, half awake, leaped over to his waist — no, it was no more than to his knees — to push off. His empty boat went on and touched again below the next reach, as the river ran then. I followed, because I knew men would come out to drag it ashore.'

'And did they do so?' said the Jackal, a little awe-stricken. This was hunting on a scale that impressed him.

'There and lower down they did. I went no farther, but that gave me three in one day — well-fed *manjis* all, and, except in the case of the last (then I was careless), never a cry to warn those on the bank.'

'Ah, noble sport! But what cleverness and great judgment it requires!' said the Jackal.

'Not cleverness, child, but only thought. A little thought in life is like salt upon rice, as the boatmen say, and I have thought deeply always. The Gavial, my cousin, the fish-eater, has told me how hard it is for him to follow his fish, and how one fish differs from the other, and how he must know them all, both together and apart. I say that is wisdom; but, on the other hand, my cousin, the Gavial, lives among his people. *My* people do not swim in companies, with their mouths out of the water, as Rewa does; nor do they constantly rise to the surface of the water, and turn over on their sides, like Mohoo and little Chapta; nor do they gather in shoals after flood, like Batchua and Chilwa.'

'All are very good eating,' said the Adjutant, clattering his beak.

'So my cousin says, and makes a great to-do over hunting them, but they do not climb the banks to escape his sharp nose. *My* people are otherwise. Their life is on the land, in the houses, among the cattle. I must know what they do, and what they are about to do; and, adding the tail to the trunk, as the saying is, I make up the whole elephant. Is there a green branch and an iron ring hanging over a doorway? The old Mugger knows that a boy has been born in that house, and must some day come down to the Ghaut to play. Is a maiden to be married? The old Mugger knows, for he sees the men carry gifts back and forth; and, she, too, comes down to the Ghaut to bathe before her wedding, and — he is there. Has the river changed its channel, and made new land where there was only sand before? The Mugger knows.'

'Now, of what use is that knowledge?' said the Jackal. 'The river has shifted even in my little life.' Indian rivers are nearly always moving about in their beds, and will shift, sometimes, as much as two or three miles in a season, drowning the fields on one bank, and spreading good silt on the other.

'There is no knowledge so useful,' said the Mugger, 'for new land means new quarrels. The Mugger knows. Oho! the Mugger knows. As soon as the water has drained off, he creeps up the little creeks that men think would not hide a dog, and there he waits. Presently comes a farmer saying he will plant cucumbers here, and melons there, in the new land that the river has given him. He feels the good mud with his bare toes. Anon comes another, saying he will put onions, and carrots, and sugar-cane in such and such places. They meet as boats adrift meet, and each rolls his eye at the other under the big blue turban. The old Mugger sees and hears. Each calls the other "Brother", and they go to mark out the boundaries of the new land. The Mugger hurries with them from point to point, shuffling very low through the mud. Now they begin to quarrel! Now they say hot words! Now they pull turbans! Now they lift up their *lathis*, and, at last, one falls backward into the mud, and the other runs away. When he comes back the dispute is settled, as the iron-bound bamboo of the loser witnesses. Yet they are not grateful to the Mugger. No, they cry "Murder!" and their families fight with sticks, twenty a-side. My people are good people — upland Jats — Malwais of the Bêt. They do not give blows for sport, and, when the fight is done, the old Mugger waits far down the river, out of sight of the village, behind the *kikar*-scrub yonder. Then come they down, my broad-shouldered Jats — eight or nine together under the stars, bearing the dead man upon a bed. They are old men with grey beards, and voices as deep as mine. They light a little fire — ah! how well I know that fire! — and they drink tobacco, and they nod their heads together forward in a ring, or sideways toward the dead man upon the bank. They say the English Law will come with a rope for this matter, and that such a man's family will be ashamed, because such a man must be hanged in the great square of the Jail. Then say the friends of the dead, "Let him hang!" and the talk is all to do over again — once, twice, twenty times in the long night. Then says one, at last, "The fight was a fair fight. Let us take blood-money, a little more than is offered by the slayer, and we will say no more about it," Then do they haggle over the blood-money, for the dead was a strong man, leaving many sons. Yet before *amratvela* they put the fire to him a little, as the custom is, and the dead man comes to me, and *he* says no more about it. Aha! my children, the Mugger knows — the Mugger knows — and my Malwah Jats are a good people!'

'They are too close — too narrow in the hand for my crop,' croaked the Adjutant. 'They waste not the polish on the cow's horn, as the saying is; and, again, who can glean after a Malwai?'

'Ah, I — glean — *them*,' said the Mugger.

'Now, in Calcutta of the South, in the old days, 'the Adjutant went on, 'everything was thrown into the streets, and we picked and chose. Those were dainty seasons. But today they keep their streets as clean as the outside of an egg, and my people fly away. To be clean is one thing; to dust, sweep, and sprinkle seven times a day wearies the very Gods themselves.'

'There was a down-country jackal had it from a brother, who told me, that in Calcutta of the South all the jackals were as fat as otters in the Rains,' said the Jackal, his mouth watering at the bare thought of it.

'Ah, but the white-faces are there — the English, and they bring dogs from somewhere down the river in boats — big fat dogs — to keep those same jackals lean,' said the Adjutant.

'They are, then, as hard-hearted as these people? I might have known. Neither earth, sky, nor water shows charity to a jackal. I saw the tents of a white-face last season, after the Rains, and I also took a new yellow bridle to eat. The white-faces do not dress their leather in the proper way. It made me very sick.'

'That was better than my case,' said the Adjutant. 'When I was in my third season, a young and a bold bird, I went down to the river where the big boats come in. The boats of the English are thrice as big as this village.'

'He has been as far as Delhi, and says all the people there walk on their heads,' muttered the Jackal. The Mugger opened his left eye, and looked keenly at the Adjutant.

'It is true,' the big bird insisted. 'A liar only lies when he hopes to be believed. No one who had not seen those boats *could* believe this truth.'

'*That* is more reasonable,' said the Mugger. 'And then?'

'From the insides of this boat they were taking out great pieces of white stuff, which, in a little while, turned to water. Much split off, and fell about on the shore, and the rest they swiftly put into a house with thick walls. But a boatman, who laughed, took a piece no larger than a small dog, and threw it to me. I — all my people — swallow without reflection, and that piece I swallowed as is our custom. Immediately I was afflicted with an excessive cold which, beginning in my crop, ran down to the extreme end of my toes, and deprived me even of speech, while the boatmen laughed at me. Never have I felt such cold. I danced in my grief and amazement till I could recover my breath and then I danced and cried out against the falseness of this world; and the boatmen derided me till they fell down. The chief wonder of the matter, setting aside that marvellous coldness, was that there was nothing at all in my crop when I had finished my lamentings!'

The Adjutant had done his very best to describe his feelings after swallowing a seven-pound lump of Wenham Lake ice, off an American ice-ship, in the days before Calcutta made her ice by machinery; but as he

did not know what ice was, and as the Mugger and the Jackal knew rather less, the tale missed fire.

'Anything,' said the Mugger, shutting his left eye again — '*anything* is possible that comes out of a boat thrice the size of Mugger-Ghaut. My village is not a small one.'

There was a whistle overhead on the bridge, and the Delhi Mail slid across, all the carriages gleaming with light, and the shadows faithfully following along the river. It clanked away into the dark again; but the Mugger and Jackal were so well used to it that they never turned their heads.

'Is there anything less wonderful than a boat thrice the size of Mugger-Ghaut?' said the bird, looking up.

'I saw that built, child. Stone by stone I saw the bridge-piers rise, and when the men fell off (they were wondrous sure-footed for the most part — but *when* they fell) I was ready. After the first pier was made they never thought to look down the stream for the body to burn. There, again, I saved much trouble. There was nothing strange in the building of the bridge,' said the Mugger.

'But that which goes across, pulling the roofed carts! That is strange,' the Adjutant repeated.

'It is, past any doubt, a new breed of bullock. Some day it will not be able to keep its foothold up yonder, and will fall as the men did. The old Mugger will then be ready.'

The Jackal looked at the Adjutant, and the Adjutant looked at the Jackal.

If there was one thing they were more certain of than another, it was that the engine was everything in the wide world except a bullock. The Jackal had watched it time and again from the aloe hedges by the side of the line, and the Adjutant had seen engines since the first locomotive ran in India. But the Mugger had only looked up at the thing from below, where the brass dome seemed rather like a bullock's hump.

'M — yes, a new kind of bullock,' the Mugger repeated ponderously, to make himself quite sure in his own mind; and 'Certainly it is a bullock,' said the Jackal.

'And again it might be — ' began the Mugger pettishly.

'Certainly — most certainly,' said the Jackal, without waiting for the other to finish.

'What?' said the Mugger angrily, for he could feel that the others knew more than he did. 'What might it be? *I* never finished my words. You said it was a bullock.'

'It is anything the Protector of the Poor pleases. I am *his* servant — not the servant of the thing that crosses the river.'

'Whatever it is, it is white-face work,' said the Adjutant; 'and for my own part, I would not lie out upon a place so near to it as this bar.'

'You do not know the English as I do,' said the Mugger. 'There was a white-face here when the bridge was built, and he would take a boat in the evenings and shuffle with his feet on the bottom-boards, and whisper: "Is he here? Is he here? Bring me my gun." I could hear him before I could see him — each sound that he made — creaking and puffing and rattling his gun, up and down the river. As surely as I had picked up one of his workmen, and thus saved great expense in wood for the burning, so surely would he come down to the Ghaut, and shout in a loud voice that he would hunt me, and rid the river of me — the Mugger of Mugger-Ghaut! *Me*! Children, I have swum under the bottom of his boat for hour after hour, and heard him fire his gun at logs; and when I was well sure he was wearied, I have risen by his side and snapped my jaws in his face. When the bridge was finished he went away. All the English hunt in that fashion, except when they are hunted.'

'Who hunts the white-faces?' yapped the Jackal excitedly.

'No one now, but I have hunted them in my time.'

'I remember a little of that Hunting. I was young then,' said the Adjutant, clattering his beak significantly.

'I was well established here. My village was being builded for the third time, as I remember, when my cousin, the Gavial, brought me word of rich waters above Benares. At first I would not go, for my cousin, who is a fish-eater, does not always know the good from the bad; but I heard my people talking in the evenings, and what they said made me certain.'

'And what did they say?' the Jackal asked.

'They said enough to make me, the Mugger of Mugger-Ghaut, leave water and take to my feet. I went by night, using the littlest streams as they served me; but it was the beginning of the hot weather, and all streams were low. I crossed dusty roads; I went through tall grass; I climbed hills in the moonlight. Even rocks did I climb, children — consider this well. I crossed the tail of Sirhind, the waterless, before I could find the set of the little rivers that flow Gungaward. I was a month's journey from my own people and the river that I knew. That was very marvellous!'

'What food on the way?' said the Jackal, who kept his soul in his little stomach, and was not a bit impressed by the Mugger's land travels.

'That which I could find — *cousin*,' said the Mugger slowly, dragging each word.

Now you do not call a man a cousin in India unless you think you can establish some kind of blood-relationship, and as it is only in old fairy-tales that the Mugger ever marries a jackal, the Jackal knew for what reason he had been suddenly lifted into the Mugger's family circle. If they had been alone he would not have cared, but the Adjutant's eyes twinkled with mirth at the ugly jest.

'Assuredly, Father, I might have known,' said the Jackal. A mugger does not care to be called a father of jackals, and the Mugger of Mugger-Ghaut said as much — and a great deal more which there is no use repeating here.

'The Protector of the Poor has claimed kinship. How can I remember the precise degree? Moreover, we eat the same food. He has said it,' was the Jackal's reply.

That made matters rather worse, for what the Jackal hinted at was that the Mugger must have eaten his food on that land-march fresh and fresh every day, instead of keeping it by him till it was in a fit and proper condition, as every self-respecting mugger and most wild beasts do when they can. Indeed, one of the worst terms of contempt along the river-bed is 'eater of fresh meat'. It is nearly as bad as calling a man a cannibal.

'That food was eaten thirty seasons ago,' said the Adjutant quietly. 'If we talk for thirty seasons more it will never come back. Tell us, now, what happened when the good waters were reached after thy most wonderful land journey. If we listened to the howling of every jackal the business of the town would stop, as the saying is.'

The Mugger must have been grateful for the interruption, because he went on, with a rush:

'By the Right and Left of Gunga! when I came there never did I see such waters!'

'Were they better, then, than the big flood of last season?' said the Jackal.

'Better! That flood was no more than comes every five years — a handful of drowned strangers, some chickens, and a dead bullock in muddy water with cross-currents. But the season I think of, the river was low, smooth, and even, and, as the Gavial had warned me, the dead English came down, touching each other. I got my girth in that season — my girth and my depth. From Agra, by Etawah and the broad waters by Allahabad — '

'Oh, the eddy that set under the walls of the fort at Allahabad!' said the Adjutant. 'They came in there like widgeon to the reeds, and round and round they swung — thus!'

He went off into his horrible dance again, while the Jackal looked on enviously. He naturally could not remember the terrible year of the Mutiny they were talking about. The Mugger continued:

'Yes, by Allahabad one lay still in the slack-water and let twenty go by to pick one; and, above all, the English were not cumbered with jewellery and nose-rings and anklets as my women are nowadays. To delight in ornaments is to end with a rope for a necklace, as the saying is. All the muggers of all the rivers grew fat then, but it was my Fate to be fatter than them all. The news was that the English were being hunted into the rivers, and by the Right and Left of Gunga! we believed it was true. So far as I went south I believed it to be true; and I went down-stream beyond Monghyr and the tombs that look over the river.'

'I know that place,' said the Adjutant. 'Since those days Monghyr is a lost city. Very few live there now.'

'Thereafter I worked up-stream very slowly and lazily, and a little above Monghyr there came down a boatful of white-faces — alive! They were, as I remember, women, lying under a cloth spread over sticks, and crying aloud. There was never a gun fired at us, the watchers of the fords in those days. All the guns were busy elsewhere. We could hear them day and night inland, coming and going as the wind shifted. I rose up full before the boat, because I had never seen white-faces alive, though I knew them well — otherwise. A naked white child kneeled by the side of the boat, and, stooping over, must needs try to trail his hands in the river. It is a pretty thing to see how a child loves running water. I had fed that day, but there was yet a little unfilled space within me. Still, it was for sport and not for food that I rose at the child's hands. They were so clear a mark that I did not even look when I closed; but they were so small that though my jaws rang true — I am sure of that — the child drew them up swiftly, unhurt. They must have passed between tooth and tooth — those small white hands. I should have caught him cross-wise at the elbows; but, as I said, it was only for sport and desire to see new things that I rose at all. They cried out one after another in the boat, and presently I rose again to watch them. The boat was too heavy to push over. They were only women, but he who trusts a woman will walk on duck-weed in a pool, as the saying is: and by the Right and Left of Gunga, that is truth!'

'Once a woman gave me some dried skin from a fish,' said the Jackal. 'I had hoped to get her baby, but horse-food is better than the kick of a horse, as the saying is. What did thy woman do?'

'She fired at me with a short gun of a kind I have never seen before or since. Five times, one after another' (the Mugger must have met with an old-fashioned revolver); 'and I stayed open-mouthed and gaping, my head in the smoke. Never did I see such a thing. Five times, as swiftly as I wave my tail — thus!'

The Jackal, who had been growing more and more interested in the story, had just time to leap back as the huge tail swung by like a scythe.

'Not before the fifth shot,' said the Mugger, as though he had never dreamed of stunning one of his listeners — 'not before the fifth shot did I sink, and I rose in time to hear a boatman telling all those white women that I was most certainly dead. One bullet had gone under a neck-plate of mine. I know not if it is there still, for the reason I cannot turn my head. Look and see, child. It will show that my tale is true.'

'I?' said the Jackal. 'Shall an eater of old shoes, a bone-cracker, presume to doubt the word of the Envy of the River? May my tail be bitten off by blind puppies if the shadow of such a thought has crossed my humble mind! The Protector of the Poor has condescended to inform me, his slave, that once in his life he has been wounded by a woman. That is sufficient, and I will tell the tale to all my children, asking for no proof.'

'Over-much civility is sometimes no better than over-much discourtesy, for, as the saying is, one can choke a guest with curds. I do *not* desire that any children of thine should know that the Mugger of Mugger-Ghaut took his only wound from a woman. They will have much else to think of if they get their meat as miserably as does their father.'

'It is forgotten long ago! It was never said! There never was a white woman! There was no boat! Nothing whatever happened at all.'

The Jackal waved his brush to show how completely everything was wiped out of his memory, and sat down with an air.

'Indeed, very many things happened,' said the Mugger, beaten in his second attempt that night to get the better of his friend. (Neither bore malice, however. Eat and be eaten was fair law along the river, and the Jackal came in for his share of plunder when the Mugger had finished a meal.) 'I left that boat and went up-stream, and, when I had reached Arrah and the back-waters behind it, there were no more dead English. The river was empty for a while. Then came one or two dead, in red coats, not English, but of one kind all — Hindus and Purbeeahs — then five and six abreast, and at last, from Arrah to the North beyond Agra, it was as though whole villages had walked into the water. They came out of little creeks one after another, as the logs come down in the Rains. When the river rose they rose also in companies from the shoals they had rested upon; and the

falling flood dragged them with it across the fields and through the Jungle by the long hair. All night, too, going North, I heard the guns, and by day the shod feet of men crossing fords, and that noise which a heavy cartwheel makes on sand under water; and every ripple brought more dead. At last even I was afraid, for I said: "If this thing happen to men, how shall the Mugger of Mugger-Ghaut escape?" There were boats, too, that came up behind me without sails, burning continually, as the cotton-boats sometimes burn, but never sinking.'

'Ah!' said the Adjutant. 'Boats like those come to Calcutta of the South. They are tall and black, they beat up the water behind them with a tail, and they — '

'Are thrice as big as my village. *My* boats were low and white; they beat up the water on either side of them, and were no larger than the boats of one who speaks truth should be. They made me very afraid, and I left water and went back to this my river, hiding by day and walking by night, when I could not find little streams to help me. I came to my village again, but I did not hope to see any of my people there. Yet they were ploughing and sowing and reaping, and going to and fro in their fields, as quietly as their own cattle.'

'Was there still good food in the river?' said the Jackal.

'More than I had any desire for. Even I — and I do not eat mud — even I was tired, and, as I remember, a little frightened of this constant coming down of the silent ones. I heard my people say in my village that all the English were dead; but those that came, face down, with the current were *not* English, as my people saw. Then my people said it was best to say nothing at all, but to pay the tax and plough the land. After a long time the river cleared, and those that came down it had been clearly drowned by the floods, as I could well see; and though it was not so easy then to get food, I was heartily glad of it. A little killing here and there is no bad thing—but even the Mugger is sometimes satisfied, as the saying is.'

'Marvellous! Most truly marvellous!' said the Jackal. 'I am become fat through merely hearing about so much good eating. And afterward what, if it be permitted to ask, did the Protector of the Poor do?'

'I said to myself — and by the Right and Left of Gunga! I locked my jaws on that vow — I said I would never go roving any more. So I lived by the Ghaut, very close to my own people, and I watched over them year after year; and they loved me so much that they threw marigold wreaths at my head whenever they saw it lift. Yes, and my Fate has been very kind to me, and the river is good enough to respect my poor and infirm presence; onlv —'

'No one is all happy from his beak to his tail,' said the Adjutant sympathetically. 'What does the Mugger of Mugger-Ghaut need more?'

'That little white child which I did not get,' said the Mugger, with a deep sigh. 'He was very small, but I have not forgotten. I am old now, but before I die it is my desire to try one new thing. It is true they are a heavy-footed, noisy, and foolish people, and the sport would be small, but I remember the old days above Benares, and, if the child lives, he will remember still. It may be he goes up and down the bank of some river, telling how he once passed his hands between the teeth of the Mugger of Mugger-Ghaut, and lived to make a tale of it. My Fate has been very kind, but that plagues me sometimes in my dreams — the thought of the little white child in the bows of that boat.' He yawned, and closed his jaws. 'And now I will rest and think. Keep silent, my children, and respect the aged.'

He turned stiffly, and shuffled to the top of the sand-bar, while the Jackal drew back with the Adjutant to the shelter of a tree stranded on the end nearest the railway bridge.

'That was a pleasant and profitable life,' he grinned, looking up inquiringly at the bird who towered above him. 'And not once, mark you, did he think fit to tell me where a morsel might have been left along the banks. Yet I have told *him* a hundred times of good things wallowing down-stream. How true is the saying, "All the world forgets the Jackal and the Barber when the news has been told!" Now he is going to sleep! *Arrh!*'

'How can a Jackal hunt with a Mugger?' said the Adjutant coolly. 'Big thief and little thief; it is easy to say who gets the pickings.'

The Jackal turned, whining impatiently, and was going to curl himself up under the tree-trunk, when suddenly he cowered, and looked up through the draggled branches at the bridge almost above his head.

'What now?' said the Adjutant, opening his wings uneasily.

'Wait till we see. The wind blows from us to them, but they are not looking for us — those two men.'

'Men, is it? My office protects me. All India knows I am holy.' The Adjutant, being a first-class scavenger, is allowed to go where he pleases, and so this one never flinched.

'I am not worth a blow from anything better than an old shoe,' said the Jackal, and listened again. 'Hark to that foot-fall!' he went on. 'That was no country leather, but the shod foot of a white-face. Listen again! Iron hits iron up there! It is a gun! Friend, those heavy-footed, foolish English are coming to speak with the Mugger.'

'Warn him, then. He was called Protector of the Poor by some one not unlike a starving Jackal but a little time ago.'

'Let my cousin protect his own hide. He has told me again and again there is nothing to fear from the white-faces. Not a villager of Mugger-Ghaut would dare to come after him. See, I said it was a gun! Now, with good luck, we shall feed before daylight. He cannot hear well out of water, and — this time it is not a woman!'

A shiny barrel glittered for a minute in the moonlight on the girders. The Mugger was lying on the sand-bar as still as his own shadow, his fore-feet spread out a little, his head dropped between them, snoring like a — mugger.

A voice on the bridge whispered: 'It's an odd shot — straight down almost — but as safe as houses. Better try behind the neck. Golly! what a brute! The villagers will be wild if he's shot, though. He's the *deota* of these parts.'

'Don't care a rap,' another voice answered; 'he took about fifteen of my best coolies while the bridge was building, and it's time he was put a stop to. I've been after him in a boat for weeks. Stand by with the Martini as soon as I've given him both barrels of this.'

'Mind the kick, then. A double four-bore's no joke.'

'That's for him to decide. Here goes!'

There was a roar like the sound of a small cannon (the biggest sort of elephant-rifle is not very different from some artillery), and a double streak of flame, followed by the stinging crack of a Martini, whose long bullet makes nothing of a crocodile's plates. But the explosive bullets did the work. One of them struck just behind the Mugger's neck, a hand's-breadth to the left of the backbone, while the other burst a little lower down, at the beginning of the tail. In ninety-nine cases out of a hundred a mortally-wounded crocodile can scramble to deep water and get away; but the Mugger of Mugger-Ghaut was literally broken into three pieces. He hardly moved his head before the life went out of him, and he lay as flat as the Jackal.

'Thunder and lightning! Lightning and thunder!' said that miserable little beast. 'Has the thing that pulls the covered carts over the bridge tumbled at last?'

'It is no more than a gun,' said the Adjutant, though his very tail-feathers quivered. 'Nothing more than a gun. He is certainly dead. Here come the white-faces.'

The two Englishmen had hurried down from the bridge and across to the sand-bar, where they stood admiring the length of the Mugger. Then a native with an axe cut off the big head, and four men dragged it across the spit.

'The last time that I had my hand in a Mugger's mouth,' said one of the Englishmen, stooping down (he was the man who had built the bridge), 'it was when I was about five years old — coming down the river by boat to Monghyr. I was a Mutiny baby, as they call it. Poor mother was in the boat, too, and she often told me how she fired dad's old pistol at the beast's head.'

'Well, you've certainly had your revenge on the chief of the clan — even if the gun has made your nose bleed. Hi, you boatmen! Haul that head up the bank, and we'll boil it for the skull. The skin's too knocked about to keep. Come along to bed now. This was worth sitting up all night for, wasn't it?'

Curiously enough, the Jackal and the Adjutant made the very same remark not three minutes after the men had left.

PART VII

'EYES OF BLUE – THE SIMLA HILLS . . .'

'Some people say there is no romance in India. These people are wrong. Our lives hold quite as much romance as is good for us. Sometimes more.' The opening lines of 'Miss Youghal's Syce' set the tone for the ten or so Simla stories that follow in *Plain Tales from the Hills*. Two stories from that slim little volume of social dynamite are represented here, both governed by Kipling's perception of the Simla memsahib as a 'Goddess of the hour', worthy of worship but fickle and merciless at heart. There is 'no sadder sight than the spectacle of a young man . . . being retained for the purposes of vivisection' by a Simla 'divinity', writes the experienced 'Uncle David' in an unsigned 'Hill Homily' carried by *The Pioneer* in March 1888, supposedly offering advice to an inexperienced nephew. It is Kipling adding insult to the newly-published *Plain Tales from the Hills*, warning that Simla in the summer season has 'one of the most unhealthy moral atmospheres in Asia'.

'Venus Annodomini' is the Simla Goddess at her most benign. Mrs 'Ted' Hill suggests in one of her letters that she can be identified with the forty-nine-year-old woman celebrated in Kipling's ballad 'My Rival', which seems to be a hint that 'Venus Annodomini' – 'as immutable as the Hills. But not quite so green' – is none other than Mrs Alice Kipling. With 'Lucy Hauksbee', who makes her first entrance in 'Three and – an Extra', we are on surer ground, it being generally agreed that the character was based on a certain Mrs Burton, the wife of an army major. Rudyard was captivated by her charm and vivacity when he first met her in Simla in 1886 and acted with her in amateur theatricals the following season. Mrs Burton was one of three older women – the others being his mother and 'Ted' Hill – to whom Rudyard wrote personal dedications on the flyleaf copies of *Plain Tales*, intimating to each that she and no other was 'The Wittiest Woman in Asia'. Besides introducing us to one of his most enduring characters, 'Three and – an Extra' also gives us that most done to death of Kipling's lines: 'But that is another story'. It pops up again in no less than seven other *Plain Tales* stories.

Although not set in Simla but in the fictional station of Kashima 'within the circle of the Dosehri hills', the third story included here is very much in the Simla vein – but taken to its extreme limit. 'A Wayside Comedy' is the most perfectly cynical of Kipling's Anglo-Indian romances. It was one of the first of the longer stories that he put into *The Week's News* and republished at the end of that same year in *Under the Deodars*, a collection of six tales that portray the Simla romance in much darker tones than before. The gaiety of the early stories has gone. Now there is pain in the laughter and sometimes we are asked to laugh at the pain.

'Venus Annodomini' and 'Three and – an Extra' appeared in the *C&MG* within three weeks of each other in November and December 1886. 'A Wayside Comedy' was first published in *The Week's News* on 21 January 1888.

VENUS ANNODOMINI

SHE HAD NOTHING to do with Number Eighteen in the Braccio Nuovo of the Vatican, between Visconti's Ceres and the God of the Nile. She was purely an Indian deity – an Anglo-Indian deity, that is to say — and we called her *the* Venus Annodomini, to distinguish her from other Annodominis of the same everlasting order. There was a legend among the Hills that she had once been young; but no living man was prepared to come forward and say boldly that the legend was true. Men rode up to Simla, and stayed, and went away and made their name and did their life's work, and returned again to find the Venus Annodomini exactly as they had left her. She was as immutable as the Hills. But not quite so green. All that a girl of eighteen could do in the way of riding, walking, dancing, picnicking, and over-exertion generally, the Venus Annodomini did, and showed no sign of fatigue or trace of weariness. Besides perpetual youth, she had discovered, men said, the secret of perpetual health; and her fame spread about the land. From a mere woman, she grew to be an Institution, insomuch that no man could be said to be properly formed, who had not, at some time or another, worshipped at the shrine of the Venus Annodomini. There was no one like her, though there were many imitations. Six years in her eyes were no more than six months to ordinary women; and ten years made less visible impression on her than does a week's fever on an ordinary woman. Every one adored her, and in return she was pleasant and courteous to nearly every one. Youth had been a habit of hers for so long, that she could not part with it — never realised, in fact, the necessity of parting with it — and took for her more chosen associates young people.

Among the worshippers of the Venus Annodomini was young Gayerson. 'Very Young Gayerson' he was called to distinguish him from his father 'Young' Gayerson, a Bengal Civilian, who affected the customs — as he had the heart — of youth. 'Very Young' Gayerson was not content to worship placidly and for form's sake, as the other young men did, or to accept a ride or a dance, or a talk from the Venus Annodomini in a properly humble and thankful spirit. He was exacting, and, therefore, the Venus Annodomini repressed him. He worried himself nearly sick in a futile sort of way over her; and his devotion and earnestness made him appear either shy or

boisterous or rude, as his mood might vary, by the side of the older men who, with him, bowed before the Venus Annodomini. She was sorry for him. He reminded her of a lad who, three-and-twenty years ago, had professed a boundless devotion for her, and for whom in return she had felt something more than a week's weakness. But that lad had fallen away and married another woman less than a year after he had worshipped her; and the Venus Annodomini had almost — not quite — forgotten his name. 'Very Young' Gayerson had the same big blue eyes and the same way of pouting his underlip when he was excited or troubled. But the Venus Annodomini checked him sternly none the less. Too much zeal was a thing that she did not approve of; preferring instead, a tempered and sober tenderness.

'Very Young' Gayerson was miserable, and took no trouble to conceal his wretchedness. He was in the Army — a Line regiment I think, but am not certain — and since his face was a looking-glass and his forehead an open book, by reason of his innocence, his brothers-in-arms made his life a burden to him and embittered his naturally sweet disposition. No one except 'Very Young' Gayerson, and he never told his views, knew how old 'Very Young' Gayerson believed the Venus Annodomini to be. Perhaps he thought her five-and-twenty, or perhaps she told him that she was this age. 'Very Young' Gayerson would have forded the Indus in flood to carry her lightest word, and had implicit faith in her. Every one liked him, and every one was sorry when they saw him so bound a slave of the Venus Annodomini. Every one, too, admitted that it was not her fault; for the Venus Annodomini differed from Mrs. Hauksbee and Mrs. Reiver in this particular — she never moved a finger to attract any one; but, like Ninon de L'Enclos, all men were attracted to her. One could admire and respect Mrs. Hauksbee, despise and avoid Mrs. Reiver, but one was forced to adore the Venus Annodomini.

'Very Young' Gayerson's papa held a Division, or a Collectorate, or something administrative, in a particularly unpleasant part of Bengal — full of Babus who edited newspapers proving that 'Young' Gayerson was a 'Nero' and a 'Scylla' and a 'Charybdis'; and, in addition to the Babus, there was a good deal of dysentery and cholera abroad for nine months of the year. 'Young' Gayerson — he was about five-and-forty, — rather liked Babus, they amused him, but he objected to dysentery, and when he could get away, went to Darjiling for the most part. This particular season he fancied that he would come up to Simla and see his boy. The boy was not

altogether pleased. He told the Venus Annodomini that his father was coming up, and she flushed a little and said that she should be delighted to make his acquaintance. Then she looked long and thoughtfully at 'Very Young' Gayerson, because she was very, very sorry for him, and he was a very, very big idiot.

'My daughter is coming out in a fortnight, Mr. Gayerson,' she said.

'Your *what*?' said he.

'Daughter,' said the Venus Annodomini. 'She's been out for a year at Home already, and I want her to see a little of India. She is nineteen and a very sensible nice girl I believe.'

'Very Young' Gayerson, who was a short twenty-two years old, nearly fell out of his chair with astonishment; for he had persisted in believing, against all belief, in the youth of the Venus Annodomini. She, with her back to the curtained window, watched the effect of her sentences and smiled.

'Very Young' Gayerson's papa came up twelve days later, and had not been in Simla four-and-twenty hours before two men, old acquaintances of his, had told him how 'Very Young' Gayerson had been conducting himself.

'Young' Gayerson laughed a good deal, and inquired who the Venus Annodomini might be. Which proves that he had been living in Bengal where nobody knows anything except the rate of Exchange. Then he said boys will be boys, and spoke to his son about the matter. 'Very Young' Gayerson said that he felt wretched and unhappy; and 'Young' Gayerson said that he repented of having helped to bring a fool into the world. He suggested that his son had better cut his leave short and go down to his duties. This led to an unfilial answer, and relations were strained, until 'Young' Gayerson demanded that they should call on the Venus Annodomini. 'Very Young' Gayerson went with his papa, feeling, somehow, uncomfortable and small.

The Venus Annodomini received them graciously, and 'Young' Gayerson said, 'By Jove! It's Kitty!' 'Very Young' Gayerson would have listened for an explanation, if his time had not been taken up with trying to talk to a large, handsome, quiet, well-dressed girl — introduced to him by the Venus Annodomini as her daughter. She was far older in manner, style and repose than 'Very Young' Gayerson; and, as he realised this thing, he felt sick.

Presently he heard the Venus Annodomini saying, 'Do you know that your son is one of my most devoted admirers?'

'I don't wonder,' said 'Young' Gayerson. Here he raised his voice. 'He follows his father's footsteps. Didn't I worship the ground you trod on, ever so long ago, Kitty — and you haven't changed since then. How strange it all seems!'

'Very Young' Gayerson said nothing. His conversation with the daughter of the Venus Annodomini was, through the rest of the call, fragmentary and disjointed.

'At five tomorrow, then,' said the Venus Annodomini. 'And mind you are punctual.'

'At five punctually,' said 'Young' Gayerson. 'You can lend your old father a horse, I daresay, youngster, can't you? I'm going for a ride tomorrow afternoon.'

'Certainly,' said 'Very Young' Gayerson. 'I am going down tomorrow morning. My ponies are at your service, Sir.'

The Venus Annodomini looked at him across the half-light of the room, and her big gray eyes filled with moisture. She rose and shook hands with him.

'Good-bye, Tom,' whispered the Venus Annodomini.

THREE AND — AN EXTRA

AFTER MARRIAGE ARRIVES a reaction, sometimes a big, sometimes a little one; but it comes sooner or later, and must be tided over by both parties if they desire the rest of their lives to go with the current.

In the case of the Cusack-Bremmils this reaction did not set in till the third year after the wedding. Bremmil was hard to hold at the best of times; but he was a beautiful husband until the baby died and Mrs. Bremmil wore black, and grew thin, and mourned as though the bottom of the Universe had fallen out. Perhaps Bremmil ought to have comforted her. He tried to do so, but the more he comforted the more Mrs. Bremmil grieved, and, consequently, the more uncomfortable grew Bremmil. The fact was that they both needed a tonic. And they got it. Mrs. Bremmil can afford to laugh now, but it was no laughing matter to her at the time.

Mrs. Hauksbee appeared on the horizon; and where she existed was fair chance of trouble. At Simla her by-name was the 'Stormy Petrel.' She had won that title five times to my own certain knowledge. She was a little, brown, thin, almost skinny, woman, with big, rolling, violet-blue eyes, and the sweetest manners in the world. You had only to mention her name at afternoon teas for every woman in the room to rise up and call her not blessed. She was clever, witty, brilliant, and sparkling beyond most of her kind; but possessed of many devils of malice and mischievousness. She could be nice, though, even to her own sex. But that is another story.

Bremmil went off at score after the baby's death and the general discomfort that followed, and Mrs. Hauksbee annexed him. She took no pleasure in hiding her captives. She annexed him publicly, and saw that the public saw it. He rode with her, and walked with her, and talked with her, and picnicked with her, and tiffined at Peliti's with her, till people put up their eyebrows and said, 'Shocking!' Mrs. Bremmil stayed at home, turning over the dead baby's frocks and crying into the empty cradle. She did not care to do anything else. But some eight dear, affectionate lady-friends explained the situation at length to her in case she should miss the cream of it. Mrs. Bremmil listened quietly, and thanked them for their good offices. She was not as clever as Mrs. Hauksbee, but she was no fool. She kept her own counsel, and did not speak to Bremmil of what she had heard. This is worth remembering. Speaking to or crying over a husband never did any good yet.

When Bremmil was at home, which was not often, he was more affectionate than usual; and that showed his hand. The affection was forced, partly to soothe his own conscience and partly to soothe Mrs. Bremmil. It failed in both regards.

Then 'the A.-D.-C. in Waiting was commanded by Their Excellencies, Lord and Lady Lytton, to invite Mr. and Mrs. Cusack-Bremmil to Peterhoff on July 26 at 9-30 P.M.' — 'Dancing' in the bottom-left-hand corner.

'I can't go,' said Mrs. Bremmil, 'it is too soon after poor little Florrie . . . but it need not stop you, Tom.'

She meant what she said then, and Bremmil said that he would go just to put in an appearance. Here he spoke the thing which was not; and Mrs. Bremmil knew it. She guessed — a woman's guess is much more accurate than a man's certainty — that he had meant to go from the first, and with Mrs. Hauksbee. She sat down to think, and the outcome of her thoughts was that the memory of a dead child was worth considerably less than the affections of a living husband. She made her plan and staked her all upon it. In that hour she discovered that she knew Tom Bremmil thoroughly, and this knowledge she acted on.

'Tom,' said she, 'I shall be dining out at the Longmores' on the evening of the 26th. You'd better dine at the Club.'

This saved Bremmil from making an excuse to get away and dine with Mrs. Hauksbee, so he was grateful, and felt small and mean at the same time — which was wholesome. Bremmil left the house at five for a ride. About half-past five in the evening a large leather-covered basket came in from Phelps's for Mrs. Bremmil. She was a woman who knew how to dress; and she had not spent a week on designing that dress and having it gored, and hemmed, and herring-boned, and tucked and rucked (or whatever the terms are), for nothing. It was a gorgeous dress — slight mourning. I can't describe it, but it was what *The Queen* calls 'a creation' — a thing that hit you straight between the eyes and made you gasp. She had not much heart for what she was going to do; but as she glanced at the long mirror she had the satisfaction of knowing that she had never looked so well in her life. She was a large blonde and, when she chose, carried herself superbly.

After the dinner at the Longmores' she went on to the dance — a little late — and encountered Bremmil with Mrs. Hauksbee on his arm. That made her flush, and as the men crowded round her for dances she looked magnificent. She filled up all her dances except three, and those she left blank. Mrs. Hauksbee caught her eye once; and she knew it was war — real war — between them. She started handicapped in the struggle, for she had ordered Bremmil about just the least little bit in the world too much, and he was beginning to resent it. Moreover, he had never seen his wife look so

lovely. He stared at her from doorways, and glared at her from passages as she went about with her partners; and the more he stared, the more taken was he. He could scarcely believe that this was the woman with the red eyes and the black stuff gown who used to weep over the eggs at breakfast.

Mrs. Hauksbee did her best to hold him in play, but, after two dances, he crossed over to his wife and asked for a dance.

'I'm afraid you've come too late, *Mister* Bremmil,' she said, with her eyes twinkling.

Then he begged her to give him a dance, and, as a great favour, she allowed him the fifth waltz. Luckily Five stood vacant on his programme. They danced it together, and there was a little flutter around the room. Bremmil had a sort of a notion that his wife could dance, but he never knew she danced so divinely. At the end of that waltz he asked for another — as a favour, not as a right; and Mrs. Bremmil said, 'Show me your programme, dear!' He showed it as a naughty little schoolboy hands up contraband sweets to a master. There was a fair sprinkling of 'H' on it, besides 'H' at supper. Mrs. Bremmil said nothing, but she smiled contemptuously, ran her pencil through Seven and Nine — two 'H's' — and returned the card with her own name written above — a pet name that only she and her husband used. Then she shook her finger at him, and said laughing, 'Oh, you silly, *silly* boy!'

Mrs. Hauksbee heard that, and — she owned as much — felt she had the worst of it. Bremmil accepted Seven and Nine gratefully. They danced Seven and sat out Nine in one of the little tents. What Bremmil said and what Mrs. Bremmil did is no concern of any one.

When the band struck up 'The Roast Beef of Old England,' the two went out into the verandah, and Bremmil began looking for his wife's *dandy* (this was before 'rickshaw days) while she went into the cloak-room. Mrs. Hauksbee came up and said, 'You take me in to supper, I think, Mr. Bremmil?' Bremmil turned red and looked foolish. 'Ah — h'm! I'm going home with my wife, Mrs. Hauksbee. I think there has been a little mistake.' Being a man, he spoke as though Mrs. Hauksbee were entirely responsible.

Mrs. Bremmil came out of the cloak-room in a swan's-down cloak with a white 'cloud' round her head. She looked radiant; and she had a right to.

The couple went off into the darkness together, Bremmil riding very close to the *dandy*.

Then said Mrs. Hauksbee to me — she looked a trifle faded and jaded in the lamplight — 'Take my word for it, the silliest woman can manage a clever man; but it needs a very clever woman to manage a fool.'

Then we went in to supper.

CHRISTMAS AT AN INDIAN HILL STATION—GOING HOME AFTER A PARTY

A WAYSIDE COMEDY

FATE AND THE Government of India have turned the Station of Kashima into a prison; and, because there is no help for the poor souls who are now lying there in torment, I write this story, praying that the Government of India may be moved to scatter the European population to the four winds.

Kashima is bounded on all sides by the rock-tipped circle of the Dosehri hills. In Spring, it is ablaze with roses; in Summer, the roses die and the hot winds blow from the hills; in Autumn, the white mists from the *jhils* cover the place as with water, and in Winter the frosts nip everything young and tender to earth-level. There is but one view in Kashima — a stretch of perfectly flat pasture and plough-land, running up to the gray-blue scrub of the Dosehri hills.

There are no amusements, except snipe and tiger shooting; but the tigers have been long since hunted from their lairs in the rock-caves, and the snipe only come once a year. Narkarra — one hundred and forty-three miles by road — is the nearest station to Kashima. But Kashima never goes to Narkarra, where there are at least twelve English people. It stays within the circle of the Dosehri hills.

All Kashima acquits Mrs. Vansuythen of any intention to do harm; but all Kashima knows that she, and she alone, brought about their pain.

Boulte, the Engineer, Mrs. Boulte, and Captain Kurrell know this. They are the English population of Kashima, if we except Major Vansuythen, who is of no importance whatever, and Mrs. Vansuythen, who is the most important of all.

You must remember, though you will not understand, that all laws weaken in a small and hidden community where there is no public opinion. When a man is absolutely alone in a Station he runs a certain risk of falling into evil ways. This risk is multiplied by every addition to the population up to twelve — the Jury-number. After that, fear and consequent restraint begin, and human action becomes less grotesquely jerky.

There was deep peace in Kashima till Mrs. Vansuythen arrived. She was a charming woman, every one said so everywhere; and she charmed every one. In spite of this, or, perhaps, because of this, since Fate is so perverse, she cared only for one man, and he was Major Vansuythen. Had she been

plain or stupid, this matter would have been intelligible to Kashima. But she was a fair woman, with very still gray eyes, the colour of a lake just before the light of the sun touches it. No man who had seen those eyes could, later on, explain what fashion of woman she was to look upon. The eyes dazzled him. Her own sex said that she was 'not bad looking, but spoilt by pretending to be so grave.' And yet her gravity was natural. It was not her habit to smile. She merely went through life, looking at those who passed; and the women objected while the men fell down and worshipped.

She knows and is deeply sorry for the evil she has done to Kashima; but Major Vansuythen cannot understand why Mrs. Boulte does not drop in to afternoon tea at least three times a week. 'When there are only two women in one Station, they ought to see a great deal of each other,' says Major Vansuythen.

Long and long before ever Mrs. Vansuythen came out of those far-away places where there is society and amusement, Kurrell had discovered that Mrs. Boulte was the one woman in the world for him and — you dare not blame them. Kashima was as out of the world as Heaven or the Other Place, and the Dosehri hills kept their secret well. Boulte had no concern in the matter. He was in camp for a fortnight at a time. He was a hard, heavy man, and neither Mrs. Boulte nor Kurrell pitied him. They had all Kashima and each other for their very, very own; and Kashima was the Garden of Eden in those days. When Boulte returned from his wanderings he would slap Kurrell between the shoulders and call him 'old fellow,' and the three would dine together. Kashima was happy then when the judgment of God seemed almost as distant as Narkarra or the railway that ran down to the sea. But the Government sent Major Vansuythen to Kashima, and with him came his wife.

The etiquette of Kashima is much the same as that of a desert island. When a stranger is cast away there, all hands go down to the shore to make him welcome. Kashima assembled at the masonry platform close to the Narkarra Road, and spread tea for the Vansuythens. That ceremony was reckoned a formal call, and made them free of the Station, its rights and privileges. When the Vansuythens settled down they gave a tiny house-warming to all Kashima; and that made Kashima free of their house, according to the immemorial usage of the Station.

Then the Rains came, when no one could go into camp, and the Narkarra Road was washed away by the Kasun River, and in the cup-like pastures of Kashima the cattle waded knee-deep. The clouds dropped down from the Dosehri hills and covered everything.

At the end of the Rains Boulte's manner towards his wife changed and became demonstratively affectionate. They had been married twelve years, and the change startled Mrs. Boulte, who hated her husband with the hate of a woman who has met with nothing but kindness from her mate, and, in the teeth of this kindness, has done him a great wrong. Moreover, she had her own trouble to fight with — her watch to keep over her own property, Kurrell. For two months the Rains had hidden the Dosehri hills and many other things besides; but, when they lifted, they showed Mrs. Boulte that her man among men, her Ted — for she called him Ted in the old days when Boulte was out of earshot — was slipping the links of the allegiance.

'The Vansuythen Woman has taken him,' Mrs. Boulte said to herself; and when Boulte was away, wept over her belief, in the face of the over-vehement blandishments of Ted. Sorrow in Kashima is as fortunate as Love because there is nothing to weaken it save the flight of Time. Mrs. Boulte had never breathed her suspicion to Kurrell because she was not certain; and her nature led her to be very certain before she took steps in any direction. That is why she behaved as she did.

Boulte came into the house one evening, and leaned against the door-posts of the drawing-room, chewing his moustache. Mrs. Boulte was putting some flowers into a vase. There is a pretence of civilisation even in Kashima.

'Little woman,' said Boulte quietly, 'do you care for me?'

'Immensely,' said she, with a laugh. 'Can you ask it?'

'But I'm serious,' said Boulte. '*Do* you care for me?'

Mrs. Boulte dropped the flowers, and turned round quickly. 'Do you want an honest answer?'

'Ye-es, I've asked for it.'

Mrs. Boulte spoke in a low, even voice for five minutes, very distinctly, that there might be no misunderstanding her meaning. When Samson broke the pillars of Gaza, he did a little thing, and one not to be compared to the deliberate pulling down of a woman's homestead about her own ears. There was no wise female friend to advise Mrs. Boulte, the singularly cautious wife, to hold her hand. She struck at Boulte's heart, because her own was sick with suspicion of Kurrell, and worn out with the long strain of watching alone through the Rains. There was no plan or purpose in her speaking. The sentences made themselves; and Boulte listened, leaning against the door-post with his hands in his pockets. When all was over, and Mrs. Boulte began to breathe through her nose before breaking out into tears, he laughed and stared straight in front of him at the Dosehri hills.

'Is that all?' he said. 'Thanks, I only wanted to know, you know.'

'What are you going to do?' said the woman, between her sobs.

'Do! Nothing. What should I do? Kill Kurrell, or send you Home, or apply for leave to get a divorce? It's two days' *dak* into Narkarra.' He laughed again and went on: 'I'll tell you what *you* can do. You can ask Kurrell to dinner tomorrow — no, on Thursday, that will allow you time to pack — and you can bolt with him. I give you my word I won't follow.'

He took up his helmet and went out of the room, and Mrs. Boulte sat till the moonlight streaked the floor, thinking and thinking and thinking. She had done her best upon the spur of the moment to pull the house down; but it would not fall. Moreover, she could not understand her husband, and she was afraid. Then the folly of her useless truthfulness struck her, and she was ashamed to write to Kurrell, saying, 'I have gone mad and told everything. My husband says that I am free to elope with you. Get a *dak* for Thursday, and we will fly after dinner.' There was a cold-bloodedness about that procedure which did not appeal to her. So she sat still in her own house and thought.

At dinner-time Boulte came back from his walk, white and worn and haggard, and the woman was touched at his distress. As the evening wore on she muttered some expression of sorrow, something approaching to contrition. Boulte came out of a brown study and said, 'Oh, *that*! I wasn't thinking about that. By the way, what does Kurrell say to the elopement?'

'I haven't seen him,' said Mrs. Boulte. 'Good God, is that all?'

But Boulte was not listening and her sentence ended in a gulp.

The next day brought no comfort to Mrs. Boulte, for Kurrell did not appear, and the new life that she, in the five minutes' madness of the previous evening, had hoped to build out of the ruins of the old, seemed to be no nearer.

Boulte ate his breakfast, advised her to see her Arab pony fed in the verandah, and went out. The morning wore through, and at mid-day the tension became unendurable. Mrs. Boulte could not cry. She had finished her crying in the night, and now she did not want to be left alone. Perhaps the Vansuythen Woman would talk to her; and, since talking opens the heart, perhaps there might be some comfort to be found in her company. She was the only other woman in the Station.

In Kashima there are no regular calling-hours. Every one can drop in on every one else at pleasure. Mrs. Boulte put on a big *terai* hat, and walked across to the Vansuythens' house to borrow last week's *Queen*. The two compounds touched, and instead of going up the drive, she crossed through the gap in the cactus-hedge, entering the house from the back. As she passed through the dining-room, she heard, behind the *purdah* that cloaked the drawing-room door, her husband's voice, saying —

'But on my Honour! On my Soul and Honour, I tell you she doesn't care for me. She told me so last night. I would have told you then if Vansuythen hadn't been with you. If it is for *her* sake that you'll have nothing to say to me, you can make your mind easy. It's Kurrell — '

'What?' said Mrs. Vansuythen, with a hysterical little laugh. 'Kurrell! Oh, it can't be! You two must have made some horrible mistake. Perhaps you — you lost your temper, or misunderstood, or something. Things *can't* be as wrong as you say.'

Mrs. Vansuythen had shifted her defence to avoid the man's pleading, and was desperately trying to keep him to a side-issue.

'There must be some mistake,' she insisted, 'and it can be all put right again.'

Boulte laughed grimly.

'It can't be Captain Kurrell! He told me that he had never taken the least — the least interest in your wife, Mr. Boulte. Oh, *do* listen! He said he had not. He swore he had not,' said Mrs. Vansuythen.

The *purdah* rustled, and the speech was cut short by the entry of a little thin woman, with big rings round her eyes. Mrs. Vansuythen stood up with a gasp.

'What was that you said?' asked Mrs. Boulte. 'Never mind that man. What did Ted say to you? What did he say to you? What did he say to you?'

Mrs. Vansuythen sat down helplessly on the sofa, overborne by the trouble of her questioner.

'He said — I can't remember exactly what he said — but I understood him to say — that is — But, really, Mrs. Boulte, isn't it rather a strange question?'

'*Will* you tell me what he said?' repeated Mrs. Boulte. Even a tiger will fly before a bear robbed of her whelps, and Mrs. Vansuythen was only an ordinarily good woman. She began in a sort of desperation: 'Well, he said that he never cared for you at all, and, of course, there was not the least reason why he should have, and — and — that was all.'

'You said he *swore* he had not cared for me. Was that true?'

'Yes,' said Mrs. Vansuythen very softly.

Mrs. Boulte wavered for an instant where she stood, and then fell forward fainting.

'What did I tell you?' said Boulte, as though the conversation had been unbroken. 'You can see for yourself. She cares for *him*.' The light began to break into his dull mind, and he went on — 'And he — what was *he* saying to you?'

But Mrs. Vansuythen, with no heart for explanations or impassioned protestations, was kneeling over Mrs. Boulte.

'Oh, you brute!' she cried. 'Are *all* men like this? Help me to get her into my room — and her face is cut against the table. Oh, *will* you be quiet, and help me to carry her? I hate you, and I hate Captain Kurrell. Lift her up carefully, and now — go! Go away!'

Boulte carried his wife into Mrs. Vansuythen's bedroom, and departed before the storm of that lady's wrath and disgust, impenitent and burning with jealousy. Kurrell had been making love to Mrs. Vansuythen — would do Vansuythen as great a wrong as he had done Boulte, who caught himself considering whether Mrs. Vansuythen would faint if she discovered that the man she loved had forsworn her.

In the middle of these meditations, Kurrell came cantering along the road and pulled up with a cheery 'Good-mornin'. 'Been mashing Mrs. Vansuythen as usual, eh? Bad thing for a sober, married man, that. What will Mrs. Boulte say?'

Boulte raised his head and said slowly, — 'Oh, you liar!' Kurrell's face changed. 'What's that?' he asked quickly.

'Nothing much,' said Boulte. 'Has my wife told you that you two are free to go off whenever you please? She has been good enough to explain the situation to me. You have been a true friend to me, Kurrell — old man — haven't you?'

Kurrell groaned, and tried to frame some sort of idiotic sentence about being willing to give 'satisfaction.' But his interest in the woman was dead, had died out in the Rains, and, mentally, he was abusing her for her amazing indiscretion. It would have been so easy to have broken off the thing gently and by degrees, and now he was saddled with — Boulte's voice recalled him.

'I don't think I should get any satisfaction from killing you, and I'm pretty sure you'd get none from killing me.'

Then in a querulous tone, ludicrously disproportioned to his wrongs, Boulte added —

'Seems rather a pity that you haven't the decency to keep to the woman, now you've got her. You've been a true friend to *her* too, haven't you?'

Kurrell stared long and gravely. The situation was getting beyond him.

'What do you mean?' he said.

Boulte answered, more to himself than the questioner: 'My wife came over to Mrs. Vansuythen's just now; and it seems you'd been telling Mrs. Vansuythen that you'd never cared for Emma. I suppose you lied, as usual. What had Mrs. Vansuythen to do with you, or you with her? Try to speak the truth for once in a way.'

Kurrell took the double insult without wincing, and replied by another question: 'Go on. What happened?'

'Emma fainted,' said Boulte simply. 'But, look here, what had you been saying to Mrs. Vansuythen?'

Kurrell laughed. Mrs. Boulte had, with unbridled tongue, made havoc of his plans; and he could at least retaliate by hurting the man in whose eyes he was humiliated and shown dishonourable.

'Said to her? What *does* a man tell a lie like that for? I suppose I said pretty much what you've said, unless I'm a good deal mistaken.'

'I spoke the truth,' said Boulte, again more to himself than Kurrell. 'Emma told me she hated me. She has no right in me.'

'No! I suppose not. You're only her husband, y'know. And what did Mrs. Vansuythen say after you had laid your disengaged heart at her feet?'

Kurrell felt almost virtuous as he put the question.

'I don't think that matters,' Boulte replied; 'and it doesn't concern you.'

'But it does! I tell you it does' — began Kurrell shamelessly.

The sentence was cut off by a roar of laughter from Boulte's lips. Kurrell was silent for an instant, and then he, too, laughed — laughed long and loudly, rocking in his saddle. It was an unpleasant sound — the mirthless mirth of these men on the long white line of the Narkarra Road. There were no strangers in Kashima, or they might have thought that captivity within the Dosehri hills had driven half the European population mad. The laughter ended abruptly, and Kurrell was the first to speak.

'Well, what are you going to do?'

Boulte looked up the road, and at the hills. 'Nothing,' said he quietly; 'what's the use? It's too ghastly for anything. We must let the old life go on. I can only call you a hound and a liar, and I can't go on calling you names for ever. Besides which, I don't feel that I'm much better. We can't get out of this place. What *is* there to do?'

Kurrell looked round the rat-pit of Kashima and made no reply. The injured husband took up the wondrous tale.

'Ride on, and speak to Emma if you want to. God knows *I* don't care what you do.'

He walked forward, and left Kurrell gazing blankly after him. Kurrell did not ride on either to see Mrs. Boulte or Mrs. Vansuythen. He sat in his saddle and thought, while his pony grazed by the roadside.

The whir of approaching wheels roused him. Mrs. Vansuythen was driving home Mrs.

Boulte, white and wan, with a cut on her forehead.

'Stop, please,' said Mrs. Boulte, 'I want to speak to Ted.'

Mrs. Vansuythen obeyed, but as Mrs. Boulte leaned forward, putting her hand upon the splashboard of the dog-cart, Kurrell spoke.

'I've seen your husband, Mrs. Boulte.'

There was no necessity for any further explanation. The man's eyes were fixed, not upon Mrs. Boulte, but her companion. Mrs. Boulte saw the look.

'Speak to him!' she pleaded, turning to the woman at her side. 'Oh, speak to him! Tell him what you told me just now. Tell him you hate him. Tell him you hate him!'

She bent forward and wept bitterly, while the *sais*, impassive, went forward to hold the horse. Mrs. Vansuythen turned scarlet and dropped the reins. She wished to be no party to such unholy explanations.

'I've nothing to do with it,' she began coldly; but Mrs. Boulte's sobs overcame her, and she addressed herself to the man. 'I don't know what I am to say, Captain Kurrell. I don't know what I can call you. I think you've — you've behaved abominably, and she has cut her forehead terribly against the table.'

'It doesn't hurt. It isn't anything,' said Mrs. Boulte feebly. '*That* doesn't matter. Tell him what you told me. Say you don't care for him. Oh, Ted, *won't* you believe her?'

'Mrs. Boulte has made me understand that you were — that you were fond of her once upon a time,' went on Mrs. Vansuythen.

'Well!' said Kurrell brutally. 'It seems to me that Mrs. Boulte had better be fond of her own husband first.'

'Stop!' said Mrs. Vansuythen. 'Hear me first. I don't care — I don't want to know anything about you and Mrs. Boulte; but I want *you* to know that I hate you, that I think you are a cur, and that I'll never, *never* speak to you again. Oh, I don't dare to say what I think of you, you — man!'

'I want to speak to Ted,' moaned Mrs. Boulte, but the dog-cart rattled on, and Kurrell was left on the road, shamed, and boiling with wrath against Mrs. Boulte.

He waited till Mrs. Vansuythen was driving back to her own house, and, she being freed from the embarrassment of Mrs. Boulte's presence, learned for the second time her opinion of himself and his actions.

In the evenings it was the wont of all Kashima to meet at the platform on the Narkarra Road, to drink tea and discuss the trivialities of the day. Major Vansuythen and his wife found themselves alone at the gathering-place for almost the first time in their remembrance; and the cheery Major, in the teeth of his wife's remarkably reasonable suggestion that the rest of the Station might be sick, insisted upon driving round to the two bungalows and unearthing the population.

'Sitting in the twilight!' said he, with great indignation, to the Boultes.

'That'll never do! Hang it all, we're one family here! You *must* come out, and so must Kurrell. I'll make him bring his banjo.'

So great is the power of honest simplicity and a good digestion over guilty consciences that all Kashima did turn out, even down to the banjo; and the Major embraced the company in one expansive grin. As he grinned, Mrs. Vansuythen raised her eyes for an instant and looked at all Kashima. Her meaning was clear. Major Vansuythen would never know anything. He was to be the outsider in that happy family whose cage was the Dosehri hills.

'You're singing villainously out of tune, Kurrell,' said the Major truthfully. 'Pass me that banjo.'

And he sang in excruciating-wise till the stars came out and all Kashima went to dinner.

That was the beginning of the New Life of Kashima — the life that Mrs. Boulte made when her tongue was loosened in the twilight.

Mrs. Vansuythen has never told the Major; and since he insists on keeping up a burdensome geniality, she has been compelled to break her vow of not speaking to Kurrell. This speech, which must of necessity preserve the semblance of politeness and interest, serves admirably to keep alight the flame of jealousy and dull hatred in Boulte's bosom, as it awakens the same passions in his wife's heart. Mrs. Boulte hates Mrs. Vansuythen because she has taken Ted from her, and in some curious fashion, hates her because Mrs. Vansuythen — and here the wife's eyes see far more clearly than the husband's — detests Ted. And Ted — that gallant captain and honourable man — knows now that it is possible to hate a woman once loved, to the verge of wishing to silence her for ever with blows. Above all, he is shocked that Mrs. Boulte cannot see the error of her ways.

Boulte and he go out tiger-shooting together in all friendship. Boulte has put their relationship on a most satisfactory footing.

'You're a blackguard,' he says to Kurrell, 'and I've lost any self-respect I may ever have had; but when you're with me, I can feel certain that you are not with Mrs. Vansuythen, or making Emma miserable.

Kurrell endures anything that Boulte may say to him. Sometimes they are away for three days together, and then the Major insists upon his wife going over to sit with Mrs. Boulte; although Mrs. Vansuythen has repeatedly declared that she prefers her husband's company to any in the world. From the way in which she clings to him, she would certainly seem to be speaking the truth.

But of course, as the Major says, 'in a little Station we must all be friendly.'

PART VIII

'EYES OF BROWN – A DUSTY PLAIN . .'

'The House of Shadows – By its Occupant' was the first 'turnover' to go into the *C&MG* after Kay Robinson had reorganised the paper, probably written to order soon after Rudyard had returned to his parents' empty bungalow from Simla. It is a very characteristic Hot Weather haunting story by the young Kipling, a delicate little tale that was never reprinted – perhaps because it was too similar in theme to 'My Own True Ghost Story', which appeared in *The Week's News* some six months later. However, it conveys very nicely the way the combined pressures of heat and isolation might prey on a lonely man's mind.

'In Flood Time' is another Hot Weather story but written from an Indian perspective, a monologue told as if to Kipling as he waits to cross a river swollen by the melting snows of the Himalayas. Returning to Allahabad from what was to be his last visit to Simla in July 1888, Rudyard was unable to ford the flooded Gugger river. He passed the time chatting to the elderly female custodian of the ford and it was this incident, linked to an old Punjabi folk tale about lovers separated by a river, that provided the basis for 'In Flood Time', published in early August 1888.

The last story also relates to night-time Lahore at the height of summer. In fact, it is more of a sketch than a story, replete with adjectives and adverbs that the older Kipling would never have allowed himself but it has a place of honour here as the story that marks his breaking out from the confines of British India and reaching across the divide into Indian India. It is 'The City of Dreadful Night', published in *The Civil and Military Gazette* on 10 September 1885 when Rudyard Kipling was still some months short of his twentieth birthday.

'The House of Shadows – By its Occupant' appeared in *The Civil and Military Gazette* on 4 August 1887. 'In Flood Time' was first published in *The Week's News* on 11 August 1888 and reprinted in *In Black and White* in December of that same year. 'The City of Dreadful Night' was reprinted in *Life's Handicap*, 1891.

THE HOUSE OF SHADOWS

A WOMAN HAS DIED and a child has been born in it, but these are accidents which may overtake the most respectable establishments. No sensible man would think of regarding them. Indeed, so sound is my common sense, that I sleep in the room of the death and do my work in the room of the birth; and have no fault to find with either apartment. My complaint is against the whole house; and my grievance, so far as I can explain it in writing, is that there are far too many tenants in the eight, lime-washed rooms for which I pay seventy-five rupees a month.

They trooped in after the great heats of May as snakes seek bathrooms through drought. Personally I should prefer the snakes, the visible, smashable snakes, to the persons who have quartered themselves upon me for the past ten weeks. They take up no space and are almost noiseless, like the Otto Gas Engines — but they are there and they trouble me. In the very early morning when I climb on to the roof to catch what less heated breeze may be abroad, I am conscious that someone has preceded me up the narrow steps, and that there is someone at my heels. You will concede, will you not, that this is annoying, particularly when I know that I am officially the sole tenant. No man, visible or invisible, has a right to spy upon my outgoings or incomings. At breakfast, in the full fresh daylight, I am conscious that some one who is not the *khitmatgar* is watching the back of my head from the door that leads into my bedroom; when I turn sharply, the *purdah* is dropped and I only see it waving gently as though shaken by the wind. Quitting the house to go to office, I am sure — sure as I am of my own existence — that it is at once taken possession of by the people who follow me about, and that they hold who knows what mad noiseless revels in the room when the bearer has done his duster-flapping and the servants have withdrawn to their own quarters.

Indeed, once returning from office at an unexpected hour, I surprised the house, rushed in and found . . . nothing. My footfall rang through the barn-like rooms, and as the noise ceased, I felt that the people who had been crowding the floor were rushing away — pouring out into the garden and the verandahs, and I could not see them. But I knew they had been

there. The air was full of the rustle of their garments.

Still an assembly is preferable to the one man — he must be a man; he is so restless — who comes in to spend the evening and roams through the house. His feet make no noise, but I can hear in the hot, still night the jar of the *chik* as he comes into the verandah, and the lifting of the *purdah* over the drawing-room door. Then he touches a book in the drawing-room, for I hear it fall, or he thrums the Burmese gong ever so lightly, for I catch the faint ring of the smitten metal, and passes on, shifting things, scratching things, tapping things, till I could shriek aloud with irritation. When he comes to the room I am in he stops, puts the *purdah* aside and looks at me. I am sure of it, for when I turn the *purdah* has always just fallen. He must be the man who takes so impertinent an interest in my breakfast. But he will never face me and tell me what he wants. He is always in the next room. Though I have hunted him through the house again and again, he is always in the next room.

When I enter, I know that he has just gone out. The *purdah* betrays him. And when I go out I know that he is waiting, always waiting, to slip into the room I have vacated, and begin his aimless strolling among the knicknacks. If I go into the verandah, I know that he is watching me from the drawing-room. I can hear him sitting down on one of the wicker-work chairs that creaks under his weight.

On Sundays, the long, hot, pitiless Sundays, when the consciousness of arrears of work prevents their clearance, he comes to spend the day in my house from ten in the morning till the hour of the evening drive. I can offer him no amusement. He cannot find me cheering company. *Why* does he hang about the house? He should have learnt by this time not to touch a *punkah* fringe with his head or to leave a door on the swing, I can track him then and prevent him from sitting down on the chairs in the next room.

I would endure the people who hide in the corners of the lamproom and rush out when my back is turned, the persons who get between the *almirah* and the wall when I come into my dressing-room hastily at dusk, or even the person in the garden who slides in and out of the *ferash* trees when I walk there, if I could only get rid of the Man in the Next Room. There is no sense in him, and he interferes sadly with one's work. I believe now that if he dared he would come out from the other side of the *purdah* and peep over my shoulder to see what I am writing. But he is afraid and is now twitching the cord that works the ventilating window. I can hear it beating against the wall. What pleasure can he find in prowling thus about another man's premises? I asked him the question last Sunday, but my voice came back to me from the high ceiling of the empty room next to my bedroom, and that was all my answer.

One of these days, perhaps, if I enter my own house very, very silently, with bare feet, crawling through a window, I may be able to catch him and wring from him some sort of explanation; for it is manifestly absurd that a man paying seventy-five rupees a month should be compelled to live with so unsatisfactory a chum as the man in the next room.

On second thoughts, and after a plain statement of facts to the doctor, I think it would be better to go to the Hills for a while and leave him to maunder about the empty house till he is tired. The doctor says he will be gone when I return; taking all the other persons with him.

IN FLOOD TIME

THERE IS NO getting over the river tonight, Sahib. They say that a bullock-cart has been washed down already, and the *ekka* that went over a half-hour before you came has not yet reached the far side. Is the Sahib in haste? I will drive the ford-elephant in to show him. *Ohe, mahout* there in the shed! Bring out Ram Pershad, and if he will face the current, good. An elephant never lies, Sahib, and Ram Pershad is separated from his friend Kala Nag. He, too, wishes to cross to the far side. Well done! Well done! my King! Go half-way across, *mahoutji*, and see what the river says. Well done, Ram Pershad! Pearl among elephants, go into the river! Hit him on the head, fool! Was the goad made only to scratch thy own fat back with, bastard? Strike! strike! What are the boulders to thee, Ram Pershad, my Rustum, my mountain of strength? Go in! Go in!

No, Sahib! It is useless. You can hear him trumpet. He is telling Kala Nag that he cannot come over. See! He has swung round and is shaking his head. He is no fool. He knows what the Barhwi means when it is angry. Aha! Indeed, thou art no fool, my child! *Salaam*, Ram Pershad, Bahadur! Take him under the trees. *mahout*, and see that he gets his spices. Well done, thou chiefest among tuskers. *Salaam* to the Sirkar and go to sleep.

What is to be done? The Sahib must wait till the river goes down. It will shrink tomorrow morning, if God pleases, or the day after at the latest! Now why does the Sahib get so angry? I am his servant. Before God, *I* did not create this stream! What can I do? My hut and all that is therein is at the service of the Sahib, and it is beginning to rain. Come away, my Lord. How will the river go down for your throwing abuse at it? In the old days the English people were not thus. The fire-carriage has made them soft. In the old days, when they drave behind horses by day or by night, they said naught if a river barred the way, or a carriage sat down in the mud. It was the will of God — not like a fire-carriage which goes and goes and goes, and would go though all the devils in the land hung on to its tail. The fire-carriage hath spoiled the English people. After all, what is a day lost, or, for that matter, what are two days? Is the Sahib going to his own wedding, that he is so mad with haste? Ho! ho! ho! I am an old man and see few Sahibs. Forgive me if I have forgotten the respect that is due to them. The Sahib is not angry?

His own wedding! Ho! ho! ho! The mind of an old man is like the *numah*-tree. Fruit, bud, blossom, and the dead leaves of all the years of the past flourish together. Old and new and that which is gone out of remembrance, all three are there! Sit on the bedstead, Sahib, and drink milk. Or — would the Sahib in truth care to drink my tobacco? It is good. It is the tobacco of Nuklao. My son, who is in service there, sent it to me. Drink, then, Sahib, if you know how to handle the tube. The Sahib takes it like a Mussulman. Wah! Wah! Where did he learn that? His own wedding! Ho! ho! ho! The Sahib says that there is no wedding in the matter at all. Now *is* it likely that the Sahib would speak true talk to me who am only a black man? Small wonder, then, that he is in haste. Thirty years have I beaten the gong at this ford, but never have I seen a Sahib in such haste. Thirty years, Sahib! That is a very long time. Thirty years ago this ford was on the track of the *bunjaras*, and I have seen two thousand pack-bullocks cross in one night. Now the rail has come, and the fire-carriage says *buz-buz-buz*, and a hundred lakhs of maunds slide across that big bridge. It is very wonderful; but the ford is lonely now that there are no *bunjaras* to camp under the trees.

Nay, do not trouble to look at the sky without. It will rain till the dawn. Listen! The boulders are talking tonight in the bed of the river. Hear them! They would be husking your bones, Sahib, had you tried to cross. See, I will shut the door and no rain can enter. *Wahi! Ahi! Ugh!* Thirty years on the banks of the ford. An old man am I and — where is the oil for the lamp?

Your pardon, but because of my years, I sleep no sounder than a dog; and you moved to the door. Look, then, Sahib. Look and listen. A full half *kos* from bank to bank is the stream now — you can see it under the stars — and there are ten feet of water therein. It will not shrink because of the anger in your eyes, and it will not be quiet on account of your curses. Which is louder, Sahib — your voice or the voice of the river? Call to it — perhaps it will be ashamed. Lie down and sleep afresh, Sahib. I know the anger of the Barhwi when there has fallen rain in the foot-hills. I swam the flood, once, on a night tenfold worse than this, and by the Favour of God I was released from Death when I had come to the very gates thereof.

May I tell the tale? Very good talk. I will fill the pipe anew.

Thirty years ago it was, when I was a young man and had but newly come to the ford. I was strong then, and the *bunjaras* had no doubt when I said 'this ford is clear.' I have toiled all night up to my shoulder-blades in running water amid a hundred bullocks mad with fear, and have brought them across not losing a hoof. When all was done I fetched the shivering men, and they gave me for reward the pick of their cattle — the bell-bullock of the drove. So great was the honour in which I was held! But, today when the rain falls and the river rises, I creep into my hut and whimper like a dog. My strength is gone from me. I am an old man and the fire-carriage has made the ford desolate. They were wont to call me the Strong One of the Barhwi.

Behold my face, Sahib — it is the face of a monkey. And my arm — it is the arm of an old woman. I swear to you, Sahib, that a woman has loved this face and has rested in the hollow of this arm. Twenty years ago, Sahib. Believe me, this was true talk — twenty years ago.

Come to the door and look across. Can you see a thin fire very far away down the stream? That is the temple-fire, in the shrine of Hanuman, of the village of Pateera. North, under the big star, is the village itself, but it is hidden by a bend of the river. Is that far to swim, Sahib? Would you take off your clothes and adventure? Yet I swam to Pateera — not once, but many times; and there are *muggurs* in the river too.

Love knows no caste; else why should I, a Mussulman and the son of a Mussulman, have sought a Hindu woman — a widow of the Hindus — the sister of the headman of Pateera? But it was even so. They of the headman's household came on a pilgrimage to Muttra when She was but newly a bride. Silver tires were upon the wheels of the bullock-cart, and silken curtains hid the woman. Sahib, I made no haste in their conveyance, for the wind parted the curtains and I saw Her. When they returned from pilgrimage the boy that was Her husband had died, and I saw Her again in the bullock-cart. By God, these Hindus are fools! What was it to me whether She was Hindu or Jain — scavenger, leper, or whole? I would have married Her and made Her a home by the ford. The Seventh of the Nine Bars says that a man may not marry one of the idolators? Is that truth? Both Shiahs and Sunnis say that a Mussulman may not marry one of the idolators? Is the Sahib a priest, then, that he knows so much? I will tell him something that he does not know. There is neither Shiah nor Sunni, forbidden nor idolator, in Love; and the Nine Bars are but nine little faggots that the flame of Love utterly burns away. In truth, I would have taken Her; but what could I do? The headman would have sent his men to break my head with staves. I am not — I was not — afraid of any five men; but against half a village who can prevail?

Therefore it was my custom, these things having been arranged between us twain, to go by night to the village of Pateera, and there we met among the crops, no man knowing aught of the matter. Behold, now! I was wont to cross here, skirting the jungle to the river bend where the railway bridge is, and thence across the elbow of land to Pateera. The light of the shrine was my guide when the nights were dark. That jungle near the river is very full of snakes — little *karaits* that sleep on the sand — and moreover, Her brothers would have slain me had they found me in the crops. But none knew — none knew save She and I; and the blown sand of the river-bed covered the track of my feet. In the hot months it was an easy thing to pass

from the ford to Pateera, and in the first Rains, when the river rose slowly, it was an easy thing also. I set the strength of my body against the strength of the stream, and nightly I ate in my hut here and drank at Pateera yonder. She had said that one Hirnam Singh, a thief, had sought Her, and he was of a village up the river but on the same bank. All Sikhs are dogs, and they have refused in their folly that good gift of God — tobacco. I was ready to destroy Hirnam Singh that ever he had come nigh to Her; and the more because he had sworn to Her that She had a lover, and that he would lie in wait and give the name to the headman unless She went away with him. What curs are these Sikhs!

After that news I swam always with a little sharp knife in my belt, and evil would it have been for a man had he stayed me. I knew not the face of Hirnam Singh, but I would have killed any man who came between me and Her.

Upon a night in the beginning of the Rains I was minded to go across to Pateera, albeit the river was angry. Now the nature of the Barhwi is this, Sahib. In twenty breaths it comes down from the Hills a wall three feet high, and I have seen it, between the lighting of a fire and the cooking of a *chupatty*, grow from a runnel to a sister of the Jumna.

When I left this bank there was a shoal a half-mile down, and I made shift to fetch it and draw breath there ere going forward; for I felt the hands of the river heavy upon my heels. Yet what will a young man not do for Love's sake? There was but little light from the stars, and mid-way to the shoal a branch of the stinking deodar tree brushed my mouth as I swam. That was a sign of heavy rain in the foot-hills and beyond, for the deodar is a strong tree, not easily shaken from the hillsides. I made haste, the river aiding me, but ere I had touched the shoal, the pulse of the stream beat, as it were, within me and around, and, behold, the shoal was gone and I rode high on the crest of a wave that ran bank from bank. Has the Sahib ever been cast into much water that fights and will not let a man use his limbs? To me, my head upon the water, it seemed as though there were naught but water to the world's end, and the river drave me with its driftwood. A man is a very little thing in the belly of a flood. And *this* flood, though I knew it not, was the Great Flood about which men talk still. My liver was dissolved and I lay like a log upon my back in the fear of Death. There were living things in the water, crying and howling grievously — beasts of the forest and cattle, and once the voice of a man asking for help. But the rain came and lashed the water white, and I heard no more save the roar of the boulders below and the roar of the rain above. Thus I was whirled down-stream, wrestling for the breath in me. It is very hard to die when one is young. Can the Sahib, standing here, see the railway bridge? Look, there are the lights of the mail-train going to Peshawar! The bridge is now twenty feet above the river, but upon that night the water was roaring against the lattice-work, and against the lattice came I feet first. But much driftwood was piled there and upon the piers, and I took no great hurt. Only the river pressed me as a strong man presses a weaker. Scarcely could I take hold of the lattice-work and crawl to the upper boom. Sahib, the water was foaming across the rails a foot deep! Judge therefore what manner of flood it must have been. I could not hear. I could not see. I could but lie on the boom and pant for breath.

After a while the rain ceased and there came out in the sky certain new washed stars, and by their light I saw that there was no end to the black water as far as the eye could travel, and the water had risen upon the rails. There were dead beasts in the driftwood on the piers, and others caught by the neck in the lattice-work, and others not yet drowned who strove to find a foothold on the lattice-work — buffaloes and kine, and wild pig, and deer one or two, and snakes and jackals past all counting. Their bodies were black upon the left side of the bridge, but the smaller of them were forced through the lattice-work and whirled downstream.

Thereafter the stars died and the rain came down afresh and the river rose yet more, and I felt the bridge begin to stir under me as a man stirs in his sleep ere he wakes. But I was not afraid, Sahib. I swear to you that I was not afraid, though I had no power in my limbs. I knew that I should not die till I had seen Her once more. But I was very cold, and I felt that the bridge must go.

There was a trembling in the water, such a trembling as goes before the coming of a great wave, and the bridge lifted its flank to the rush of that coming so that the right lattice dipped under water and the left rose clear. On my beard, Sahib, I am speaking God's truth! As a Mirzapore stone-boat careens to the wind, so the Barwhi Bridge turned. Thus and in no other manner.

I slid from the boom into deep water, and behind me came the wave of the wrath of the river. I heard its voice and the scream of the middle part of the bridge as it moved from the piers and sank, and I knew no more till I rose in the middle of the great flood. I put forth my hand to swim, and, lo! it fell upon the knotted hair of the head of a man. He was dead, for no one but I, the Strong One of Barwhi, could have lived in that race. He had been dead full two days, for he rode high, wallowing, and was an aid to me. I laughed then, knowing for a surety that I should yet see Her and take no harm; and I twisted my fingers in the hair of the man, for I was far spent, and together we went down the stream — he the dead and I the living. Lacking that help I should have sunk: the cold was in my marrow, and my flesh was ribbed and sodden on my bones. But *he* had no fear who had known the uttermost of the power of the river; and I let him go where he chose. At last we came into the power of a side-current that set to the right bank, and I strove with my feet to draw with it. But the dead man swung heavily in the whirl, and I feared that some branch had struck him and that he would sink. The tops of the tamarisk brushed my knees, so I knew we were come into flood-water above the crops, and, after, I let down my legs and felt bottom — the ridge of a field — and, after, the dead man stayed upon a knoll under a fig-tree, and I drew my body from the water rejoicing.

Does the Sahib know whither the backwash of the flood had borne me? To the knoll which is the eastern boundary-mark of the village of Pateera! No other place. I drew the dead man upon the grass for the service that he had done me, and also because I knew not whether I should need him again. Then I went, crying thrice like a jackal, to the appointed place which was near the byre of the headman's house. But my Love was already there, weeping. She feared that the flood had swept my hut at the Bahrwi Ford. When I came softly through the ankle-deep water, She thought it was a ghost and would have fled, but I put my arms around Her, and — I was no ghost in those days, though I am an old man now. Ho! ho! Dried corn, in truth. Maize without juice. Ho! ho!

I told Her the story of the breaking of the Barhwi Bridge, and she said that I was greater than mortal man, for none may cross the Barhwi in full flood, and I had seen what never man had seen before. Hand in hand we went to the knoll where the dead lay, and I showed Her by what help I had made the ford. She looked also upon the body under the stars, for the latter end of the night was clear, and hid Her face in Her hands, crying: 'It is the body of Hirnam Singh!' I said: 'The swine is of more use dead than living, my Beloved,' and She said: 'Surely, for he has saved the dearest life in the world to my love. None the less, he cannot stay here, for that would bring shame upon me.' The body was not a gun-shot from Her door.

Then said I, rolling the body with my hands: 'God hath judged between us, Hirnam Singh, that thy blood might not be upon my head. Now, whether I have done thee a wrong in keeping thee from the burning-*ghat*, do thou and the crows settle together.' So I cast him adrift into the flood-water, and he was drawn out to the open, ever wagging his thick black beard like a priest under the pulpit-board. And I saw no more of Hirnam Singh.

Before the breaking of the day we two parted, and I moved towards such of the jungle as was not flooded. With the full light I saw what I had done in the darkness, and the bones of my body were loosened in my flesh, for there ran two *kos* of raging water between the village of Pateera and the trees of the far bank, and, in the middle, the piers of the Barhwi Bridge showed like broken teeth in the jaw of an old man. Nor was there any life upon the waters — neither birds nor boats, but only an army of drowned things — bullocks and horses and men — and the river was redder than blood from the clay of the foot-hills. Never had I seen such a flood — never since that year have I seen the like — and, O Sahib, no man living had done what I had done. There was no return for me that day. Not for all the lands of the headman would I venture a second time without the shield of darkness that cloaks danger. I went a *kos* up the river to the house of a blacksmith, saying that the flood had swept me from my hut, and they gave me food. Seven days I stayed with the blacksmith, till a boat came and I returned to my house. There was no trace of wall, or roof, or floor — naught but a patch of slimy mud. Judge, therefore, Sahib, how far the river must have risen.

It was written that I should not die either in my house, or in the heart of the Barhwi, or under the wreck of the Barhwi Bridge, for God sent down Hirnam Singh two days dead, though I know not how the man died, to be my buoy and support. Hirnam Singh has been in Hell these twenty years, and the thought of that night must be the flower of his torment.

Listen, Sahib! The river has changed its voice. It is going to sleep before the dawn, to which there is yet one hour. With the light it will come down afresh. How do I know? Have I been here thirty years without knowing the voice of the river as a father knows the voice of his son? Every moment it is talking less angrily. I swear that there will be no danger for one hour, or, perhaps, two. I cannot answer for the morning. Be quick, Sahib! I will call Ram Pershad, and he will not turn back this time. Is the 'paulin tightly corded upon all the baggage? *Ohe, mahout* with a mud head, the elephant for the Sahib, and tell them on the far side that there will be no crossing after daylight.

Money? Nay, Sahib. I am not of that kind. No, not even to give sweetmeats to the baby-folk. My house, look you, is empty, and I am an old man.

Dutt, Ram Pershad! *Dutt! Dutt! Dutt!* Good luck go with you, Sahib.

'THE CITY OF DREADFUL NIGHT'

THE DENSE WET heat that hung over the face of the land, like a blanket, prevented all hope of sleep in the first instance. The cicalas helped the heat; and the yelling jackals the cicalas. It was impossible to sit still in the dark, empty, echoing house and watch the *punkah* beat the dead air. So, at ten o'clock of the night, I set my walking-stick on end in the middle of the garden, and waited to see how it would fall. It pointed directly down the moon-lit road that leads to the City of Dreadful Night. The sound of its fall disturbed a hare. She limped from her form and ran across to a disused Muhammadan burial-ground, where the jawless skulls and rough-butted shank-bones, heartlessly exposed by the July rains, glimmered like mother o' pearl on the rain-channelled soil. The heated air and the heavy earth had driven the very dead upward for coolness' sake. The hare limped on; snuffed curiously at a fragment of a smoke-stained lamp-shard, and died out, in the shadow of a clump of tamarisk trees.

The mat-weaver's hut under the lee of the Hindu temple was full of sleeping men who lay like sheeted corpses. Overhead blazed the unwinking eye of the Moon. Darkness gives at least a false impression of coolness. It was hard not to believe that the flood of light from above was warm. Not so hot as the Sun, but still sickly warm, and heating the heavy air beyond what was our due. Straight as a bar of polished steel ran the road to the City of Dreadful Night; and on either side of the road lay corpses disposed on beds in fantastic attitudes — one hundred and seventy bodies of men. Some shrouded all in white with bound-up mouths; some naked and black as ebony in the strong light; and one — that lay face upwards with dropped jaw, far away from the others — silvery white and ashen gray.

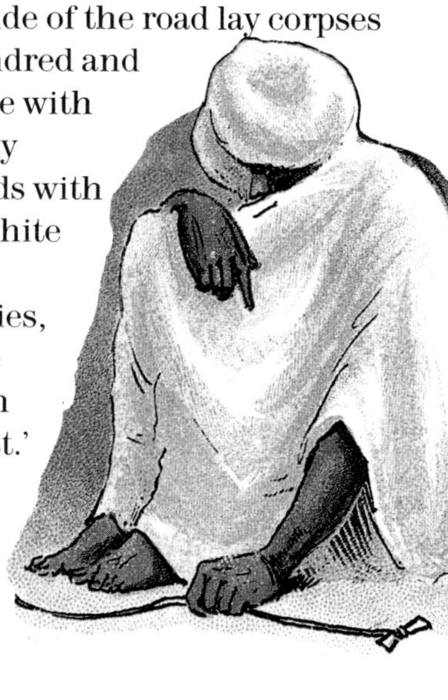

'A leper asleep; and the remainder wearied coolies, servants, small shopkeepers, and drivers from the hack-stand hard by. The scene — a main approach to Lahore city, and the night a warm one in August.' This was all that there was to be seen; but by no means all that one could see. The witchery of the moonlight was everywhere; and the world was horribly changed. The long line of the naked dead, flanked by the rigid silver statue, was not pleasant to look upon. It was made up of men alone. Were the womenkind, then, forced to sleep in the shelter of the stifling mud-huts as best they might? The fretful wail of a child from a low mud-roof answered the question. Where the children are the mothers must be also to look after them. They need care on these sweltering nights. A black little bullet-head peeped over the coping, and a thin — a painfully thin — brown leg was slid over on to the gutter pipe. There was a sharp clink of glass bracelets; a woman's arm showed for an instant above the parapet, twined itself round the lean little neck, and the child was dragged back, protesting, to the shelter of the bedstead. His thin, high-pitched shriek died out in the thick air almost as soon as it was raised; for even the children of the soil found it too hot to weep.

More corpses; more stretches of moonlit, white road; a string of sleeping camels at rest by the wayside; a vision of scudding jackals; *ekka*-ponies asleep — the harness still on their backs, and the brass-studded country carts, winking in the moonlight — and again more corpses. Wherever a grain cart atilt, a tree trunk, a sawn log, a couple of bamboos and a few handfuls of thatch cast a shadow, the ground is covered with them. They lie — some face downwards, arms folded, in the dust; some with clasped hands flung up above their heads; some curled up dog-wise; some thrown like limp gunny-bags over the side of their grain-carts; and some bowed with their brows on their knees in the full glare of the Moon. It would be a comfort if they were only given to snoring; but they are not, and the likeness to corpses is unbroken in all respects save one. The lean dogs snuff at them and turn away. Here and there a tiny child lies on his father's bedstead, and a protecting arm is thrown round it in every instance. But, for the most part, the children sleep with their mothers on the housetops. Yellow-skinned white-toothed pariahs are not to be trusted within reach of brown bodies.

A stifling hot blast from the mouth of the Delhi Gate nearly ends my resolution of entering the City of Dreadful Night at this hour. It is a compound of all evil savours, animal and vegetable, that a walled city can brew in a day and a night. The temperature within the motionless groves of plantain and orange-trees outside the city walls seems chilly by comparison. Heaven help all sick persons and young children within the city tonight! The high house-walls are still radiating heat savagely, and from obscure side gullies fetid breezes eddy that ought to poison a buffalo. But the buffaloes do not heed. A drove of them are parading the vacant main street; stopping now and then to lay their ponderous muzzles against the closed shutters of a grain-dealer's shop, and to blow thereon like grampuses.

Then silence follows — the silence that is full of the night noises of a great city. A stringed instrument of some kind is just, and only just, audible. High overhead some one throws open a window, and the rattle of the wood-work echoes down the empty street. On one of the roofs, a hookah is in full blast; and the men are talking softly as the pipe gutters. A little farther on, the noise of conversation is more distinct. A slit of light shows itself between the sliding shutters of a shop. Inside, a stubble-bearded, weary-eyed trader is balancing his account books among the bales of cotton prints that surround him. Three sheeted figures bear him company, and throw in a remark from time to time. First he makes an entry, then a remark; then passes the back of his hand across his streaming forehead. The heat in the built-in street is fearful. Inside the shops it must be almost unendurable. But the work goes on steadily; entry, guttural growl, and uplifted hand-stroke succeeding each other with the precision of clock-work.

A policeman — turbanless and fast asleep — lies across the road on the way to the Mosque of Wazir Khan. A bar of moonlight falls across the forehead and eyes of the sleeper, but he never stirs. It is close upon midnight, and the heat seems to be increasing. The open square in front of the Mosque is crowded with corpses; and a man must pick his way carefully for fear of treading on them. The moonlight stripes the Mosque's high front of coloured enamel work in broad diagonal bands; and each separate dreaming pigeon in the niches and corners of the masonry throws a squab little shadow. Sheeted ghosts rise up wearily from their pallets, and flit into the dark depths of the building. Is it possible to climb to the top of the great Minars, and thence to look down on the city? At all events the attempt is worth making, and the chances are that the door of the staircase will be unlocked. Unlocked it is; but a deeply sleeping janitor lies across the threshold, face turned to the Moon. A rat dashes out of his turban at the sound of approaching footsteps. The man grunts, opens his eyes for a minute, turns round, and goes to sleep again. All the heat of a decade of fierce Indian summers is stored in the pitch-black, polished walls of the corkscrew staircase. Half-way up, there is something alive, warm, and feathery; and it snores. Driven from step to step as it catches the sound of my advance, it flutters to the top and reveals itself as a yellow-eyed, angry kite. Dozens of kites are asleep on this and the other Minars, and on the domes below. There is the shadow of a cool, or at least a less sultry breeze at this height; and, refreshed thereby, I turn to look on the City of Dreadful Night.

Doré might have drawn it! Zola could describe it — this spectacle of sleeping thousands in the moonlight and in the shadow of the Moon. The roof-tops are crammed with men, women and children; and the air is full of undistinguishable noises. They are restless in the City of Dreadful Night;

and small wonder. The marvel is that they can even breathe. If you gaze intently at the multitude, you can see that they are almost as uneasy as a daylight crowd; but the tumult is subdued. Everywhere, in the strong light, you can watch the sleepers turning to and fro; shifting their beds and again resettling them. In the pit-like courtyards of the houses there is the same movement.

The pitiless Moon shows it all. Shows, too, the plains outside the city, and here and there a hand's-breadth of the Ravi without the walls. Shows lastly, a splash of glittering silver on a house-top almost directly below the mosque Minar. Some poor soul has risen to throw a jar of water over his fevered body; the tinkle of the falling water strikes faintly on the ear. Two or three other men, in far-off corners of the City of Dreadful Night, follow his example, and the water flashes like heliographic signals. A small cloud passes over the face of the Moon, and the city and its inhabitants — clear drawn in black and white before — fade into masses of black and deeper black. Still the unrestful noise continues, the sigh of a great city overwhelmed with the heat, and of a people seeking in vain for rest. It is only the lower-class women who sleep on the house-tops. What must the torment be in the latticed zenanas, where a few lamps are still twinkling? There are footfalls in the court below. It is the *Muezzin* — faithful minister; but he ought to have been here an hour ago to tell the Faithful that prayer is better than sleep — the sleep that will not come to the city.

The *Muezzin* fumbles for a moment with the door of one of the Minars, disappears awhile, and a bull-like roar — a magnificent bass thunder — tells that he has reached the top of the Minar. They must hear the cry to the banks of the shrunken Ravi itself! Even across the courtyard it is almost overpowering. The cloud drifts by and shows him outlined in black against the sky, hands laid upon his ears, and broad chest heaving with the play of his lungs - 'Allah ho Akbar'; then a pause while another *Muezzin* somewhere in the direction of the Golden Temple takes up the call — 'Allah ho Akbar.' Again and again; four times in all; and from the bedsteads a dozen men have risen up already. — 'I bear witness that there is no God but God.' What a splendid cry it is, the proclamation of the creed that brings men out of their beds by scores at midnight! Once again he thunders through the same phrase, shaking with the vehemence of his own voice; and then, far and near, the night air rings with 'Mahomed is the Prophet of God.' It is as though he were flinging his defiance to the far-off horizon, where the summer lightning plays and leaps like a bared sword. Every *Muezzin* in the city is in full cry, and some men on the roof-tops are beginning to kneel. A long pause precedes the last cry, 'La ilaha Illallah,' and the silence closes up on it, as the ram on the head of a cotton-bale.

The *Muezzin* stumbles down the dark stairway grumbling in his beard. He passes the arch of the entrance and disappears. Then the stifling silence settles down over the City of Dreadful Night. The kites on the Minar sleep again, snoring more loudly, the hot breeze comes in puffs and lazy eddies, and the Moon slides down towards the horizon. Seated with both elbows on the parapet of the tower, one can watch and wonder over the heat-tortured hive till the dawn. 'How do they live down there? What do they think of? When will they awake?' More tinkling of sluiced water-pots; faint jarring of wooden bedsteads moved into or out of the shadows; uncouth music of stringed instruments softened by distance into a plaintive wail, and one low grumble of far-off thunder. In the courtyard of the mosque the janitor, who lay across the threshold of the Minar when I came up, starts wildly in his sleep, throws his hands above his head, mutters something, and falls back again. Lulled by the snoring of the kites — they snore like over-gorged humans — I drop off into an uneasy doze, conscious that three o'clock has struck, and that there is a slight — a very slight — coolness in the atmosphere. The city is absolutely quiet now, but for some vagrant dog's love-song. Nothing save dead heavy sleep.

Several weeks of darkness pass after this. For the Moon has gone out. The very dogs are still, and I watch for the first light of the dawn before making my way homeward. Again the noise of shuffling feet. The morning call is about to begin, and my night watch is over. 'Allah ho Akbar! Allah ho Akbar!' The east grows gray, and presently saffron; the dawn wind comes up as though the *Muezzin* had summoned it; and, as one man, the City of Dreadful Night rises from its bed and turns its face towards the dawning day. With return of life comes return of sound. First a low whisper, then a deep bass hum; for it must be remembered that the entire city is on the housetops. My eyelids weighed down with the arrears of long deferred sleep, I escape from the Minar through the courtyard and out into the square beyond, where the sleepers have risen, stowed away the bedsteads, and are discussing the morning hookah. The minute's freshness of the air has gone, and it is as hot as at first.

'Will the Sahib, out of his kindness, make room?' What is it? Something borne on men's shoulders comes by in the half-light, and I stand back. A woman's corpse going down to the burning-*ghat*, and a bystander says, 'She died at midnight from the heat.' So the city was of Death as well as Night after all.

The real epilogue to Kipling's years in India is his novel *Kim*. Here we must make do with second best in the shape of the last article that Kipling wrote for the newspaper on which he learned his craft. It is an account of his journey across India in December 1891 from Tuticorin in the South up to Lahore, 'where I was snatching a few days' visit with my people. They were coming "Home" for good soon: so this was my last look round the only real home I had yet known.' The article was written in haste while in Lahore. When it appeared in *The Civil and Military Gazette* on 25 December 1891 he had already set sail from Bombay for England.

For reasons of space I have cut many paragraphs, indicated by ellipses in the text.

EPILOGUE: HOME

THE LONGING BEGAN began at least a league off shore from Colombo, when the *Chusan*, Calcutta bound, swung out round the breakwater under the *Valetta's* nose, and we who were Anglo-Indians separated ourselves a little from the crowd. A smell came up out over the sea — a smell of damp earth, coconut oil, ginger, onions and mankind.

It spoke with a strong voice, recalling many things; but the most curious revelation to one man was the sudden knowledge that under these alien skies lay home and the dearest places in all the world; even the first sniff of London had not caused so big a choke in the throat or so strict a tightening over the heart . . . [ ]

With me, sole survivor of a scattered card party, was the Post Officer of Vizagapatam, and he promised me breakfast on shore in the old casual Anglo-Indian fashion. 'I know the Post Officer here,' he said, 'met him once. No, I didn't, by Jove — he was out when I came — but I can put up at his house. He'll give us breakfast.' By this I knew where I was and rejoiced. Then we stepped on to Indian soil under the green fig trees that face the beach, where the cotton trains go to and fro, and the Tamil women weave onion baskets of green reeds while their babies hang like cocoons in the bight of a loin-cloth flung over a branch. Allah be praised, we stepped straight into India again. It was not quite the real India, but the India that the English knew — the *Little Henry and his Bearer* country, all paddy, palmyra, and coconut-palms as the books draw it. Hindu temples jostled old Dutch-built Roman Catholic Churches where the Virgin, I believe, has twelve arms and the saints are rather like Krishnas. The people, too, were hereditary Christians, and spoke English, many of them. Small wonder that the South Indian papers point out that the writer at least does not describe India — their India. Could a Swede from the Baltic write of Algiers? But the beautiful smell was there, the brown, slow-moving crowds were there (white is rather a leprous tint when you come to think of it, and it doesn't match backgrounds), the crumbling *kutcha* walls and the deep-bowed bungalow were all waiting there. Best of all there was the Post Officer, first met of the breed, a khaki-clad Anglo-Indian, not one whit disturbed because two utter strangers from the sea demanded breakfast.

Oh! that breakfast, eaten under the slow-swinging *punkahs* with the white-robed butlers behind our chairs — the fresh fish from the sea that was lapping twenty yards away outside in the glare, the teal bagged yesterday, the Madras curry with its rich allowance of spices, and the first long pull of Pilsener, the ice clinking in the tall glass. Afterwards — this was even more perfect — there came the self-assured and confident flop into the long chair — our long chair — where you put up your feet by right and not by permission, and jamming a black rank Dawson No. 1 between your teeth puff the well remembered incense and thank Heaven you are back among your fellows once more. There were no 'Misters' in that bungalow after the first introductions, we keep 'Mister' for the Globe-Trotter . . . [ ]

We loafed through the bazar to the train, paralysed booking and telegraph clerk by trying to get a ticket, and send a telegram, in under half-an-hour, and at noon in the brilliant moist sunshine slouched off by the S.I.R. on a four hundred mile run to Madras.

The warm rain began to fall steadily, and in an hour or two the flat red soil was under water as far as the eye could reach. Then came the perfect tropical moon turning the embankment aloes to frosted silver, and the frogs sang songs at the stations where we halted, and palms dripped heavily and gave out all their smell. Moreover, Asia, taking me back without reserve, flung her mantle over me from head to foot. To think that a man should be thankful for prickly heat!

After interminable hours — twenty-eight of them — and flood all the way, there was Arconum and a parting. The Post Officer of Vizag went his way to the harbour, and I to mine, hopping from train to train and wrestling with booking-clerks who denied the existence of Lahore. [ ]

Then north to Raichur and Wadi where the look of the land changed, and there was a prophecy of drought in the air. Two men entered, one a Major of seventeen years' service and the other a Subaltern of two. He was on transfer to the Staff Corps, had bagged his five tigers, desired more *shikar*, and more than *shikar* lusted for Active Service. [ ]

All this time India was rolling back behind the wheels — level, burned and dusty. We ploughed through the Assergurh jungle in company with a Forest Officer and a young 'Stunt two months out from home, a little bewildered at the new life, but very resolute to make the best of it. The Forest Officer melted nearly to tears at the sight of an English half-crown, handled it lovingly and offered three rupees in exchange.

Now, was it yesterday, or ten years ago, that in a railway carriage by Neemuch I found a Globe-trotter and sighed when he showed me an English penny? It must have been the better part of ten years; and today it is our poor one and four penny rupee that makes me home-sick.

The first suggestion of the cold weather — our own real cold weather began at Bhopal, where the train ran through the dank white layers of evening wood smoke and there came a smell of dried earth and burned cowdung. Morning — a clear dry morning — brought 'the hottest town in all this land of Ind'. Agra, with her red Fort and disreputable monkeys. There was a 'homey' look about the fields; the village boundary-pillars were familiar, and the cattle such as one knows.

But the people on the platform were only North-West men — down country folk and they did not carry the proper kind of *huqqa*. By noon we should be in our proper territories, and it was more than likely that some old faces . . . Now observe the kindness of Providence! Three years ago it was the Lord of the Iron Horses of the North-Western Railway who saw me off the premises in his inspection carriage. Therefore it was right and proper that the first train into Ghaziabad — Ghaziabad with its awful tiffins and vault-like refreshment rooms — should bring up from Ajmir on his way to Lahore that same Lord of the Iron Horses.

'Back again?' said he. 'Back again,' said I. 'Well, you're a nice sort of Globe-trotter!' said he. I pocketed the insult for there were three years' arrears of news to make good of what had happened up at home. Who was dead, married, transferred, promoted or gone under? In the evening light, flying up to Meerut, my questions were answered simply and monosyllabically as is our custom. Thus—'A?'

'He's dead. Didn't you hear?' 'B?' 'Transferred — Poona.' 'C?' 'Still at Guardespore.' 'D?' 'He married Miss Such an one. They've both gone home on six months.' 'Mrs E?' 'Dead — died of typhoid last July. It was a bad hot weather.' 'And you yourself?' I said, knowing he had had no leave for eleven years. 'Oh, I don't care. I know that the weather can't be worse than I've known it, so I stick it out. I say, though, what a fuss you kicked up at Home about that Manipur business; might have thought all India was being sacked.'

'You at home' sticks unpleasantly in the throat; confound the Lord of the Iron Horses. 'What have I to do with the people at "Home"? I am here and the North-Western Railway is running disgracefully late as usual.'

'Don't you fret,' he answers calmly. 'She'll leg it in the night. Look at Meerut. There's a Cavalry Camp on.' [ ]

She legs it. After Saharanpur she lies down to her work in earnest with an hour and a half to make up. The Jhelum bridge rings and rattles under her heels. There is a glimpse of lean, dry sand under the moon, and with a whistle, she sails into the Punjab. The rest is easy. How do the Stations run? Umballa, Phillour, Beas East, Jullundur, Amritsar and Ataree, and then Lahore. Colder and colder grows the Northern night. Somebody shouts Umballa through my dreams — Umballa of a hundred Simla memories before you went to Kalka by rail. Now that I know every tie and fishplate from here to home I will sleep.

'Hi! Ho! We're past Amritsar. Here's Ataree. There's *chota hazri* in K's carriage.'

It is the diamond clear cold weather dawn — dawn among the ferashes, the creaking well-wheels and the Jats — the huge thighed Jats — each man's head blanketted from the cold and each trailing his lumbering *huqqa*. The land looks sick and droughty, but it's home — every dusty inch of it. [ ]

Now, certainly, I have never been one day absent. There was an agricultural Exhibition at Jullundur yesterday which I was sent to describe, and after breakfast there will be just time to get back to office, send in the report and take the day's mail. The old life will begin again . . . after breakfast. Up start the brown faces in the familiar verandah that takes the dust of the Mozung.

'Yes, by the Sahib's favour, we be all well. Others of the Sahib's household be coming to make salutations after breakfast. Yes. He that was the scullion is now promoted to be butler by the Honoured One's favour and' — Kadir Baksh, pearl among *khitmatgars*, the voice was thine! — 'there is *Hursaini kebab* for *hazri*.'

A pious Mussulman would be shocked if he were violently hugged by a Kaffir. None the less, I should like to dance sarabands with Kadir as he grins and hands the curry. There is only one curry in the world, and Kadir Baksh makes it, and — oh, the forgotten decency that the English cannot understand; — sets out the finger bowls after meat. For the rest, looking round the old home there is not much of the luxury we read about in books. How would an English memsahib approve whitewashed walls, raw timbered roofs split and cracked with old summers, the whitewash splashed impartially over the timbers, doors that never shut, and glass puttied as for an outhouse? But these things, with the old jail *dhurries*, the ruggled *chitai* in the verandah, the cock-eyed *almirahs*, the *choukuts* that catch a forgetful foot on the threshold, and the rude printed cloth dadoes make homes. To clinch everything, the Very Dearest Dog in all the world recognises a long lost master, and behaves accordingly. Vixen, do you remember the hot weather we shared together when you lay in the thermantidote and panted? Do you remember the wet tonga-drives to Simla, and rat-catching in this office? Vixen, it's nearly seven years since I bought you at the sale of a dead man's kit and you are getting old. 'Take me out,' says Vixen, 'show me a squirrel and see.' [ ]

'Sahib, this is indeed the office of the *Charpar Kargaz* and I was your old *chaprassi*, but the paper itself is printed at another office and elsewhere.' This is really pleasant. It reminds you who you are, to go to your own office and find that it isn't there any longer, and that you don't know where it is. Once before, the mother-paper changed her place, but then one knew all about it. Now, one is only a rank outsider — a Globe-trotter who must be piloted about Lahore. Yet it is good to think that the paper has prospered. To the new office, therefore, with a big, big lump in one's throat. No man can put in his seven years on an Indian Journal when he is half the staff, and the sheet is part of his being, without loving her dearly. The smell of the office comes out through the orange trees, and

there is the thump of an old columbiard (I think I know which one it is) running off the galley proofs for the editor. There, through a cautiously lifted *chick*, the old scene stands revealed and there rush back on the memory the names of a score of natives buried for a time under the drift of the months. The brown comps are bending over the cases, the little distributing boys are sitting cross-legged on the floor and yes! *He* has not changed in the least — the man who broke my heart daily for years in getting together the standing matter. What would happen if one called out '*Kitna* in hand *hai, kul si*?'

The lemon and green turbans shake like a bed of tulips in a high wind, and they come up by the dozen, from the foreman, whom nothing could flurry, to the man who locks up the formes and has a detestable trick of doing it at least ten minutes too soon. One cannot say much, but one thinks a great deal. Of the old staff of '82, the foreman, perhaps three other hands and myself are the sole survivors. And now I am on the staff no longer. No word of mine can make the old wheels spin, and Mahmud would only grin if I rated him for his sins. It isn't a nice feeling, but I know it will be worse this evening among the men at the Hall and the Club.

Into the office and the piles of the dusty exchanges, to fall over the eternal *duftir* and to watch with envy the loaded and littered table. There is a long talk here — talk of the old days, reminiscences of catchwords, bygone practical jokes, and all the intimacies, squabbles and crises between two yoke-mates for years and then — it had to come, but it hurt — 'Well, I must get through the *dak*, old man. Can you give us something while you're here?'

'*You* give *us*! Yes, I think so. An epic if I had it in hand.' 'There is no demand for epics in the Punjab: men live there; but anything else will do' . . . I comforted myself with that thought, and went off to the happy hunting grounds in the City [ ]

As second wind to a runner, or wine to a wearied man, has been this second view of the City of Lahore — the oldest and surely the most picturesque city in the world. Thomas of the K.O.S.B.'s was on guard at the main gate of the Fort (I wonder which of us two knew better the guardroom in the wall) and the sunlight was splashing the mouldering tile work of the main face — the gay tile wrought angels and elephants of Akbar. The minarets of Shadera where Jahangir lies dead, and with him the memories of many moonlight picnics and wild words under the roses and the orange trees, showed above the belt of green by the Ravi. Thomas — a spot of vermilion — was loafing down the sunk way to the gate, his dog at his heels. Thomas with a *chilumchee* and bareheaded — will nothing teach Thomas that he must not play with the cold weather sun? — was scuffling from barrack to barrack, and Thomas — (fever stricken Thomas) in his greatcoat was hanging over the balcony of the hospital, half-a-dozen superb Pathan soldiers in undress were swinging across the path by the glaring native guardroom where Sikh sepoys rested near their speckless rifles, rising to salute and standing one bar of blood red against the whitewashed wall. It is awful to think that in England they have never seen any of the primary colours, and that they know nothing of drapery, the folds of well worn unsewn clothing that falls in great laps and curves, gathered round the neck and under the armpit in robes of richest deep shadowed wrinkles. [ ]

There was a glimpse of the Fort barrack room with its monstrous understrutting of masonry — and the spider-legged cots disposed in the hall of the dead kings, the pillars of black and white marble defiled with whitewash, and the marvellous relief work daubed out of all knowledge. [ ]

If the Civil station hinted at the memories of years, the city shouted them aloud. House upon piled house, the time-worn tracery standing askew on the rotten brick-work, well, gulley-mouth, ruinous dead wall and crumbling heap of sheer stark red-rotten rubbish overrun by the crowd, the cattle and the asses – all spoke with the voice of the years.

Here lived the Jews of Shushan, there, the arrogant and unashamed was Lalun's naughty little house, Azizun of the Douri Bagh was a little beyond and the house of Suddhoo was not far off the ringing roaring gulley of the coppersmiths, where the lean traders sat by piles of beaten gold vessels selling the splendour of the East for a few annas. Here were the Pathan horse-dealers chaffering with the seal-cutters for a new signet ring. Not till one understands in some small measure the heart of the city, does one realise how much the poorest country in the world has to spend of fripperies – four annas embroidered caps for the babies, cheap jewellery, bats and stumps (a new industry since my time – cricket is more than ever naturalised with us), kites, cheap photographs of the gods, tinsel-stuck shoes and slippers, necklaces, beads, mirror-rings and a hundred other toys. Here and there through the jostling crowd where buffalo calves and led ponies share all the rights of way with men, a face passed that I knew, and once or twice an old friend stops me to give greeting. The Dubbi Bazar is full of old friends, from the fat *bunnia* among the turmeric heaps to the policeman with the *kullam* and the green glazed inkpot in his hand. They don't know me but I know them.

How shall one descrive the sunlit river of people whose daily passage has oil polished the wooden posts of the shop boards, smoothed the angles of the brickwork and faced the very ground with glair as a glacier polished a rock. As if its own beauty were not enough, the dyers have spread filmy muslins of palest blue and pink across the street, and you look upon the old witchery of the old life through the pearl tinted mists of dawn. It is noon and past, and high overhead a boyu's paper kite is sawing and jigging into the restful blue like a big sulphur butterfly. Below there is the hurry and the shouting, the broken waves of colour, the deep shadows that heighten colour as velvet displays the diamond, and above all, and apart from all, as a prayer from a tortured heart, the mosque of Wazir Khan flings up its four minars to heaven. What need to cry five times a day that God is Great?

At the shadow of the Delhi Gate the picture of the city ends for the sight – to be graven deeper on the mind. Again comes the memory of the urmurs of a little city called London – a city where there is neither colour nor light nor air. Who was the particular *pagal* over there who wrote of extravagance of description and the Lord knows what else? If he were here now – between than broken-hatted, unbottoned English loafer slinking red-nosed in the sunshine and the dusty swaying plantain leaves of the Badami Baghere where I stand looking at the heaped-up roofs of the city, the proud arch of the gateway and the torrent of turbulent colour that rolls beneath it, what would he write? And if he had seen that Jubilee night in '87, when the City of Lahore flamed out of the dusk as a jewelled Queen from the door of the palace of night – dome, minaret, bastion, wall and house-front drawn in dotted fire, what would he have said of extravagance then? But who can show a blind man colour?

GLOSSARY

Kipling's spelling of Urdu, Punjabi and Anglo-Indian words is given throughout. His use of 'native' in place of 'Indian' deserves fuller explanation. The former has been a 'taboo' word in the colonial context for several decades now but in Kipling's day it carried no pejorative overtones. From the start of the nineteenth century, Britons living in India had referred to themselves as 'Indians' and to Indians as 'natives'. By Kipling's time 'Anglo-Indian' had largely replaced 'Indian' but not so completely as to allow it to replace 'native'. When in 1900 'Anglo-Indian' was officially adopted to describe persons of mixed race efforts began to be made to ease out 'native' in favour of 'Indian' – though it must be said that right up to 1947 the majority of Britons in India went on calling themselves 'Anglo-Indians' and Indians 'natives'.

A.D.C. – Aide-de-Camp
Adjutant-crane – largest stork of N. India, so-called for its upright stance and measured martial gait
'Afghan business' – Second Afghan War 1878–80
ahir – ancient (?)
Ai, Ahi – Ah
'*Allah ho Akbar*' – 'God is Great'
almirah – wardrobe (orig. Portuguese)
amratvela – sunrise
Andamans – Andaman Islands, where long-term convicts were confined
Anglo-Indian – (1) Briton living in India; (2) after 1900 person of mixed Indo-British ancestry
ayah – native nurse

baba – baby
babu – properly a term of respect, to Anglo-Indians a term of disrespect used to describe English-speaking native clerks
barrick-damages – compulsory deductions from soldiers' pay to cover barrack repairs
beastie – *bhisti*, water-carrier
bhai – brother
Bhil – main aboriginal tribe of Central India
bhusa – chaff and straw
bivoo-whacking – bivouacing, camping out
Black Tyrones – Mulvaney's first regiment before he transferred to the 'Ould Regiment'
Bobs – Lord Roberts, known as 'Bobs *Bahadur*' – 'Robert the Champion'
boorka – *burqa*, garment with eye-holes worn by Muslim women
bootgall – septic blisters
box-*wallah* – door-to-door pedlar, thus derog. term for European businessman
bracelets – handcuffs
bradawl – bayonet
Brahmin – high-caste Hindu priest
budmash – rogue
bull-oont – bull camel
bull's wool – leather
bumblepuppy – casual whist
bundobust – arrangement
bunjaras – nomadic tribe of grain-carriers and cattle-drovers
bunnia – corn merchant, money lender
bustee – town quarter, slum area
byle – Indian bullock

Cantonment – army standing camp, thus military quarter of Station
chaprassi – office messenger, from brass badge or *chapras* worn by government staff
charpar kargaz – printed paper
charpoy – wooden frame cot with webbing
cheroot – truncated cigar, chiefly from S. India
chik, chick – (1) split bamboo screen; (2) six rupees
chilumchee – metal wash bowl
chitai – rush matting
chota hazree – 'small meal', thus morning tea
chota-sahib – 'small master', thus junior European or boy
chotee bolee – 'little talk'; thus children's talk
choukut – mat
Chucks – character in Marryat's *Peter Simple*
chunam – shell and sand cement
chupatty – unleavened bread pancake
Civil Lines – area of Station given over to government offices and quarters
clink – guardroom cells
Cold Weather – winter season from October to February
Collector – chief administrator of District or Division
Commissariat – supply branch of the army
competition-*wallah* – member of the Indian Civil Service after competitive examinations introduced in 1856
compound – area enclosing bungalow, servants' quarters and garden, from Malay *kampong*
comps – compositor
Coppersmith – familiar name of the Copper-Breasted Barbet, or *Chhota Basanth*

dak, dawk – mail, transport by relays of horses or

carriers; thus *dak*-bungalow – travellers' rest house
dandy – open litter used in Himalayan foothills, poss. der. sedan chair
Darzee – tailor, name given to sparrow-like bird that stitches leaves together to form its nest
'Dawson No. 1' – long Trichinopoli cheroot
deota – god
deodar – 'tree of God', tall Himalayan cedar
dewanipagal – prince of madness
dhak – jungle shrub known as Flame of the Forest, *Butea Frondosa*
dhoby – washerman
dhurrie – rough cotton rug, usually made by prisoners
dikh – *diqqat*, trouble
Din – 'the Faith', cry of Muslim worshippers
Directory – Government Directory published annually listing all government officers with details of rank, service and salary
District – basic administrative area of British India, 250 in number
Division – administrative area comprising several Districts
doolies – hammocks suspended from poles for carrying sick or wounded
Doon – vale in the Siwalik foothills of the Himalayas
duftar, duftir – office, from *duftar khana* or 'book room'
dugubashi-exercises
Durbaris – those attending Viceroy's court
Dutt – command to go forward given to elephants and bullocks

ekka – two-wheeled cart, described by Kipling as 'a bundle of tortures'
Englishman, The – Calcutta newspaper
E.P. tents – Army Tents, India Pattern, European Privates, for the use of

ferash – species of date tree; a tamarisk tree acc. to Hobson-Jobson
fire-carriage – steam locomotive
full regimental – Number One regimental dress
furlough – leave of absence

gavial – *gharial*, long-snouted fish-eating crocodile
gentleman-ranker – gentleman enlisted as a private rather than an officer
ghari – vehicle
ghat, ghaut – river landing or crossing place
goglet – pottery water cooler
Gunga – river Ganges, Mother Ganges
gunny-bag – jute-fibre sack
gymkhana – sports meeting

hathi – elephant
Hazur – 'Presence', a title of respect
Heidsieck – brand of champagne
helmet – pith helmet made from the fibre of the *sola* plant
Hills – mountains, usually taken to be the Himalayan foothills
'*Hitherow tum*.' – 'Come here you.'
'Holy Christians' Hotel' – guardroom of a certain regiment
Hot Weather – summer season from mid-March to September
huqa, huqqa – hookah, pipe in which tobacco smoke is sucked through a container of rose water
Hursaini kebab – spiced mutton kebab

Indian – in Kipling's time still taken to refer to Britons living in India
Issiwasti – *Iswaste*, therefore

Jail-*khana* – jail-house
jalousie – shutter
Jat – peasant of Punjab
Jehannum – Hell
'*Je han. Such hai*.' – 'Yes sir. It is true.'
jeldi – *jaldi*, quick
jhampani – *rickshaw-puller*
jhil – swamp

Kafir – non-Muslim infidel
kaparia-bawaria – low-caste rag-collector
karait – *krait*, one of the few snakes in India whose bite is fatal to humans, its venom being 15 times more lethal than that of the cobra
Kasi – 'city of light', Benares
khana – meal; thus *khansamah* – cook
khitmatgar, khit – 'one rendering service', thus table servant, usually a Muslim who also performs the duties of a valet
kikar – alluvial mud
King's Peg – champagne with a peg or tot of brandy
'*Kisiwasti*' – 'For whom?'
kite – common pariah kite, a city scavenger
'*Kitna* in hand *hai, kul si*?' – 'How much is there in hand, was it all?'
kos – Indian mile, between one and two English miles
K.O.S.B. – King's Own Scottish Borderers
Kowl – protection
Krab goshe – bad meat
kullam – pencil
kutcha – raw, unfinished

lakh – one hundred thousand
'landos an' b'rooshes an' brooms' – 'landaus, barouches and broughams'
lao – 'Bring.'
laonee – ballad
lathi – bamboo staff
Little Henry and His Bearer – well-known Anglo-Indian nursery classic by Mrs Sherwood published in 1815
'Locomotus attacks us' – locomotor ataxy or creeping paralysis (as a consequence of venereal disease)
log, logh – people, species; thus *sahib-log* – Europeans
Lord of the Iron Horse – Chief Commissioner for the N.W. Railway
Lord Sahib – Viceroy

mahout – elephant keeper and driver
Mahratta – Maratha race of Western India
Mair – tribe of Central India

Malik – master, proprietor
mashing – dandified courting
Mata – Goddess of smallpox
mangi – boatman
memsahib – madam sahib, commonly denoting European women, *mem-log*
minar – tower of Muslim mosque
Mohurrum – Muslim festival commemorating the death of the martyrs Hasan and Hussain
mohur – Mughal gold coin
muezzin – Muslim caller to prayer
muggur – marsh crocodile formerly found throughout India, flesh-eater but rarely a man-eater
mullah – learned Muslim priest
murrain – cattle fever
murramutted – repaired
Mussulman – Muslim, lit. 'submitting oneself (to God)'
must, musth – state of periodical sexual excitement affecting bull elephants

nag – common name for cobra, of which the black variety is only found in N.W. India
native – born inhabitant of the country, thus Indian
naygur – nigger, much used by British troops in reference to Indians
neem – variety of ash tree whose twigs are much favoured as tooth-brushes and whose leaves, bark, fruit and sap have various healing properties
netschies – low types
Nine Bars – passage from the Koran
noncoms – Non-Commissioned Officers
Nuklas – Lucknow
nullah – dry water course
numah – Kapok tree
nungapunga – naked

Ochterlony monument – tall pillar in Calcutta supporting statue of General Sir David Ochterlony

padri – padre, Christian priest
pagal – mad; thus madman
pahari – hill-man
pariah – pariah dog, common yellow dog of Asia regarded as a scavenger
'paulin – tarpaulin
Paythan – Pathan, N.W. Frontier tribesman
peepul – pipal tree, *ficus religiosa*, a variety of fig tree often found shading focal point of village
Peliti's – tea shop on the Mall at Simla
pleader – see *vakil*
Prayag – 'confluence', Hindu name for Allahabad
pukka – 'ripe'; thus proper, completed
Pundit – religious teacher of Brahmin caste
punkah – fan suspended from ceiling and pulled by *punkah-wallah*
Purbeeah – 'one from the East'; in this context, sepoys of the Bengal Army
purdah – curtain across doorway in place of door; thus 'behind the *purdah*' – a state of (female) seclusion

Quane – Queen (Victoria)

Rains – monsoon season in N. India from June to August
Rest House – simple one-roomed bungalow used when touring
'rickshaw – hand-pulled cart, *jin-riki-sha*, introduced to Simla from Japan in about 1880
ryot – agriculturalist, thus *ryotwari*

Sahib – 'companion'; thus lord, commonly used to denote a European
sais – groom
salaam – salute, greeting
'Shia nor Sunni' – two rival sects of Islam
shikar – hunting and shooting
Silver's Theatre – scene of hand-to-hand fighting recounted in 'With the Main Guard'
sinthry-go – sentry duty
S.I.R. – Southern Indian Railway
Sir Garnets – models of perfection, after General Sir Garnet Wolseley
Sirkar – Government (of India)
Snider – army rifle superseded by Martini-Henry in early 1880s
Sobraon – battle that ended the Anglo-Sikh war in 1846
sowar – trooper
Station – district headquarters
stringers – handcuffs
subadar – chief native officer
sungar – *sangar*, stone breastwork
sunud – *sannad*, grant, patent
surki – red brickwork (?)

takkus – tax
'*talaam, tahib*' – '*salaam, sahib*'
tamarisk – feather-like shrub covered with thorns
Tarka Devi – Tara Devi, Goddess of the Dawn
tatoo – pony trap, from *tat* – pony
terai – jungle belt south of Himalayas; thus *terai* hat – broadbrimmed jungle hat of double felt worn mostly by memsahibs
theek – alright
thermantidote – early air-conditioner fitted to a window-frame in which air is blown through screens of wetted mats
thunder suruk – central passage (?)
Thursday – rest day in the army, known as '*buckshee* day' or 'old soldiers' day' without parades
ticca-gharri – hired carriage
'Tini – Martini-Henry, the newest army rifle of the mid-1880s

Urdu – 'language of the camp', lingua franca of Northern India
'*uttee* – *hathi*, elephant

Vakil – legal pleader, native attorney
Vizier – see *Wazir*

Wahabi – Arab fanatic
Wah, Wahi – exclamation of satisfaction
Waler – cavalry horse imported from New South Wales
wallah – person; thus *punkah-wallah*
Wazir – chief minister

'*Ya illah*' – 'By Allah'

NOTES ON THE ILLUSTRATIONS

In this selection we have sought to illustrate themes and settings rather than directly illustrating the stories themselves. Only a few pictures – Lockwood Kipling's illustrations for 'The Undertakers' and Detmold's magnificent painting of Rikki-Tikki-Tavi and Nag the Cobra – come directly from Kipling's stories. Our thanks to all those who provided us with illustrative material, in particular, the Kipling Society and Niall Hobhouse.

Sketches from Beast and Man by J. L. Kipling pp1, 52, 53, 105, 134, 149, 176, 181, 260

Sketches of Indian Life by W. Lloyd pp3, 19, 30, 31, 46, 56, 87, 94, 74, 78, 271, 275, 278

Sketches from Behind The Bungalow, 'EHA' pp41, 47, 101, 115

Sketches from People of India, W. Mempes pp36, 56, 98, 202

Sketches from Second Jungle Book, J. L. Kipling pp221, 227, 238

Sketches from Caine's Picturesque India p279

Courtesy of Christies, South Kensington p6 The Girgaum Road, Bombay, Horace Van Ruith

Courtesy of Victoria & Albert Museum p11 Street Scene Lahore, William Carpenter; p214 Itinerant Snake Catchers, Captain J. Luard; p259 Dust In The Plain, William Simpson; p276 A Street in Lahore, A Lady

Courtesy of India Office p15 The Tent Club at Tiffin, Percy Carpenter (from Hog Hunting in Lower Bengal); p16 Officer in Mess Dress; p67 PWD Bungalow at Pakyong; p71 Artist's bedroom Ambala, N. V. L. Rybot; p42 A Bungalow; p108 Sketch; p118 Drawing; p122 The Rest House at Jatingri; p173 A Kulu Woman; p209 DC's House, Jullundur; p242 Sketch; p250 The Government Bungalow at Purwain; pp281, 282 Sketches A. F. P. Harcourt; p63 The Burning Ghats at Benares, Edward Lear; pp135, 143, 144 Diary of Expedition against the Mohlaing, E. A. Smith; p123 Guide's Cavalry; p164 the Jumrood Fort, Entrance to Khyber Pass, C. J. Cramer-Roberts; p172 The Temple at Kanawar; p239 Travellers Near Simla, Walter Fane; p178 Side Street, Sringar, Mary P. Blyth; p191 Mess House and Barracks, Lahore; p198 Lahore Gateway, H. A. Oldfield; p217 Rikki-Tikki-Tavi, M. Detmold; p230 The Ganges Canal, W. Simpson; p243 Simla, H. B. A. Poulton; p247 Mrs Gladstone Lingham at Borhampore, Anon

Courtesy Niall Hobhouse, Eyre & Hobhouse p39 Nursery Scene, Patna Artist c 1830; p185 Kashmir, William Carpenter; p205 Verandah of House on Adyar River, S. J. Delafour

Courtesy BBC Hulton Picture Library pp48, 49, 55 P&O Pencillings, W. Lloyd; p60, 61 La Famine Aux Indes, A. Willett; p80 Captain Butler Receiving Native Chiefs, Anon; p82, A Tiger Hunt in India, Graphic Magazine; p97 Wedding Party; p186 and p196 Sketches, Captain E. R. Penrose; p169 Christmas In The Jungle; p212 An Unwelcome Visitor, Anon; p258 Christmas Greeting by the English Mail, J. C; p267 The Collector's Bungalow, Anon

Courtesy Mary Evans Picture Library p50 Christmas In India, Anon; p65 Tunes of Long Ago, Anon; p248 Going Home after a Party, Anon

Courtesy Charles Allen p26 Graphic p110 At An Indian Kucherry, Graphic Magazine; p137 Afghan War, Italian Illustrated; pp154 and 159 A Sudden Attack, p166 Wounded Soldiers at Allahabad, Illustrated London News; p206 Indian Bathroom, L. Raven-Hill; p255 Travelling in the Hills; p257 Early Morning Ride, Graphic Magazine; p262 Phantom Rickshaw, cover by J. L. Kipling

Courtesy The British Library p224 Chasse Au Crocodile, M. Andrasi; p235 Halottegetes Kalkuttaban, M. Andrasi

Courtesy J. A. Mills p130 Afghan Galop, Anon; p201 Polo in India, R. Caton-Woodville